C.C. Humphreys was born in Toronto and grew up in Los Angeles and London. A third generation actor and writer on both sides of his family, he is married and lives with his wife and son on Salt Spring Island, Canada.

BY C.C. HUMPHREYS

*Novels*
The French Executioner
Blood Ties
Jack Absolute
The Blooding of Jack Absolute
Absolute Honour
Vlad: The Last Confession
A Place Called Armageddon
Shakespeare's Rebel

*Writing as Chris Humphreys*
The Fetch
Vendetta
Possession

*Plays*
A Cage Without Bars
Glimpses of the Moon
Touching Wood

*Screenplay*
The French Executioner

# THE FRENCH
# EXECUTIONER

## C.C. HUMPHREYS

An Orion paperback

First published in Great Britain in 2002
by Orion
This paperback edition published in 2002
by Orion Books,
an imprint of The Orion Publishing Group Ltd,
Orion House, 5 Upper St Martin's Lane,
London, WC2H 9EA

An Hachette UK company

3 5 7 9 10 8 6 4
Reissued 2004

A CIP catalogue record for this book is
available from the British Library.

ISBN 978-0-7528-4830-3

Typeset at The Spartan Press Ltd,
Lymington, Hants

Printed and bound in Great Britain by
Clays Ltd, St Ives plc

The Orion Publishing Group's policy is to use papers
that are natural, renewable and recyclable products and
made from wood grown in sustainable forests. The logging
and manufacturing processes are expected to conform to
the environmental regulations of the country of origin.

www.orionbooks.co.uk

# AUTHOR'S NOTE

The idea for this story first came to me as I worked out in a gym in Vancouver, Canada, in 1993. I was doing a shoulder press, facing a mirror and studying my form. This internal dialogue followed:

(Lift weight) 'God, I've got a long neck.'

(Lower) 'If ever I was to be beheaded, my neck would be a really easy target for an axe.'

(Lift) 'Or a sword. Anne Boleyn was executed with a sword.'

(Lower) 'Anne Boleyn had six fingers on one hand.'

The seed was sown, and it soon sprouted. I wrote a short story, a little horror piece that required no research. I worked on it for about a week, then abandoned it. I had already written one play which had won a local competition and I was about to be commissioned to write another. A third was to follow. I was, just barely, a playwright. No way was I a novelist. That was too big a mountain to climb.

Other images came to me over the next few years, other fantasies (I remember yelling 'Fugger!' at my surprised wife on an island once). We moved to London, England, where I'd grown up. My career as an actor waxed and waned. I toyed with a fourth play. Then, in a cottage in Shropshire in the autumn of 1998, I realised why this most recent play wasn't working. It wasn't the story I needed to tell. I needed to tell the story of Anne Boleyn's executioner.

I researched for about a month. I'd bought books over the years that I thought would be useful if I ever came to write the novel, but had never read them. I read them now. *Reformation Europe* by G. R. Elton I'd studied before at A level and it gave me the background, along with *War and Society in Renaissance Europe 1450–1620* by J. R. Hale. *A World Lit Only by Fire* by William Manchester was wonderful on mindset and sixteenth-century smells. *Religion and the Decline of Magic* by Keith Thomas reminded me how very different people's beliefs were the best part of half a millennium ago, in a world where magic was ever present. *The Galleys at Lepanto* by Jack Beeching taught me battle tactics and slave conditions.

When the month was up I decided that, though I needed to learn a lot more, what I needed most was my characters to start telling me their stories. After twenty-three years as an actor I was grounded in Motivation: Why does he want to do this? What stops him achieving it? How does he feel then? What does she want now, and who is stopping her getting it? It's the same writing plays – objectives running into obstacles create action.

The great thing about a minor figure in history is that no one knows much about him. I discovered that Anne Boleyn's executioner was named Jean Rombaud, that he lived in St Omer near Calais, that he killed with a sword – far quicker and cleaner than the axe, and so the kindest stroke in a brutal world – and that Henry VIII paid a great deal of money to bring him over as a final favour to his soon-to-be ex-wife. That was all there was to know about him.

Anne, of course, was different. Many books have been written about her, who she was, what she did. She was important. Without her, Elizabeth would never have been born and England might still be a Catholic country. Nearly everyone I asked had heard of Anne Boleyn. And nearly half of them knew she had a six-fingered hand.

So I began with a rough cast of characters, ideas of their

journeys through the novel, a few images. I love film, the power of a striking visual. As a young reader I always loved epics, the more adventurous the better. I decided that since this was my novel I would put into it everything I loved. I have always been a storyteller, so many of my characters are too. I was my school's sabre champion at sixteen; I became an actor so that I could leap around with swords. In Canada, I became a fight choreographer in theatre. So I wanted lots of swashbuckling and derring-do. Battleaxes and slingshots and scimitars. I like visionaries, kaleidoscopes and altered states of consciousness. Fortunately, I found my research dovetailing almost perfectly with these imaginative desires. I was writing an adventure, not an historical document, but it all seemed possible. And who *really* knows what happened back then anyway?

Here are a few examples of my images and ideas coinciding with character and history (and one example where it didn't quite and I kept it in anyway).

**The Fuggers** They truly were the greatest banking family in Europe. They bought the Emperor-ship for Charles V. And bankers did have their hands chopped off by vengeful, bankrupt knights.

**Haakon** I am half Norwegian and I love the sagas, so I had to have a Viking figure. I have also studied the runes, the Norse system of divination. I have one of Haakon's runes – UR – tattooed, uh, somewhere on my person. And I wore a silver axe around my neck for about fifteen years.

**Beck** I love Shakespeare, women dressed as men. I also played a Jewish zealot in the Biblical-Roman TV epic *A.D.* – Anno Domini. I am probably the only member of British Actors Equity who knows how to use a slingshot. And since you still see them used today, in news footage of riots from Jerusalem, why not in 1536? (I still have my slingshot.)

**Giancarlo Cibo** Entirely made up, and I'm probably libelling the Archbishop of the time as well as Pope Alexander whose bastard son Cibo could not have been. But I needed a debauched, Borgia-like prelate and I always wanted to go to Siena. So, for my second draft I did and rewrote accordingly.

**Dancing a galliard** The captain of a galley did dance a galliard going into battle, except it happened at Lepanto in 1571.

**St Anthony's Fire** I have long been fascinated by this phenomenon. The last recorded instance of this mass hallucination was in the eighteenth century – or so I thought. Then I found a book called *The Day of St Anthony's Fire* by John G. Fuller which described in detail the hallucinogenic horrors that swept over a town called Pont-Sainte-Esprit in France in 1951. The poisoning is caused by ergot, a fungus that grows on rye and from which LSD is derived. Eating ergot-infected bread was like taking ten or more doses of LSD.

**Kaleidoscopes** The idea of a Black Mass within one within a dungeon was a wonderful image. But my editor wishes me to point out that kaleidoscopes weren't invented until 1816. Then again, modern research is showing that Caravaggio must have used camera lenses to paint his hyper-realist paintings in 1600, so there!

Finally, a definite example of wrong history. The siege of the Anabaptists in Munster took place in 1535, six months before the death of Anne Boleyn. But when I read about Jan Bockelson I remembered watching live on television the tragic events at Waco, Texas, in 1993 and learning of the messianic madness of David Koresh. And as they say in journalism, never let the facts get in the way of a good story. Their sacred texts and the hymn I quote I got from a religious encyclopedia at the British Library. All genuine Munster Anabaptist. Fortunately, they were as obsessed by resurrection as I needed them to be.

There are many more incidents in the novel that come from my fascinations or, in some cases, my experiences. I would be happy to answer any questions on them. For now, though, I'd like to end by thanking some people without whom I would not have written this novel. All women, strangely. Or perhaps not.

Firstly, there is my wife, Aletha, who encouraged me when I began, pushed me when I faltered and forgave the odd peculiarity of behaviour in the name of research. The time when she came home to discover me leaping around the hall with an umbrella trying to behead imaginary chickens comes to mind.

Next, my wonderful agent, Anthea Morton-Saner at Curtis Brown, who took me on because of this novel and has proved again and again the truth of the old dictum: Get an agent!

I'd also like to thank Jane Wood, publishing director at Orion, who turned my fantasy into reality and made me believe that I might have more than one book in me by giving me an advance for two.

Penultimately, there's Rachel Leyshon, my editor, who not only will drink beer with me but whose penetrating notes and brilliant eye guided me on my final edit to help me achieve my true vision, and whose enthusiasm for the story continually reassured this self-critical newcomer.

Finally, there's one person without whom nothing would be possible. Anne Boleyn. She must have been quite extraordinary. I hope I've done her justice. And whoever it is who places a bunch of white roses on her tombstone in the chapel of St Peter ad Vincula in the Tower of London every 19 May, the anniversary of her death, I would like to thank them too.

Hoch! Hoch!

C. C. Humphreys
London, February 2001

*For Aletha*

PART ONE

# THE VOW

# ONE

# THE GIBBET

It was unseasonably cold for a late May night, but the gibbet's former occupant was too dead to care and his replacement too unconscious. It was the three men-at-arms who grumbled about it, and though the removal of the skeleton from the torso-shaped cage required some strenuous snapping and pulling, they were not grateful for the warmth of the exercise. With their prisoner finally wedged in and the cage's key replaced on its hook, they returned to their horses. Pressing themselves against the warm flanks, the soldiers brushed the gibbet's leavings from their cloaks, and grumbled still.

'Such a beautiful night.' The voice came silky and warm from beneath folds of cloak and fur, the breath a steady stream into the frosty air. 'Look, a comet! In Siena we'd say: there's another virginity gone.'

There was a laugh, as silken as the voice, followed by a cough. A piece of red cloth dabbed at the lips.

Heinrich von Solingen turned towards the man who had just spoken, the man whose every command he obeyed. Heinrich was confused. He liked things ordered and simple. They had got what His Holiness wanted. Wrapped in velvet, it rested now in His Holiness's saddle bags. Confusion made him angry and bold enough to question.

'I don't see why we are here, my Lord. Why didn't we just kill the Frenchman back at the inn?'

'I think you tried, didn't you?'

'I mean after, when he was unconscious.'

The smaller figure shifted in his saddle. Moonlight fell on a sharp forehead, a long straight nose, fleshy lips. There was a touch of something sad in the silkiness now.

'Really, after what he did, we should have tried him as a heretic then given him to God's redeeming fire. Alas, the time is not right for his story to be told abroad. So we give him here, into God's hands.'

'But my Lord Archbishop—'

The blow surprised Heinrich because the Italian was neither young nor, he thought, especially strong. Pain contradicted that impression.

'I've warned you about using my title in a public place.'

'I am sorry, my Lord, but there is only the prisoner and my men—'

The hand emerged again from within the cloak and moonlight glinted on heavy rings, which explained the blood now running down Heinrich's chin.

'Enough! You are a fool and I another to let you question me. There may be a gibbet keeper nearby who would recognise the rank. And your men did not know it till now. I must think. Get them to find the keeper.'

A curt command and the three soldiers began to search where they could, yet there was little there: a bare crossroads a league beyond a village with neither tree nor bush nearby. Little for the full moon to shine upon but the dangling, vaguely human iron form, the cross-beamed support and the midden of gibbet filth on which, in six parts now, sprawled the cage's last tenant.

The men reported their failure.

'Very well.' The Italian coughed, a gout of blood caught in the swiftly raised cloth. There was little he could do now; and even if the keeper did lurk and had somehow heard Heinrich's indiscretion . . . Well, how could a creature of such an occupation threaten a Prince of the Holy Church?

Giancarlo Cibo, Archbishop of Siena, decided he could take the risk. He didn't take many – it was how he survived the hurly-burly of life back in Italy after all. He wouldn't take another with Heinrich's men. Heinrich would have to deal with them himself, later, a fitting punishment for his indiscretion. Perhaps incorporating some unusual methods. The Archbishop would like to see that. It would truly upset the surly German. The Archbishop would like to see that too.

'Put double the usual coins in the offertory. Let's pay the keeper well,' he said, all silk and smoothness again.

Ducats were dropped into a small box at the base of the gibbet, and Heinrich went back to join his men. There he listened to his blood drip onto the pommel of his saddle, kept his silence, and watched from a distance as the Archbishop pushed his horse right up to the gibbet.

The Italian leant forward until it looked as if he was almost kissing the cage's iron-slatted face. Until he could feel the breath of the man inside on his own lips. The man's breathing was erratic; Heinrich's men had beaten him badly when they finally felled him. Not surprising, as the Frenchman had killed two of their number and incapacitated two more, his strange, square-headed sword dancing graceful and deadly among the suddenly leaden-footed Germans. Heinrich had said it was an executioner's sword, much favoured in France as a more humane way of despatching traitors, if their rank and purses deserved it. The sword would make a fine trophy on his palace wall, for he knew just whose neck had last been severed with it. A neck and something far more unusual – a six-fingered hand.

'Why did you do it, Jean?' Cibo whispered into the cage. 'A belief that it could heal, like the bones of St Agnes? Is that what you thought she was, Jean, a saint and martyr for the new religion? Or was it gold? The most powerful relic in the world would have fetched more than you could have earned in a lifetime of headtaking.'

The unconscious man had no answer for him, beyond his

5

shallow breaths. The Archbishop studied the face before him. Features somewhat finer than was common among the French, a smaller nose, thick black hair now slick with the blood and sweat of the fight. It was ordinary. He was always surprised when ordinary men did extraordinary things.

'I do wonder about you, Jean. Sadly, I will never know. But it's mine now, a greater weapon than any executioner's sword for myself and for Mother Church. We'll have to see how best we two can use it.'

And with that, Cibo turned his horse and broke straight into a gallop. He was proud of his horsemanship and his steeds were trained to respond to his instant whim. The Germans were surprised and, with Heinrich bellowing orders, followed as swiftly as they were able.

Such was the speed of their departure, such their pleasure in forsaking that dismal place, that no one even glanced back at the gibbet cage and its new occupant. If they had, they would have seen that the first effects of their beating had worn off.

Jean Rombaud, master executioner and recent slayer of Anne Boleyn, had woken up.

# TWO
# THE FUGGER

The first thing to be done, he knew, before opening his eyes, was to tally the injuries. He had learnt on a battlefield to take stock blind, because moving without knowing who's around you could mean ending up worse off.

Begin with the chest, breathe a little deeper. Christ preserve me, there's pain, maybe a rib broken, others bruised. The taste of iron. Probe with the tongue. No, shit! Two more gone. Worse than the ribs, that. Ribs heal, but teeth left on battlefields across Europe made it harder each day to chew meat. One leg curled up under – the pain of constriction, or a break? Among the many blows, a memory of being kicked on the shin. Kicked hard.

Trace the body, look for wounds. Head? Battered yet intact. Guts? There was always that smell when they were pierced. Groin? Seemingly unswollen. And he'd have remembered the entrance of metal anywhere. He'd felt it before, after all. It was a distinct sensation.

All in all, and considering the odds, he wasn't doing too badly. So now, fall to listening. Anyone breathing out there? Anyone watching him for a trace of life, blade poised, waiting to snuff it out? No? Then open the eyes.

No. Close them again, dismiss what they've seen. There has to be another explanation. Move the hands, shift the legs, measure the space. No. It can't be.

'Jesus!' Jean Rombaud blasphemed solidly for a minute.

7

He was imprisoned. Worse, far worse, he was in a gibbet cage. Hung up like a common thief, left to rot and die. It wasn't possible, he was still unconscious, dreaming . . .

The cage was swinging wildly now in his panic, grating, screeching. That would do him no good. The last thing he needed was to draw attention to his position. He was outside the village but he didn't know how near it was. He did know how the villagers would treat him if they found him. At best jeer, pelt him with muck, make bets on his endurance; at worst . . . well, it had been a hard winter, and the salted mutton would be running out.

'No,' he said again, firmly, and managed to still the lurching cage. He had been put there silently by men who did not want witnesses. There was time to think, in these few hours before dawn. This could not be his destiny, to die from torment or starvation, or more likely from a cannibal's knife, in a cage in the middle of France.

He used his limited movements again to explore his confines, glad he was slightly smaller than most men, for he had little enough room, none to raise his arms above his head to where the lock held the front and back of the cage together. Yet even if he could twist himself to get a hand through the slats and up, the lock looked rusted but solid.

He bit down on his despair. This couldn't happen. He wasn't a man who gave much thought to death, it would come when it must. But swifter, surely? Not like this, not when . . .

Then the memory of what had led him to this place came scrabbling back and, cursing again, he reached out to squeeze the slats, find their weakness, force himself through them. These men had stolen from him, and thus from Anne Boleyn, the most precious part of herself, bound by sacred vow to the care of Jean Rombaud. His oath to his Queen would surely give him the strength to snap mere metal!

Long after the certainty that it was futile, he squeezed and pushed and beat upon the unyielding iron, till the blood ran from his fingers. As his struggles became weaker, the executioner did something he'd not done since the day he'd laid his wife and child in the plague pit, picked up his sword and took again to the mercenary's road. He wept. His tears fell from the cage, splashing droplets onto the gibbet midden below.

Salt-blinded as he was, he didn't notice the first stirrings amid that filth, of something beginning to work its way up from within, from the very depths of muck, rotting clothes and bones picked clean, didn't see what looked like a worm break through the crust, to be followed by another worm, then a third, then five. Fingers they were, joined to a hand, an arm, a shoulder. Then a head burst out of the earth and a voice, mud ridden and muck-choked cried out, 'DAE-MON!'

Jean set the cage swinging again, his face turned from this vision spewed from hell. He'd long since forsaken the Church he was baptised in, disgusted by what he'd seen done in the name of God on battlefields and in the palaces of the Princes of Religion. Tales to frighten children he'd called their stories, their rules and penalties. Well, he was no child and he was terrified now.

The demon worked its shoulders clear, then, resting a moment to glance up at Jean, threw back its head and shrieked: 'He's got my legs! I'm trapped. The foul fiend nips my ankles. Help me! Help! Pull me up, why can't you? Ohhh!' It gave a piteous wail and cried 'Dae-mon!' once again.

As if answering a summons a raven, a blue-black brute, flew down and circled the gibbet, cawing a series of short cries, descending in darting runs to flap round the head of the embedded demon. The two of them made hideous harmony, alternating in pitch and volume, and Jean suddenly, forcefully, realised that all the tales he'd denied, all the visions that had merely troubled a few sleeps since his priest-ridden childhood, they were all true. There *was* a hell, and he was descending into it.

Then the demon ceased its wailing. The raven stopped

screeching and landed on its shoulder. The two of them tipped their heads to one side and four eyes regarded Jean. Then, like a cork from a bottle, the whole hideous shape popped out of the hole in the ground and stood, feet splayed, upon the midden. The skull of the gibbet's former occupant, which had perched precariously atop the midden, now rolled down and lodged between the creature's ankles, seeming to make a third set of eyes to gaze upon the prisoner.

'Well, well, well,' said the demon, after a moment and in quite a reasonable tone, 'and who is our guest for tonight, Daemon?'

A mud creature stood there, black with filth, its eyes reflecting the moon the only flicker of light. Garbed in some sort of tattered dress, a shapeless sack hanging from shoulder to ankle, one arm bare and one encased. Wild, spiralling locks hung from the encrusted head, falling in shanks down to the shoulders to meld with a rat's nest of a beard. The bird was as clean as its perch was filthy.

In the silence of their stares, Jean regained his defiance.

'Be gone and torment me not. I am not for you yet.'

The two heads swivelled to look at each other, then back to him. The raven gave a cry and took to the air, while the mud beast leant forward and spat.

'Do you hear that, Daemon? Orpheus tells Charon when he chooses to cross the Styx!' It threw its head back and laughed, a ghastly rattle. It then reached up to the cage and said, in its formerly reasonable tone, 'It's for me to decide, you know. Daemon and me' – it bent down to pick up the skull – 'and my friend Felix here makes three. What shall we do with him?' Fingers moved the fleshless jaw up and down as if in answer.

Bowing to the skull, the creature began a strange shuffling that Jean realised was a dance, of sorts. Humming a tune, it moved across the midden, back and forth, words and laughter emerging.

'He wants to be left alone. But that can't be. Such a long

time since we had a visitor! Last one was you, dear Felix, and how boring were you? They did for you before you arrived, few breaths, no stories to pass your passing. I like a story with my supper, and if I can't have one at least I can have . . . but this one looks healthy, this one looks good, he won't be leaving till I tell him he should! A rhyme. A rhyme! I still have the gift, oh yes. Papa would be proud.'

Jean listened and calculated as he did. The creature was mad, that much was sure, but there were bits of sense within the ramblings, even a way of speaking that sounded less than brutish.

'You dance well,' he called down, 'but your partner lacks something in the leg.' The creature had stopped its swaying to listen. 'Why don't you let me down? I can cut a finer caper than your Felix.'

The creature dashed the skull to the ground then rose up next to the gibbet and hissed, in a whisper as devoid of mirth as its dance had been full of it, 'Death is all you have coming. The time is God's to choose. I am God's helper. I keep his clock. Tick tock. Tick tock. Tick . . . tock.'

The creature sank silently back down to the midden and began to collect up the bones that lay there.

Jean knew now he was at the mercy of no demon, but one who sinks as low as any human can. To be a gibbet keeper was to survive on scraps dogs would shun, with an occasional coin thrown from a justice's hand or prised from a victim's family to swiftly end a loved one's suffering. It was life, but barely, and Jean knew the best he could expect was that same swift slitting of his own throat.

And yet, how could he accept such a death? Was this a fitting end to his career, a last cruel joke in a life that had witnessed many? No. While he had breath, and a tongue in his head, there was hope.

'What are you doing with those bones?'

The keeper started, as if he'd forgotten his prisoner was there.

'Soup,' he muttered without turning around. 'Do you believe me?'

'No.' Jean shifted in the cage. 'Why would you want old bone soup when you have such fresh meat hanging by?'

The keeper made a snuffling sound that Jean realised was laughter.

'Is that what you want? A swift release provided by my little trusty here?' He patted a small scabbard at his side. 'But that would be a sin – isn't that what your friend the Archbishop would say? Ooh . . .' He broke off and gazed up at Jean. 'An archbishop, eh? What illustrious senders-off you had. We don't usually get such company here. Why should you interest His Holiness, I wonder?'

Affecting calm, Jean said, 'Why were they interested in me? Oh, now there's a story.'

The keeper stopped scrabbling and tipped his head to one side, bones and skull cradled in his arms.

'A story?'

'Aye. I heard you say you like a story over supper. Well, there's a tale in me, if you choose to hear it.'

'Oh, yes, we do like stories, Daemon and I. Do you speak any Raven? No matter, he speaks some French and, of course, German. Don't you, beloved?'

The raven swooped down upon the crossbeam, opened its beak and said, 'Save the eyes! Save the eyes!'

'You see! And I can translate the rest. We would like to hear your tale.'

Jean forced a smile. 'And what price do you offer for this night's entertainment?'

'Some food, some wine, and a swift good night if you so choose. But only if your tale pleases us.'

'I do not drink bone soup.'

'And neither do we,' the keeper cried. 'Do you think the Fugger has lost all his civility? I have eaten off silver trenchers in my time. And now I have cold root stew. I have wine. I may even have some old, old bread.'

'A meal, then a swift passage from one hell to another? That is not a fair return for this story.'

'And what would young Orpheus want? Nothing less than your lover back from Hades, I presume?'

'Oh no, nothing like that.' Jean leant his face against the slats. 'Only the chance to carry on the story.'

White eyes flashed at him from the darkness.

'You mean, this story has no ending? The Fugger hates stories that don't end. Hates them! All stories must have an ending, and all endings must be sad.'

'Well, that will be for you to judge. You can make it end the way you want. For you are in it, and Daemon too.'

'You hear that, Daemon? A story that includes us. This we must hear.'

'A bargain, then. If my story pleases, you will set me free to continue it, for this story is so powerful it cannot be allowed to die here with me. If it does not . . . well, maybe I'll take some of your wine and a little relief from that friend you keep at your side. Is it a bargain?'

The Fugger leapt up from a squat, grabbed the cage and thrust an arm through the bars to support himself. He hung there, swinging, causing the metal hook to grate in its socket. His face was matted with filth, but within that grime eyes shone out in the moonlight. They fixed on Jean now, and a whisper came.

'A bargain made! But know this, young Orpheus. Daemon and I, we have heard all the tragedies, yes we have, seen a hundred men and more wedged in where you are now. Every one with a story of love lost, murder unavenged, maidenheads plundered, and not one has ever gone free. Not a single one. Daemon thinks I would listen to his tale from our Lord's own mouth and, like Pilate, wash my hands.' The eyes lowered and he continued softly, 'Maybe he's right. So far am I sunk in sin, so great my degradation.'

He dropped down then and crouched, muttering, on the midden, reaching into its filth and scrabbling around until

13

there emerged from within it an encrusted flagon and a sack. He uncorked the bottle with his teeth, drank, spat out something, drank again.

'So sing us your song, young Orpheus, pluck at our hearts. But beware! We like a story with a beginning, a middle and an end. A proper story. And then, who knows? Do you understand the challenge?'

'I do,' Jean replied. 'And if I finish my tale and the key is not in the lock a moment later, may God have mercy on both our souls.'

'Amen,' sighed the Fugger, stretching out on the midden, settling himself into the soft earth to hear the tale.

But how to tell it? Jean thought, hopelessness growing within him with the creeping dawn light. A story told to a madman and his bird through the bars of an iron coffin, an impossible tale of the killing of a queen and a last request to her killer to do an impossible thing. A sane audience would think him mad; a mad audience . . . well, perhaps it was the only one that could think him sane.

He wondered where to begin. At his lodgings in St Omer, stubbornly sober despite the endless wine, receiving the summons? With an explanation of why he was chosen, his skill with the executioner's sword?

He was not good with words, his trade rarely required them. But then, suddenly, it came to him. Once upon a happy time he'd lulled his precious daughter, Ariel, to sleep with little stories. She'd always liked them best when they were simple and true in the telling. So, taking a deep breath, he began.

# THREE

# THE EXECUTION

Mist encased the small boat and, along with water like spoiled milk, seemed to force against the bow, preventing swift progress to their landing. The boatman was as reluctant as his vessel, muttering warding words against the witching hour and this midnight mission. Jean thought limbo must feel this way: body and will suspended, approaching a place one could never quite reach.

When they did, even he, who rarely made the gesture, aped the boatman and crossed himself. He had spent much of his life in such places, his trade demanded it: prisons and the cells within them where light never reached, where there was only the stench of the doomed, the cries of the despairing. But this fortress! All the evil and unhealth of a realm seemed to be lodged within it. It squatted over the water like some giant, venomous toad, and as they passed under the walls Jean felt he was being sucked into its maw.

'The Bloody Tower!' the boatman muttered, crossing himself again. Languages were useful to a mercenary and Jean had picked up enough English on campaign to understand both meanings.

The boat, entering under a portcullis raised slowly ahead of them, scraped against a wooden dock where the boatman paused just long enough for Jean and his meagre baggage to be placed ashore before pushing off, eagerly seeking the open water, never looking back. Unseen hands had raised the iron

15

grille and now let it drop. Jean knew he was expected, but he was still left there long enough for a deeper chill to settle within him, while the water lapped against the dock, seeming to speak in various tongues, echoing in the low roof overhead.

Eventually, there were heavy boots on stone, metal jangled, and flickering light barely pierced the gloom.

'Rombaud?'

'Monsieur.'

'Follow me.'

The phantom officer led Jean through a maze of passages and finally up a long spiral staircase. The room at the top dazzled with its sudden light, its warmth. He'd been expecting no more luxury than a palliasse in the corner of a cell or a nest under the scaffold. Here there was a truckle bed, a good fire snapping in the grate and a sheepskin on the stone floor, even some wine, bread and cheese on a table.

'I am grateful, Monsieur,' he said to the officer he now saw to be a tall, sandy-haired Englishman whose voice had seemed to come from someone far older.

'Tucknell is my name and all this is not my doing,' the man replied in that French the English always seemed to use, entirely without song. 'You may thank the Queen—' He broke off and flushed in a way that revealed his youth still more. 'I mean, Anne, your . . . she's no longer Queen, of course, as you know, or you wouldn't be . . .' He paused, then looked down and added, 'Wouldn't be here, I suppose.'

Caught out by this unexpected emotion – he really was no more than a boy – the officer made to leave. Jean stopped him with a raised hand.

'Monsieur, would you be so kind – when am I to meet my client?'

Startled by the word, Tucknell looked at the executioner as if for the first time.

'In the morning, after her prayers. It is . . . you will do your work the morning after.'

A nod, and he was gone.

Jean ate and drank. The wine was excellent – it had been heated and flavoured with honey and some unknown herb. The sheepskin rug was more comfortable than the bed and it could be pulled closer to the fire. Wrapped in his cloak, surprised by this good fortune, he swiftly fell into a deep sleep. It was largely dreamless until near dawn, when someone seemed to be dragging him down a dank corridor. There was something unsettling in the grip and when he awoke the hand he'd been pulled by ached.

Tucknell brought him some food and small beer soon after, then returned to lead him back down those twisting stairs and out into the light.

It was the laughter he heard first. Then he saw her, in a patch of bright sunlight, emerging from a chapel, leaning on the arm of a priest, four ladies in attendance. It was no distance across the small lawn and Jean's reaction, as always in this situation, was practical. He studied her neck, clearly visible in the low-cut dress she wore.

Long, slender, no trouble there, of a strength that would almost have suited a man better. Her hair was thick, a horse's mane of it barely tamed by the French hood that held it. It was of a lustrous black, though with silver threaded through like filigree. Its length would be a problem for his sword and he reminded himself to suggest a coif.

So far, he had allowed his professionalism to rule, but now curiosity overcame him. This was a queen, after all, who had gathered legends about her even Jean Rombaud of St Omer had heard. Ballads were sung of her beauty, of eyes that could melt the stone of statues and a body to make angels yearn for earthly life. Yet to Jean, across the green was a tall, thin woman with greying hair who showed her more than thirty years and the toll they'd taken, the daughter she'd given birth to and those babes she'd lost in her struggle to produce a male heir for her King and husband.

*So this is the temptress who has led a good Catholic prince to break with the Church he loved?* Jean thought. *This, the second Eve who has caused such a schism between heaven and earth?*

He felt a slight itch of disappointment, then remembered: he was there to do a job, nothing more. A swift introduction, the usual mix of terror and embarrassment, a swifter dismissal. He would see her only once more, through the slits of a headsman's mask. He would do well what he was well paid to do and he would be gone on the next flood tide. His reputation enhanced by the quality of the head he had taken, he would be able to up his fees, future clients flattered at the attentions of the Queen's Own Executioner.

*And what will you do with all the extra gold?* he asked himself briefly as the entourage approached across a lawn suddenly cooler with the disappearance of the sun. She was still leaning on the arm of her confessor, who was trying to look solemn but failing, walking with him across to where Jean and Tucknell waited.

When she turned to them, even as Jean was bending his knee, he glanced up and saw them! Eyes of such intensity, pools of immaculate blackness, sinking to unimaginable depths. Within the deeper darkness of one of them the pupil was slightly offset, as if there were a question there, while an answer awaited in the other. All this he saw in one brief glimpse, a lightning blast so powerful he faltered as he sank and was grateful for the knee pressed to the damp turf.

Beside him, Tucknell knelt and then rose, stuttering Jean's name in his flat French, failing to find the correct title, dubbing him 'Slaughterer' as if his trade was in cattle. Laughter vanished as the sun had and Jean waited, head bent, for them to quell their emotions while he tried to quell his. He knew this moment well, was used to waiting some time. Yet he was to be surprised again. Firstly by the voice, the deep richness of it, like cream clotting in the pails on his father's farm.

'Oh no,' said Anne Boleyn, 'his title is Doctor, for he has

come to spare me pain. Honour him as you would every man of science.' The French was as flawless as the sentiment.

A hand reached out. Jean took it and bent his head to kiss it. A hand much like any other noble lady's. Delicate, flushed like a musk rose, nails like perfect half moons, with neither blemish nor wrinkle, mole nor scar to disfigure the beauty of it. It also had six fingers. He had forgotten this one legend among her many. And because he had forgotten he was startled, and reacted with an oath from his native valley, an obscure one concerning the unusual habits of farmers and their pigs.

Silence again, with Jean aghast. His meetings with his clients were usually brief, formal; they were embarrassed or defiant, he was polite, calming. Here, he had acted improperly and he coloured with the shame of it. Dismissal awaited. Disgrace.

But this silence was short-lived because into it came a laugh from the belly. 'I have not heard that . . . phrase in a very long time,' she said, her laughter seeming to draw the sun back from behind the clouds. 'I . . . oh, forgive me! I spent many, many happy summers in the Loire, is that not where you are from?'

Jean nodded, still too distracted to speak.

'Not from Calais, then?'

Jean cleared his throat, spoke without looking up. 'I live in St Omer, Majesty, in the Pas de Calais. But I grew up in the Loire.'

She studied him for a long moment. He kept his eyes lowered.

'Well then, we *do* have a lot to talk about, dear Doctor. Will you honour me with your conversation if I promise no more little jokes? You would have thought I would be tired of that one by now, but it's not often I find someone who can still be tricked by it. Ah well! Please, forgive me and walk with me?'

Sometimes, rarely, this happened – a client wanting more

from him, almost befriending him. He had often noticed, in the time just before or just after death, how words would flow. As if those about to die could anchor their place in this world with the tale of their life. Or the bereaved, how they would talk, as Jean had talked after he laid his wife and child in the ground. Waves of words, weeks of them, seeking to hold them in his life with his recollections. And when he realised he couldn't, when he knew nothing he had done or said or prayed had saved them, he had stopped talking, and the great silence had fallen on him. He'd barely had a conversation in the five years since.

But he was to have one now. Anne Boleyn dismissed her ladies and her confessor, only the moon-faced Tucknell and one maid trailing at a discreet distance. Around and around the green she led Jean, showing her delight when the ravens swooped down on them if they passed too near hidden caches of food, telling him the history of the Tower as if he were some gawping visitor and not the man who had come to take her life. She talked of her childhood in France, of the times spent in happiness in those same vine-clad valleys that had been his childhood home.

They fell into an even pace. She talked, he listened and asked no questions, for there was no need, his task was clear before him. He had seen the lords who spoke so bravely only to blubber and sway so much on his scaffold he had to have them bound and blindfolded. Or the drunk ones who couldn't keep upright. But he looked at Anne Boleyn and knew she would kneel as calm and erect on his scaffold as ever she had before the thrones of France and England.

They had taken a dozen turns about the small green when she stopped and said, 'And you? What of you, Jean Rombaud? Tell me of the roads you have taken from the Loire to bring you to this place.'

It was rare that clients asked anything of him, so concerned were they with their own mortality. Yet Anne Boleyn was unlike any client he had met, for the curiosity in her offset eyes was genuine, and after his blunder he was prepared to do anything to please her. So he talked, his voice at first hesitant from disuse, growing stronger in the quality of her attention. She listened, prompting occasionally, her strange hand now and again drifting to press his arm in a six-fingered grasp, lingering there and then moving just before he could grow uncomfortable.

The chapel bell sounded ten and to his surprise Jean realised two hours had passed in this exchange of histories, an exchange that had become curiously one-sided. She went once more to her prayers, but not without extracting his word, gladly given, that they would meet again at sunset.

His quarters were warm enough, and there was food and wine laid out. He ate and drank sparingly, then slept surprisingly long and well. When he awoke, there was only a little he could do while he waited, but he could do that little. He took the sword, the whetstone and the oil from his bag. Settling in a patch of sunlight at the entrance to his tower, he drew his treasure out, for treasure it was to him, his fortune and the maker of such reputation as he had.

Longer, just, than the length of his arm, thus shorter than most swords then in fashion, its blade doubled their width and weight. A craftsman in Toledo had folded the metal over and over Jean could not tell how many times, such was its weight, while its counter-balance was perfection, residing within the double-handed grip Jean re-tied in green leather each time, and within the apple-sized pommel. A handspan from its square tip, and no more than a handspan in length, lay the killing zone. Though its entire length on both sides was of an equal and extraordinary sharpness, it was this neck-wide section that divided life from death, became the focus of his swing and timing. The rest was a reminder of battle, where a back edge and a sudden cut could, and had, saved him more than once.

He swung it above his head and around his body, letting

the weight of it pull and stretch his shoulders. It was their sudden uncoiling which produced the single killing stroke that was his speciality, that had spread his fame. The condemned would pay well for that skill rather than submit to the crudeness of axe and block, trussed and bent over, rump in air, neck a scrunched target for an often drunk butcher to hack away at. There was no such indignity on his scaffold. His clients knelt upright, hands and eyes free if they so chose.

*Henry of England obviously still cares enough for his soon-to-be former wife to give her this farewell*, Jean thought. Yet remembering the woman he'd met that morning, the thought did not make him smile.

The sword was a tool, practical, deadly, and Jean rarely considered it beyond that. But today, with the spring sun glittering off its facets, it seemed to him again like a doorway, a swift conduit to another world. Jean had long since lost track of the numbers because so many had gone under the blade during the wars. Yet the sword seemed to him to carry a memory of all it had done, of every person it had moved on, connecting their last look at this world with their first glimpse of the next, retaining in its planes something of their fevered prayers, their shouted curses.

He had been dipping the whetstone in water and moving it with angled, sharp strokes down the length of both sides for some time when a shadow took the sunlight away.

'Do you have everything you need?' Tucknell was staring at the sword on the Frenchman's lap.

'Everything I could wish for,' Jean replied and slipped the weapon back into its soft leather sheath. 'Is it time?'

'Time?' Tucknell looked startled.

'For my second meeting with the Queen.' Jean spoke gently. 'She asked for me near sunset.'

'Yes. It is. You are to follow me.' The officer made no move to leave, just kept gazing at the sword. Jean waited. There was always someone who needed to talk to him about what he was to do. More often than not a relative, sometimes a servant or friend. 'But I told you, she's no longer a queen. The King stripped her of the title yesterday.' The voice's attempt to be calm betrayed the opposite.

'It is often the way,' Jean said. 'Reducing an enemy to a commoner makes them—'

'She is no commoner,' Tucknell burst out. 'She is noble beyond estimation, beautiful beyond all reckoning, and he . . .' He turned away, struggling to pull back the anger and the pain that distorted his face. In a voice like a little boy's, he said, 'I would give my life for hers, gladly.'

'I don't think the exchange would be accepted.' Jean gently laid his hand on Tucknell's arm. It was immediately pulled away. Pity was the quickest way to harden most men, Jean had always found.

'Do your job well, Frenchman,' Tucknell growled. He turned and, once Jean had put the sword away, led him back to the green.

She was waiting there with two of her ladies. They broke off their conversation as soon as she saw him.

'Monsieur Rombaud, I hope my gallant Tucknell is treating you well.'

'Excellently, Majesty,' he replied, at which she raised a six-fingered hand.

'I am not to be addressed as such. The King has ordained it so and he is not a man to anger, or disappoint.' She glanced around at the embarrassed, averted faces. 'Why are you all so glum? Do you not know the relief it is to be a woman again after a thousand days of woe as Queen? My head is lighter for the loss of a crown and soon my shoulders will be lighter—' She broke off. 'I am sorry, Monsieur Jean, dear Doctor, my Englishness shows most in my terrible habit of joking in the face of all adversity, which may do for me but not for those who care about me. Forgive me,' she said to them all. 'Yet we still have this problem of titles. If I am not a queen I am still perhaps a lady? Lady Anne – sounds now like the heroine of

23

some terrible ballad, which I have been, of course. What about plain old Anne Bullen? They call me that in my native Norfolk, where they don't hold with airs and graces. No? Well, what did you call your love, Jean Rombaud, your childhood sweetheart from the Loire valley? Maybe I could steal her name, since I am to steal a last caress from her love.'

She laughed at that, even if the others didn't, and in the laugh Jean heard something that reminded him of Lysette, of the first time he'd seen her chasing chickens in her father's yard, aged ten. Or again at fourteen when he'd kissed her on the riverbank, or at sixteen with the betrothal wreath in her hair, or at twenty-five when he'd been gone to war so long and she'd waited, though many considered her an old maid by then. And their last five wondrous years together.

He'd closed his eyes momentarily, and when he opened them again he was plunged straight into the depths of hers, for she had stepped close. She spoke, but her lips seemed not to move, the words instead sounding directly inside his head.

'Lysette? It is a beautiful name. Yet too precious to borrow, I think.'

Once more he felt himself unsteady, for he was sure he had not spoken aloud; yet this woman had read his mind as easily as he could tell the approach of rain. She had plucked the thought from him. Him, the faceless, the masked man, exposed.

'Walk with me,' Anne Boleyn said. 'We will discuss names and titles later, I think.'

They circled the green again and again, long after the sun had set and a chill reclaimed the Tower. He did not seem to feel the cold, it was outside them, for they spoke again of a warmer place removed in time and distance, of days of endless summer beside a river, of the taste of the young wine made in the Loire as nowhere else, of festivals and frolics and the adventures of being young. Hers had been a very different world. She was of the court that often stayed there, he of the fields and the village even if his father had grown from mere peasant to landowner, innkeeper, army supplier. The memory of the land though, that they could share – the quality of its light, the colour of its earth.

He found himself telling her things he had never spoken of before, of his wife and daughter, their sudden deaths of the plague. In turn, he was at first disconcerted, then fascinated by tales of her life at the French and English courts he only, rarely, came into contact with. She was funny, indiscreet, occasionally shockingly coarse. And when she gave that deep belly laugh, bent over in her glee, he'd laugh too, then look at her and remember she was to die the next day. He had come to take her life. To spare her pain and give her some dignity, undoubtedly, but to kill her nonetheless. And remembering, he was confused. He'd had noble clients who seemed to want to befriend him before the end, who had revealed more intimate things than are often heard in the confessional. Yet this was different; Anne Boleyn sought to achieve an intimacy and succeeded. There had to be a reason, but he could not think of it.

Some hours passed before Tucknell came to lead her away, and in that time Jean had learnt precisely why a king had overthrown his beloved Church for this woman, for she deserved no less than the uproar of heaven and earth. It was not a beauty of face or body. What he felt was not desire as such, though she was seductive beyond the price of paradise. It was something he'd never known before, something of the spirit and holier than anything he'd ever met in a church.

Back in his quarters, good food and delicious wine were again laid out but Jean had an appetite for neither. He was disturbed, angry with himself. Clients were not meant to evoke feelings. He did not think it would make his job harder, he knew his duty and the only kindness he could show lay in the precise performance of his duties. Usually, though, his thoughts on an execution's eve were his own, easy ones that allowed him to sleep. He felt he would get none of that relief tonight.

He was wrong. He did sleep, but fitfully, spirits his companions, dying clients, dead lovers and a six-fingered woman lingering there long after his eyes were open to dismiss them. It took him several moments to realise the hand shaking his shoulder was real, that Tucknell was bidding him rise. It was long before his time – no hint of dawn in the sky – but he threw a cloak over his shoulders and followed the impatient Englishman down the stairs and then along unfamiliar grey stone corridors.

Suddenly they plunged into a dead-end passage where Tucknell disappeared into the rock. Jean stood, shocked, till a gauntlet materialised and pulled him into the niche and on into the darkness of a narrow stairwell, boots splashing through fetid puddles. Half blind, he slammed into the officer's back as Tucknell cursed and fumbled at something ahead of them. There was a chink of light, a doorway, and then he was standing in a sparse bedroom with Anne Boleyn before him. Alone, for Tucknell had vanished again.

She simply looked at him for some moments while he stood, off balance once again, as if she were the executioner, he the client. At last, she spoke.

'Jean Rombaud, when I heard Henry had granted me the last favour of a French swordsman's death, it was the first good news I had received in many a day. It was not that you were coming to spare me pain, though I do not doubt your skill. No, my tiny hope was that you would be the man you are, a man of honour. That you also come from the Loire is beyond anything I could have hoped or prayed for. Because it was there, in the land we share, that I learnt to be who I am. Not a queen. No, not even the daughter of a noble house.'

She poured some wine into a goblet, brought it across to him. It was similar to the wine from his chamber: hot, redolent of herbs, honey-sweet, heady. He drank, then passed the cup back to her.

She drank too, spoke again.

'For it was there, in your groves, in your fields, by your river, that I learnt to believe in something older even than this.' She gestured to a crucifix on the wall behind her. 'And something just as holy.'

She refilled the one goblet with the honeyed wine and each drank before she continued.

'I tell you this because I need your help and, if you will give it, a vow sworn on whatever you believe to be sacred that you will do as I bid you. There will be gold enough, but gold will not buy what I ask of you now.'

'Ask,' Jean said softly.

'You have heard the stories. Anne Boleyn, Witch, the Six-Fingered Hag. Well, there's a truth hidden there, though not in the way people fear, consigning all to the shadows where they keep their supposed sins. I am of both light and dark, of earth and fire, air and water. My so-called witchery lies fully, and only, in them. Do you understand, Jean Rombaud?'

'I understand.'

'Very well.'

She smiled then, and looked away, and there was something terrible, beautiful, so sad in that smile. The wine was affecting his vision, not making him drowsy but altering the light, making shapes of the shadows cast by the fireplace. He would have liked to lean back and study those shapes. Yet when she raised her hand, her six-fingered hand, it pulsed, drawing in the light of the reed torch, harnessing its flame. It commanded his eyes. He could look nowhere else, could only listen.

'When you have struck my head from my shoulders, you must strike again, once and secretly. You must cut off this hand.'

He stumbled forward then, towards her. He had not expected this, of all the things she could ask.

Her eyes never lost his.

'You must cut it off, then take it to the Loire, to our land.

There is a village called Pont St Just, near Tours. To the south of it lies a crossroads. There, at the next full moon, bury my hand at the exact point where the four roads meet.' She smiled. 'That is all I ask of you. It is much, and it is dangerous beyond your imaginings, for there are those who will hazard all to stop you. Will you do this for me?'

Jean was unable to speak, to breathe. The cell vanished, he was floating on smoke, nothing in his sight but six fingers and two eyes, black pools of immeasurable depth. Something stirring within them, another pair, then another, an infinity of eyes stretching back in an unbroken line to a time before, on and on, generations of women looking out at him, dark-eyed, six-fingered. He was exposed, naked, waiting to be born. Needing a word for that, to come back into the world. One simple word.

'Yes,' he said.

'And will you swear it? On what could you swear such an oath?'

He did not know. He was not a religious man, the faith he'd been baptised in long since ripped away by the desecrations of war and his terrible loss. He knew a lot about death, and maybe once, for a time, a little about love. Maybe enough.

'I will swear it on love. On that love I had – have – for my Lysette and my little Ariel. On their blessed eyes I vow: I will do what you ask of me.'

She stepped close and his knees wavered under him as, silently, she measured the depths that gave birth to such a promise. Then suddenly she smiled, a smile of such joy, such radiance.

'I did not fear my death except in this, the harm I could do after I passed over were this vow not spoken. And I could not offer anything to buy this of you. But now it is freely pledged, there is something I can give.'

She reached up, touched him on either side of his head, held him with those strange, uneven hands – with her uneven eyes the only reason he was still standing. She whispered, 'Be ready. For your reward will come the moment your sword sets me free.' And then she kissed him, a kiss which burnt onto his lips and through them to what he could only call his soul. A kiss that turned all memory to mist, in a room drowsy with reed-torch smoke and wine heavy with secret herbs.

When he woke, the hand on his shoulder was a man's, shaking him roughly awake. Anne was gone, light was in the sky and Tucknell had returned to lead him back to his chambers. There was not much time to wait.

He saw her again not an hour later as she mounted the scaffold with a step that seemed to spring, a smile on the lips whose kiss yet burnt him. Her serenity calmed a restless mob, and if she were not a beauty, she had a light that caused all to gasp. A weeping maid took off her French hood, the hair under it prettily coiled into a white linen coif. Her robe was of grey damask trimmed with fur with a low, square neck, as simple as the speech that followed. She blamed no one, admitted nothing, put her faith in God and asked all present to pray for her.

Through the slits of his leather mask, Jean looked out at the small, eager crowd. King Henry was not going to risk a public riot beyond the walls on Tower Hill. He needed this act, this state-sanctioned murder, to be hidden away, as so many had been within this evil place. All those drawn from the inner court that were there had schemed, begged and bribed to be at this most fashionable of occasions. Courtiers who had bent before her to kiss what they saw only as her deformity, gallants who had flirted and composed odes to her beauty, ladies who had fawned while they seethed at her rise and rejoiced in her fall – all had gathered now to share in the ritual of her destruction.

His problem lay there, in those hundreds of ecstatic eyes, for they would follow his every gesture. However distracting the sight of her head separating from her shoulders, however

29

swift his stroke, someone would note the second rise and fall of the blade that took the hand.

Before Anne now knelt the confessor, urging her to join him on her knees, to make one last atonement. Yet she was more concerned with feeling the breeze on her face, standing there, eyes shut, palms spread wide. Jean watched the man raise his own clasped hands to his face . . . and saw, in that instant, what must be done.

He stepped before her, his shadow falling on the priest who started, crossed himself and moved away. Taking his place, Jean knelt and publicly began the penultimate stage of the ritual.

'Forgive me for what I must do.'

Anne's eyes opened at his voice and a smile came into them.

'I forgive you all, Master, and I thank you.'

The weeping maid handed her the fee and she held it out to him. He grasped but did not take it, and they were joined across that velvet purse while the promise and the memory coalesced in her eyes.

He whispered, 'At the last, raise your hands to pray.'

'But why?'

'Raise them, my lady. And when I say "now" leave just the one there, the thumb resting upon your chin. Do you understand?'

'Ah, yes. Yes, I do.'

'And so . . . goodbye.'

He made to take the purse, but now she held it, held his eyes.

'Not goodbye, Jean Rombaud. Au revoir. For if there is one thing certain in this world, it is that we two shall meet again.'

She let go of the purse, and the shock of her words, of no longer being joined to her, left him breathless. He stood, she knelt, looking up into the sky for a last time before accepting the blindfold. Then she raised her hands to her face, her lips moving in prayer.

Jean reached for his sword, hidden behind him under his cloak. He swung it back, feeling its beautiful weight, its perfect balance. He bent at the knees, inhaled and, as he coiled his arms still further, said, 'Now.'

One hand dropped away as he released his shoulders, the blade gliding perfectly flat towards that perfect neck, gliding through with not a second's pause to mark the border crossed between life and death. Through to the other side and through the hand, though it seemed to all there as if he had touched neither.

All was frozen – faces on the scaffold, faces in the crowd, caught in joy or horror – and in that frozen moment the sun broke from its cloud prison, dazzling everyone, shimmering off the sword resting at the end of its swing. To Jean it was a weapon no more but a key, unlocking the door between this sphere and the next. And in its glittering planes he saw two figures.

A shard of exquisite pain, a tremor of indescribable happiness, surged through him. For there, lit by celestial light, were his Lysette and his little Ariel. Jean saw faces so calm, so at peace, that he felt a near irresistible urge to join them in their bliss. It seemed they saw him too, for they smiled and then, hand in hand, they turned away.

He had the reward she had promised. But he only had time to say thank you before the door closed gently upon them. A thin red line had appeared at Anne Boleyn's throat and wrist and the voice of the crowd, suspended for those seemingly eternal moments, returned now in full roar.

It seemed that a world starved of air suddenly breathed as Tucknell stepped forward and pulled Anne's head from her shoulders by the hair. All eyes looked to its rising, the blood spurting at last in a high arc out over the crowd. The body fell sideways, the severed hand dropped at Jean's feet and Tucknell, tears flowing into his beard, in a voice thick with grief, cried, 'Behold the head of a traitor! God save the King!'

The crowd surged forward then, shrieking, and as they did

Jean bent down and scooped up hand and purse together, slipping the one into the other, bending over the body to wrap it swiftly in his cloak, binding it tightly. He thrust the purse under his executioner's apron, sheathed his sword and pushed his way off the back of the scaffold, away from the civilised courtiers and decorous ladies transformed into snarling animals in their struggle to soak their handkerchiefs in a dead queen's blood. His departure was unimpeded.

And nearly unnoticed. For one pair of eyes must not have been drawn by the head's bloody rise as Jean, wedged in the gibbet cage, now knew. One pair of eyes had followed the progress of the hand from scaffold to purse to apron, then followed it all the way to a crossroads in the Loire. There the possessor of such keen sight had left Jean hanging from a gibbet to die, his only hope of salvation the tale he'd just told to a madman by the light of a waning full moon.

# FOUR

# JUDGEMENT

Jean, who had kept his eyes closed while he concentrated on his story, opened them now and struggled to turn in the cage to see his audience below.

'The wretched creature is asleep!' he cried, the sound choking in his throat. To have told that tale, to have relived it again, all for nothing? Such little hope had burnt within him, and even that was now extinguished. *I will die here. My vow to Anne Boleyn is broken.*

He eyed the Fugger in despair.

Then the Fugger stirred beneath him. A flick of the right arm knocked Felix's skull down the midden's slopes. Shaking spread through his body until all was a-twitch – arms, legs, head. With a leap, the Fugger was on his feet and whirling. All the while sounds poured from his mouth, words in a multitude of tongues, shrieks, moans and gibbers.

With a mighty croak, the raven rose to circle above, adding its harsh voice to the cacophony. Slowly, slowly, the din died, the caws of man and bird became muted, the caperings eased. When it had come down to a mere shuddering, the Fugger suddenly leapt up to the cage, thrust his left hand through the bars and, swinging there, fixed Jean with a maddened stare.

'Who told you?' he shrieked. 'Heh? Come on, come on, someone has sent you to torment me, told you my life, given you this weapon to use against me.'

'I do not know—' Jean began, but the Fugger began swinging the cage hard.

'Then you saw!' he yelled. 'You saw, then fashioned your story, so clever. Admit it and it will go easier for you, I will give you a swift end. Your story was all lies! Lies, lies!'

'Monsieur,' Jean said as calmly as he could, 'I know nothing of your life. I have told you the truth of mine. That is all.'

The Fugger swayed there, staring at Jean for a moment longer. Then he cried out, 'Tell me you didn't know about this!' And he thrust his right arm into Jean's face. It ended in a stump.

A moment of choice for the caged man. The Fugger in reach of his cramped arms. Grab, twist, hurt, force him to swing the cage over to the crossbar, force him to grab the key. Decisive actions, and the seizing of a chance, any chance, had meant survival on a score of battlefields.

*Come*, thought Jean, *seize another now*.

And yet, in that moment's hesitation he remembered another savaged wrist, transforming the one before him now; and seeing it somehow made him recognise, deep within the maddened, moon-bright eyes of the Fugger, the same pain, the same appeal he had seen just a week before in the Tower of London.

Slowly, Jean closed his fingers on the tortured flesh before him, held it gently for a moment. It was the nearest thing to a caress he could manage. The Fugger fell back as if struck and lay again on the midden. There was no movement save for the tears cascading down his face.

In the long silence that followed, broken only by the Fugger's crying, Jean wondered if he'd just let his one chance of freedom fall from the cage. To put his trust in the humanity of a madman? What had he been thinking? And he was not reassured when the sounds below him changed from muffled weeping to a rasping, crackling sound that he came to realise could only be laughter.

'Oh Daemon, dear,' laughed the Fugger. 'It really is such a good story. And so unbelievable that it could only be true.'

As suddenly as the laughter had begun, it stopped. The Fugger sat up, wiped a grimy sleeve across his face and said, 'These men who put you here. They have taken the hand of the Queen?'

'Yes.'

'Why?'

'I do not know. It is said there is power in relics. If so, there must be a great power in this one.'

'And who has stolen it?'

'You said before one was called "the Archbishop". She warned me there would be those who sought to use her after death for their own ends.'

'He was called "Archbishop" by the other. It made him very angry. Such illustrious visitors, I thought. That's when I knew you were special.'

'An archbishop makes sense. Do you know where from?'

'No. But I heard him talk of Siena.'

'And this other, the soldier?' asked Jean.

'I didn't see him. But from his voice I could tell he was a countryman of mine. German. But from the south. One of those accursed Bavarians, for certain.'

'Well.' Jean stared through the slats along the road the horsemen had taken. 'I begin to know my enemy.'

'And I know mine,' said the Fugger. He jumped up, thrusting his good arm through the bars again. 'What will you give me if I free you now?'

'I gave you the story. Was not that my part of the bargain?'

The Fugger let out that strange, crackling laugh, like sheets of rough parchment rubbed together.

'Only if it pleased me, you said. It does. But I want something more.'

'I have nothing more. I never had much and they have taken everything. Even my sword – which is the first thing I plan to get back. I have no gold.'

35

'Gold?' The Fugger turned and spat on the midden heap. 'As a banker's son my life was all gold before, and look where that has led me.' Before Jean could question him, the Fugger went on. 'No, a duke's ransom would not free you from this cage. I ask for the one thing you are able to give me – another vow.'

'And that is?'

'That you will let me help you fulfil yours.'

'By setting me free, you help me.'

'No. I want to help you regain what is taken from you. You see, I too have lost a hand. It seems fitting that I find another.'

Jean looked into the Fugger's crazed eyes and thought, *All I have seen so far is his madness. I have not seen the person at all. Now I see both the man and his need. A need as great as mine, perhaps.*

Still, he said, 'I will not lie to you. My promise to my Queen is all to me. Help me and somehow I think you will be blessed for it. Cross me, and I'll abandon you in an instant.' It was a brave speech for a man swaying on a gibbet. Which the other recognised.

'You drive a hard bargain. And from such a strong position,' laughed the Fugger. 'I accept.'

One leap fetched the key from the crossbeam and the Fugger turned it in the lock. With a scream of metal, the iron cage opened and Jean tumbled out. The raven set up a loud croaking.

'Oh yes, how could I forget? Daemon comes too! What a force we will make, the three of us. Let the quest begin!' And the Fugger started his strange, twitching dance.

As Jean lay on his back on the midden heap, fire rushing through his cramped, bruised limbs, he watched the caperings of a madman and the cawing swoops of a raven.

'God help us,' he groaned.

'Amen!' yelled the Fugger, whirling round and round.

# FIVE

# TO THE VICTOR, THE SPOILS

To the innkeeper of the village of Pont St Just, it was very clear: the Germans had made a mess of his inn when capturing their quarry and they had not paid a sou for it. Furthermore, the two wounded comrades they had left behind in his barn for his wife to tend on the promise of recompense when the rest returned had, shortly after dawn, suddenly, simultaneously and mysteriously died. This was not his fault, but he now had to deal with the bodies, scrub away the stains on floor and palliasse, repair or replace the furniture and pots smashed in the mêlée . . . and then there was the waste of the wine spilled and the stew now feeding the cats among the floor reeds!

'And so, my sweetness,' Guillaume Roche declared to his wife, his sausage fingers fluttering under his fat chin, 'since they have not returned to pay, by ancient right their goods are forfeit.'

'Oh good!' said his equally plump wife. 'More prize weapons to rust on our walls, more big boots to use on our fire. If you stood more by cash up front and less by "ancient rights", we might have something worthwhile now. How many times must I tell you?'

Guillaume sighed, nodded and agreed, but remembered the shock of a group of large, exotically dressed Germans at his tables demanding food and wine. There hadn't seemed to be a moment to ask before. And he assured his wife that they were just about to reach into their purses, they truly were. But then the stranger had walked in.

'It must have just slipped their minds afterwards,' he reasoned, and his wife snorted and walked away, leaving him, broom in hand, to contemplate the damage.

One man against eight – you'd have thought it would have been over much quicker, with a lot less fuss. Guillaume would gamble on anything, from the quickness of rats to logs burning in a fire, so when the man with the square-tipped sword had reduced his enemies by half within seconds, well, he'd have given quite good odds on him finishing them all off. And he would have done too had it not been for that plate of stew and a misplaced foot, a moment off balance.

Once down, a search of the loser's possessions had yielded a purse from the saddle bags, heavy with coin; but the real yell of triumph came when they found a velvet bag, shouts which stopped abruptly at the upraised hand of a figure as slight and drab as the Germans were bulky and colourful, dressed in a cloak that had a monastic air until one noticed the richness of its cloth, the lush fur around the hood. This hand had silenced all except the two wounded men, though even their groans subsided a little. And when it felt what was in the bag, the slight figure gave out a moan that was . . . well, the memory still made Guillaume shudder, for it had reminded him of love-making and death at the same time.

He assessed his limited haul. The bag of the vanquished stranger had yielded a spare set of clothes, a complete barber's set of scissors, combs and knives, and a leather mask. All this might fetch a few sous in the market in Tours at month's end. The clothes from the four dead Germans were more of a problem, though. Not only were they somewhat stained with blood, they were also of the type worn by mercenaries the world over.

'Peacocks!' Guillaume spat, raising one scarlet and blue jacket by its puffed, blistered and slashed sleeve, eyeing with distaste the clashing interior lining, pulled through the cuttes, of vivid yellow. The breeches were golden, a horrible contrast to the black-and-orange hose stocking that rose through them. Aside from these fripperies, there were two huge Landsknecht swords (conversion to ploughshares possible), two pairs of very large boots (use the leather again or burn them as fuel), some serviceable cloaks and shirts, and two hats which, when stripped of their ostentatious plumes, might suit a farmer.

'Twenty sous, the lot,' he grumbled. Hardly worth the trip to town. Probably wouldn't even cover the damage. His wife, annoyingly, was correct. So much for ancient rights!

Then he realised what he could do with these items, and the thought made him beam. It was Sunday, the priest was adamant about Sabbath rest, and many in the village would be around with nothing to do. If he could offer them some entertainment such as an auction, he could barter these goods away and sell some extra wine and beer into the bargain.

Much cheered, he went round the back to water down both immediately.

The sight that greeted Jean when he limped into the inn was one of frenzied bidding. He had spent the morning binding his ribs – bruised but not broken – and shin, tending the nasty sword slash to it, eating such food as the Fugger could provide, resting and thinking. His impulse was to run in the direction the Germans and the Archbishop had ridden, but the feeling soon passed. He had campaigned long enough to know that an attack in haste and in a weakened state always failed. He needed supplies and a weapon, and to regain some strength.

Walking into the inn, he doubted his enemies would have left his possessions, certainly not the hefty fee he'd earned the week before in London. But they might have left some clue as to their identity and their next destination.

The Fugger was waiting on the edge of the village. Once his euphoria had passed, the strange man had become very upset, tearful even, at the thought of leaving the kingdom he ruled and returning to the world that had taken so much from him, including his hand. It had only been Jean's determined strides away from the crossroads that finally prised him loose, although he darted back to pick up some little trinket, a scrap of food and, fortunately, the coins Jean's assailants had left in the offertory box. When they reached the village, the Fugger had slunk away into the shadows. He would not enter the inn, for he looked like what he was, the gibbet keeper, reeking of his trade, an offence to nose and eyes, body parts thrust through his gaping rags, hair and beard a nest of lice, a now silent raven perched on his shoulder. As he contemplated him, Jean feared he would have cause to curse this latest vow of his many times.

'Two sous . . . and a cockerel!' someone yelled as Jean stepped quietly through the partly open door. There was much cheering at the bid, some oaths, tankards raised and clinked loudly.

'Come come, Messieurs.' Guillaume waved the sword above the heads of those nearest him. 'Two sous for such a fine piece of weaponry?'

'And a cockerel!' the bidder reminded the landlord and began to crow in imitation of his bid.

A slight man with rat-like eyes caught Guillaume's attention and declared, 'Three sous!'

'Three sous is bid. I say, three sous,' called the landlord. 'Come, come gentlemen, surely one of you has a son who wants to go a-warring, to bring back honour and loot from foreign scum? Why not give him the advantages of this fine German weapon? Look at its length, its keen blade, its superb balance. I'll even throw in a Landsknecht jacket to give the little master strut. Or if warring's not to your taste, think of the ploughing! A little hammering at the forge at La Fontiane and your furrows will be deeper and straighter even than Gaston's here.' A derisory yell went up. 'Who will give me five sous?'

Guillaume was enjoying himself. It wasn't often he got to use his city wiles on these peasants. Seven years as an apprentice to that brewer in Beaune had not been wasted time.

It was then that he saw the stranger, and the moment their eyes met, Jean began to move through the crowd. Guillaume knew he'd seen the fellow before and recently, but for a fateful second's delay he didn't recognise him, so completely had he dismissed the idea that the Germans' victim could still be alive. By the time he remembered, Jean was in front of him, one of his hands resting beside the landlord's on the hilt of the sword.

'May I?' he said quietly, his eyes never leaving Guillaume's, and he lifted the sword away.

'Hey,' said the rat-eyed man, 'that's mine.'

'I don't think so.' Jean was still looking at the landlord. 'You know who I am. Tell them.'

'But Monsieur,' the big man stuttered, 'they left without paying. By ancient right—'

'By ancient right the man they robbed and tried to kill is entitled to restitution.'

'Ancient right be damned!' The frustrated bidder had risen and turned to his friends. 'I put in the highest bid. Are we to let a stranger cheat us of what's ours? Let us—'

He'd got that far when the flat of the blade caught him just above the ear. Only a short backswing followed by a sharp pull, but it was enough to tweak Jean's sore ribs and he uttered a small prayer to St Vincent that it would suffice. They may have been peasants but there were ten of them, on their own ground and full of cheap wine. Each was sure to have a cudgel about him somewhere.

It was enough. Caught in mid-sentence, the man hung in the air a second longer than his words, then suddenly sat down on the floor. As he sat down, Jean swung the sword back to rest on his shoulder.

'I am not here for trouble,' he said evenly. 'The landlord

will tell you how I was wronged. If you will join me in a flagon to toast the miracle of my survival and the recovery of my possessions, we may all part friends.'

They didn't care for strangers in Pont St Just. Even if this one held a weapon, they were still ten against one.

'A flagon on the gentleman!' yelled Guillaume, suddenly realising that a little wine sold was better than a room destroyed. Again. Besides, he had already seen what this man could do with a sword. He didn't want to see it a second time. He had few enough paying customers as it was. 'Did I not tell you, Messieurs,' he hurried on, 'what this one Frenchman did against ten – no, wasn't it at least twenty? Against twenty Germans, only yesterday? Madeleine, the wine, quickly. Ah, what a sight . . .'

The landlord's well-spun story, and the free wine, soon had good cheer restored. Even Jean's victim revived, choking on his share of the handout. And when the story had been told and retold – how Jean, a native hero, had despatched at least thirty Germans – five extra flagons lay upended on the floor.

Later, Jean took the landlord aside to negotiate a swift exchange.

'Are you a surgeon, then?' Guillaume laughed nervously, handing over the set of knives and scissors.

'In a way,' said Jean, remembering his time in the army. Before he found his true vocation, before he found his sword, he'd been the closest most soldiers got to a doctor. A barber-surgeon, cutting hair, extracting musket balls, stitching wounds.

He took just the one Landsknecht sword, his own meagre gear and the least stained set of clothes from the Germans. He gave Guillaume one of the gold coins from the offertory box at the gibbet for the flagons and some food and wine for the journey. And he learnt from him all the landlord knew about his assailants, who apparently had arrived just before him from the local town, Tours. Guillaume had recognised the marks on some of their pack horses from a stable there.

Finally, Jean went and looked at the German corpses. They were naked and blue in the inn's stable, and he briefly studied the wounds. What had undoubtedly done for the wounded men was a knife thrust between the six and seventh ribs. He doubted the landlord would have the skill or stomach for that. So the others had been back and taken care of their own. It told him a little more about his enemy. In war he had seen this often – when retreating, never leave a comrade to be taken and killed more slowly by the foe. But this was a time of peace, the wounds not so serious that these soldiers could not have been moved by cart. His enemy was in a hurry. And so was he.

Yet it was mid-afternoon before he was able to leave. The weather, as was customary at that time of year and especially in that part of the world, had changed again, the last chill of a cold spring gone, a warmer wind sweeping in from the south bearing scents of Africa. It was a day for beginnings, and if his destination weren't so important, Jean would have savoured it more. Now, he merely set his eyes on the horizon and walked towards it.

He'd reached the edge of the village when something whirligigged out of a bush, the black shape splitting into two, the top section cawing and flapping, the bottom leaping and scratching.

'Caw caw!' yelled the Fugger, echoing Daemon's cries. 'Which means, roughly: How found you the village – brought us some food? – how far do we travel and when will we get the hand hand hand?'

Jean reached out and grabbed the Fugger by the throat. He held on through a few more shudders and squawks until all was calm. Then he slowly loosened, but did not quite release, his grip.

'Never,' he said quietly, 'never again declare our goal.'

The Fugger hung limply and nodded. 'We will be silent, Daemon and I. Not once shall we mention the hand.'

'Hand hand!' cawed the bird, circling above them.

'By the soiled seat of a saint!' yelled Jean, bending to pick up and cast a stone at the raven, which floated gently over it. 'What have you done?'

'Well, you were gone so long.' The Fugger's tone was accusing. 'We had to talk about something.'

'Jesu spare me!' spat the executioner and strode off down the road.

He didn't look back. He didn't need to. The warm wind that blew up the valley carried with it the unique scent of the gibbet keeper, refining and ripening under the hot sun. It didn't help his temper for he knew that any unobserved progress with the Fugger through this land was doomed: the nostrils of those ahead would tell that something rank that way came long before the sight caused all to reach for cudgel and stone. If he kept his promise to the Fugger – and he didn't see how he could start breaking vows now – he would have to find some way for them to proceed in amity together.

About an hour's walk from the village, Jean could bear it no more. He suddenly left the road and made his way down to the stream they'd been following. It broadened into a little pool shaded by three willows and surrounded by sweet-smelling rosemary bushes, which he thankfully sank his head into, rubbing the prickly leaves to release the scent. Then, as he bent down to cup his hands into the water, he heard the whirligig approach a second before the stench hit him. When the Fugger began to lap the water like a dog, Jean stood up, stepped sideways and planted his boot straight up his back-side.

The Fugger plunged into the water, surfaced, spat water and let out a mournful wail. 'I drown, I drown! So cold, so chilly on my bones! Let me out!'

Jean stood square on the bank and unsheathed his sword.

'You are not coming out until you have washed some of that stench from you.'

'No!' howled the Fugger. 'I'm drowning!'

'Nonetheless,' said Jean, and as the Fugger tried to pull himself out, he sliced at the two shoulders of the Fugger's clothing sack and the whole thing fell off him, leaving nothing but a bare, blackened creature flailing around. The flat of a blade on his haunch sent him sprawling again, soon to be joined by two large clumps of rosemary Jean had quickly sliced from the bushes.

'Use them to scrub off that filth. Then use the river mud. Rub it all over your body, and especially through your hair.' It was how he used to bathe as a child.

'I'll die of cold.'

'You will if you don't keep moving.'

Shivering, quaking, emitting a steady moan, the Fugger began to do as he was told, at first with little vigour. But as the layers began to drop off and cloud the water around him, he ceased his noise and began to use the rosemary branches more forcefully. A noise began again, and Jean made out a song under the Fugger's breath as he began to range around the pool in search of cleaner water. When Jean was satisfied, he allowed the Fugger out and gave him the newly acquired cloak.

Sitting the shaking form down on a stone, he said, 'And now Monsieur is clean, perhaps a new hairstyle?' and, without waiting for a response, began to ply his barber's shears around the unfortunate's head. Shanks, knotted locks and rat's-nest curls tumbled to the ground as he trimmed the head right down to the pate, the only way to get rid of such undergrowth. He then began on the beard, cutting it to a soldier's fashionable length.

Finished, he stood back to study his work.

Before him sat a very frightened young man with a high forehead fringed by cropped hair that was actually of a reddish hew, and a red beard that tapered to a point two fingers' width below his chin. The sharp features were not just the product of hunger; high cheekbones were divided from each other by a long thin nose and piercing blue eyes darted nervously about.

'What have you done to me?' the Fugger cried.

'See for yourself.' Jean gestured to the pool.

Lowering himself cautiously as if expecting another shove, the Fugger glanced down once, quickly, then looked away for a long moment. When he looked again he held his gaze, running his fingers up and down, exploring his face. After a while, he just stopped and stared, tried to pretend that was all he was doing. Seeing water flow from the eyes to join the pool, Jean turned away to pack up his barber's gear.

'Thank you,' said the Fugger at last. 'I thought this person was gone for ever. His soul was stolen, do you see, along with . . .' He raised the stump of his arm to Jean. 'Now he has come back.'

Then the tears really came, and he made no attempt to conceal them. Jean moved away, sat and waited; for though time was pressing he knew that some men who had emerged from a great madness, as from battle or the terrible sack of a city, needed to howl like this. He had done it once himself, in a burning church in Tuscany, a lifetime before. There was nothing to do but wait, as someone had once waited for him.

Eventually, he could tell the shivering came more from cold than emotion so he went to his bag.

'Here.' He threw the German soldier's clothes across.

'For me?' A voice filled with wonder, hands turning the material over and over.

'They may be a little large, and gaudy,' Jean said, 'but they are of good quality. He obviously lived well.'

The Fugger slipped his head into the wool shirt, found the arm holes. Jean had chosen the smallest set of clothes but the breeches were still vast. A length of rope restrained some of the bagginess, while clumps of grass filled in the front of the heavy boots. The scarlet-and-black jerkin's sleeves were rolled up and the cloak over the top disguised the irregularities, hiding the worst of the peacock display.

'Not bad,' said Jean as the Fugger moved around him. 'And the smell's an improvement. Even if it has a touch of German sweat about it.'

'Well, I will add to it then,' the Fugger spoke softly, 'for I am German too.'

'A German, eh? From where?'

'From Munster.'

'And did you not say, when we were, uh, negotiating back there at the gibbet, that you were a banker's son?'

'I did.'

Jean scratched his head.

'I am not one for questions. A man's business is his own,' he said. 'But how, by the useless balls of a Dominican monk, did a German banker end up running a gibbet in France?'

The Fugger laughed. It seemed a strange sensation until he realised he was doing it for no reason other than pure pleasure.

'You have a very mixed way of cursing, Monsieur.'

'I have been in too many countries' armies, perhaps, Monsieur Fugger.'

With the laughter came another feeling, and the Fugger raised his one good hand to Jean.

'The Fugger who kept a gibbet in France?' he said. 'It is a long tale and a strange one.'

'That is good.' Jean rose. 'The longer and stranger the better, for we have a night's march ahead of us. We must be in Tours by dawn.'

And with that, hefting sword and pack, he headed back to the road.

The Fugger stood for a moment alone on the stream bank. Stooping suddenly, he scooped up some tangled skeins of hair, running them through his fingers before throwing them back into the fast-moving water. As the last traces of his recent life swirled away, caught and burst through a small dam of reeds, he murmured, 'And wash my sins away.'

Then he turned and hurried after the Frenchman.

# SIX

# ORGIES AND AXES

Giancarlo Cibo, Archbishop of Siena, was enjoying all the hospitality the church in Tours could offer him, which for a small provincial town wasn't so bad. His host, the Bishop of Tours, knew the favour of so powerful a churchman as Cibo would help him in his quest to secure the recently vacant See of Orleans. So he was making a strenuous effort to see his noble guest was well entertained.

The orgy, while not reaching Roman levels, was nonetheless of a high standard. The Bishop's mistress had overseen it, from the elaborate feast – swans roasted and dressed again in their feathers, a whole bear cooked in its skin and clutching a wild boar in its arms, a suckling pig in its mouth – to the after-dinner antics. Some of the town's most expensive whores, who counted the Bishop's mistress as a former member, together with a troop of the palace guard, re-enacted the biblical story of Sodom and Gomorrah, with a strong emphasis on the Sodom. The climax came when the mistress herself, as Lot's wife, was covered in 'salt', which turned out to be confectioner's sugar, soon to be licked off by two muscular soldiers dressed as Satan's satyrs, cloven-hoofed and horned, who then proceeded to take her simultaneously, thus demonstrating the true penalty for looking back.

The Archbishop was invited to join in at any stage, but since he never liked to be second in anything, three virgins were produced, dressed as noviciates. He knew they were neither by the expert way they plied their scourges, causing him just the right level of pain yet never drawing blood. However, they looked young enough and gave suitably virginal screams when he 'deflowered' them one after the other. Under their habits they too were sugar-coated.

Altogether a most satisfying night. Especially after all his tribulations in achieving his victory. He'd had to stay in disguise for so long, for Princes of the Roman Church were not popular in England, to say the least. The week spent pursuing that damned executioner through France! Sleeping in flea-ridden inns or roadside encampments, his cough had worsened considerably.

And yet, what lay now in his saddle bags made all the suffering worthwhile. Anne Boleyn's distinctive hand was a mighty weapon to control men's minds. Cibo understood the power of such symbols even if he was not a believer in them as literal facts. How often had he mocked the credulous fools he bent to his will with the healing touch of St John's cloak or the laying on of St Agnes' femur? Belief in the symbol was all, faith so touching, so often effective. But he knew it was the belief, not the piece of moth-eaten cloth or crumbling bone, that had the effect. That belief gave him the power to control men's minds.

It was why he'd gone to that chill, damp island of Britain. When he'd heard of Anne's forthcoming execution he'd remembered all the curious tales connected with her, not least the oddity of her six-fingered hand, and the fact it had shaken the Holy Church by leading that most Catholic monarch, Henry, away from his faith. He knew that if he took it, embalmed it or even just kept it as a skeleton, it would be a far more potent weapon than most of the bogus relics floating around Europe.

*Yet perhaps, as an archbishop, I should have more faith. After all, since I took the hand my cough has got better!* The absurd thought made him laugh. And the man waiting

49

patiently on the other side of the room took that as a signal to come forward. Watching the German approach, he thought, *Heinrich von Solingen believes in the power of her hand. He believes in it all, for only total belief can justify his terrible need to savage and kill.*

Cibo smiled. He had discovered early on that this man's propensity for violence was a superb weapon and he had channelled it accordingly. All he had to do was make Heinrich believe his sins were washed away by his service, his loyalty to whatever Christ's representative on earth – himself – needed him to do. It had led to some very special sinning, in the years of their association. He felt happy that he could offer the man such spectacular opportunities for transgression and redemption.

*But the man himself? How dreary he is,* the Archbishop thought, *standing there with his eyes studiously averted. He does not even dress like a mercenary any more. With his black, dull clothes, his white-blond hair close-cropped, he looks more like a priest.*

The puckered pink scar running from the right eyebrow to just above the jaw was hardly priest-like though. And neither were the many memories Cibo had of Heinrich with a weapon in his hand, the most recent one when his captain had erased the witnesses his former soldiers had become. Not as showy as the Archbishop would have liked, mere swift throat-slitting of drunken fools. But death was the best preliminary to any orgy, he always felt.

'Pain and pleasure, eh, Heinrich?'

Heinrich von Solingen kept his eyes fixed above his reclining master and the naked whores draped over him. He had followed this man for eight years and performed the most unspeakable acts for him. As a loyal son of the Church it was his duty – more, his personal crusade, to defy the Protestant heresy. *But why,* he thought for the thousandth time, *does Mother Church allow herself to be defended by men like this?*

It was always a problem for him, the contrast between flesh

and faith. That holy rebel Luther – who was, at least, a good German through and through, he thought – is right in that. Rome is corrupt beyond estimation. But loyalty to the Church isn't a changeable position, he told himself again. Heinrich was aware his master knew he believed that to his core. It gave the degenerate power over him. He hated that.

'My Lord?'

'Heinrich?'

'Shall I make the preparations to depart at dawn?'

'Dawn? It's a hideous idea. It must be mere hours away. And my kittens here have not allowed me to rest.'

One of those kittens reached up and ran a painted finger-nail down his exposed thigh. Heinrich looked quickly away.

'But my Lord wanted to move in haste. The . . . artefact is needed in Rome.'

'It is. But not yesterday, nor tomorrow. If we take the ship that awaits us in Toulon we can be there in ten days. It will suffice. And besides, the Bishop, my new friend over there' – he gestured to a bare rump just visible under a pair of sugared thighs – 'has requested my official presence at an execution tomorrow evening . . . I mean tonight. Six heretic weavers are to burn, and a heretic count is to have his head removed as a climax. Who would have thought a Catholic prince would turn away from his Mother Church like that?'

'Fat Henry of England did.'

'Exactly, my knowledgeable friend. There must be no more Henrys. So my attendance is important. Rome sends a message. Unless, of course . . .' He beckoned Heinrich closer and the tall man reluctantly bent towards him. Whispering now, the Archbishop continued, 'I had a rather intriguing message during the feast last night, from a rival of my dear host over there. The Bishop of Angers wants the See of Orleans for himself. He thinks I can influence that. Go there in the morning and find out what he's offering me.'

'My Lord.'

'You may leave. Go on, man, it's time for a little more

entertainment. Unless, perhaps, you would care to watch and learn?'

'I will go to church, my Lord, and pray for my sins.'

'What a good idea.' The Archbishop was gently kicking his kittens awake. 'Do say one for me.'

If the Archbishop of Siena was relaxed, the Bishop of Tours, a few hours later, was the opposite. All had gone to plan so far, the orgy had been a great success. Now, he was dragged from the arena of pleasure to hear the news that the centrepiece of his festival was in jeopardy.

'What do you mean? He can't be dead! He's my executioner,' he roared, somewhat illogically. He had a headache like a hammer pounding on an anvil. 'How did he die?'

His steward, Marcel, shrugged. 'Apparently he tripped over his sword, Milord. He was trying to piss out of the window.'

'How dare he?' screamed the Bishop. 'Have him flogged immediately!'

'Yes, Milord,' Marcel said nervously. 'Um, he is dead.'

'I don't care. He's left us in a very bad position with his carelessness. The execution is tonight.'

'I could send to the Bishop of Angers?'

'Idiot!' The Bishop struck his steward hard across the face. 'Is this the sort of advice I pay you for? The Bishop of Angers wants Orleans for himself. He will come with his executioner and he will steal my glory. No, you must find someone here in Tours.'

'Here?'

'Yes. There must be an executioner out there among that rabble of discharged soldiers. Mercenary scum, most of them, not even French. Find one.'

'Eminence,' Marcel spoke carefully, while backing out of range, 'I doubt we'll find a skilled swordsman at such short notice.'

'I don't care,' screamed the Bishop, turning the same colour as his purple hat, 'if he takes off the head with a sword, an axe or my tailor's pinking shears! Find me someone to do it!'

And with that, clutching his own head, the Bishop sank back onto his bed. He wasn't used to panicking. He had people to panic for him.

By the time Jean and the Fugger reached Tours mid-morning, the town was abuzz as an ever-changing crowd gathered at the main church's doors to read the poster hung there.

'"Due to the unexpected and sudden demise—"' the Fugger read swiftly, 'uh, "only men of true worth and experience need apply." That's you, isn't it?'

'It is,' said Jean, 'but I had not thought to ply my trade again so soon, if at all.' He looked across at the young German. 'I thought, perhaps, a new career in barbering.'

'Either way,' mumbled the Fugger, rubbing his shorn head, 'you're a butcher.'

Jean laughed and turned back to the poster.

'Wait! What's this?' He gestured to the words scrawled near the bottom of the paper.

He could not read as quickly as his companion and by the time he'd finished the Fugger was hopping from foot to foot in excitement, humming the while. He stopped when Jean looked at him.

'I know. I'm drawing attention, but think of it. He's here, he's here! That's what it says, "In the presence of his Holiness the Archbishop of Siena".'

'I can read.'

Jean turned away down the alley to the left of the church, quickly entering the rancid, sweating, crowded heart of Tours on a festival day. The Fugger followed, the raven perched on his shoulder. The lane was so narrow and the opposite houses overhung so much that they nearly touched two storeys above, making flight impossible.

'We've caught up with him. It is here, what we seek. We can take it back,' the Fugger whispered excitedly.

53

'Indeed.' Jean was straddling with his steps the line of sewage running down the middle of the lane. 'And how would you suggest doing that?'

The Fugger grabbed him by the arm and pulled him into an alcove.

'I have a plan. My fine, educated mind has worked on the problem and come up with an answer instantly, yes it has. It's a golden opportunity. You take the job of the executioner. You will be up there, shrouded and armed, right beside the Archbishop.'

'Fugger, you want me to steal the hand in front of a thousand people?'

'Why not?' The Fugger's darting eyes finally settled upon Jean. 'It's not as if you haven't done it before.'

The second gold coin from the offertory box bought them a share of a palliasse, unoccupied now it was day, a hunk each of bread and meat, some sour beer, and gave them a little change. Consuming his food swiftly, Jean straight away lay down and tried to sleep. The Fugger, delighted to find his mind working once more along relatively straight lines, was determined to share the results. He sat up and uttered a continuous stream of words.

'What we'll need is some sort of diversion. Well, that will be my job, mine and Daemon's. We will direct the eyes away for a moment from the block – oh, I'm sorry, I know you don't use a block – well, from the stage anyway, while you pin that little worm of Satan against the wall and force him to give up the hand. Or, better still, maybe a fire, just a small one, around some bales nearby – nothing like a fire to get a town moving, of course, terrible things. I was in that great one that burnt down half of Basle. Yes, a fire to draw them away, your sword to His Eminence's throat and—'

'By the scrotal beard of Suleyman, will you shut up!' roared Jean. 'I need to rest. I cannot think for lack of sleep.' He flipped onto his side. 'What time did they call on volunteers for this job?'

54

'Three bells, at the abattoir. The execution is at nine in the main square.'

'Wake me at two bells, then. And, by the weeping Madonna, be silent,' Jean said, and closed his eyes.

The Fugger watched him for a while, twitching, scratching, his mind as agitated as his body. He couldn't sleep, felt he'd been asleep for a thousand years; now there was so much he wanted to say, so many plans he had to share. He wanted above all to be useful, to belong to this noble quest, as more than a hindrance to be dragged around. He owed this barbering, barbarous headsman that much.

Just then, one of the headsman's eyes opened.

'If you want to be useful, go and find out what happened to the dead executioner's sword.'

Not twenty paces from where Jean began to snore, another headsman was lying down, but this one had given up all hope of sleep, his mind too full of the images Angelique had brought back from the Bishop's palace where she'd been one of the inhabitants of Sodom. He'd waited outside the palace all that rainy night to escort her home at dawn, and now he lay awake while she slept next to him, his arm growing stiff under her head, trying to conjure other images. Failing.

A shout from the street below, an argument breaking out, curses, the sound of blows exchanged. Carefully withdrawing his arm, Haakon moved to the window, stooping to peer out into the murk. The source of the dispute was hidden, but enough light penetrated through the almost joined roofs of the houses to allow a distorted reflection to appear in the thick, grimy glass – the outline of a curling beard, of thick golden hair pulled back and held in a clasp at the neck. The angle of the head, the strength of nose, brow and forehead, all these reminded him, inevitably, of his father. For a tiny moment, if he closed his eyes he could almost hear him again, recounting the sagas of the heroes and the old gods Haakon had struggled so hard to memorise, sitting with his back to the legs of a huge oaken chair, his father's rich voice resonating through the wood and on into the heart of a boy, words stored up against the day foretold when he also would speak them to his people, to his own son. The day that had never come.

A groan from behind him, a little laugh. Haakon turned slightly and the reflection turned with him, his father disappearing to be replaced by a satyr, licking sugar from fleshy lips. A satyr, yet still himself, the man who now lived by the profits of the licked.

'Odin's blood,' he whispered, and the act of whispering reminded him how he was no longer someone who spoke his truth out loud. Men were going to die in this town tonight for doing just that. Braver men than Haakon had become.

He went into the second of the shabby rooms he shared with Angelique. There, in a nest made from a jumble of boxes, deep in some dream of hunt or battle, his hound, Fenrir, growled and shuddered the length of his grey-white body. His only true companion, they had been inseparable since the day Haakon had found the puppy, mewling and still blind, in a pillaged farm in Flanders five years before. He was bred of both wolves and their fleet-footed hunters but, like his master, he was getting fat in the idleness of town life.

Haakon bent to scratch behind the large ears and Fenrir thumped his tail on the wooden floor, his strange, square wolf eyes alight with pleasure at the touch. Reaching past him, Haakon rooted through the debris of his former life, the clothes, satchels and trinkets he'd accumulated in his years as a mercenary. Buried deep among it all, somewhere, was his inheritance. If he could not remember his father's tales, at least he had this much of him.

He heard the familiar chink of bone, dug deep within the cavernous bag and came up with the frayed pouch of brown wool. A linen cloth, its green faded with age, lay in the neck. He pulled it out, spreading it between his dog and himself. Then he tipped the rest of the bag's contents out upon it.

There were twenty-four runestones, each disk the size and shape of the circle of thumb tip to forefinger. When his father had killed a narwhal instead of the sought-after whale he'd seen it as a sign from Odin himself and carved Odin's runes upon disks made from the tusk. Haakon had watched as his father spent days shaping and polishing them, then more days in contemplation and fasting, before finally seizing his finest chisel and cutting the shapes themselves into the bone. The dye was already prepared, his own blood and extracts of muds and iron mixed, and the freshly cut-out symbols were soaked in a red that blazed from them still.

Turning each of them slowly over, so that all showed their cracked and yellowing backs, Haakon sought the stillness he'd need if the runes were to whisper to him rather than just show him their faces. He'd had the skill once, like his father before him, and his before that. Yet he feared it was another skill gone, like his ability to weave tales, from disuse, from separation from the land from which both he and they came.

Uttering a short invocation to Odin, he brought to his mind his question, banishing all other thought. There could only be one question: was it possible for him to escape this world he had settled in and return to a life where tales were both made and told? He began to move the runes, and the clack of bone on bone, bone on floor, filled his ears, their redness seeping, as mist, into his eyes.

His hand was drawn without hesitation to one of the disks, the same as all the rest. Different. Picking it out, laying it down, he moved again till another lay beside it, then another, and as he did so he went beyond the room, beyond the present, to past and future, all time one in his belief. Time that is and time that is becoming.

He turned the first rune over and it was FE. He knew it stood for cattle, effort expended for gradual reward, opposition overcome if you prepare till you are ready. He'd seen it once before, four years to the day since his father's murder, the day he'd first picked up his father's legacy, these rune-stones. Haakon had just turned fourteen, grown strong as he hid from his father's murderer among his woodcutter cousins. Holding a vision of vengeance at his axe's edge.

The second rune was UR, the Wild Ox, the beast to be slain by a boy who in the slaying becomes a man. It meant a sacrifice, of childhood, of much that was good and safe, and thus a leave-taking too. Something must be slain, and the fourteen-year-old boy, on seeing UR, had reached for his father's only other legacy, his axe.

The third rune was HAGALL, a hailstorm, striking the land from nowhere, sudden destruction, the same rune that had sent him without a word of farewell, with only rune-stones at his waist and an axe in his hand, back over the fells of Hareid by night, to stand in his father's house, before his father's bed, where the murderer slept who had stolen both. A boy had raised an axe, struck, the sacrifice made. A man had left the house and headed for the harbour, the first step on a path that had led, by various ways, to the mercenary road.

The red mist fading, Haakon stared down at the three symbols, unsurprised that they were the same as those that had sent him vengefully into the night fourteen years before. Since then many crossroads, many choices between left and right, forward and back, like the choice made by Angelique, his lover, to ply her trade in her home town of Tours at war's end. Choices ending up here, on a road leading nowhere.

And yet, the runes whispered again of choice, of opportunity, there if he could but see it. He knew what was behind him, the feeling that all of any importance in his life had been accomplished with one clean axe-stroke half a lifetime before. To set out again, all he needed was the will, the putting of one foot before the other. That and perhaps some coins to help him on his way.

Then a voice drifted up from the street and crept into his ear. It belonged to one of the Bishop's men, standing before

Haakon's lodgings where the lane widened a little, and it spoke of gold to be had by a man who knew how to wield an axe.

# SEVEN

# WINGED SLAUGHTER

As the first of the two bells rang, the Fugger nudged Jean in the chest with something hard; and when, grumbling, he opened his eyes, the Frenchman found an executioner's sword lying across his chest.

'How in the name of . . .' coughed Jean, but the Fugger was off, moving around the room.

'So Daemon and I are flying down the street,' he began, 'the one where I had been told the late headsman lived, and we come across a throng in a doorway. "You shall not enter!" yells a stout woman in the entrance. "What little he had is mine, for the six months he was under my roof." "But he owed me for three casks of beer!" shouts one man. "And he owed me for an army's share of my bread!" says another. "And he owed me for days on my back!" screams a thin woman, thrusting two ragged children forward. "These mites are his too. He was to buy them new clothes after he took the Count's head tonight." This brings an angry roar from the small crowd, who were siding now with one claimant, now with another. But the stout woman will not be budged from her doorway. Meantime, Daemon – yes, yes, come forward, my dear, take a bow – Daemon is above me and lets out a caw, and I look up to see him sitting on a hoist under the window up above. There's a hoist opposite too, and the houses so close there's almost a bridge between them. The shop owner is out watching the fun so without a second's pause I slip past him, through his shop, up the stairs and into the room on the street, open the window – and walk right over the arguing heads and into Old Stouty's residence.'

The Fugger, who had enacted every part of the story along with the words, now leapt from his imaginary bridge near the window and fell into a room.

'There did not seem much in the room worth fighting over, but I didn't linger. The sword sat on the window ledge so I grab it, teeter back across the hoists, and am down the stairs and through the crowd just as the two women are coming to blows.'

Jean slipped the weapon from its sheath. It was slightly heavier than his own, longer too, and not so exquisitely forged. But he had used worse, far worse.

'Fugger,' he declared, 'you've done well.'

'And Daemon too,' laughed the Fugger.

'And Daemon too,' said Jean.

The bird, occupied among its feathers, looked up at the mention of its name. 'Hand hand!' it cawed.

Jean stiffened, then after a second smiled grimly.

'We're coming to that,' he said. 'But first, we need to find this abattoir.'

When ordered to find a replacement executioner at such short notice Marcel, the Bishop's steward, had had one of his panics – or what his lover, Jacques, called a 'blue whirlwind'. Arranging orgies was one thing. He relished the detail involved in creating the tableaux, finding the perfect compli-mentary bodies; his years of travelling with the players of Poitiers had given him a taste for spectacle and a relish for surprising effects – the confectioner's sugar for Lot's wife had been his idea. But having to deal with real life in the form of the killers and thugs who would answer a call for the role of executioner – well, it would agitate the nerves of less sensitive men than he. Especially when so much was at stake. If the finale of the Archbishop's entertainment was a success and led to his master's rising to the See of Orleans, he knew his own rise was guaranteed too.

It was Jacques, the brutish boy with more than a touch of the gutter about him, who suggested the competition. Test the headsmen's skills *and* make some extra money from the spectacle of it all. A cousin – there was always a cousin with Jacques – owned an abattoir at the edge of town, an enclosed stockyard where you could crowd people in at a few sous apiece and take a cut from the profits of the beer and roast offal traders who were bound to set up.

Marcel felt he could leave the cruder details in the rough hands of his young friend. But the spectacle would be his. He had played in enough small towns to know what people craved. Violence, as brutal as possible, and comedy. He had some ideas for both.

When Jean, the Fugger and Daemon arrived at the abattoir, they found a small carnival taking place. The notices and criers had called forth not just the participants and their entourages but a host of spectators and the people to service, entertain and prey on them – fire-eaters, stilt walkers, magicians, pickpockets, whores, all moving through the throng. It was a good warm-up for the main event of the evening.

They could see the abattoir comprised a series of animal pens, with an outer track along which the beasts could be driven, itself surrounded by a circular stockade. Every plank of this was already occupied by children from the street, hopping down to dart among the smoking braziers of the meat sellers, the casks of the beer men, and the legs of the apprentices and artisans who had paid a few sous to enter by the main gate.

It was from there that Jean regarded the scene. Through the hurly-burly he could see a raised dais on which a man in gaudy hose was gesticulating extravagantly to a large, bearded man beside him. Before them stood a group of men in eye masks or makeshift hoods.

Mask and sword gained Jean admittance, and he pushed through to the dais.

'Name?' said the little man with the lacy shirt, frills of which sprouted around his tunic at collar and crotch, spilling there around one of the largest codpieces Jean had ever seen. *The larger the codpiece* Jean thought, but said, 'Blanc. Gaston.'

'Really?' tittered the man. 'It seems to be a family trade. These two are also Blancs.' He gestured towards two men with hoods. 'Do you require an axe as well?'

'No, Monsieur. I have my weapon here.'

Marcel leant forward and his eyes widened.

'A swordsman, eh? Do you have the requisite skill?'

'We shall see.'

'Are you experienced?'

'I have used it before, yes.'

'Any famous heads we would have heard of?'

'Probably not, Monsieur. With the army. Here and there.'

'I see,' sighed Marcel, already bored. Executioners always bored him, they had no small talk. 'Well, Blanc G., you can show us your talents in a moment. Wait with the others.'

Jean went and stood in the small group of shrouded men and looked over his rivals. The two Blancs were in animated discussion, raising their hoods to babble at each other. Another three men in eye masks stared silently ahead, but the last man in the line returned his gaze evenly. He was huge, in height and girth, and obviously experienced for a golden beard spilt out from under a leather mask, well stitched and fitted over the nose, weighted down with metal bands at the neck, with slashes for breathing and hearing. The kind he wore himself.

Two other things caught Jean's eye. In giant hands the man was holding an axe, but not such a one as he had ever seen before. It had not the usual huge, heavy, curving blade but a smaller half moon set into a slim shaft that was bound tightly in red leather straps. This was not an axe for wood or animals, but by the way he held it Jean knew it had been well used on something. The second thing was the huge hound, at least part wolf, that sat quiet and alert at the man's feet, eyes flicking constantly over the crowd.

The axe, the dog, the beard, the size of him. It brought one word to Jean's mind: Norseman.

Haakon had followed his rival's movements, from the moment he saw the mask pulled on at the gate. He too noted the quality of the mask, the man's easy stride, most of all the sword held lightly in the scabbard to his side. He knew in that instant who his main opponent would be.

He had seen an executioner's sword used many times on campaign. In the right hands it was a fine tool and weapon, but he had rarely seen it in the right hands. More often he had seen men blunder and fail with it, for it took a rare eye and a skill in timing. Haakon was confident he would not encounter such skill in a backwater like Tours.

Nevertheless, Fenrir had growled when the swordsman stepped down from the dais and Fenrir was a good judge of enemies. So he returned the man's stare evenly. Lifting the axe, he let it dangle over the ground. The victory, the client, the client's purse would soon be his. And then the tales would begin again.

A fanfare announced the start of the competition. Marcel, becoming more fatigued each minute by the noise and smells of the crowd, gestured Jacques forward.

'Be advised!' he bellowed. 'His Eminence, the Most Holy Bishop of Tours, seeks this day a man worthy to take the place of our late, lamented executioner.' A chorus of hoots and boos erupted at that. Rising above it, he continued, 'And so the Bishop has ordained this holy competition to find the right man. These honoured competitors' – he waved at the dozen men below him – 'will each display their skill through a series of tests and one of their number will win the ultimate prizes – the head and purse of the Count de Chinon – before supper.'

This last provoked more noise, cheers in approval and curses from the many there who liked the young and handsome Count and felt that, his unfortunate heresy notwithstanding, they were not looking forward to watching him die.

The first round consisted of nothing more than the chopping of fruit. A dozen melons were placed on the small-fowl cutting blocks. Each headsman took his position and each, in turn, his swing.

Before they began, betting was intense. The Fugger, who'd scrambled through a small gap in the fence at the back, took a bet from the brother of the competitor before Jean that his axe would triumph over Jean's sword. Having nothing to stake, the Fugger risked all his nothing and called it two sous, and at the drop of Marcel's handkerchief found himself that much the richer. Hardly difficult, this first round had still eliminated half the competitors who through nervousness or lack of technique had missed, flattened or bobbled their melons. Four others had achieved their goal, along with Haakon and Jean.

The second set of targets were at least alive. Six bullocks were brought out of their pens and held in position by chains through their nose rings and a rope around their haunches. Terrified by the noise of the crowd, their squirming provided a suitable test, the aficionados of executions agreed, for a moving target was often what you got on the scaffold. This time the Fugger got odds, five to his two, so confident was the man in the prowess of the butcher, whose bloodstained leather apron beneath the eye mask gave his trade away. This was what he did every day, the Fugger reasoned to secure the odds. Surely he would defeat a mere swordsman?

He didn't. By the time Marcel's scented handkerchief had floated to the ground all killing had to be complete. Never mind the number of strokes used, heads had to be on the ground. Only two were. Two bullocks wandered around bleating from the blows they'd received, another had an axe head lodged in its skull, while the butcher was still hacking away in a furious and blood-spattering frenzy long after money changed hands.

So far, Jean had used two strokes of his sword. He thought that the Norseman had used three of his axe, understandable without the block to oppose the blow. As he'd expected, it had come down to the two of them.

Jacques bellowed again, 'And now, Mesdames and Messieurs, by the great kindness of our loving father the Bishop, we have a special treat to decide this contest. He has provided us with two of the heretics who were to die tonight in God's holy flame!'

And with that two men, as bound and terrified as the beasts before them, were herded like them into the arena. The crowd surged forward, delighted to have such a good view of what they usually only saw high above them on a scaffold. They watched as the younger fellow's head was thrust down on a block, the older, greying man forced to kneel before the swordsman, both of them spitting prayers out between their chattering teeth.

For a moment, looking down at the kneeling figure, Jean returned in his mind to that other, recent place of execution. To what he'd done there and why he'd done it. In the silence of the crowd's anticipation, he looked into the shrouded eyes opposite him and said, 'The triumph is yours, Monsieur. I do not kill men for the sport of others.'

'Neither do I,' growled the big man, and stepped away from the block.

There was uproar, some applause, threats. Marcel stamped angrily on the dais and complained loudly at this thwarting of his spectacle, after all the trouble he'd taken. The butcher, mask off, his apron covered in bullock's brains, lurched forward to say he would take care of them both. The victorious executioners just rested on their weapons.

Within the tumult, Jean became aware of a small voice beside him. It was the prisoner's, and he had to lean close to hear him.

'Monsieur,' said this greying man whose face betrayed the treatment he'd received in prison, his voice and manner a class above the rabble's now screaming for his blood, 'my son and I were destined for the flames tonight, for the pleasure of the Bishop, the education of the people, and in full view of our wives and families. All because we chose to read the words of the Lord in our own tongue. Now He who sees all has chosen you to spare us that pain and our loved ones that vision. I implore you, even if you do not share our faith, share our humanity.'

Jean moved across to the figure opposite him. 'They will burn instead. He asks us to prevent that.'

'That is different then,' Haakon grunted, immediately kneeling to ask the weeping lad's forgiveness. On the other side, Jean did the same.

'I bless you for your kindness, Monsieur. And God will bless you for it as well.'

There was no ceremony to it. The crowd were distracted by their arguments, and while Marcel whined about betrayal an axe and a sword rose and fell and two heads rolled on the ground.

At being thus cheated, the mob's disapproval threatened to turn violent, discarded melon husks already flying towards the dais where Marcel had failed to provide the show some of them had paid for, and all desired.

The Fugger knew a distraction was necessary before spectacle was abandoned in favour of riot. For Jean had to win the prize, had to be on the scaffold tonight beside the man who'd condemned him to his slow death, had to take back what was stolen. So he pushed his way to the front, climbed up and grabbed the melon-dodging Marcel.

'Monsieur, the final test!'

'There is no other,' Marcel said, wiping pulp from his lace.

'I had thought to get the mob to choose between their headstrokes, but now—'

'I have a test for them. They are matched in efficiency. Try them for speed.'

'Speed?' said Marcel disdainfully. 'How can we test their speed?'

'Look!' The Fugger pointed into the chicken pens behind them. 'Fifty each. First man to finish, wins.'

It was a straw, and Marcel grasped it. Jacques, who had just punched the drunkest of the protesters, had a moment to shout the proposition. Loud laughter greeted it and the mob swayed behind the idea. The action would be fast, furious and faintly ridiculous and it was something in which they all could share. They were chicken killers to a man.

Details were quickly arranged. The two executioners would stand in separate pens whose fences would prevent the chickens fleeing their fate. Each could have two assistants to chase, catch and place on the block; as Jean did not use one he was free to move as he chose, and he put his assistant, the Fugger, atop the fence to keep him informed as to his rival's count. Each bird had to be severed at the neck, with only five mistakes allowed.

In the frenzy of betting that followed the Fugger, who had doubled his money on an evens bet on the prisoners, now placed his twenty sous at two to one with a man who believed utterly in the axe and block – as most people did.

Crowding round the extremity of the pens, climbing on every elevated part of the abattoir, the crowd cheered each group of chickens thrown in, like gladiators entering some ancient arena. Haakon stood at his block, massive, calm, certain. If the two boys he'd selected did their job in supplying him with chickens – helped by a now agitated Fenrir, snapping at the frightened birds – he felt certain the prize would be his. Only when he looked across at his opponent standing calmly, legs apart and sword resting on his shoulder, did he have a moment's doubt.

A handkerchief fluttered, a roar split the sky, and the two men began executing chickens. With a one-handed, shortened grip, Haakon grabbed, placed, steadied, chopped and discarded. The boys, awed by the huge Norseman and desirous of a twin for the coin already in their breeches, kept his block awash with birds. Fenrir, snapping and snarling, drove the fowl into their arms.

When the handkerchief dropped, Jean brought his sword down from his shoulders, removing in the stroke the heads of two startled birds. Changing the angle and swivelling on his right foot he brought his left around and swept sideways, his blade making a T with the ground, adding another three heads to the dust. Untwisting his wrists, he brought the blade up and over while lunging, catching a chicken that had realised, too late, the place it occupied was not a healthy one. Bringing his right foot over he swivelled on his left, scything parallel to the ground, taking two that tried to escape and one that threw itself forward onto the blade.

His enemies were much smaller, but it was not unlike the tactics he would use in a mêlée. His size, his ability to move swiftly and low, had always been an advantage and was doubly so here. As in battle, he blocked from his mind all the extra sounds – here, the cheering, the maniacal laughter, the frantic clucking, the disturbingly rhythmic and speedy thud of axe on block – and focused on opponents who duly sought to avoid him and whom he hunted down and despatched as ruthlessly as he had any enemy.

The problem with his method came with the tendency of headless chickens to still run around. He often held up strokes to avoid splitting one of these, but there were the inevitable mistakes. He'd used up four of his five by the time he had only three chickens left.

It was then he became aware of the Fugger on the fence. He was frantically signalling the score from the other pen. His one hand was raised, and two fingers were down on it.

Time slowed then for Jean, as it had on Tower Green, as it

always did in such moments. He took in the thumb and two fingers raised, the two remaining chickens with heads in one corner, the last one behind him in the diagonally opposite one. It was like the game they often played in the army camps, throwing heavy wooden discs at pins set up in formation. With them split like that, two and one, what was his choice? He needed all three.

Another of the Fugger's fingers dropped. Jean felt he was moving ever slower, but to the onlookers he became a blur of man and metal as he hurled himself to the two, took the first with a downward swipe and the second with that valuable back edge. Only the Fugger's thumb remained upright. Jean saw the axe rising up over the top of the fence and then, miraculously, pause. Haakon's last chicken had slipped temporarily through bloodied fingers, and it took a moment to jerk it back into position.

That moment was enough. In that half second, though his bruised ribs protested Jean used his back and outstretched leg and the weight of the sword moving forward to spin around, complete a half circle with the blade, uncurl his bunched shoulder muscles and send the sword spinning across the compound to the other corner where the last chicken obliged him by craning up to look at this possible source of flying food. It caught, but did not hold the sword halfway down its neck.

Haakon's axe had just begun its descent when the crowd screamed at Jean's throw. The axe bit into the wood a hair above the mottled flesh and, knowing it was too late to remove and strike again, Haakon glanced back over the fence in time to see Jean's sword end its journey. The Frenchman was sprawled in the feathers and the blood, and it was then that the Norseman realised he'd seen this man before. There had been blood then too, and pain. But neither had come from chickens.

When the Fugger had collected his winnings, he fetched water to the hut where Jean had taken refuge from the congratulations of the mob. There Jean cleaned himself, sipping the wine he'd been given by all his new friends.

'I knew, I knew, I knew you could do it!' The Fugger danced before him. 'Such a flashing, slashing, blinding victory!' He moved around the hut, imitating some of Jean's cuts and thrust. 'I bet that hulking brute . . .' he started, then stopped, for his lunging hand had encountered something hard that had stepped between him and the sunlight.

'You were saying?' The Norseman was there, making the doorway look small.

'Nothing,' said the Fugger, 'nothing at all. Now where is that Daemon? Excuse me – such a nice . . . ooh, uh, dog is it, yes? Daemon! Come away from those chickens!'

The Fugger scrambled out of the hut, leaving the two unmasked headsmen to regard each other for a long and silent moment.

'Wine?' Jean offered a flask.

The Norwegian took it and drank, his eyes never leaving Jean's, then handed it back with the words, 'I know you.'

'Indeed?'

'Not your name. But we have met before.'

'Indeed?' Jean said again. 'When?'

'In twenty-five. I was with Frundsberg at Pavia.'

'And I was with King Francis.'

'Mercenary?'

'Not then. For King and country then. But I took my first step along the mercenary road there. It was where Frundsberg recruited me.'

'I remember.' The Norseman paused, then added softly, 'The Landsknecht whose place and sword you took. His name was Tomas. He was a friend of mine.'

'Of course,' said Jean. 'You were the man with the musket.'

'Yes. I was the man with the musket.'

For just a moment, both their minds returned to that day.

71

France's army had been annihilated on the plains outside Milan and in the ensuing rout Jean had been cornered by a squadron of the enemy. Their executioner had come for an unarmed Jean, who had taken the man's sword from him and killed him with it. It was the first time he'd ever held one of the square-headed weapons, and he could still remember the shock of it, as if it had been born somehow to his hand but had been taken away at birth. While marvelling at what felt like a reunion, Jean had suddenly realised someone was preparing to shoot him, so he'd flung the sword at the assailant from twenty paces. Being unused to the weapon then, it was the pommel not the blade that hit the man with the musket, whose bullet had then gone through Jean's cap.

The same man, it seemed, who stood before him now.

'That blow changed my life,' Haakon continued. 'I was unconscious for a day and a night. Some Swiss found me and took me to fight in Flanders.'

Jean smiled. 'And, as you say, I took the place of the man I'd killed. Frundsberg sent us to Hungary to fight the Turk.'

Haakon smiled also. 'I always hoped I'd meet you again.'

'Indeed,' said Jean for the third time, and reached for his sword.

The giant did not move.

'Have no fear.'

'I am not afraid,' replied the Frenchman.

'Good. For I do not seek revenge. I used up my share of that many years ago.'

'Then what do you seek?' Jean's hands were still light upon the sword's guard.

'I seek . . . a way out. I thought the execution was that way, but I misread the signs. They spoke of a man who would change my direction. They spoke of you.'

'I do not know what you mean. For I am not a leader.'

'The one-handed one follows you.'

'Well.' Jean looked out into the stockyard, where the

72

Fugger could be seen trying to prise a carcass away from a determined Daemon. 'I rescued him from something.'

The big man smiled, sadly. 'Then rescue me.'

Jean looked at this man's open face, the cascading flow of golden hair and beard, eyes the blue-green of one of his native streams. It was a face without guile.

'What is your name?'

'Haakon Haakonsson.'

'Well, Haakon, listen. I am . . . on a quest. I have made a vow, and my loyalty is only to that. But it may be a short one and could well kill me, even as soon as tonight.'

The Norwegian thought for a moment.

'I like the sound of a quest,' he rumbled. 'Quests make for good stories. Is there a hoard of gold at the end of it?'

'Probably not.'

'A woman?'

'A . . . woman, yes. The vow was sworn to her.'

'Better and better. And a fight to be had, did you say?'

'I didn't. But there will be a fight, for sure. Perhaps many, perhaps just one, tonight.'

'Then I am indeed your man.' Haakon lowered himself onto the bench beside the Frenchman. 'I would ask just one thing, the only favour I will ever ask of you. In return for it, I will offer you my loyalty, total and complete.'

'And that is?'

Haakon smiled. 'When I have proved myself worthy, you will tell me the tale of this lady and this vow.'

Jean scratched his head. For a man who always worked alone he somehow was attracting followers at every stage of this journey. And both seemed bereft in some way. Well, that made three of them, he supposed. A quest for the lost.

Then it occurred to him that maybe their coming wasn't to do with him at all. Maybe it was to do with Anne Boleyn.

'Well,' he shook his head, 'we can discuss this over some food. Would you like to eat?'

'Yes,' said Haakon, 'I would. Just as long as it's not chicken.'

Both men laughed. It felt good after such an afternoon, so they kept doing it for a while.

# EIGHT

# HERETIC'S REVENGE

When Jean met his client two hours later, he found a man unprepared to die. But not for the usual reasons.

'Ah yes, the executioner.' The Count de Chinon barely glanced at Jean, instead gesturing to the man who sat opposite him. 'The Count de Valmais plays a particularly vicious game of royales. You must excuse me while I watch him like a hawk. You see?' He'd laid down a card which was snatched up in triumph by his equally youthful opponent.

Jean studied de Chinon. Scarcely eighteen, an attempt at a beard around chin and upper lip made him look even younger, while his black hair was longer than the close-cropped regal style of King Francis' court, probably due to its thickness and sheen. The azure bonnet was jewelled, the ostrich feather that circled it ending in a golden nib. His clothes were dazzling, in the Swiss mercenaries' style so eagerly appropriated by the aristocracy: the striped vest embroidered with gold, alternating white satin and black, the sleeves matching, hugely puffed, white taffeta pulled through the slashes. The sleeveless overvest of vivid crimson was held only at the waist, opening wide at the chest, giving the desired effect of broadness. His legs were crossed, their hose a riot of contrasting shapes and colours. Thankfully, the youth's surcoat of turquoise blue silk was lying on the table at the side, for the addition would have been overpowering.

Studying this latest client who ignored him in favour of his friend, Jean thought, *There is nothing of the religious fanatic in his manner, no glow of the soon-to-be martyred. His heresy probably has more to do with the romance rebellion holds for the young.*

There was something else about the Count though, his face flushed with wine and the enthusiasm of the game. Jean was used to bravado from his noble clients, used to the denial of approaching death from men who felt they were too young, too handsome and too important to die. It sometimes lasted right up to the point of kneeling before the sword. Yet Jean had always been able to penetrate even the strongest of brave fronts to expose the true fear beneath. This Count de Chinon seemed completely lacking in it.

It perturbed Jean. He was there to do a job, whether he actually got as far as carrying it out or not. But there was a protocol to be gone through, questions asked, answers received.

He waited silently, until the last card had been slapped down, a triumphant de Chinon snatching the final trick. Victorious, he finally turned his attention to Jean, while his friend de Valmais, his exact counterpart in clothes and hairstyle, if of a lighter colour and fuller beard, watched in amusement, shuffling the pack.

'And so, Monsieur Headsman, what is it we need to discuss?'

'Well, Milord, I wanted to tell you the procedure.'

The Count lazily waved a hand. 'It is not necessary, really, I have attended enough of these events to know how they go. I make a brave speech, I accept God's will, I kneel, you strike. . . . Pft! It is over, and so dies another traitor. What else is there to know?'

'If Milord would care to be blindfolded—'

'No.'

'And something must be done about Milord's hair.'

'Oh, I don't think so. Florian thinks my hair my best feature.'

76

At which both men burst out in loud guffaws.

'But the blade, Milord, it—'

Again the hand. 'Really, do not concern yourself with any of that. It will all be dealt with on the scaffold. I will see you there.'

Resisting his dismissal, Jean had one more question, a somewhat awkward one.

'Money?' drawled de Chinon. 'Really, you'll have to wait to discuss that with my friend here afterwards.'

'It is not customary, Milord—'

Now the Count reacted angrily. 'I do not care for custom. It is my execution and I shall do as I like. You may go.'

Something was not quite right about this execution; the Count was unlike any martyr he had ever seen. But a waved hand and a little smile at his companion dismissed Jean. The whole interview had lasted barely a minute, and it violated Jean's sense of professionalism. As he said to Haakon, who awaited him outside the cell, he hadn't been planning on taking the Count's head anyway, if he could avoid it.

'But there are certain understandings in our work, are there not? This young braggart seems to wish to violate them all.'

'I don't know about you,' said Haakon, 'but I think there has been a definite decline in the quality of clients in recent years.'

'Well, what do you think?'

The Bishop wasn't happy with the Archbishop's appearance. It didn't fit in with the careful staging he'd ordered Marcel to create. He would have much preferred His Eminence beside him on the scaffold the entire time, having emerged together from the palace in full pomp and splendour, thus displaying the Bishop's status to the world. However, one didn't contradict a man like Cibo when he'd obviously set his mind on something.

'Are you sure you wouldn't like my tailor to line it? Some rabbit's fur, perhaps?' he suggested.

'Rabbit's fur? In a cassock?' The Archbishop let out his silky laugh. 'I think that might stretch our friends', the Dominicans, tolerance a little far. I think they already suspect my motives for joining their parade. Besides,' he added, twirling back and forth in the plain brown, sack-like dress, 'I rather like the feel of the rough wool on my skin. And I won't be wearing it for long. Mostly I shall be like this.'

He dropped the heavy cassock off his shoulders. It was held at his waist by a simple rope belt. The Bishop smiled nervously at the suddenly exposed flesh, faint traces of his kittens' scourging still dappling it in a web of rosy lines. Suddenly he wondered if he had what it took to be an archbishop. If it wasn't for his mistress and her grand plans for Orleans . . .

'Now.' Giancarlo Cibo moved across to a small table. 'Which scourge shall I use? I did like those ones from last night, but leather might be a little . . . formal? Simple knotted rope for a monk, don't you think? Like this?'

And he hit the Bishop over his back. Even through his heavy surplice he could feel the bite.

'Ah, ha ha!' he stepped back, nervously. 'That's quite, um . . . do you, uh, do you think the people should see you, um, in the flesh like this?'

'Oh yes, that's the whole point. Well, most of it,' said Cibo. 'We are burning men who claim, like Calvin and Luther, that Rome is all decadence and corruption. Now we know how sadly mistaken these men are.' He raised the scourge again and the Bishop took another step away. 'But if the people see me like this, merely another barefoot, suffering priest who happens also to be Archbishop of Siena, well, the heretics' argument is undone. And then they see me step into my robes of office to witness the punishments, side by side with their own Bishop, well, the contrasting nature of the Holy Church's teaching is most beautifully demonstrated. You are pomp, I am poverty. And then I am God's Anointed again.'

The most opposition the Bishop could muster to this was a

sigh. Moving surprisingly quickly, the Archbishop hit him again.

'Besides,' Cibo smiled, 'you want me to end my visit well, don't you?'

The Bishop could only nod, mesmerised by the softness of the Italian's voice. He could feel the skin swelling where he had been last hit. He felt the blow had perhaps even drawn blood. Well, at least tonight his guest would be gone, for his taciturn German bodyguard had insisted they leave immediately after the execution.

*Not before time*, thought the Bishop. He didn't know how much more sin he could stand.

That same German had now silently entered the chamber. Rubbing his shoulder, trying to keep a smile on his face, the Bishop said, 'I'll leave you to your, um, preparations.'

When the door had closed behind him, Cibo turned to Heinrich.

'Well? What does my friend the Bishop of Angers say?'

A servant entered, bringing wine and fruit. Cibo beckoned his bodyguard forward and Heinrich bent down to whisper in his ear.

'Really?' Cibo smiled. 'That much? You know, I definitely must have a word with the Pope. We can't be taxing the French Church enough.'

He moved across to the table where the servant, bowing, handed him a goblet of wine. Cibo sipped and ran his finger slowly down the rope scourge.

'Pity,' he murmured, 'such a pity.'

They had been assigned an antechamber to an antechamber at the back of the palace. Stale bread and some indifferent wine had been provided. The Bishop cared little for the comfort of his executioner and it suited Jean to be thus overlooked, to rest and think and make adjustments to the plan, such as it was. They would use the distraction of the execution and the heretic's flaming pyres to kidnap the

Archbishop, then force him to give up or lead them to the hand.

A small window gave on to the lane at the rear of the palace. Pushing open the shutters, Jean leant through the bars and whistled, was answered by a familiar caw. Daemon settled onto the ledge and immediately began to groom his feathers. A moment later, the Fugger was crouched below.

'Is all ready, Fugger?'

The German hopped from foot to foot in his strange shuffling dance.

'Oh yes, oh yes, the finest three horses that my winnings could buy await us.'

'If all goes well, you will hear the commotion from the square before you see us. Be ready.'

'I will, oh, I will.' The Fugger disappeared down the alley.

'Will he be all right?' Haakon was occupied in honing his axe blade.

The risk of the next few hours, the poverty of the plan and the sudden weight of having even two men to command had made Jean edgy.

'Perhaps you would prefer to join him and hold his one hand?' he snapped.

Haakon smiled. 'Oh, I think not. Sounds like there's more fun to be had in the square.'

'Fun?' Jean snorted. 'You have a curious way of having fun, my friend. You're more likely to leave that square dead than alive.'

The big man let out his rumbling laugh. 'To die fighting is the Norwegian way of having fun. Death or glory and a speedy passage to Valhalla. What a story that would make!'

Jean snorted again and turned away so the other man could not see him smile. *Jesu save me*, he thought, *pagans and madmen are my followers. And animals*, he added, as Fenrir echoed his master's humour with a bark.

The door was flung open and in swept Marcel. He had

changed clothes since the abattoir, his hair gleamed now with oil, his slashed velvet jacket a blue and yellow shimmer.

'Amateurs!' he wailed. 'Why will they not leave it to those who understand these things?'

'Monsieur is having a problem?' Haakon offered the distraught man a chair.

'A problem? Yes! It was all so perfect. The Archbishop was to march with my master from the palace here, preceded by those beautiful boys singing the "Te Deum" in their angelic soprano, the golden cross aloft, incense filling the air. And now . . .' He sobbed, regained control of himself and went on. 'Now the tedious man has decided to join the Flagellants.'

'Flagellants, Monsieur?' Jean brought Marcel some wine.

He gulped at it and continued, 'Yes, Flagellants. Dominican monks. Twenty of them, they were to lead the Count de Chinon and the four heretics from their cell, scourging themselves every step of the way. Now this . . . this Cibo has joined them. They are to be the very last to appear, with the Archbishop the last of all. Such vanity. Such an . . . amateur!'

Wiping his eyes, he started fussing around the execution party. He had reluctantly agreed that Haakon should be Jean's assistant on the scaffold but was appalled at the state of their clothes, their drab grey cloaks, unadorned brown jackets and vests, single-colour leggings. Headsmen, he was reminded, dressed not to be noticed. But what truly incensed the steward was that the hound would be accompanying them, although he ceased complaining when Fenrir's jaws closed in on the waving arm that came too close and gently applied some pressure.

Marcel led them down narrow corridors to the palace's great hall. Doors swung open upon a babel of shouting, flailing preparation.

Leaning down to Jean, Haakon whispered, 'Should we not warn the Fugger of this change?'

'No, it doesn't alter the plan. You heard this Marcel say the

81

Archbishop will be the final Flagellant, so we will know him then. And there is another man to watch for, a tall German, looks like a priest, a scar down his face. He was the one who felled me at the inn when I was captured. I think he is the bodyguard. I know he is dangerous.'

Haakon's grip tightened on his axe. As the gates of the palace were opened on to the square and the crowd roared its excitement, he said, 'Then I look forward to seeing him.'

Behind the palace, the Fugger already had.

Checking on his horses, he was muttering to Daemon when the Archbishop's bodyguard entered the stable. He could hear what the tall, scarred warrior was saying to the grooms – at least he heard words spoken, orders given, but the power of understanding speech had been removed from him by the appearance of the speaker. For this was not the first time he had seen Heinrich von Solingen.

His right hand began to throb, always a strange sensation since it wasn't there. The last man ever to hold it, however, was. His mind throbbed too, in a burst of white-light pain that merged with the flare of the groom's reed torches, removing both the Fugger and his countryman from a stable in Tours to a tavern in Bavaria seven years before.

'A Fugger?' the mercenary with the long fair hair and a wound running from brow to chin had cried. 'That family of Jews who bankrupt honest knights with their usury?'

'Not Jews, Sir. We in Munster follow the word of Luther. And money-lending is now legal, thanks to the Emperor's favour,' the sixteen-year-old Albrecht Fugger had bravely said, the last brave thing he'd ever said.

'Worse and worse, and worst for you.' The face leant in, eyes afire with hate. 'Seize him!'

No matter that it was a public place, no matter that Albrecht was a gentleman on his first mission for his illustrious family, entrusted with bringing coin to their tin mines in the south. A table was swept clear of platters and beer, his body thrown upon it, stretched out by willing helpers.

That face again, the scar livid in the fire glow, the mouth speaking foul words.

'If I'd met you alone on the road, you'd be dead by now. You are lucky in that. But your money-grasping hands have ruined many of us. No one here can deny a Catholic son of Bavaria the right to give you fitting punishment.'

The blade had glittered so high above him and fallen so fast, bringing the first flash of that white-light pain, blanking out the world. When he returned to it, his servants, his money, his hand were gone. Gone too his former life, severed as surely as his flesh. There would be no taking the road back to Munster, a cripple, in disgrace. His father, Cornelius, would not see a maimed son, he would see only his lost gold. And he would reach up into the ceiling of his study and pull down the hazel wand he kept there for special punishments.

No, the road could only lead away from that. Lead eventually, by diverse lanes and crossroads, to a gibbet in the Loire.

Cowering back into the stall, lowering his pulsing head upon his pulsing wrist, the Fugger wept.

The crowd had been waiting and drinking for hours. Now, as the first notes of the choir reached them, they surged against the rank of guardsmen who, pikes at port, kept the space before the scaffold like a storm break in a harbour. As the headsmen ascended the ramp, through the eyeslits in his leather mask Jean saw other soldiers in two lines forming a channel across the square to the gates of the town hall, like the parting of the Red Sea for Moses.

Reaching the platform, the parade dispersed across it, Jean and Haakon to either side of the two thrones that sat centrestage. The Bishop placed himself before one of them, the other occupied by an archbishop's robes and mitre. Behind him ranged ten priests, each with a boy chorister before him, their white surplices a background to the Bishop's of brilliant red. Before them the trumpeters, in their tunics of blue studded with fleurs-de-lis and the town symbol of mace and key, blew a fanfare that gradually hushed the crowd.

In the silence, the doors of the town hall opposite slowly opened and a single drum struck up a steady beat. The Count de Chinon did not so much walk as stroll from his gaol. His hands, as was customary for his rank, were free and he used them to acknowledge the crowd. He looked more like a triumphant general than a man marching to death, and his attitude, youth and handsomeness had an effect on the crowd. The soldiers in the lines had a hard time beating them back with their pikestaffs.

He mounted the platform with easy strides. Raising his hands, he tried to calm the crowd to hear his final speech, but a gesture from the Bishop brought guards to the Count's side, pulling him away, forcing him to kneel with his back to a mob whose frenzy increased when the four heretic weavers were swiftly led out and tied to their stakes before the scaffold.

Another trumpet blast, another near silence. Then, from within the darkness of the hall's entrance, two new sounds clearly carried: a sharp snap and a groan poised between pleasure and pain. Figures appeared, shrouds hiding the faces, torsos bared, cassocks cinched at the waist. Pausing, each raised a thin, knotted-rope scourge high above his head then brought it down, sharply and in unison, across his shoulders. The crack as the scourges bit into flesh made the crowd collectively wince. The twenty Dominican monks moved forward in a huddle, one shrouded figure trailing slightly behind. With every strike and step, they intoned the penance of guilt: 'Mea culpa, mea culpa, mea maxima culpa.'

They beat themselves along the Via Dolorosa created by the soldiers. The odd oath or drunken laugh that had greeted their appearance died away now, leaving only the dirge of voices and the crack of whips biting home.

The rhythmic blows, the chanting, the pulse of the drums; Jean felt himself slipping again into familiar ritual. His hands began to clasp and unclasp on the sword hilt, his mind to focus on the stroke that was to come.

No, he told himself angrily, *I am not part of this. I am here for Anne Boleyn.*

He tried repeating her name like a chant. But on this scaffold, the memory of that other one seemed a mere dream, the voice in his head dying away. There was no vow, no six-fingered hand, no moment when a door opened and revealed his lost loves. There was only this ritual of death, and his function in it. He looked ahead to a kneeling man, a sword raised, a perfect swing.

The Dominicans, on reaching the scaffold, lowered their shrouds then took their places by the wood bundles that surrounded the four stakes, each lighting a torch from the braziers there. All save the last man, their still-shrouded leader, who stood dripping blood at the scaffold steps. The trumpets sounded again and the Bishop walked forward, spreading his arms wide in blessing.

'Brothers in Christ,' he shouted, 'we welcome this, your example of true faith and sacrifice. It shines forth as a beacon to those who would accuse the one true Church of sin and decadence. And see, see, oh my flock, how even a prince of our faith is prepared to take on the pains of our Lord.'

Jean found he was gripping Haakon's arm.

'This is him,' he said, through his teeth. 'At last, I will know my enemy.'

The bloodstained man had raised his hands to the shroud on hearing the Bishop's words. Now, as he lowered it, all on the scaffold heard the puzzlement in his voice as he said, 'I am flattered by the title, my Lord Bishop, but I am simply the Abbot of the Dominicans.'

The Bishop of Tours stood staring, his mouth opening and closing like a freshly caught fish on a river bank. Jean had stumbled forward, sword and scabbard gripped tight. In the shocked silence that greeted the Abbot's voice, Haakon's whisper came clearly to him: 'Look there. There! At the centre, where the lines meet.'

Still dazed, Jean followed the Norseman's pointing finger. A group of some twenty men, each in a large hat and cloak, had massed at the junction of soldiery directly before the scaffold. As Jean and Haakon looked, they saw each man reach within his cloak and hold his hand there.

One of the men looked up. For a moment their eyes met, and Jean recognised the Count de Chinon's companion, the Count de Valmais.

The explosion shattered the first floor of the town hall, flames bursting through the crumpled leaded glass, a huge column of smoke belching into the night air. Everyone ducked and Jean heard a single shout of 'Now!' Looking down, he saw each of the muffled men pull a dagger from beneath his cloak and stab the soldier directly in front of him.

Instant mayhem. Those at the back surged away from the explosion and the flames, while those nearest the front, witnesses to the soldier's sudden assassinations, tried to go the other way. They imploded into the middle and the guards who had lined what had been the path simply dissolved into the crowd. Those on the fringes rushed for the side lanes, swiftly blocking them, rebounding into the only gap that now existed – the area around the scaffold. The potential martyrs were engulfed in the wave, picked up bodily, still attached to their posts, and swept along in the torrent.

Only the men in cloaks knew exactly where they were going. They moved forward over the writhing bodies of the soldiers to the stairs.

The Bishop had regained his voice. 'The Count! Heretics come to free the prisoner. Seize him!'

These orders were shouted at Jean and Haakon. Neither had any intention of obeying, the cause was not theirs. But the rescuers were not to know that, for de Chinon was still kneeling at the centre of the scaffold behind the executioners.

And there were now swords as well as daggers in many of the rescuers' hands.

Crouched beneath his horses, locked into foul memories, the Fugger was only startled back to consciousness by the sudden explosion, the sound crashing down the lane from the square, causing his animals to whinny and pull against their tethers. In calming them, he calmed himself a little. He had returned so utterly to the gibbet midden, its safety and familiarity, that he did not want to come back fully to this world.

The man who had caused him thus to slip back had stepped outside the stables, where the Fugger had heard him pacing up and down. A few minutes after the explosion, he came back inside. He was no longer alone.

For yet another moment the Fugger thought he was truly back, safe again, within the gibbet midden, for it was while lurking there that he'd first heard the seductive voice that he heard again now.

'I couldn't resist seeing the Bishop's face,' Giancarlo Cibo was saying, 'but it seems he has received an even greater shock than the one I intended for him. Are the horses prepared?'

'Here, my Lord.' Heinrich untethered the Archbishop's stallion. 'And here are your travelling clothes. But the rest of our possessions, they are in the palace.'

'We will have to leave them. We need to get through the city gates before they are blocked. This town is closer to the heretic than we thought, something else I will have to discuss with the Pope. I will shed my Dominican garb on the road to Toulon.'

The Fugger saw the two men straddle their horses. He ducked down lower into the hay of his stall.

'Do you have the Bishop of Angers' gold, at least?'

'Here, my Lord, in my saddle bags.'

'More importantly, where is the witch's hand?'

'In your saddle bags, my Lord. As always.'

87

The Fugger heard leather being patted.

'Good,' came that voice, 'then let us ride.'

The horse's shod hoofs clattered on the cobbles, the sound swiftly swallowed by screams, by the crackle of wood on fire and the clash of arms, all coming from the direction of the square. The Fugger could tell that men were fighting and dying down there.

Jean's weapon was still in its scabbard, so it was the haft of Haakon's axe that deflected the first two swords away from the Frenchman. Then the scabbard was shed, and with a sharp uppercut Jean took the third sword away from Haakon's exposed flank and threw it high into the air, reversing the arc to bring the flat of the blade down on the assailant's head. The man fell back with a cry, arms flailing, blocking the approach of five more of de Chinon's rescuers.

'This is not our fight, Norseman. Our quarry has fled,' Jean yelled.

'Tell them!' Haakon gestured at the men now leaping over their comrade's fallen body.

There was no time for debate. Five men were trying to kill them and three of them died, the last two pulled off by their fellows who had reached and freed the Count de Chinon. Swept into their midst, his white shirt disappearing under a cloak and hat, the remainder of the Count's men pushed away from the scaffold, moving as solidly as only a body of determined men can through chaos.

The lane from the square, though a major route out of it, was still no broader than a cart, putrid and greasy from the sewer running down its centre, piles of garbage clogging the edges. Many fled the carnage with Jean and Haakon, slowing them down, and it took a while to reach the rendezvous of the stables.

'Fugger?' Jean pushed the doors open with his square-tipped blade. 'Are you here?'

It was Daemon who appeared first, surging out of the pile

of hay where the Fugger had hidden. The bird's master followed, paler than ever, eyes moving as if they would leave his head.

'What is it with you, Fugger? You look like you have seen a devil.'

The teeth chattered still, but words came out.

'I have, oh I have. One such as I thought I'd never see again. And I heard another, though he has the voice of a fallen angel.'

'We have no time for this, Fugger,' Jean snapped. 'The Archbishop has gone.'

'He . . . he has. He rode from here just now. He—'

'Then let us follow. No, no more words. We can talk when we are clear of the town. They will be closing the gates soon to try and keep the Count and his followers inside.'

They rode through an unguarded town gate, the watch called to quell fire and riot in the square. They halted on a hill just beyond the city walls to confer.

'Even if we knew their destination, how can we pursue them on these?'

Haakon spoke from the back of the biggest horse and his feet almost reached the ground. With their big bellies and slung backs, they knew the animals were fit for the working farm but not for a pursuit of thoroughbreds down country roads.

'But we do know their destination.' The Fugger's breath was coming easier now, though his eyes still moved about. 'I heard him say it. Toulon.'

'Toulon?' Jean looked into the darkness ahead. 'So they make for a harbour and a boat back to Italy, do they?'

'How far is Toulon?' Haakon asked.

'Three nights and a day if you ride by the main road. But' – Jean smiled – 'there is more than one way to Toulon, to a man who knows his way. These horses might not move fast, but I'll bet they are bred for the hill paths.'

They mounted again, Jean ahead, the Fugger struggling

with the most docile horse in the middle, Haakon at the rear, Fenrir at his stirrup. They followed the main road south for a while, then Jean turned his horse onto a trail just perceptible in the weak moonlight. It twisted up into the hills, and as they climbed they became aware of the noise from the distant town. Looking back, they could just see that fire had spread from the square and was consuming a considerable section of the crammed streets.

'Look, Daemon,' the Fugger whispered to the bird nestled on his shoulder, 'they got their cleansing flames after all.'

After a few minutes, the trail widened to a farm-cart's width, and Haakon pushed his nag up beside the Frenchman's.

'Is now the time to remind you of your promise?' he said.

Jean grimly indicated the path ahead. 'You believe I think of anything else?'

'Not to your lady,' Haakon grinned. 'Your promise to me.'

'And what was that?'

'If I should prove myself worthy, you would honour me with the tale of your quest. Have I fulfilled my share of that bargain?'

It was Jean's turn to smile.

'You might have stopped me dying on a heretic's blade back there, I suppose. But do you truly want to hear this tale now, on a hard night's ride?'

'I can think of no better time. Besides, and I have thought much about this during our short acquaintance, you are a very dangerous person to be around. And I suspect you have more hazards in mind for us. So now might be the only time.'

Jean laughed. That was twice in a day, and this man was responsible both times. The horses had their heads and would follow the dark trail better than he. So he sat back in his saddle and for the second time told the tale of his promise to Anne Boleyn.

# NINE

# AMBUSH

The moon was on the wane, but still gave off enough light to show them the path. They rode without break through the nights, rested for a few hours each morning, then rode or walked out the day before a short evening rest. A final night ride ended with them, near dawn, wearily tethering and feeding their horses on a small knoll overlooking the main road to Toulon.

'They will not have passed here yet,' Jean told them.

'How can you be sure?' The Fugger was bent with exhaustion, and had fallen to the ground as one dead. It was many years since he'd straddled a horse and he'd forgotten which parts of the body were required. They were reminding him in fire now.

'The man we hunt is no fool. He will not want to kill his horses and leave himself a long walk, not in this country.' Jean looked about him, scanning the little valley in the growing light. 'A man on a horse might outrun the brigands who thrive here. A man on foot, never. We have three hours at least, by my reckoning.'

He threw himself onto the ground beside the Fugger, covering the both of them in one cloak.

'You'll take the first watch, Haakon?' he said.

The big Norwegian was laying out a blanket.

'No need. Fenrir!' he called, and the huge hound came and curled up beside his master, who threw the blanket over the two of them. 'Fenrir will tell us when someone approaches. Horse!' he instructed, and the beast growled an acknowledgement. 'Otherwise every rabbit and wolf will have us reaching for our weapons.'

Despite the immediate duet of snores around him, Jean lay for a while watching the morning star wink into nothingness. The point he had chosen overlooked a narrowing of the road to the width of a farm cart, the surface showing the signs of a wet spring, deep ruts filled with glutinous mud. A horse would have to be led through it. It was the perfect spot for an ambush.

That thought disturbed him just a little before deep exhaustion took him and he began to snore too.

Almost opposite Jean's rise, and slightly higher, was another hill crested by a few stunted pines arched over by the force of the wind that blew up from the sea. Downwind, and thus beyond the sensitive nostrils of Fenrir, a body shifted very slightly on its bed of pine needles. Two eyes glared down at the intruders.

*Three. I can take three.*

Fingers reached out to the weapon stretched over a rock, checked each stitch that held the leather pouch in place, continued down the tightly coiled ropes to the knots and loop at the ropes' ends, an arm's length away. Satisfied, the fingers moved on to the twin piles of stones. Two kinds had been gleaned from the riverbed nearby. The larger ones were the size of a gull's egg; heavier to heave, they would travel slower and arrive with a force designed to stun. The smaller, a wren's egg of a stone, would kill any approaching Goliath, if the aim were true. There were ten stones in all.

*Double what I need. There's only these three, and the two who come.*

*Five. I can take five.*

The Archbishop was in a foul mood which a beautiful dawn

did nothing to alleviate. Mortification of the flesh was something he preferred in short, intense shocks, such as might be provided by a scourge or the long fingernails of Donatella, his mistress in Siena. It was not the drawn-out, numbing pain of three nights' hard riding with little food and no wine, no luxurious cloaks to sleep under – all left behind by Heinrich in the Bishop's palace when they'd fled Tours.

'How much further, dolt?' he called to the broad back ahead of him.

The only satisfaction to be had was to goad his bodyguard. Yet even that pleasure had palled, for Heinrich had learnt to say nothing in response. Cibo liked to keep men around who hated him, who were forced to endure his ceaseless baiting yet could sometimes be prompted into a foolish response to be punished in some ingenious way. Fear and hatred were far easier to inspire than love, he'd always found – and far easier to control.

'Not far,' came the sullen reply, called over the shoulder.

Cibo scrunched down in his saddle, his many pains agonising him, his cough wrenching small gobbets of blood from deep within him. His cough had lessened since the crossroads, that was sure, but it never ceased completely.

Heinrich von Solingen smiled at the sound. 'Hate the master, love the cause'. The phrase came again to his mind, oft repeated, like a Latin chant in a cathedral.

A dog howled, almost wolf-like in its drawn-out note. It was coming from a couple of rises ahead. People could be about, yet Heinrich had no fear of brigands, not at this time of the day. He'd been a robber-knight himself, before he became Christ's warrior and began the long penance for his thousand sins in the Archbishop's service. He knew that dawn for brigands inevitably meant lying drunk somewhere. No, a dog simply showed they were drawing close to some outlying village, the beginning of the descent to the port of Toulon. Still, just in case, he put on his helmet and loosened his sword in its scabbard.

'No, not far,' he said again, hoping to hear the cough.

'Kill the bodyguard, leave the Archbishop,' Jean had told Haakon when the Norseman had convinced him he could hit a target as big as Heinrich from forty paces. Now, watching the two men lead their horses into the trap, he hoped Haakon was as good as his boast, that no arrows went astray. He needed Cibo alive – at least until the hand was again in his possession.

'Then again . . .' Jean had wondered if there was a gibbet short of a tenant nearby.

The two men had, as Jean predicted, dismounted to enter the gap, their horses treading carefully over the ruts. They were at the head of the small passage made by the two hillocks, and fifty paces ahead of them the road emerged and opened, the mud cleared, a rider could mount and be off on the last stage to Toulon. Here, though, was as fine a killing ground as either of the two mercenaries had seen.

The German bodyguard had stopped as he entered the pass, also noting the land, sensing its potential. Cibo, focused on avoiding the worst of the mud, suddenly found himself shoved into the rump of his bodyguard's stallion, and was about to let out another stream of insults when he noticed the quality of Heinrich's attention.

'What—' he began to say.

'Ssh!'

Jean, seeing the enemy hesitate, hissed 'Now!' and turned to watch the arrow's despatch. He saw Haakon rise up, draw back the small hunting bow to full stretch, then suddenly leap in the air as something struck him. He tumbled forward, the arrow deflecting to the right, thumping into the Archbishop's saddle bag, just missing the man.

Jean had half stood and now jerked his sword up in a defensive reflex. This saved him from the fate of his felled comrade, but only just, as something smashed into the blade, crashing it into his face, knocking him backwards and into the lee of the rock again.

'Mount, for the love of Christ!' He heard the cry from the defile.

Peering cautiously out, he saw both men trying to achieve just that, their horses circling in sudden terror. As he looked, he saw the German's horse rear, whinnying in pain as a rock struck it on the mouth. It jerked its rein out of the grasp of the bodyguard and bolted down the road.

'Haakon!' Jean yelled, to no avail. The man was not moving.

Seizing on the fleeting cover offered by the galloping animal, Jean sprinted for Haakon. A stone clipped him as he weaved, a glancing blow to the shoulder that drew forth a gasp of agony. Someone was hurling projectiles at them with more power than he'd felt with anything that didn't have gunpowder behind it. There was no explosion though, no gunshot, and as he ran he caught a very quick glimpse of where they were coming from – the hill opposite, amid the stunted pines.

He rolled behind Haakon and over him, snatching up the bow as he went. The quiver, with half a dozen arrows in it, was placed behind a nearby rock. Swiftly fitting one of the arrows to the string, he released it at the pines. He was not aiming at a target but he hoped to delay the onslaught of stones.

*Who is up there?* he thought, reaching for another arrow.

His own horse gone, Heinrich was just three paces behind Cibo's. He made two of them before a stone the size of a wren's egg crashed into the side of his head. He didn't stumble so much as drop straight down at the Archbishop's feet.

With arrows flying from his left and stones from his right, fleeing on the horse was no longer a safe option for the Archbishop. At the cry 'Down!' the horse, used to responding instantly to his master's commands, lay on its side, providing shelter from the stone thrower above while Heinrich's body sprawled before him gave him some protection from any arrows.

And then he saw one of those arrows fly up towards the trees, a stone hurled back in reply. *There is more than one set of brigands here, and they quarrel over the prize*, he thought. This brief respite from being the target allowed him to reach into his saddle bags. The crossbow he pulled out was designed for hunting small birds rather than humans, but it could be loaded quickly, it was a weapon, and he was no longer toothless prey.

As Jean raised his head to loose yet another arrow at the trees, a crossbow bolt ricocheted off the rock in front of him. It had come from the direction in which he'd last seen his intended victims. A quick peek told him that although the German was down, maybe dead, the Archbishop had managed to bring his horse to the ground and was hiding behind it. He knew he wasn't good enough with a bow to hit a lying target, or one hidden in trees. *What devil is up there anyway?* he thought, putting his back against the rock and closing his eyes in momentary despair. He had fought in enough wars to know a stalemate when he saw one.

Missiles round, short and long had all whirred in the time it took the Fugger to draw three deep breaths, skitter around the edge of his hillock and over to the back of the other.

'Oh Daemon, oh my dear, what can we do?'

The bird landed beside him and began to pick at a worm that crawled along there.

'Yes, yes, you are oh so right. Let the warriors fight it out, eh? Wait till it's all over, nice and safe, eh?'

The raven looked up and said, quite distinctly, 'Hand.' Then, its prize in its beak, it flew up to dine among the trees on top of the other hill. The one from where the stones were being hurled.

'Hand!' the Fugger muttered to himself. 'Daemon reminds me.'

He had no choice. Even a brain less educated than his could see that he was the only one not trapped in the crossfire. And if he could not envisage grappling with a muscular assassin amid the stunted pines, at least he could cause some form of distraction. Long enough for Jean to figure out what to do.

Moving carefully upwards, he became aware of an almost constant noise, either a very faint roaring or the buzzing nearby of a hive of bees. Yet when he saw the source of the noise, he was perplexed. A dark-haired man, no, a boy really, stood in the trees facing downhill, every now and then whirling what looked like a small roped basket above his head. And as he watched, the boy hurled one end of this basket while keeping hold of the other, and a stone whipped down the hill.

*A boy*, he thought as he moved up quietly behind him. *Perhaps even I can take a boy.*

The last stone hurled had altered the precarious balance for it shattered the bow Jean had raised towards the Archbishop. Cibo saw this and fired a bolt that passed before Jean's face, forcing him to fall back under cover. Both men's weapons were thus unavailable to react to the sudden appearance of the assassin from the pines tumbling down the slope, wrestling with a screaming Fugger. Over and over they fell, crashing finally into the stump of a dead tree with a force that winded them both.

Cibo could not load and fire swiftly enough to deal with three enemies. So he shouted 'Up, up!' and his stallion scrambled to its feet with him half-slipped into the saddle. A moment to gain control, a jab of heels into soft flanks, and the beast went straight from a standstill into a gallop, its hooves pounding the ground a hand's breadth from Heinrich von Solingen's head.

Jean, bursting from behind the rock, leapt up as the horse hurtled by. For a moment he clung to the Archbishop's saddle bags. Then something slipped from them, a long shape wrapped in hessian sacking. His hands held on to it as he fell.

Standing ankle deep in the gelatinous mud, spitting out dirt and curses, he watched the hand of Anne Boleyn snatched away, almost from within his grasp. He saw himself bending to kiss those six fingers again and saw them pulled back, turned into a fist that struck him. He deserved such punishment and worse, for he kept failing. Once more he felt the burden of his responsibility, his own inadequacy.

Looking down in his despair, he noticed the object in his hands. Green leather strapping peeked from the sacking, beneath an apple-sized pommel. Pulling the cover off, he once more drew his own executioner's sword from its scabbard.

He had no time to wonder at the reunion. There were enemies still to deal with, comrades down.

The enemy first, for the enemy could still do harm. One glance at the bodyguard, face down in the mud, showed that he wouldn't be causing any problems for a while, if ever. The other was a different matter, trapped under the dead weight of a stunned Fugger, struggling to drag a leg clear. Jean saw now the stone-hurling assailant was little more than a boy, strong of nose and jaw, black hair close-cropped around an olive brow, eyes of charcoal, flaming now as they watched Jean unsheathe his sword. As he slowly approached, Jean saw the boy redoubling his efforts to extract his pinned leg and, when the struggles still failed, saw him reach into his doublet.

Pulling out a long, thin dagger, the youth yelled in a voice high-pitched yet strong, 'Take another step and I'll slit your comrade from arse to throat.'

'Comrade?' Jean didn't even break stride. 'I thought he was with you.' And swinging his sword two-handed from his shoulder, Jean hit the dagger, knocking it twenty paces back up the hill.

The youth unleashed curses in a guttural language Jean had never heard, then spat at him, before reverting to French. 'Well, kill me then. Come on, I deserve to die anyway. Finish me off, if you have the guts. You footpads are always at your best when a man is down.'

There was silence for maybe three seconds, broken suddenly by a shout of laughter.

'Sweet Mother of God! Who is calling who a footpad?'

Jean knew it was probably just the release after combat, but the boy seemed so annoyed. He couldn't help but laugh, an urge that only increased when the Fugger rolled over, opened one eye and moaned, 'I will never drink brandy again, O Daemon dear.'

And when the raven flew down, sat solemnly on the Fugger's shoulder and deposited a puddle of white on it, Jean's laughter became uncontrollable.

The mirth stopped the instant he heard the groan.

'Son of a whore!' Haakon was trying to sit up. 'Who has broken my head?'

He sank back. Jean could see the lump swelling beneath broken skin on the forehead, an eye already halfway to closing.

'Your whoreson's here, Haakon,' he called.

'Keep your filthy tongue off my mother,' the youth spat.

At the third attempt, the big man managed to stagger over. He looked at the young man before him.

'You tried to kill me,' he said in a sad voice, rubbing his eye. 'What did you hit me with?'

'This.' The youth held up the slingshot. 'And if I'd wanted to kill you, you'd be dead.'

'A David! A David is come among us,' said the Fugger.

Jean took the weapon, running his fingers down the ropes.

'I used to hunt birds with one of these when I was a child. Why would you use them on men?'

'Why don't you ask your friend here?' Turning to Haakon, the youth said, 'I used the large stone on you so it would just stun you. Him I wanted dead, and he is. Look!'

The youth gestured towards Heinrich and, while they all turned to look at the body in the mud, quietly rose from the ground and took one step up the hill.

'No, my David,' said the Fugger, grabbing an ankle, 'I've had enough of rolling down hillsides, if you please.'

And then the dead man moaned, and each of them turned

99

again, a sword and an axe poised. And since both men had served with the English on campaign they both understood the youth's next words in that language.

'Fuck! Fuck! Fuck! How could this happen?'

The moan was all they got from Heinrich. The smaller stone had caught him in the killing zone at the temple, but had caught the edge of his helmet too, halving its force. He was in more danger from drowning in the muddied rut, so Jean turned Heinrich's head towards them while he considered what to do.

'We may need him later,' was how he explained this act of seeming kindness.

The laughter had been a release, but now the situation returned to Jean, and with it some of his determination. His comrades were suffering the various after-effects of battle. All, including himself, were bruised, if not bleeding. Pursuit of Cibo had to be swiftly undertaken. Yet he had some obstacles to that and he dealt with the one he could speak to first.

'Are you English then, young man?'

'I was born there. In York. But I wouldn't call myself English. My people have a faith not a country.'

'Ah, a Jew.' Jean smiled. 'Now the slingshot makes more sense.'

'Yes, a Jew.' The strong jaw was thrust forward. 'Any problems with that?'

'No.' Jean returned the other's look. 'My problems are all to do with the man we just let escape. We pursue this man not because we are "footpads" but because *he* has stolen something from *us*.'

'We are equal in that. Giancarlo Cibo has something of mine as well.'

Jean paused at the naming of his enemy, and at the determination that underlay that naming. It seemed a match for his own, and it decided what he said next.

'I am not in the habit of leading, but perhaps this common

cause can bind us. Our quarry will go to ground in Toulon, in the Bishop's palace or some other place where it will be hard to flush him out. One with skill such as yours could be useful. And perhaps our skills will prove useful to you.'

There was silence, appraisal in the dark brown eyes. Finally, the youth spoke. 'I am not in the habit of following. But if your paths and mine are the same, I will walk with you for a while. And if your orders serve my turn, I will even obey them. Yet I am on my own quest, and someone's life depends on me. To that mission my ultimate loyalty is bound.'

'Good enough. My name is Jean.' Jean spat on his hand and held it out. 'To common cause.'

The youth spat and reached up. 'Beck. Yes, common cause.'

Jean saw the young man before him and felt a young man's grip, a squeeze of equal measure to his own. But there was another quality to the touch that made him think instantly of Anne Boleyn, of that moment when she'd laid her hands on either side of his head. It was strange. Was it the darkness of the eyes, similar to his Queen's? He tried to look at them more closely, search them for a reason for this disquiet. But Beck had become suddenly busy, retrieving stones, so Jean set about his own preparations. Yet he found himself glancing continually at the young man, looking swiftly away if in danger of his glance being met.

The second obstacle was the unconscious bodyguard. Haakon had been for killing him there and then, but Jean disagreed.

'We think this Cibo will seek the protection of the local Church. But he is cunning and knows he will be followed. If he goes to ground, this man' – Jean raised Heinrich by the hair – 'will lead us to him.'

The party assembled. Fenrir was in front, sniffing excitedly at the scents wafting from the sea ahead. Daemon rode on the Fugger, Haakon had the unconscious Heinrich lying on the biggest horse before him. When Jean mounted, he looked again at Beck, who waved them on.

'My horse is tethered over the rise. I'll catch up with you.'

Beck watched the party set off.

*Why am I joining them? I always work alone. Was it this Frenchman's handshake? Was it his laugh? Something as ridiculous as that?*

Climbing the hill to the trees, hidden there from anyone's sight, the youth began to adjust clothing. Things had come badly undone in the tumble down the hillside with the Fugger. Removing the baggy shirt, Beck fully unwound the cloth wrapped six times around the chest. Then, pausing only for a moment to rub her long-constricted breasts, she began to bind them tightly again into their linen prison.

# TEN

# UNSAFE HARBOUR

The Archbishop had not taken refuge with the Bishop of Toulon for two reasons. Firstly, he was known to be religious and it would mean hours of ceremony and prayer, plain food and watered-down wine. More importantly, this religiousness meant the fool kept only priests around him, and they would not be enough to stop his pursuers.

Cibo headed straight for the port. It was the first time he lamented the loss of his bodyguard, for Heinrich had arranged the passage, knew the captain and the boat by sight and was used to harbours such as these. Knowing only the ship's name, Cibo had to search among the hundreds of mastheads himself, mixing with sweating humanity, the villainous swill of Europe and Africa concentrated in a small area with too little to do and too little money to do it with. He'd taken the precaution of dressing in the cassock lent to him by the Dominicans for the scourging. Their vow of poverty meant they were usually poor fare for robbers. Had any known that under the simple woollen shift he carried a saddle bag with the Bishop of Angers' generous bribe, Cibo would not have survived the walk.

He found the ship after an hour. The Genoese master, a surly dog named Rudolpho reeking of sweet Malaga wine, who knew only that his nameless passenger wanted swift and secret passage, deposited him in his 'accommodation', a hammock stretched out in a hold that had recently contained dried fish, a feeble light coming from one open porthole.

Yet, once swinging, with an evening and a night to pass before they could sail with the dawn tide, Cibo was strangely content. True, he had lost the bodyguard he so loved to torment and, even more sadly, his beautifully trained horse, Mercury – a monk leading a stallion through the port would not have made his ship – but he had survived an ordeal that would top even the best story his mad brother, Franchetto, could tell. And it had been a welcome, active change from the labyrinthine politics of the Papal court, where ploys were more esoteric, betrayals a mental rather than a personally physical exercise. One didn't administer poison oneself, or feel the joy of a dagger stealing a life. One had people to do that for one.

Of course, the main thing was that he had won, again! The hand was his, the witch's hand, that monstrosity taken from a queen – what, could it be no more than a couple of weeks before? – in that crude island of Britain. That the hand had a great power over men he already knew – for wasn't it the executioner, Jean Rombaud, the man he'd left to rot in a gibbet cage, who had leapt at his horse this afternoon? If the hand could encourage a man thus to cheat his lawful death and seek revenge on Giancarlo Cibo, what else could it do?

Glancing over at his saddle bag, he noticed something curious. He'd broken off the arrow shaft that had embedded itself in the bag at the ambush, but had not yet had time to dig out the iron tip. He realised now that there was a dark stain on the leather where none had been before. It wasn't sweat but something thicker, and potent enough to penetrate cow hide.

He pulled the bag up onto the hammock and worked the arrow head free. The pocket beyond held the velvet bag which in turn held Anne Boleyn's hand. He'd only looked at it briefly once, by moonlight, outside that inn. Now, he needed to see it again, despite the putrid flesh that would be clinging to it by this time – which smell, oddly, he'd yet to notice.

He sniffed; still no trace. *Must be the fish.*

Undoing the strap of the pocket, pulling out the velvet bag, fumbling with the drawstring, his hands shook with excitement. He reached in and touched the hand cautiously, then quickly withdrew his probing finger.

It was cold, which was understandable, but it was the smoothness that made him gag more than any putrescence would have done. It seemed to be stuck somehow in the bag, and shaking would not dislodge it.

'Enough!' he said, and reached in. After some twisting, he pulled it into the light and saw where the arrow head had pierced it, saw the trail of fresh blood oozing down to the six fingers, pooling in the nails there.

It was not the blood, where there should have been none, nor the unnatural freshness of the hand that caused him to scream. It was the way the fingers suddenly bunched into a ball, the way just one slowly uncurled, pointing, in red and bloody accusation, straight into his eyes.

On deck, the sailors heard the scream and it froze them where they stood. After a moment, as the drawn-out wail died away to be replaced by a desperate sobbing, even the drunk of a captain began feverishly to cross himself. A mad priest was one of the most terrible things you could have on a boat. A mad monk was worse. Far worse.

There was next to nothing going on in the festering stew of Toulon harbour that Maltese Gregor did not know about. It was his business to know which ship was bringing in hashish, and which was bringing in slave girls. The price squid could fetch that day in the market, and who was trying to undercut that price. Which passengers were leaving, openly or in disguise, and which were arriving and might need expensive assistance or the thrust of a fee'd assassin's knife. Knowledge was profit and power, and if he, the King of Thieves, did not earn the one and control the other, who would?

He knew one of the ships bound for the Indies contained

twenty heretics in its stinking hold. They had paid hand-
somely for his silence. He knew a quantity of near-perfect
fake ducats had just arrived from the silversmiths of Izmir. He
had taken a handsome handling fee. And he knew that a
Dominican monk had paid *in gold* to take ship to Livorno,
the free port of Tuscany. Inconsistencies like monks with gold
disturbed him and he felt a personal midnight visit might be
required. He liked to handle inconsistencies himself because it
was so hard to find people who would not try to cheat him.
He'd personally garrotted a servant that morning for that
very offence, and the memory of the incredulity on the man's
face made him smile.

There were always people looking for signs of weakness in
him to exploit, and a good garrotting reminded them that
he'd been in charge for five years and would be for some
considerable time to come. He knew it couldn't last for ever.
Just till he'd amassed enough gold to return to his home
and live out the rest of his life in luxury. And when he
thought of Bavaria – for 'Maltese' was a title only from the
days when that tribe ran Toulon – he smiled again. His
personal fortune would already guarantee him the life of a
successful burgher. Five more years, three if they were very
good, and he could buy himself a title. Not bad for the
bastard son of a butcher.

All it required was knowing everything there was to know,
with no surprises. So when Heinrich von Solingen walked
through his door, he was less than pleased for all sorts of
reasons.

'Heinrich!' he beamed. 'It's been a long time.'

Inwardly, he had a vision of another garrotting. Someone
would pay for letting this man near him unannounced.

Since the German bodyguard had never seen Beck, Jean had
let the youth do the close shadowing, while he and the others
followed from a safer distance. They'd managed to keep
Heinrich in sight through the increasing frenzy of the town,

and now met in the lee of a waterseller's awning opposite the stairway their quarry had just ascended. Unnecessary caution, perhaps, for Heinrich was still shaking and rubbing his head, and had done from the time they'd dumped him outside the town walls at the moment when his groans indicated returning consciousness. On his weaving walk in, he'd failed to look back more than once.

While the Fugger went off to bargain for food and wine, the other three watched the only door of the house. Many came and left.

'Judging by the activity,' said Haakon, 'I'd say he's in a brothel.'

'A pretty low-class one,' Jean commented, observing the tenth man they'd seen in as many minutes go in. 'All the scum of the docks. And they don't seem to stay very long. Must be Dutch.'

Both men laughed and for some reason, Beck blushed. At that moment the Fugger came back and began to hand out bread, peaches, wine, pig's trotters and roast chitterlings. The fruit basket he'd carried it all in, upended, made a table.

The Fugger was pleased with more than the food.

'Daemon and I have news. Where do you think our quarry has gone to ground?'

'A brothel,' came a joint reply.

'A good Catholic Bavarian like this fellow? How could you think such a thing? No, no, according to my friend the offal salesman – isn't the pig's intestine delicious, young David? – according to him, our fellow keeps illustrious company. Royal company!'

'How's that then, royal?' Haakon was already well on the way to devouring his own pile, after sharing some with Fenrir, and was beginning to eye up the others'. Beck, who'd spat while the Fugger talked, shovelled her offal before the Norwegian and ate just peaches and bread.

'Can you not guess?' Feeding crumbs to his raven, the Fugger was enjoying himself. 'Let me riddle it for you. Who's the highest and the lowest and keeps his court to keep out of court?'

'The King of Thieves,' said Jean.

'Bravo, Master, in one,' said the Fugger. 'Cunning and strength together. With you as our leader, how can we fail to triumph?'

Jean spat out a particularly chewy bit of gristle, jarred less by its consistency than by the Fugger's jesting. He got up, stood with one hand raising the awning and stared at the doorway opposite.

*A leader, he calls me. What have leaders to do with me? I who have always been led – to battle, to scaffolds. That's the way for a man such as I. Responsibility for no one but myself. To fight the man in front of me, then the man after that, to strike at the neck presented. That has been my life. The Queen of England, the King of Thieves, the Archbishop of Siena. And I, Jean Rombaud, peasant of the Loire!*

'Do you ever think of failure, Frenchman?' Beck's voice was pitched low beside him, inaudible to their bickering companions at the table.

*If I am a leader*, he said to himself, *then I must speak only of success, never doubt.* But before he could frame words into an encouraging lie, Beck continued, 'For I do, often. Sometimes it feels as if I have challenged the whole world. Then I can see no other end but failure. And seeing it, I despair.'

There was something else in the voice, something hidden in the eyes.

'And how do you keep going then, when the despair comes?' He turned, noticing peach juice glisten on lips.

'I concentrate first on my cause, then on the strength of my good right arm.'

'I wonder if that will be enough for me.'

A hand reached up and squeezed him just below his shoulder.

'I cannot speak as to your cause,' Beck said softly, 'but your arm seems strong enough to me.'

The pressure lingered for a moment, and then the touch was gone. The boy returned to the table. Jean felt suddenly bereft, then instantly renewed.

The strength of the cause and the strength to pursue it. He had both. All he had to do was answer the simple questions one at a time. The first one being, what was the bodyguard of an archbishop doing with the King of Thieves?

Calling in a favour.

Heinrich had spoken the one sentence he needed to speak and now he leant on the table, resting his weight on his palms, staring down into Gregor's eyes.

It was strange how memory worked. Maltese Gregor had spent years forgetting the last time he had seen the man before him now. It was a good night to forget, or a bad night depending on how one viewed it. He hadn't considered it in years. Sometimes a bed companion would tell him he'd whimpered in his sleep, but what of that? Everyone whimpered sometimes. It didn't mean anything. It didn't have to mean he was remembering Rome.

Like he was remembering it now, conjured fully formed in the cold eyes of his old comrade in arms, Heinrich von Solingen.

Remembering how, before he became Maltese, he had been part of the same squadron of mercenaries as Heinrich. Even remembering the reason for going to Rome, for in 1527 the Pope had switched allegiances again, allying with the French, betraying the Emperor. And the Emperor, Charles, had failed to pay his soldiers for too long. They decided to get the money he owed them from his enemies and, despite all entreaties to turn back, had marched on the city. A lot of them were of the new faith of Luther and slaughtering Catholics was the closest they came to holy war, give or take the odd foray against the Turk.

Gregor remembered how he and Heinrich, as good Bavarian Catholics, had limited their pillaging to unconsecrated ground, their rapine to anyone other than nuns, salving their consciences thereby. The pickings were too easy to pass up. There was almost no resistance.

It was that 'almost' Gregor was trying most not to remember, hoping that the man opposite him would say something beyond 'You owe me.' But he didn't. He just stared, and Gregor, for whom speech was never a problem, couldn't think of anything to say. So he carried on remembering.

How at night, gorged with excess, soldiers would fall asleep wherever they happened to be and how it was then that the despoiled inhabitants would take such revenge as they could. How two sisters, brutally raped by Gregor and his cronies some nights before, had been left for dead in the smoking ruins of their house, alongside the bodies of their parents. How Gregor had made the mistake of revisiting the scene alone, sure he'd overlooked some booty, unwilling to share any of it. How those sisters had clubbed him to the ground, stripped him naked, bound him, hung him upside down and burnt and cut him, one starting at the head, the other at the feet. How they were just about to meet at the middle when Heinrich arrived. The sisters swiftly joined their parents in heaven or hell, while a blood-and-shit-smeared Gregor babbled eternal gratitude and the granting of any favour.

Nine years! And Gregor had nearly managed to forget about it all. But that one night in Rome had decided him that the mercenary life had lost its savour and began him on the road that led to Toulon. To the good life. To be reminded so suddenly of the inauspicious start to that journey was deeply unpleasant. To be immediately reminded that a favour was also owed was even worse. Hence his thoughts turning to garrotting, for if his lookouts had warned him of this man's approach he might have had time to make arrangements for a dagger in an alley. For Heinrich von Solingen was not a man you said no to face to face.

Gregor decided he could take the silence no longer. 'What? What is it, Heine, old comrade? Why do you stare so?'

The cobalt-blue eyes never left him. 'I just wanted to make sure you remembered.'

Hastily pouring him some wine, Gregor said, 'Heinrich, my friend, let's not talk about old times, eh? Sit. Sit! Here, drink this. What happened? You look terrible.'

The stone had caused a giant swelling at his temple; it throbbed violently, causing pain to shoot throughout his head. Blood was still caked in his ear, which he hoped was all that accounted for his faulty hearing, the ringing that dominated all other sound. He drained the wine, gestured for more, said, 'It does not matter what happened. All that matters is what's going to happen. You owe me.'

'You already said, Heinrich, and of course, do you think I would ever forget? An oath, an oath I swore to you, old comrade. Here, some food, more wine, of course. Ask, and if a poor man with limited means can oblige you, you know he will.'

Von Solingen looked at the smile that never reached the pig-like eyes, the face that had doubled in jowl and fat since he'd last seen it. He'd never liked Gregor, indeed had enjoyed watching from the shadows as the sisters plied their knives and firebrands, only stepping from them at the last because Gregor had a rat's nose for things hidden and if he was in the house there was booty to be had there. Yet he also knew how much a man could hate being bound by an oath of loyalty. He'd cursed his to Giancarlo Cibo every day, and while he would not waver from it, he could not be sure of the dog before him. He knew he'd have to throw him a bone as well.

'I need some people killed.'

'Easy. Name them.'

'I do not know their names. There are three, possibly four, and they are hiding outside, waiting for me.'

'I will call my men. Six should do.'

'Make it twelve. These enemies are strong, and clever.'

'Twelve men?' Gregor sucked in his lower lip. Twelve was expensive, because he'd have to go outside his own group.

Heinrich saw the calculation, the hesitation. He threw the bone.

'And there will be gold in it. Plenty of gold.'

'Heine,' said Maltese Gregor, beaming at last, 'it really is such a pleasure to see you again.'

On his provisioning expedition, the Fugger had gleaned other information from his talkative new friend the offal vendor.

'Two fleets sail at dawn, of equal size. One to the Indies and the other to Livorno.'

'Tuscany.' Beck's voice had a strange timbre to it, eyes clouding.

Jean noticed, looked away and nodded.

'So our search is narrowed down to half the vessels. We know which fleet the Archbishop sails with. He'll be making for Siena.'

'And the fleets contain slaves. You can always tell by the aroma.' Haakon sniffed and threw down a last pork bone in disgust. 'Of all the fates a man can face, chained to an oar on one of those death galleys must be the worst.'

'Wait!' Jean stood swiftly. 'Here comes our man.'

The trail they took was short, for Heinrich went to ground again in another, larger brothel. It was harder to cover, for there were three entrances, out of sight of each other. Beck, Jean and Haakon took one each while the Fugger scurried between them with messages.

Jean watched the front, his anxious mood heightened by the parade that passed before him. The town was seething with the sailors and soldiers of both convoys, attempting to get into as much trouble as they could before returning to their ships. Every inn was crammed with a writhing mass of humanity; ale, wine and brandy was churned out as fast as it could be watered down. Only the more expensive whores operated under a roof; the others despatched clients in every back alley, in every nook with the slightest of shadows, just one of the many causes of fights which broke out everywhere. It was bacchanal and battle, orgy and riot, lit by firebrands, with musicians vying with drunk and full-voiced sailors to provide the musical accompaniment.

'Come on, come on!'

Jean's hand clutched and unclutched on the grip of the sword hidden under his cloak. But his desire could not speed the night. It wore on, hour after noisy hour, while men staggered into them, offered drink or violence, rutted within their sight. Many came and many left the house of pleasure, but not their man. And as the hour got later, or earlier, the crowd thinned as more and more headed for their boats, staggering, carried, accompanied by cheers or curses.

'Haakon wonders if the blow to the head has finally killed the bastard and that's why he hasn't appeared,' the Fugger said, the tenth time he'd come round. He was the only one who seemed less than exhausted by another night without sleep; but the way he saw it, he'd been asleep for a thousand years under a gibbet.

Jean had wondered the same.

'I could go in and see.'

The Fugger was doing the strange shuffling dance he called standing still, and Jean thought that of them all, he'd attract the least attention. The town was mad tonight, so it was the sane and the sober who stood out.

'I don't think that will be necessary,' he said, for over the Fugger's shoulder a party of particularly raucous seamen poured out and behind them the tall figure of Heinrich loomed in the brothel doorway. Ducking down, Jean watched him speak briefly to someone out of sight, then turn and head down the street towards the harbour, along the same route the mob had taken.

'Go, tell the others the direction and take up your post,' he whispered, and set off after the German.

'Let me come, please.' The Fugger's face twisted in appeal. 'I know I'm not much of a fighter but I . . . I . . .'

Jean paused just long enough to squeeze the young man's shoulder.

'We need you to speed our escape, you know the plan. And our rendezvous, if things go awry. Each to his own strength, Fugger, remember? We'll be coming back fast. Without you, we wouldn't make it.'

And with that he turned and followed his prey.

The Fugger quickly passed the word to Haakon and Beck, then made for the stables where their horses lay. Fenrir greeted him with the growl that had seen off anyone nosy enough to poke among the hay, where the saddle bags lay hidden. Sitting on one, he tried to still his limbs for the wait.

A raucous caw came from a beam above.

'Aye, Daemon,' he said, 'I hope so too.'

Heinrich had turned three corners by the time Beck and Haakon caught up with Jean.

'At last,' the Norseman muttered as he fell into step. At his side he clutched the axe in one hand and in the other a large jar filled with lamp oil. Beck held a covered lantern in which a flame burned. They had decided that they might need some distraction at the dockside if they were to slip aboard a boat and steal what they'd come for, and nothing distracts a sailor as quickly as his boat going up in flames.

What was strange was that their quarry's turns first seemed to be moving them parallel to the waterfront rather than towards it, then away into an area of rotting wharves and abandoned warehouses. Little light shone here, only as much as the approaching dawn and their own small lamp could shed. At times Jean thought they'd lost their quarry, and he was aware, as the noises of the town faded behind them, of their quickened feet making more and more sound in the growing silence, lightly though they were trying to tread. Then, just when he'd begin to truly worry, he'd catch sight of the broad back striding on, turning ahead of them, taking them ever deeper into a labyrinth of roadways.

Beck said, 'He must be deaf as well as stupid,' when they rounded a corner into a long straight strip and saw that they were now following air. The German had indeed vanished.

They rushed forward, careless of noise now. In the dimness before them they could see a large, broken cart in the middle of the lane, a wheel gone, down on one axle. As they ran towards it, they realised it was the only place that could hide a man. They were right and they were wrong, for indeed the man they sought appeared from behind it, sword in hand, but six other men followed him, three armed with halberds – the half pike, cutting and slashing weapon favoured by mercenaries.

A crossbow bolt pinged off the axe Haakon jerked up, another thumping into a doorframe beside them. Beck reached for the slingshot slung around her shoulders, got it into her hands and loaded in two heartbeats. Forefingers found the loop, left hand placed the killing stone in the pouch, the right grabbed the knotted end and the left pulled the cords taut. The others ducked as leather and rope whirled over them, the stone unleashed finding an immediate target in one crossbowman, reeling him backwards with a cry.

'It's a trap!' yelled Haakon, somewhat obviously, weaving to create a moving target.

Jean grabbed Beck, shoving the youth the way they'd come. He was not going to stand and fight, not against crossbows, not until he knew more about the odds. They ran.

'Now!' called Gregor from behind them, and from the end of the street they'd entered seven more figures emerged from the shadows to block their path.

Hesitation is death in a street fight. Jean and Haakon were among this new enemy in a moment, following the large vessel of oil the big man hurled into the foe. Beck stopped, spun, hurled a stone at the eagerest of those behind them. He pitched backwards, arms flailing into two of the others. Ducking under a whirling sword and axe, she drew her long dagger. She slipped to the side as a sword thrust at her, dragging the knife in a swift cut across the lunging hand.

Blade rang against blade, axe haft blocked cudgel and bill, momentum going with the charging headsmen. Adopting a low stance, stepping under an overhead blow from a halberd, Jean swept a cut at knee height, severing the tendon. The man, carried forward by the momentum of his own weapon, fell over him. A sword cut downwards. Jean blocked with a sloping parry that swept the man's blade to the ground, drawing the head level to the hilt of the square-headed sword. Jean smashed it into the face before him.

Yelling like his berserker ancestors, Haakon's charge had carried him deep into the enemy, his axe swing scattering men into a semi-circle before him. Moving lightly for his size, he dodged to his left as blades came snickering in, then planted his front foot and swung the axe back, catching two of the weapons in a sweep that sent them flying off into the dark.

They held their brief advantage but Jean, with a swift glance back, knew that it could not last. Six wraiths were gliding up the alley, Heinrich among them.

Ducking under another swinging axe, Jean found his head close to the boyish one of Beck.

'Get out. Now!'

'I cannot—'

'Remember your cause. The Fugger knows ours. And he knows where to meet. If we are not there in a month, then—' Jean parried a sword thrust from one of the two men left in front, his weapon forming the upright of a cross with it. Launching himself off the ground he headbutted the man between the eyes. 'Then your right arm is all your own again.'

Jean had opened a gap and reluctantly Beck took it, leaping the body on the ground, running ten paces then stopping to glance back. The other group had hesitated at the decimation of their comrades, but now, urged on from behind by Heinrich and another man, fat and shouting, they began to advance again. The two disarmed men had regained their weapons and were circling, keeping out of range of the axe, awaiting the reinforcements. One of them turned towards her. Still she hesitated, before a crossbow bolt hummed past her ear and another cry from Jean sent her running towards the town.

The renewed enemy closed on them. Haakon, burying his axe head in an enemy's arm, wasn't able to remove it in time to parry the swing of a halberd shaft. Turning his head, a glancing blow caught him and sent him reeling to the side, his weapon left behind. Jean, who had turned aside two thrusts, spun in a circle, sweeping his blade at head height round and around, causing all to duck. There was even a moment when a gap opened up for him and he too could have followed Beck's route away. But then he saw Haakon go down, their eyes meeting.

'Go!' cried the big man.

But Jean hesitated – and that is death in a street fight. The butt of a halberd caught him hard in the stomach, and then they were on to him. But the enthusiasm of the kill made them get in each other's way. Buffeted, knocked to the ground, he took a slash to the shoulder, another to the thigh.

'Enough!' shouted Maltese Gregor, and his own men, used to the repercussions when he was not instantly obeyed, stepped backwards. One of the hired men, swept up in the bloodlust, aimed a killing blow at the felled Haakon and received a pike butt in the face from Gregor himself, who yelled, 'I said enough! What sport is there in spearing hogs? Besides' – and here he turned to the tall man beside him – 'we have our client's wishes to consider.'

Heinrich von Solingen had taken no part in the fighting, though he'd stood there with sword in hand. His head still throbbed as if a thousand anvils were being beaten inside it, and his vision added a shadow figure to any real one before him. He felt like he was going to vomit, as he had been doing intermittently all day. He couldn't remember when he had last eaten and wondered if he ever would again. So when they all turned expectantly to him, looking to him to provide the death strokes, he looked back at the two dozen faces swimming before him, down at the writing snake bodies on the ground, and couldn't even find the strength to lift his sword. He closed his eyes to steady himself and staggered. Somewhere within he thought he heard a bell strike four times, then some distant cheering.

'What hour?' A swollen tongue made speech hard.

'Four bells,' someone said. 'The fleets make ready to sail with the tide.'

The fleet. The Archbishop's boat. Heinrich knew he had to be on it. He took one step towards the harbour and stopped. Someone had asked him a question. Two jowly, greased faces swam into view.

'How would you like them to meet their end?' Maltese Gregor smiled at him. 'It's your choice.'

Of course, the enemy. He had succeeded once again in ending a threat to his master. This dog had been hung in a gibbet but had lived to plague them. It was an outrage, to escape his just punishment in this way. He should be put into the embrace of the iron cage again, as an example to all.

But there was no time. Four bells. Noise from the harbour growing. The fleet departing.

'Hang them,' he muttered, then the words came more clearly. 'Hang them high like the dogs they are.'

He watched as the two semi-conscious men were pulled into position under a beam, hands bound, nooses placed around their necks. Four men gathered at the end of the bigger man's rope, three for the Frenchman. Both men were hauled upright until only the tips of their toes remained on the ground. At a signal from Gregor, the rope men heaved again. Jean and Haakon were hoisted off the ground.

The wriggling and writhing turned Heinrich's stomach again. He retched, and sour bile filled his mouth. He knew he could only stay upright a short while longer.

Four bells. The harbour. He turned and headed away.

Gregor watched him go, calling, 'Farewell, Heine, old comrade. You are welcome. See you again . . .' and turning to his men adding, '. . . in hell.'

Dancing in the air, unbelievable pain filling his body, wide awake now and dying, Jean watched his enemy walk away, so slowly, raising and lowering his feet as if it took minutes to complete each action. His head was being wrenched from his shoulders. He thought of his neck lengthening, expanding, growing into the perfect target for a sword cut. His insides churned and voided, he had no control, nothing left to call his own, his whole frame emptying and pouring his life out into this alley. Suddenly, somewhere in a distant world the other side of agony, two eyes appeared, huge black pools, and he started to swim towards them. Someone opened a door behind them, flooding them with light, an infinite brightness that yet contained some tiny darkness, shapes growing from wriggling circles of form into bodies, into a woman and a child, into Lysette and Ariel. They were smiling and waving to him, beckoning him on to a world where all this terrible pain would disappear. It was already receding when the man whose identity he no longer remembered placed a foot around the corner and began to move beyond it, and it seemed like Jean himself built up speed at that moment, rushing now to flow into the light.

Only one thing disturbed him: behind his wife and child a hand was growing, overshadowing them, reaching up to tower over them. It had six fingers, and when the man finally turned the corner and disappeared, the sixth one, the little crooked finger, bent in to fold his loved ones in a crushing embrace.

And then he was tumbling down, falling from his great height back to agony. In the moment before oblivion, he heard a harsh voice bellow, 'Easy, you scabs. We don't want to damage the merchandise.'

Louis St Mark de la Vallerie, captain of His Majesty's ship the

*Perseus*, clutched a scented handkerchief to his extraordinarily large and very sensitive nose in a feeble attempt to dissolve the smells engulfing him. It was always the same when he rejoined the galley. It took him days, sometimes weeks to get used again to the sickening stench of shit, urine and sweat floating up from the rowers' benches below. A few warm days had doubled the foulness, and he knew it would only grow worse. He was just relieved it was a relatively short run to start with, thanks to a last-minute order diverting his ship to Valletta where he was to subvert certain Knights of St John with the considerable amount of gold he had on board, to lure them away from their allegiance to the Emperor. He did not question the order – he was His Majesty's servant after all. In truth, he relished the little break before the true fighting season began, when he'd again be shepherding convoys around the Mediterranean, spending weeks out of any port or civilisation. In a fleet the stench was always worse. Your own ship's foulness you gradually got used to.

The reek was not his only source of irritation. Four bells had just sounded, and he would be under way before the fifth without the full complement of gutter filth needed to man his oars. The magistrates in the town had been too generous of late, or had dropped their usual requirement on bribes, because far too few men had been sentenced to the fleet, and those who had were of a poor quality. And even these he'd been forced to pay a high price for in order to snatch them away from his rival captains.

In the end he had to turn, yet again, to Maltese Gregor. He hated dealing with the man, mainly because he knew him to be a German peasant through and through, yet one that could buy and sell the captain a dozen times. More. It was an unfair God that allowed such men to thrive, forcing men of the class of de la Vallerie to seek their favour. The man was obsequiously polite, of course. Too polite, for there was always a glint of humour in his eyes that showed he knew too well who had the upper hand in the relationship.

Pacing irritably, he was about to give up on the scum when he noticed a dog cart being wheeled down the dock and recognised the man walking behind it as the one he had lately been cursing. The cart stopped at the gangway and Gregor, catching de la Vallerie's eye, took off his hat and made an elaborate formal bow.

'Greetings, my Captain. I trust the morning finds you well.'

'You're late, Gregor. I was about to start beating the drum.'

'Ah, and when have I ever let you down, my Captain? Well, just that once, but that wasn't my fault, as you know. But here, I more than make amends. See what I have brought you.'

He drew a cloak back from the cart and there, sprawled and tangled in a heap, lay two men, one large, one smaller.

The captain came down the gangplank.

'They look dead, Gregor.' He prodded the bodies with his stick, then stepped back, raising his handkerchief. 'And they reek. From what gallows did you pluck this scum?'

'Your Excellency's nose is as sharp as his sword, as usual.' Gregor's eyes twinkled at him. 'How fortunate France is to have such men to defend her. Alas, the town used up all its noble volunteers when the army came through last week. But look at the muscles on these two, eh? Your ship will out-row any corsair with men such as these on your benches.'

'And these? What are these weapons they are lying on?'

Gregor spat. 'They tried to ambush us with them. I was going to take the dogs to the magistrates to be hung, when I remembered your need. Yes, it's unusual, the sword, is it not? An executioner's.'

De la Vallerie had picked it up, weighing its balance with a few strokes in the air. He was proud of the collection of weapons he kept in his cabin. Some day they would line the walls of his great hall – once he'd won enough booty in war to buy one.

'How much for the sword?'

Gregor smiled. 'Oh, it is a valuable piece, my Captain, but not as valuable as you are as a customer. Take it for three ducats, and I'll throw in this assassin's axe as well.'

The captain grunted acceptance. He didn't have time to haggle with the rogue. A man stood close by, naked to the waist where a whip hung. He was heavily muscled and on his distended belly danced a tattooed snake. His thick black hair and beard almost met, obscuring a face where one eye glittered and the other was covered with a leather patch.

'Corbeau, take them below. Chain them up. When they wake, shave them.'

'Yes, my Captain.' The brute half turned, then turned back. 'Slave or criminal?'

'They are thieves, not Turks. Leave them their tufts.'

It took two men to carry Haakon aboard, while Corbeau himself hoisted Jean over his shoulder. As they disappeared up the gangplank, the money was counted out and handed over. Gregor had been promised gold by Heinrich and had felt cheated when his old comrade offered none, just staggered off into the night without so much as a farewell. Still, sixty or so ducats was not a bad night's work. And he had lost five men in the skirmish, so that was five less to pay. Fifty to him and a debt forever cancelled.

'Bon voyage, my brave Captain. Take some infidel heads with that sword, eh? The hopes of Christendom go with you.' He bowed and laughed all the way back to his brothel.

It was only at the moment just before he fell asleep, his head drowsy with celebratory wine, that he realised he'd forgotten to visit the Dominican monk, the one with the gold, bound for Tuscany.

'Oh well,' he yawned, 'it couldn't have been that important.'

The captain returned to his quarterdeck and shortly afterwards Corbeau came to the foot of the stairs to tell him that all slaves were safely chained in position. De la Vallerie glanced around the harbour at both fleets streaming out, boats of every shape and size, oared and sailed, weaving round each other as they caught the tide.

Removing his handkerchief from his nose for the briefest of seconds, he called down 'Valletta' and waved his new sword in the air. Executioner's, Maltese Gregor had said. Well, there was sure to be an occasion to try it out before the trip was over.

The cry was taken up by the men on the deck, the first time they'd heard the ship's destination. Soon the vessel had moved out of its berth and joined the stream heading towards the open sea. They were using short oars to avoid collisions, so progress was slow.

'Valletta!' De la Vallerie sighed to himself. 'Another stinking port, ripening under a June sun. And with those oh-so-holy knights to deal with as well.'

He hated religious warriors. There was no fun or booty to be had with them. Thoroughly depressed, he went to his cabin to begin drinking.

# PART TWO
# HOLY WAR

# ONE

# AT SEA

Beck was not used to obeying orders.

'Anyway, the Frenchman's weren't clear,' she had muttered to herself, trying to shift her twisted limbs in the small, rotting water barrel. 'He told me to flee the battle, not the war.'

The enemy was behind her, and Jean's plan was still good: the shadow would seek the form. Heinrich von Solingen would pass this way, and go to the boat his master rested on. She would follow, stow away, or catch another vessel bound for the same port. The chase was on again, and anything could happen at sea.

Yet when the bodyguard had lurched past her, his sword dragging behind him, screeching on the cobblestones, she hadn't moved. Half of her had yearned to be off in pursuit but the other half had held her.

'Comrades,' she'd thought. 'Enemies I have always had, comrades never. I have to know what happened to them.'

She didn't narrow 'comrades' down any further than that.

A few minutes later, they had wheeled Jean and Haakon by on a dog cart. She had moved from shadow to shadow, keeping pace with the procession, following them down to the docks where she'd watched the whole transaction between a naval officer and the fat man who had been one of their assailants. The unconscious bodies had been taken aboard.

Her nostrils had told her what manner of voyage they were embarking on.

'May God protect you, Jean Rombaud,' she'd whispered.

Water had filled her eyes but she'd immediately turned away from the galley, clamping down on this unaccustomed desolation. Anger was easier to understand and direct. *Remember the cause*, she'd thought, and brought Giancarlo Cibo into her mind's eye. He was still here somewhere, and his shadow, Heinrich von Solingen, was weakened from her stone. She could still find and kill Cibo, steal his seal of office as she'd planned to do in the ambush. The forgers of Venice still waited to do her will. She would just have to beat the news of his death back to Siena.

She had spent a futile hour walking the dockyard, keenly watching the departure of every ship. But the fleets sailed with no clue given as to the whereabouts of the enemy. Reluctantly, she returned to the barn.

'A galley?' the Fugger wailed. 'Oh Daemon, oh no!' The bird flew down to sit on his shoulder, while Fenrir began to whine and scratch at the stable door. 'Then there is no hope, none, for they are doomed. No one returns from that hell. No one.' He fell onto the floor, his body contorting, his groans filling the small barn.

Beck had given way to sadness once. No more. 'He said you had a rendezvous arranged.'

'We have, we have, but what good is a rendezvous when only one side comes? Ayee!'

'Listen. Stop that moaning and listen to me, will you?'

The writhing Fugger stilled.

'You told me a little of your meeting with Jean last night.'

The Fugger came to his knees, swaying. 'So?'

'So, if a man can escape the certain doom of a gibbet, he can escape anything.'

'But a galley?' came the wail. 'A ship of death?'

Beck knelt beside him, grabbed his shoulders, sought and held the dancing eyes with her own.

'A ship that goes to war, with all the hazards that can present. To me, hazard is another word for opportunity. If you want something enough – you haven't told me what Jean Rombaud wants, but I can see his desire matches even mine – then anything is possible. All you can do—'

'All I can do is keep my pledge.' The Fugger had all but ceased his twitching and was now thinking. 'He told me of this town amid the vineyards. He knew it from the Italian wars. A man who owes him a favour runs an inn there. Montepulciano, it is called.'

'Montepulciano? I know it. It is near Siena. So the Frenchman and I had the same thought: if we lose Cibo's tracks here we follow the beast to his lair.'

'Then we will go there now? We will wait for him in Montepulciano?'

Beck rose and went to the stable door. A fireball sun beating down upon the anvil of the town made her squint. She said, 'You must keep your pledge as you see fit. But I have an older one to honour.'

'But Jean—'

She spoke over her shoulder. 'I promised I would walk his path as long as we headed in the same direction. But he has taken one that I cannot tread. I must return to my own.' She turned to him, saw the twitching begin again. 'But you and I can travel together, Fugger. Our roads are the same. With the sale of our horses we can buy passage on a boat to Livorno. From there, it's a day's ride to Siena.'

The young man scratched his red beard, then slowly rose to his feet.

'Well, Daemon, it looks like we follow another for the while. Lead on, brave young master. I will go and sell our livestock.'

Bird and man departed, leading horses. The sight of Fenrir, still whining for his master, brought a strange pain to Beck's stomach which she quickly realised heralded the onset of her bleeding. It was one of the reasons she avoided company, this monthly curse. Her disguise became that much harder to maintain.

'Provisions,' she muttered, half to the dog, half to herself.

She fondled his ears and went outside, only to double over as another wave of pain hit her guts. All she wanted to do was curl up and sleep for a few days. Yet the pain made her think of Jean, of the greater pain he must be in now. An image came to her, of him standing over her, sword on shoulder; that laugh. It made her smile, and feel something else she couldn't place. More womanly feelings, she decided. That thought made her straighten up and, with an old Hebrew curse on her lips to ward off the pain, she went in search of supplies.

Maybe it was the rocking that first woke Jean, but it was the stench that kept him awake, that and the drum beat he felt inside his head before he heard it. He tried to stand but something gripped his left ankle and a hand hauled him down by the shoulder.

'Eashy, comrade. Wake up and you work. You work, we work. You don't want to do that to your new shipmates, do you? We've only jusht met.'

The neck! It felt as if someone had tried to wrench his head from his shoulders and had only just failed to do so. His eyes fluttered open and a heaving world of rigging and slack sail filled it, dipping and rising, a sky-silhouetted face before him shifting in and out of vision. His guts heaved, he started to throw up, and as he did the hand on his shoulder turned his face sharply downwards.

'Have shome mannersh, mate. That'sh it, down there with the resht of it.'

When the first heave passed, Jean made the mistake of opening his eyes again. Below him swam a fish head in a sea of putrid muck, brown, yellow, bedaubed now with the contents of his stomach, spotted with patches of what could only be excrement, rolling back and forth with the motion of the ship. He tried to turn his head away but another convulsion seized him and he vomited again and again until there was nothing left in his stomach and his tortured throat filled with a bitter liquid that burnt as it passed from him. The pool below him absorbed it all into the festering expanse that he now saw formed the entire deck below the hard bench on which he sat, stretching into the distance, broken up only by the legs that hung down into it, scores of them, diverting the flow like log jams in a river.

'Better, matey? No, no, you jusht resht there a moment, do ush all a favour. They'll be calling on ush soon enough, I reckon. Unlesh the wind picksh up.'

Jean tried to speak, but couldn't. He gestured vaguely around and the face, so brown and wrinkled it was impossible to tell the age, a little silver moustache atop a toothless gash of a mouth, once more came into view.

'Necksh a problem? Looksh like a gallowsh haul to me. Cutting it a bit fine weren't you, my shon? Well, you're a shervant of Hish Majeshty King Francish now. Or maybe a shlave. They didn't cutsh your hair yet so it'sh hard to tell.'

Sinking back onto the bench, trying to absorb this confusing statement amid all the other confusion, Jean began to observe, slowly, his immediate environment.

*I'm on a boat. I'm lying on a bench and there's a chain around my leg, and an oar on my thighs. There's a steady rhythm of both movement and sound, and a drum being hit somewhere behind me, towards . . . that's the prow of the ship, and I'm chained to face away from it.*

He counted the drum beats. After six there was a rattling of chains as men stood up, a whistle blasted on eight, then the grunt of many men falling back. The ship, when they fell, lurched forward, while the drum beat began again.

He was almost directly below the sail which, even as he looked, bellied with a strong gust of wind. A voice cried, 'The breath of St Christopher! Ship oars!' Immediately there was a rolling sound as the oars were pulled in, to rest across the laps of the rowers ahead, as theirs already did. The rhythmic drumming ceased.

He looked at the men, breathing hard and easing their cramped limbs around him. They were, for the most part, completely naked. Here and there a back was swathed in a sack shirt, or loins were girded in cloth, but the majority had nothing save skin to oppose the elements. Jean was still wearing the clothes he'd come aboard in but they were soiled from the effects of the hanging, the breeches especially wet and uncomfortable. He decided to try to shrug them off carefully, but his movements drew attention to him, despite the hissing of his toothless benchmate.

'Well, well, so my little master has had his fill of sleep.'

A grizzled face, obscured by hair, beard and a leather patch, loomed above him, a snake swaying sickeningly on the man's bare belly.

'Perhaps he'd want some breakfast now? A little bread and milk, some wine maybe?'

Sycophantic laughter greeted this statement, mainly coming from a fat, bare-chested seaman to the hairy man's left, but swiftly taken up by Jean's toothless companion and two other men on the same bench. Only a younger, lithe man at the oar's end kept his head down and remained silent.

'And he's soiled his pants,' the hairy man continued, to more laughter. 'Wants out of them, does he? Well, we can help him with that.' He barked at his fat follower. 'Strip him. Then shave him.'

Rough hands descended and tore off his clothing. Jean submitted to this since it was his desire anyway, but when the same hands reached down and yanked up a lock of his hair, when shears were poised above him, he took the wrist of the fat man and squeezed until there was a gasp of pain and the shears dropped.

Jean Rombaud had finally regained his voice.

'Touch my hair,' Jean croaked, 'and I'll gut you like a fish.'

'Corbeau, help me,' the fat man gasped.

The hairy man, Corbeau, who had begun to patrol up the central raised walkway, returned swiftly, uncoiling a short, many-tailed whip as he came. He raised this high above him, brought it down hard. The pain, as it lashed across Jean's tormented neck, was like bands of molten iron being laid upon fresh cuts. He dropped the hand immediately and the fat man slunk back to his master, rubbing it and glaring back.

'So we have a fighter on our benches, do we? We don't like fighters here. Unless it's us.'

Corbeau raised the whip and brought it down once, twice, again and again. Jean shielded his face as best he could and made no further noise, letting the knotted tails do their damage. It was a lighter whip, designed for pain but not serious injury. He had been whipped once in the army and knew the difference. So he waited, and finally Corbeau, breathing heavily, stopped.

'Enough, my bantam cock?' he gasped.

Jean just nodded and picked up the shears. For a moment, Corbeau and his corporal stepped back in fear, for any weapon in the hands of a slave could be deadly. But Jean merely wiped the filth of the deck from them and began to cut his own hair off. The fat man moved to take over, but Corbeau stopped him and they, the other slaves on the bench, indeed all the slaves within sight, watched as Jean began to wield the shears.

He did not just cut away madly, as the fat assistant would undoubtedly have done. He'd kept his thick hair somewhat longer than the current fashion so he had some length to work with. He began with a series of short snips, then longer passages of raising and sculpting, playing with the hair, something he'd learnt to do as a youth in the army to while away the tediousness of camp or siege, to earn a few extra sous with this entertainment. He had rarely performed on himself but the image he had within his head seemed to be translated pretty exactly onto it. There were appreciative grunts all around at his artistry.

When he had reduced his hair to all but the bare fuzz, there remained only one lock, and he'd left that because he'd observed men around him sporting such a plume. He met the eyes of the man who had lately been whipping him.

'Well, Master, do I clip the last of my feathers? I wouldn't fly far on these anyway.'

There was laughter, quickly suppressed by the raising of Corbeau's whip. The big man, glowering down at Jean, said, 'You are a criminal, justly sentenced for your sins. But I presume you are a Christian and so cannot be enslaved as these Muslim dogs around you can. They are shorn to baldness. You may keep your . . . plumage.' And with that he spat, bent down and snatched away the shears. As he did so, he said, 'When that other son of a whore you were brought aboard with wakes, you can attend to him too.'

He strode off down the gangway; lashing out at those who had failed to stow their oars fast enough. He was confused. Usually the victims of his lashings just bent over their oars and wept in pain. He felt his talents had been slighted somehow.

'Well, my friend' – the mouth of the wizened man beside him was twisted into a toothless grin – 'rarely doesh shomeone get the better of Corbeau. But I'd keep out of hish way for a while. He'sh not the man to have for an enemy.'

But Jean had already dismissed the encounter, was more concerned with the last of Corbeau's statements, that Haakon was nearby. Scanning in front of him, towards the back of the ship, he spotted the big man, three rows ahead, slumped over and leaning into the gunwales. He could see shallow breathing so at least he knew his friend was alive. Turning back to his companion, he said, 'How long have we been aboard?'

The old man smiled. 'Tired of ush already? You wash chained up not ten minutesh before the tide took ush out of Toulon a few hoursh ago. Unlucky, eh? Though by the look of your neck, maybe the galley washn't shuch a bad option.'

With the pain of the whipping, Jean had forgotten about

134

the rope burn, the stretched muscles. He rubbed his neck carefully now, before he spoke again. 'And where am I?'

'In the sheventh region of hell. Where they shend all the worst shinners, the hereticsh, blashphemersh and the shodomitesh; where Jewsh row beshide Mohammedansh and Lutheransh beshide defrocked Francishcansh. All gathered under God'sh open shkies on the deck of His Majeshty's galliot, the *Persheus*.'

Some of the man's words were hard to understand.

'Did you shay . . . say "galliot"?' Jean received a nod. 'What's that? I thought this was a galley.'

'It ish a type of galley. Shmaller, lighter, twenty oarsh inshtead of forty, shingle shail, jusht the one gun, up front. Built for shpeed, for meshagesh and quick actionsh. A beauty, besht I've shailed on.'

'And where are we bound?'

The old man leant in, the red gash of his mouth opening into a smile of sorts. 'Now there'sh a shtrange thing. We were heading with the resht of the fleet to Livorno. But Captain Big Noshe got a late meshage altering the plan. Sheems we're now bound for Valletta. Which pleashesh me, for one of my five wivesh livesh there. It'd be three year shince I sheen her.'

Malta! Jean sank back onto the bench. The naming of a destination suddenly brought to him the full truth of his situation. He was chained to a bench on a galley, or galliot – a stinking prison hulk anyway. A waking nightmare, fate of anyone who transgressed the laws of France, opposed some more powerful man's will or was simply unlucky. He had heard of men whose sole crime was being too drunk in the wrong kind of inn at the moment when a recruiter with a roll to fill passed by. You heard of such unhappy souls going. No one ever heard of them coming back.

The sentence of the galleys was a sentence of lingering death.

Every child in France was frightened to sleep with the threat of the horrors of the oar that awaited further disobedience. For how long could one survive ankle deep in this pool of pestilence? If exhaustion didn't weaken you and make you sick, the lashings, the scorching sun or freezing rain, the lack of good food and clean water would all take their toll. And then there was the not inconsiderable danger of the corsairs, the pirate fleets that preyed on all shipping in the Mediterranean from their bases in North Africa. If their ship was sunk in combat, their chains would pull them rapidly to the fathomless depths. If captured, they would swap Christian chains for those of Mohammed, the conditions and the risk exactly the same.

In a mere six days – *six!* – he had swapped a gibbet for an oar. Despair seized him. Bile filled his throat again, and he began to choke on it.

Then something strange happened. His companion said, 'You'll be needing shome water,' then got up, slipped the chain from his ankle and marched the dozen paces to the water barrel under the mast. When he returned, and Jean had stilled the retching with the cupful, he tried his own chain, which would not shift.

'How are you able to go free?' he croaked.

'They don't lock up ush volunteers. Well, only in some portsh, where the temptation might be too great to shtay away. Ash it would be in Valletta if I could shee my shweet Pancha. Jusht for fifteen minutesh, mind. I may be old but I shtill have the shtuff,' he cackled.

'Volunteers? You volunteer for this?'

'Shertainly. About a tenth of the company are here of their own free will.'

'Why?' was all Jean could manage.

'Onesh you've been behind the oar, what elshe ish there for you? I have been a shlave, a criminal and a free man, have rowed for Moshelman and Chrishtian, but even as a shlave I've never had to eat grassh as I have back in my home village, nor lain in a ditch in midwinter wanting to die, not jusht for the cold but for the lack of shomeone to talk to. Any life ish good enough if you accshept there'sh nothing better. That'sh what I'd do if I were you, shon – accshept the oar and get on with it.'

During the voyage towards Malta, Jean had time both to ponder this good advice and to learn the running of the ship. He knew that his and Haakon's lives, and any hope of escape from this hell, would depend on it. His gummy companion was called Da Costa, originally a Portuguese but a native of the galleys for some twenty years and all too willing to share his experience and knowledge. Jean found his toothless speaking became more comprehensible the longer he listened to it. And he had plenty of practice, for the old man had no sooner exhausted his wisdom of the sea than he began on tales of his adventures upon it. And Januc, the young, dark rower at the gangway end of their bench, had stories too. As befitted his age, they especially concerned women. He claimed he'd had three wives, all at once, had lived with them in a blue-tiled villa on the shores of the Mediterranean. Yet when questioned as to how he'd swapped such luxury for the roughness of an oar, he just shrugged and began another tale of jasmine-scented nymphs.

It was Haakon who revelled most in these tales. Da Costa had managed to get Haakon transferred to his, Januc's and Jean's oar, replacing the two others, telling Corbeau that it would save him many whippings, for the little man could control the big. For Da Costa, such strength beside him meant he could rest more, as the Norwegian could pull for both of them – all of them, it seemed at times, for despite the obvious horrors of their situation Haakon was delighted to be once again on a boat, to be pulling on an oar as he had done for years in his homeland. The sea air invigorated him, the body that had started to run to fat in the indolence of his life in Tours was getting hard again, and the hair cut that Jean had performed on him, reducing the long, golden hair and thick beard to the single lock that denoted the criminal, had also removed the years. And coming from the land of sagas and epic tales, Da Costa's stories of perilous life before the mast touched the Viking within him, while Januc's, of indolence, sweet sherbet and harem maidens, aroused something else. Jean would smile to see the Norseman lean forward, as if he were sat in a chair in some smoky lodge on his native island, not chained to a bench on a prison hulk, ankle deep in filth.

But rowing was what they were there to do. When the wind dropped they were worked hard, in twenty-minute bursts that left them all gasping. Big Nose, as Captain de la Vallerie was universally known, had a fondness for speed and manoeuvre and anyone who did not 'pull their weight', as the expression went, was brutally disciplined by Corbeau and his lackeys. The grumbling and cursing were continuous, the stench of bodies tethered in their own filth appalling, the rations of water and food barely adequate. But the oarsmen, for all their differences, had a kind of camaraderie, for one man not working meant more work for others, and the more experienced impressed upon the less that speed and instant obedience were all that would save them from sinking to Neptune's floor when it came to a fight. As it inevitably would.

'Ah, the battlesh I have sheen!' Da Costa declared as he spat out the larger of the worms that infested that morning's hard bread.

It was early on the fifth day and the wind was at last carrying them along steadily. Around them men leant on their oars and snored.

'It wash in nineteen that I landed with Cortez at Vera Cruz,' began the Portuguese, 'the firsht time ever I shaw New Shpain—'

'Wait, old man,' interrupted Januc, laughing. 'I thought you told us yesterday you were with that mad Genoese Columbus in ninety-two. Make your mind up.'

'I wash with Chrishtof, ash I called him then and would now, if he were shitting beshide me,' replied the older man with dignity, 'but I'm sure you'll remember me shaying that I only got ash far ash the islandsh when I wash taken with the green shicknesh and Chrishtof shays to me, he shays, "Paulho, I need you with me, but Portugal needsh you more", and he shent me back. Sho I never shaw the mainland.'

'Oh,' said Januc, smiling still, 'and there I was sure you told me weeks ago you were the first man to set foot in the New World.'

'I wash. I rowed Chrishtof ashore and leapt onto the beach to shecure the boat for him.'

This was greeted with a roar of disbelief by all within range, for more than just their bench enjoyed listening to the old man's tales. The hubbub was so loud it attracted the attention of Corbeau. He was swiftly over them, lashing out with his whip. 'If that's you telling lies again, Da Costa,' he yelled, but Haakon managed to take most of the blows aimed at the old man's frail shoulders upon his own broad ones and the bearded brute swiftly tired.

As he huffed up the walkway, Haakon stared after him, a reckoning in his eyes. Then he leant in to the Portuguese and said, 'Tell it just to me. Whisper it. What happened at Vera Cruz?'

As they murmured together, Jean turned to his other oarmate, Januc. He knew little of him, for the younger man's tales amused but revealed little of the teller. Yet Jean had the feeling there was much to the man, a power held back behind the mask of his grey eyes and strong Roman nose. He also knew that when the time came to strike, to escape and pursue the quest – a time that must come – it would be good to be able to trust the man chained beside him.

'And so, Januc. We have heard of your scantily clad maidens. Have you no battle tales to share, like our friend Da Costa?'

'A few.' Januc smiled, leant in. 'But I have found the men with the best stories rarely tell them. Those who taught me to fight also taught that silence and scars are the true testament.'

'I would agree. We've had your silence, on that score at

least. And I can see some of your scars.' He pointed to a puckered dent in his companion's shoulder. 'Arquebus or musket? Longish range I would say, because there's no exit scar. Must have had a good surgeon to get that ball out.'

'I did. The best.' Januc spoke very quietly, drawing the Frenchman in. 'A janissary always gets the best.'

Jean whistled softly. 'Janissary? So you were a mercenary, as we were. Though you fought for the Turk.'

'Is "mercenary" the right term? My parents in Dubrovnik sold me to the Sultan's recruiters when I was eight.'

'But I thought janissaries were the Bloodguard and thus the Sultan's pampered pets?'

'Pampered perhaps. But a slave is a slave, however well he's looked after.'

'A slave who had three wives at once?' Jean smiled. 'Sounds unlike any slavery I've heard of.'

He saw the grey eyes flick towards the horizon.

'That was in another, later, life.'

Jean realised he was pushing the younger man too far. 'Still, a janissary. I'm impressed.'

'I hope you'll keep your esteem to yourself.'

'Of course. Some others here might not be as forgiving as me. For I got this from one of your fellows.'

Jean lowered his head and showed the curved line that ran from the back of his left ear, under the tuft of hair and across to the apex of the crown.

'Scimitar,' observed Januc. 'Must have been a poor janissary if you're still breathing.'

'He was dead even as he struck the blow.' Jean rubbed his head. 'I think he did quite well enough.'

'And where was this? A sea battle, no doubt.'

'I have never fought at sea. Though I hope to change that, and soon.' He looked across to see if Januc had picked up the hint but there was no reaction, so he continued, 'No, this was, oh, ten years ago, one April morning on a plain in Hungary. The one that's called Mohacz.'

It was Januc's turn to whistle.

'You were at Mohacz?'

'I was. One of Frundsberg's lambs, God rest the commander's soul.'

'Forgive me if I do not join you in that blessing. That German demon and his "lambs" nearly cost us the day.'

'You were there?'

'I was.'

'You look too young.'

'It was my first battle.'

'As you can see, it was nearly my last.'

'And mine,' said Januc, pointing to the musket scar.

Both men fell silent and just looked at each other. Both, simultaneously, shook their heads and both for a moment returned to that April morning in 1526 when the armies of Suleyman the Magnificent swept out of the conquered Balkans to meet the pride of Bohemia and Hungary on a mist-filled plain called Mohacz.

In their silence there was the immediate bond of honourable foes.

*It is very strange*, Jean suddenly thought, *but both the men I now sit chained between I have met in battle. That must mean something.*

A huge row broke out behind them before any words could fail to sum up their memories. It came from the benches occupied mainly by the Muslim slaves. Corsair pirates to a man, Da Costa had said, taken in various actions across the Mediterranean.

'Infidel dogsh!' The old man spat, drool running down his chin. 'They feed thoshe bashtardsh lesh than the resht of us and whipsh 'em more, and shtill they fight.'

'So much for the camaraderie of the oar!' Haakon joked.

'Camaraderie with my arshe. Look, it'sh that Ake again. Corbeau will love thish. He hatesh thoshe blacksh. Shays they don't pull their weight. Callsh them hish Niger baboonsh!'

Jean saw a huge black man crushing a smaller white man against his chest. 'Who's that he's wrestling with?'

'I can't shee . . . Hah! It'sh Mute! No wonder the black-amon'sh shqueezing him. He'sh from Nishe and the worsht thief on the ship. Vicioush too!'

'Pull them apart!' Corbeau was screaming and he and his three assistants went in, whips flailing. Rowers on surrounding oars pulled back to the limit of their ankle chains but were still struck in the indiscriminate lashing. They set up a huge roar, blending with the partisan support for black and white.

Ake was shaking Mute back and forth as easily as a child's doll; indeed, the smaller man seemed lifeless, for the air had been squeezed out of him and he'd lost consciousness – but obviously not before he'd buried a shard of wood, prised from beneath the filth of the deck and sharpened to a wicked point, into the black chest. This was, even now, causing a thick spurt of blood to shoot from the giant. An inch lower, Jean thought, a slightly slower reaction from the African, and this Nicean gutter trash would not now be feeling the steady crushing of his ribs.

It seemed that blood loss had weakened Ake, or perhaps he felt he'd killed the little rat who, Da Costa maintained, had probably tried to steal the Negro's already meagre ration; but suddenly Ake dropped him and sat back on his bench, clutching one hand over the wound in his chest and one to his head to ward off the whips.

The shouting went on. Opinions, in nine languages and many more dialects, were delivered as to who was to blame. Ake's fellows, fifteen members of the same tribe, merely stamped in rhythm and uttered a low chant, rattling their chains in unison, while Corbeau's assistants moved among them delivering blows left and right. This did nothing to calm the hubbub; indeed, it seemed to build and build in volume, especially after Mute, whom everyone presumed to be dead, so still had he been, suddenly rolled over and vomited over Corbeau's feet.

'Quiet, you dogs!' screamed the latter, enraged, kicking the unfortunate Nicean in the face, returning him to unconsciousness. But his command went unheeded and the noise doubled and spread to other parts of the boat until everyone on the deck seemed to be yelling.

Seven oars back, Da Costa was leaping up and down beside Jean. 'Yah! Kick him again!'

'Whose side are you on?' laughed Haakon.

'I hatesh that little wharf rat Mute. Shtole a fine shet of wooden teesh I'd had carved in Algecirash.'

'Why's he called Mute?' Haakon liked to get the characters in any story right.

'Tongue ripped out. Blashphemy, probably. Yah! Give him back to the blackamon!'

And with that Da Costa slipped out of the shackle and ran forward, as all the freemen did, to get a better look.

'This piece of bread against your salt fish that the big man bleeds to death when they take that splinter out.' Haakon held out his hand.

Jean took it. 'Done. He looks like he's survived worse than that.'

The noise was still building and Corbeau and his gang were powerless to stop it, their yells and whip cracks lost in the furore. They had retreated to the gangway, Corbeau shouting for his arquebus, when there was an explosion of gunpowder. All men ducked instinctively.

'What is the meaning of this outrage?'

A nasally voice spoke into the sudden stillness. Captain Louis St Mark de la Vallerie, universally known as Big Nose, stood on the afterdeck. Behind him, twenty soldiers lowered smoking guns.

He had been on deck as little as possible during the voyage, only appearing to supervise manoeuvres. He hated it up there, the stench was intolerable. Only in his little cabin with its small promenade, the wind coming from aft and blowing them along, something scented always clutched to permanently flared nostrils, was there some respite from it. Corbeau and Augustin, the sergeant-at-arms in charge of the eighty soldiers, could receive their orders just as well away from the putrid smell. Of course, they always brought some with them, and were quickly dismissed. Louis was happy to be left alone to play with the weapons that lined the cabin walls, shooting arrows he made himself with the Turkish bow he'd seized in a sea fight at a float tethered to the ship's aft, and reading the outrageous writings of that bawdy ex-monk Rabelais.

He had been part way through a delicious passage in Gargantua that pierced, delightfully, the pomposity of so much Church humbug when the steady build of noise distracted him, making him lose track of the complex argument. Then Augustin had appeared at his door, yelling in his excitable way about 'rebellion at the oars'.

'Nonsense,' said Louis and, clutching a large metal pomander filled with dried violets in one hand and a pistol in the other, strode to the deck.

The volley, fired high, had been his idea of course. He had few enough rowers as it was, and Augustin wanted to shoot some of them? The man was incapable of organising an orgy in a brothel! As the smoke cleared from the raised platform that dominated the aft end of the galliot, the chaos below was brought into full view. The full stench came with it. He clutched his pomander ever closer to his face and spoke around it.

'Well, Corbeau, can you explain why I have been called up here to restore the order you have so obviously lost?'

Corbeau's one eye glimmered in fury. 'It was that bastard baboon,' he stuttered, drawing a chorus of ape noises from the freemen now gathered around, 'and this piece of Provençal gutter filth.'

Corbeau was from Gascony, and proud of it. He took another kick at the prostrate Nicean, who yelped.

'Get that scum back to their places,' the captain shouted, and the freemen dodged back from the swinging whips as they ran, making snorting noises through their noses. Corbeau hoped the captain didn't understand. He was angry enough.

He was also oblivious. The only thing that concerned him was the instant restoration of order. These men had to be taught to obey commands the moment they were issued. It was the difference between victory and defeat in a sea fight. Defeat was something that preoccupied his mind, because he knew that if he was unfortunate enough to survive one, his impoverished drunk of a father would never come up with any ransom money and he would probably end up chained to one of these benches himself. It wasn't the brutality he feared. It was the stench.

'Bring the offenders before me!'

Locks were unclasped, the chain that linked each man to the other was slipped through, and Mute was thrown easily onto the gangway below the captain. Ake proved a more difficult proposition. The loss of blood had caused him to faint and he was a large weight to move. Corbeau and his two subordinates finally managed it, and the big man lay beside a now wide awake Mute.

'And who started this?'

There was instant uproar as most of the white men yelled that it had to be the black's fault. Flailing whips soon quietened them, but one voice emerged from the Muslim benches. It belonged to Mugali, youngest of the Niger tribesmen, who had managed to pick up some French.

'Steal!' he cried out. 'He steal!'

He repeated this in his own tongue, which drew full vocal assent from the others, quickly again silenced by the whips.

'Are you a thief, man?' said the captain.

Mute's tongueless denial was overwhelmed by the roar of laughter and repeated snorts that greeted the question.

Colouring in anger, de la Vallerie nonetheless carefully weighed up the options. All rowers were scum, and if he could punish them all now, he would. But he was already twenty short of a full complement and he needed every man who could row. But guilty or not, it was obvious the Negro was bleeding to death while the gesticulating mute was recovering. Blaming and punishing minorities had the weight of tradition behind it and could be used as a good example to discourage the rest of the scum. There was a long summer of campaigning ahead and such an example now would be most salutary. Really, in the end, like most decisions, it was an easy one.

The pomander was removed briefly from before the nose. 'Hang the black hog by his ankles from this railing. Flay him alive.' There was some cheering as Corbeau and his minions struggled to hoist Ake into position at the captain's feet, who added, 'Oh, and tie his hands behind his back. If he pulls that stick out he'll be dead before the sentence can be carried out.' De la Vallerie had had a weapon stuck in him once, in a duel. Its removal had nearly killed him.

When they were done, and a bucket of sea water had been thrown over Ake to revive him for his torment, the captain spoke again. 'You will see now what happens to those who seek to disrupt the proper working of the *Perseus*. Row well, keep out of trouble, obey orders. If anyone fails me just once, that man will repeat this fate.'

With a nod, he signalled Corbeau to begin.

Haakon, Jean and Januc were in the small minority of people who looked away as the knife point was slipped into the first few layers of skin on the back and a large flap was torn away. They could not block their ears though, and even if they'd made this weakening gesture it would not have kept out the high-pitched shriek, more animal than human, like a weasel in a trap gnawing its own leg off. Most men, including a delighted Da Costa, watched in awe.

Sickened, Januc turned his gaze to the horizon. He was thus the first person on the ship to see the three sails. His eyes had always been sharp and even at that distance he could recognise the distinctive curves of Arab corsairs. *I should know them*, he thought, his heart beating quicker, *for I have captained a few*.

He didn't tell anyone. News travelled fast around a ship and would, too swiftly, reach the ears of his gaolers.

*Praise be to Allah*, thought Januc. *May my silence be another breath in your sails.*

# KALEIDOSCOPE

## TWO

# KALEIDOSCOPE

Giancarlo Cibo, Archbishop of Siena, had every reason to be happy. With a following wind from Toulon, the crossing to Livorno had been mercifully short, a mere three days. There his discomfort and false poverty came to an end, for his manservant, Giovanni, was at the dock to meet him with the palace carriage and the trip to Siena had taken less than a day on roads unusually empty, clear and dry under a burning Tuscan sun. He'd even got his bodyguard back, for Heinrich had staggered aboard the boat just prior to its sailing with the tale of their enemies' hanging, swiftly told before oblivion took him.

Now he lay in a bath, a thing he did occasionally in the old Roman fashion, with a feast of welcome planned for the evening and an orgy to follow, organised in her usual impeccable fashion by his voluptuous mistress, Donatella.

So he had won again! Even against the unexpectedly serious opposition. Winning always brought him pleasure, despite the fact that he did it so often. Yet he wasn't content and the reason for this lay in the saddle bag, road- and blood-stained, resting on a chair less than an arm's length from him. Even now he thought he saw movement from within it, a slight pressing outward of the leather. Cursing, he looked away; but just as they had been when he'd seen the hand four days earlier on the ship, his eyes were drawn back now to the dreadful prize of his victory.

'I don't believe in you!' he shouted, the cry drawing a servant tentatively into the room, dismissed with an angry wave.

It had been the exhaustion, that was the only explanation. The hard journey, little rest – he hadn't eaten properly in days. Hermits who fasted, mutilated their bodies, deprived themselves of sleep, wouldn't they then soar to ecstatic heights where wondrous visions danced before them?

'And if they can see the Madonna or Our Lord himself . . .'

Yes. His hardships could explain the horrifying vision of the unputrefied hand reaching out to him, the finger that pointed in bloody accusation.

But there was one thing hardships could not explain – quite the reverse. Where was his cough? His sickness had been a part of him for several years now – some days better, some days worse, but always a continuous presence. Until now.

Cibo shifted in the cooling water, aware of his puckering skin.

There had to be another explanation. Maybe the appearance of the hand was coincidental, his illness due to disappear anyway. The combination of his surgeon's treatments, the mercury and herbs, the letting of his blood, the prayers of his priests, all these had finally effected the cure. He was not some credulous peasant raised from his sick bed by the touch of St Mark's collar bone. The six-fingered hand was a symbol only, a method of controlling minds.

And yet . . . Cibo raised his own hand to his lips, tried to cough. Nothing. No blood flowed unchecked through his lips, staining his endless supply of handkerchiefs. He knew. It was not prayers, or his doctor's ineffectual ministrations.

'No!' he screamed at the saddle bags. 'No one has power over me. Not popes, not princes . . . and not the Witch Whore of England!'

The servants came again and this time he let them stay, rub him dry with soft linens, anoint him with oils to ease still

149

aching flesh, wrap him in clean robes. While they ministered to his body, his mind worked.

Perhaps he was looking at it wrong. The hand had power as a symbol, yes, but could not its true power lie *within* the strangely uncorrupted flesh? Just as gold lay within baser metals?

Of course! He had been ignoring the obvious. The answer lay in alchemy, the quest he passionately pursued to transform mere metal into gold, which was itself only part of the true quest. If the Philosopher's Stone were found, the ultimate substance from which all other substance, flesh and form derived, it would give the finder untold riches. But what it would truly yield was the quintessence of life itself, with the power to cure illness, restore youth.

Or bring the dead back to life.

The idea entranced him. God and his mind working in harmony. There was one man who could verify this for him. And he . . . existed, would be the correct word, not very far away.

Dismissing the servants, Cibo seized the saddle bag and held it as far from his body as he could manage, with his other hand plucking a torch from its socket on the wall. Its light surrounded and comforted him a little.

*I'll need it*, he thought, *for dungeons are always dark and the lowest levels the darkest of all.*

There was the world and there was its shadow, and Abraham had long ago lost the ability to differentiate between the two. When he was first imprisoned he used to struggle with it, striving to place an object on one of the planes, to grasp its form, to quantify it with all the acuity of his scientific mind; but then something previously solid would lose all cohesion, or an empty space would suddenly be colonised by a shape. This would distress him, for he was a man who had always needed to know the world around him. Gradually, though, he realised just how fragile was this thing he used to think of as reality. It no longer mattered that he could not subject the phenomenon he encountered to all the rigorous tests he would have applied in his own laboratory. That was not the point. It was not why he was there. Rigid laws of science only applied in the so-called real world outside. Not here, never here.

Some phenomena could still be felt though. He was always burning himself on the crucible because he would sit too close to it, observing the shifting patterns on the melting metal surfaces, molten worlds created and destroyed in an instant, as Yahweh had created, as Yahweh could destroy. There was a key there and sometimes he felt he could reach in and pluck it from the bubbling depths, had almost done so on more than one occasion, until some little remnant of restraint stopped him. As it was, his skin was traced with the scars gleaned from too curious reachings.

There was no time within this world, so now he sat back on a chair he had not realised was there. The lead was not near the point where it could be useful, where he would be able to siphon off its essence in the form of its smoke, capture and distil its emanations in his glass retort. Waiting was easy though, for he had only to look up and once more see the kaleidoscope.

Cascades of colour, greens plucked from a forest, magentas and blues hauled from an ocean's depths, fired Tuscan umbers and ochres, more vibrant than any seen in the country outside, shifting constantly and not just in the reflection of crucible heat nor the flickering of reed torches placed beyond the translucent walls. Shifting of themselves, glass taking breath and moving, now a steady pulse, now a ripple of falling shards. As his world turned, the petals of a rose realigned themselves into a butterfly's wings, into a crimson angel now bearing apples, now the helms of fallen warriors from whose eye sockets poured streams of river pearls. Droplets of silver, lozenges of emerald and agate. The jeweller Abraham had been linking the tumbling stones into a necklace of flame.

The ceiling revolved above him, bringing new riches. He knew beyond the torchlight was a great darkness, but he was not to dwell on that, he had been told it no longer concerned him. His whole world was within the shimmering kaleidoscope, bounded by glass without and the bubbling contents of the crucible within. Only these should occupy him. He had no other wants, not food nor drink, of which there was plenty, though he had little appetite. Above all there was the pipe that so smoothed over the inconsistencies of his life with its sweet smoke, blurring the false line, showing him the lie of existence as it seemed, enabling him to focus on the real truths within this kaleidoscopic world.

The secrets were apparent to him with every turn of his head. His task was to make them manifest to the man who had placed him there. The man who even now descended the dank stairwells under his palace, a reed torch in one hand, a saddle bag held carefully away from his body in the other.

The final stairs were especially treacherous, crumbling and damp, and Cibo took his time. The slow pace allowed his breathing to calm, his mind to turn slowly inwards, as it always did on the descent to this netherworld where the usual laws of time and space, and perceived truth, simply failed to apply. His torchlight flared off dripping walls, off the seams of agate within the harder rock from which this special place had been carved.

A masked gaoler struggled with keys to the first of two doors. When it finally creaked open Cibo entered another ill-lit corridor with three cells lining each side. There was rustling from within them as he strode past, but whether of man or beast he could not tell. Both, probably, and a mix, for the enemies who occupied these dank regions had been hidden from the light long enough to have become half-beast. He couldn't even remember who they were or why he'd condemned them. Good, prudent reasons, he felt sure.

He glanced to each side and feral eyes glimmered back

through bars in the flicker of his torch. Something slammed hard against the cell door furthest along and a growling was heard as he waited for another faceless guard to open the second iron-studded barrier.

*At least they do not lack for water.* The idea amused him. He'd ordered an underground stream to be diverted to flow through his dungeons. It was so wearisome to carry tortured bodies up the stairs and get them away from the palace with no one seeing or raising an alarm. Now, a trap-door lifted and a mangled corpse was dumped; it would career through the subterranean waterways that criss-crossed Siena and fetch up leagues away, on river bank or pondside, and no one could tell where it had come from.

He laughed, and the guard, thinking it was impatience, muttered something apologetic and fumbled with another key. Then the second door screeched on its rusty hinges and admitted him into a world that was very much his own invention. He never failed to feel the pride of the creator when he returned to it after an absence and looking around now, he smiled.

The geometry of the vaulted chamber was flawless. Yet the aesthetics were incidental, the light from the dozen reed torches failing even to illuminate the ceiling. It was the astrological alignment that mattered far more, a hard trick to get right so far below the surface of the earth. The apex of the vaulted roof was both a chimney to bear fumes away and a funnel of power to draw down the forces of the heavens. Directly beneath its centre, aligned to the accuracy of a hair, lay a glass room.

Layer upon layer of glass rose above this centre, with chambers the width of a hand in between, filled with fragments of coloured glass in every shape from diamond to lozenge, arrow head to star. Each chamber was connected to a water wheel, and each moved with the rising and falling of liquid levels in glass amphorae positioned at each end. From the outside, it looked like a random tumbling of misshapen pieces. From the inside, it looked like what it was. A kaleidoscope.

Within the kaleidoscope lay the source of the heat whose glow could be made out through the shifting chambers. It came from a huge cauldron whose lower half was buried in the floor, heated to a white intensity by unseen flames beneath.

Peering through the walls, Cibo made out the swaying figure of a man beside the cauldron.

The Archbishop felt within his robes for a piece of purple and yellow glass. Inserting it in a hidden vent, a portion of glass swung upwards and he ducked underneath it and entered the translucent room.

'Well, Abraham,' he said, 'Have you been making progress?'

The old man in the skull cap swung his head in the direction of the voice. He heard so many in the course of his day that he wasn't sure if this was just another golem sent to plague him or distract him from his work. But then he recognised the man as his . . . patron was the only word he could come up with. When had he seen him last? That night? The day before? A month ago? Time had little meaning for him in a world where the sun never rose and set. Time was just a scribble on the page of his calculations. He was given the movements of sun and moon daily, for that was important; you couldn't hope to track down the Philosopher's Stone without the most accurate of data.

Cibo looked down at his former colleague and present prisoner. It was ten years since he had changed Abraham's status from one to the other and they had not been kind to the Jew.

Cibo remembered the energetic young scientist he'd first met, experimenting with different metal fusions to create his wondrous jewellery, using that to fund his real passion: delving into the mysteries of alchemy. How they had worked together at the beginning, sharing the delights of discovery!

What progress they had made, eclipsing much of the work even of Paracelsus in Basle and Apollonius in Wittenberg. But one day Abraham had wanted to take his daughter to their relatives in Venice, unhappy she was being raised outside their faith, and Cibo could not be sure that he would ever return. He needed the Jew's superior knowledge. So Cibo had imprisoned his body in this glass world and his will with an opium pipe – necessary coercion after the daughter had somehow escaped and Abraham had grown rebellious.

The drug had aged the Jew, together with the heat and fumes of the crucible he constantly attended, the lack of air and sunlight. His world was only this kaleidoscope, devised by Cibo to combine with the narcotic and focus the power of his brilliant mind. Amazing things had been seen and achieved inside this magical chamber, for Cibo knew alchemy to be far more than merely a scientific process.

Which was why he dropped the saddle bag on the table now.

'I've brought you something that might help,' he said. 'Go on. Open it.'

He wanted to turn away, couldn't, managed a step backwards, then waited as the Jew slowly reached for the straps and just as slowly undid each one. When he reached inside and paused, Cibo shuddered, expecting Abraham to recoil in horror from the touch. Yet all he did was carefully pull out the velvet bag and place it before him on the one clear space on a table covered in charts and instruments of calculation. He made no move to go further, just sat and stared at the object before him.

'Go on,' the Archbishop's voice cracked, 'take it out.'

He was obeyed. The six-fingered hand was brought into the light and the two men gasped for different reasons.

Anne Boleyn's hand lay on the table. It did not move, as it had in the cabin of the ship, yet it did not seem completely still. For Abraham, it was the shock of the six fingers; for Cibo, it was the look of it, changed from a mere four days before. Then, there had been a bleeding gash, for an arrow had pierced leather to pierce flesh, leaving a wound that should have taken weeks to heal in someone alive and even then left a jagged scar. Yet where the wound had been there was not a trace, not the faintest hint of a blemish to mar the rosy sheen of the skin. It was the same at the wrist, where the sword had taken it from the arm. Nothing there but pink and healthy flesh.

The gasps hung in the air and lengthened into silence. Finally, Abraham said, almost wearily, 'Oh, Giancarlo, what have you done now?'

The Archbishop did not tolerate criticism. He was always right and that was an end to it. Yet somehow here, in a world without time, with a man who was the only equal he'd ever known, there was a need for some kind of explanation.

'It is not what you think,' he said. 'It is beyond anything you could think, or even dream.'

'You killed this person to take this hand?'

'I did not. I saw her killed. Yes, it's from a woman. A queen.'

'Then how—'

'The how does not matter. It's the why of it. How long do you think it is since this hand was joined to the body?'

Abraham reached out to the hand, turning it to get a perspective. Cibo sucked in his breath when he saw that, but the hand remained inert, a passive object, while the Jew examined it carefully. At last, he spoke.

'It still feels almost warm to the touch, and no rigor mortis has set in. For those reasons I would say it was no less than three hours since this unfortunate lost her hand. Yet . . .'

A great yawn swept over him, he seemed to lose focus, and Cibo had to wait impatiently. It was a part of the imprisonment that was necessary, chaining him to the opium, bending the scholar to his will. It led to some huge imaginative leaps but it also distracted him.

'Yet?' Cibo barked finally.

Abraham carried on as if there had been no pause. 'Yet the severing wound shows signs of healing, indeed it looks like it has healed entirely. That's not possible.'

'We may have to change our opinion of what is and is not possible, Abraham. For it is two and a half weeks since this hand was struck off, in the same instant as the head. If only we had that here as well, maybe we could ask her to explain herself. As it is, we have to make do with what we possess.'

Cibo had started to speak slowly. He couldn't stop staring at the hand. The light of the torches outside the chamber, filtered through the glass, was making patterns and colours weave across it and it didn't need to move to pull his eyes. The light and heat seemed to be sucked into it and it took a huge effort for him to say, in a thick voice, 'Put it away. Put it back in the bag.'

Moving very slowly, Abraham did as he was told, and a weight and a shadow seemed to leave the room. They both breathed out. Cibo's knees gave, so he pulled up a stool and sat down heavily to stare into the haggard features opposite him.

*I look as old as you*, Cibo thought. *I can no longer shake off the hardships of travel with my former ease. And my illness . . .*

The lack of a cough again made him strangely angry. All the more reason to proceed swiftly with their experiments, for it was possible that rejuvenation and cure lay ahead.

'Do you see what we have here?' he said. 'It could be the bridge we have been searching for, the link between the planes of existence. How often have we tried to create a homunculus, a replica man, from the remains of another?'

The reply, as ever, was infuriatingly slow. 'It was your desire to do that. I never thought it was necessary.'

'You never dared to think it. You hesitated from reaching for the one thing that could lead us truly on. We both know life and matter are inextricably linked. Well, I have seen the miracle confirmed. This hand could pluck out the Philosopher's Stone for us. It may be the key to freeing man from the shackles of flesh, to the true transformation of spirit.'

Cibo could sit no more. He got up and began preparing the pipe for the opium, mixing the powdery lumps with a little liquid, cramming the paste around the hole at one end of the thick, hollow, teak cylinder. When he was ready, he pulled Abraham gently by the elbow and made him lie down on the cot, his head raised up on a blanket and turned to the side. He placed the mouth of the pipe to Abraham's and touched a taper to the side of the glowing crucible. It flared instantly. Holding the flame just above the opium paste, Cibo continued in a soft voice.

'Today we begin the quest that will lead to the last discovery worth making. Tell me what you need and it will be brought to you. Dream it and it is yours. I will ransack the world for you.'

He lowered the flame. Abraham sucked, and Cibo pushed the lumpy liquid to the hole, watching it catch, transform to smoke and disappear, watching it transform the concern on the Jew's face to contentment. Five breaths he took, until the paste had been burnt away. Then Abraham curled up, bony knees reaching up to bony chest.

It was when Cibo was halfway through his ascent of the dank stairwell that the pain seized him. He bent over, a great wrenching cough seeming to take possession of his whole frame. Weakened, he leant against the dripping wall. Something was at his lips, on his chin, and he reached a hand up to touch; they came away warm and sticky and he needed no flickering torchlight to tell him what was there.

'Hurry, Abraham,' he murmured, wiping the blood away on his robes. 'Hurry.'

But Abraham could not hurry. The opium that bound his will bound his intellect too. Experiments were conducted at a slower pace. So it was two weeks later that Cibo, a daily visitor to the only place where his coughing seemed to abate, finally lost all patience.

'Enough!' He rose above the Jew, who sat at the table, the hand laid out before him at the centre of the chart showing the stars that had governed at Anne Boleyn's execution. 'Enough,' he repeated. 'We have tried your way. Now we will try mine.'

'Three weeks we've been in Siena. And how many times have we seen him?'

It was a question Beck already knew the answer to, but the Fugger gave it anyway. 'At least a dozen.'

They'd seen him going to officiate at the cathedral, borne in a litter up the few steps from his palazzo past the baptistry. They'd sat in the Duomo and heard his sonorous voice declaim the Latin prayers. They'd watched him ride in his gilded carriage the three hundred paces down the Via del Pellegrini through the Piazza del Campo to the town hall, the Palazzo Pubblico, where the business of running Siena was conducted.

'And how many chances have we had to get inside his palazzo?' Beck queried.

The Fugger sighed. They'd have this conversation at least once a day. 'Just the one.'

'Exactly. One! And who stopped me taking it? You did.'

'Our David would have got himself killed, would he not, Daemon?' the Fugger said, feeding the raven bread from a huge round of it in his lap.

Beck snorted. Yes, leaping on the back of Cibo's carriage would have been a risk, but she was well used to those. What annoyed her was that it wasn't the risk that had stopped her. What stopped her was the mentioning of a name.

'Let's wait for Jean,' the Fugger had said.

And the woman in her, the one she hid, suppressed, tied down as firmly as she tied down her breasts, had reacted to that name, to those feelings so instantly evoked by a touch, the memory of a laugh. A couple of days, mere hours really, and one fight at his side, ending in that final look as he saved her life. Her head told her that no one came back from the galleys, that she would never see those eyes again, never be able to confirm the promise or answer the question within them. Yet her heart hesitated at his name, and she missed the chance her courage told her was there.

'And that's why I always work alone,' she said, snatching some bread.

They were sat once more in front of the Palazzo Pubblico, having watched Cibo being delivered there again. They were on the other side of the Campo with their backs to the fountain, the Fonte Gaia. The Fugger was enjoying the summer sun and the sound of water gushing from the mouths of the stone wolves behind him. After his initial shock, he was even enjoying the other statues on display, several of whom were women only partially clad. One was bare-breasted, an infant with questing fingers reaching out to touch an elegantly carved nipple. He'd pretended a good Germanic outrage at the decadence, for they would never have allowed such a sight back in Munster. But while Beck splashed some cooling water on an agitated brow, he looked again.

'Beautiful, is she not?'

Beck had caught him staring. Anger banished, the teasing smile and fresh water transformed the face of the boy before the Fugger. He shook his head, remembering his own watery transformation in the stream on the way to Tours, marvelling at this change in his life, fearing that still, somehow, it was merely one of the dreams sent to torment him, visions of heaven as he lay in the hell of the gibbet midden. Could he really be sitting beneath a lewd fountain in a decadent Italian town with a bright, mad boy as a companion? With a purpose once more to his life? On the road to some sort of redemption for his sins? The tentacles of the hell he'd escaped still reached out for him sometimes, in his dreams, occasionally when he was wide awake, phantasms and ghouls and sword-wielding barons bursting out of shadows to pursue him, to hew his body, to imprison him in filth. But somehow he'd retain his grip on the world and the demons would shriek off into the sky. He still found it hard to look anyone in the eye, but more and more he could talk to them directly. Even tease back.

'Look at you,' he said. 'When you smile you look like a fresh-faced girl. Doesn't he, Daemon?'

Beck scowled, turned away. But it was hard not to smile in Siena, for the town possessed a magic that even the occasional evil of its rulers could not overpower, in its bells, its fountains and arcades.

The Fugger had turned back to watch the scurrying of people round the piazza. They emerged from the long shadow cast by the giant tower, the Torre del Mangia, carrying all manner of objects: weapons, bolts of cloth, flagpoles, huge cured hams, butts of wine. 'Looks like they're preparing for a party.'

'They are. It's the Palio.'

'Ah yes, I heard the bread seller talking of it. It's a race, yes?'

'Everyone talks of nothing but the Palio, and it's far more than a race.' Beck smiled again and leant in. 'It's the heartbeat of the city, a festival to celebrate some victory over the Florentines hundreds of years ago. The *contrade*, the local boroughs – there must be thirty of them – each has an emblem such as the eagle, the boar, the lion, the rooster and the viper. They parade through the streets under banners and in the uniforms and colours of their band. And here in the Campo, on the first night of the celebrations, two of the *contrade* have the honour of fighting each other. Fifty men a side in the *pugna*, as it's called.'

'Fighting? Are they gladiators? Have we returned to the bloodsports of ancient Rome?'

Beck smiled and held up a hand, with fingers bunched.

'Almost. But these gladiators fight with fists wrapped in cloths. People get hurt, few die.'

'Few?' The Fugger rolled his eyes. 'These Italians claim they are so civilised, that we Germans are the barbarians. Then they punch each other to death in the street.'

'Yes, Fugger, but more die in the bullfight.'

'They have a bullfight as well? Is there no end to this Roman depravity, oh Daemon?'

The raven cocked its head at the mention of its name, stretched its huge wings, then went back to pulling at something wedged between the street stones.

'Oh yes, there is an end. It ends in the horse race. That starts and finishes here in the Campo, twists through the streets, each *contrada* with its own horse. Then, of course, the real bacchanal begins, for winners and losers.'

'And when does this pagan ritual commence?'

'The second of July.'

'That's two days away. Will we get an invitation?'

'Everyone's invited. It's the biggest party you'll ever see. Everyone dresses up. You see that man carrying all that rich cloth and silk? A Sienese would rather starve for a week than be underdressed on the big day. It's a race, orgy, fight and feast, all in one.'

'What about these Italians, Daemon? What are a modest German and a good French raven to do?'

'Join in, of course.' Beck's smile was back. 'And if you can keep your head clear, there's a lot of money to be made. Purses dangle, men and women too drunk or too lost in the throes of lust to notice when they go missing.'

The Fugger feigned shock. 'You are not suggesting a life of crime, young master?'

'Not a life of it. A night will suffice. We are going to need more money if we are to . . .' Beck broke off and stared at the town hall opposite.

'Are to what? Are you still not ready to tell Daemon and I why you need to get into Cibo's palace so badly?'

'It's better that no one knows, not yet. Just know that my need is great,' Beck sighed. 'I have tried assault, I have tracked

162

that man throughout Europe in the hope of catching him unawares. Perhaps with the money we can make at the Palio I can bribe my way into his palace. People always need more money at this time. Besides—' She broke off again. 'Fugger, are you listening to me?'

He wasn't. Fenrir, who had been dozing in the sunshine at their feet, now rose, a low growl in his throat. Someone had emerged from the shadow of the tower. Someone all too familiar. 'Von Solingen,' he whispered. 'Turn away. Hide your face. He has seen you before.'

The Fugger need not have worried. Heinrich von Solingen had barely been able to focus in that street fight in Toulon, and he was not completely recovered now from the stone Beck had hurled with such force at his head. It ached, and his vision was still somewhat blurred, along with much of his memory. But his master required his recruiting skills, and his master had to be obeyed. So it was that he accompanied Giovanni, the Archbishop's manservant, whose silvery Italian tongue he was to back up with his Germanic brawn. Between them, they had men to hire. Special men.

'What's happening here?' said the Fugger as the little Italian set down the box he was carrying right in front of the fountain not a dozen paces away then stood on it while two servants began to dispense wine from a cask, gathering an immediate crowd. Von Solingen waited behind, arms folded. Giovanni began to speak.

'Honoured citizens of Siena,' he declared in a shrill voice that carried across the Campo, 'Your benign, gracious and all-loving Holiness the Archbishop – who, as you know, is a son of our fair city just like yourselves – the Archbishop wants to make this Palio even more spectacular than any that has gone before.' A small cheer greeted this statement. 'To begin with, he will reach into the heart of his magnificent wine cellar and produce barrels of nectar of which this is a mere taster.' Another, larger cheer came and more wine was dispensed. 'But more than this, he is planning an event in this very square as a prelude to the race, to dramatise that most glorious episode of our city's history – the taking of the standard bearer's hand at Montaperti, which turned the tide of war against the Florentine foe and delivered us the victory we celebrate at the Palio.'

A mixture of cheers and boos greeted the naming of the old and current enemy. The Florentines had besieged the town again, not five years before.

Raising his voice above the tumult, Giovanni went on. 'To achieve the right theatrical effect, and to show kindness to those who strayed from God's honest path once in their lives and paid such a heavy price, the Archbishop has requested that all one-handed men, I say those who through accident or punishment have lost one hand and who want to earn honest coin for three days and nights and partake of good food and wine even better than this – yes, let's crack open another barrel now – and sleep on feather beds right in the heart of the Holy Residence attended by the maidens of the Arch-bishop's household' – the largest roar of all greeted this offer – 'I say these lucky, handless men should immediately, or even sooner, present themselves to me. Redemption awaits the sinner, comfort and luxury the reformed. And a chance to be at the centre of this spectacular retelling of our heroic history.'

One-handed men abounded in any town in Europe, un-lucky thieves mainly whose lives might have been spared but whose existence was bleak after such a maiming. The free wine had lured a few such already and they eagerly rushed forward to surround Giovanni at the prospect of more.

'Where are you going?' Beck whispered, for the Fugger had got up and was divesting himself of his sack.

He knew that discussion or too much thought would weaken him, so he said quickly, 'You wanted to get into his palace. This could be the way.'

'You'd put yourself into that demon's clutches? Are you mad?'

The Fugger dropped the sack at her feet. 'As mad as you. For it's what you've been trying to do.'

'But I have a . . . a very important reason. Why would you do this?'

The Fugger thought for a moment. 'I have a reason too. The Queen's hand is in there. Wouldn't it be wonderful if, when Jean arrives, we could have it for him?'

The mention of that name again. A vision of his arm holding up the waterseller's awning. She'd said something that had made his eyes narrow, and look within her own. And then he was gone.

'He's on the death galleys. He'll never come back.'

The Fugger just smiled and said, 'But of course he will.'

'Fugger!' Beck grabbed him by the handless arm. 'People never return from Cibo's dungeons. Never. I will not hear of you again. Just as I have never heard from my father.'

She had blurted it out, something she had not told anyone in ten years.

'Your father is in there?'

'Yes. Yes, I think so. If he is still alive, which I feel he is, he is in there. Cibo's prisoner. He makes him do . . . terrible things.'

'All the more reason for me to go.'

'And never return? Are you so eager to be lost again? How can I help you if I do not know where you are?'

He thought for a moment.

'Wait!' he said, then whistled, and the raven, who had flown off to harry pigeons by the tower, flew down and settled on his shoulder. He stroked its head, just between the lustrous sable eyes, and it curved down to his touch, lulled by the caress. Carefully he reached up, took the whole glossy body in his cupped hand and tucked it under his clothes into the small of his back. 'Daemon will fly between us. He will bring you news of me.'

'You are mad,' was all Beck could manage.

'That's what I've been told.'

165

She watched him walk right up to the Archbishop's manservant, and as he walked she saw him begin to adopt the cringing, hopping, shuffling gait she somehow knew had been his life before.

'Master,' said the Fugger. 'Ooh, kind master, look what I have for you here.'

And he thrust the stump right into Giovanni's face.

Heinrich caught the recoiling Italian and thrust him back towards his latest recruit. He had the oddest sensation that he'd seen this gibbering fool somewhere before, but his head still hurt badly, his vision was still blurred and he put it down to that. He hadn't chopped off any hands in Italy after all. That activity had taken place years before, back in Bavaria.

Shaking himself to clear the mists, he barked, 'Come on, this will do for a beginning.' And, using the big club he always carried in these streets, he none too gently began to shepherd his half dozen or so recruits out of the Campo and along the Via del Pellegrini towards the Archbishop's palace.

Beck followed, watching the Fugger spinning round and round, doing his little dance. Pausing before the baptistry, for a moment he froze and raised his one hand in a gesture that could only have been a farewell. Then he was through the archway, and the black gates swung shut upon him.

# THREE

# THE SEA FIGHT

'A sail! Three sails! To larboard!'

It wasn't the fact of the cry but the tone of it that froze every person on the *Perseus*, Muslim and Christian, freeman and slave. Sails were a common sight on this busy sea. They did not draw forth the edge of terror that all could hear in the lookout's voice.

Ake heard it, suspended upside down, bleeding from his chest wound and the three gashes where the skin had been torn from his back. Corbeau, poised above him, knife in hand and deciding where to make his next incision, heard it. Jean, Januc, Haakon and Da Costa heard it, and their eyes swivelled to the source of the fear. On the quarterdeck, de la Vallerie heard it and reached for his telescope.

'Hell's minions!' he thundered and, without removing the instrument from his eye, bellowed at Corbeau, 'When this is over I want that lookout flogged to death. How did he let us get this close?'

He studied the red curved sails tacking against the wind that filled the *Perseus*'s own sail. With that behind him and more notice he could have outmanoeuvred, then outrun, these three. They had more rowers, but they were heavier galleys and a galliot would always take them with a following breeze. But they were spaced wide, a net thrown out to trap him. Now it might have to come to a fight in which he was heavily outnumbered. Unless . . . De la Vallerie had served on these waters for twenty years. He knew a trick or five.

'Corbeau, get onto the gangway. Double time.'

'Aye, Captain.' Corbeau stuck his flaying knife into his belt and turned back to the deck. Then a thought came to him, and his one eye gleamed up at his leader. 'Captain? Which direction?'

De la Vallerie smiled. Corbeau hated it when he did that. 'Straight at them, of course. Ramming speed.'

Cursing him for a big-nosed lunatic, Corbeau nonetheless did what he was told. He wanted the flaying knife to stay in his belt, not to be used on his own skin.

'Drummer! Strike double time!' he yelled as he ran aft. 'Row, you swine! Row till you burst!'

'Augustin.' The captain turned to his sergeant-at-arms standing nervously at his side. 'Get your gun crew forward and your arquebusiers in position. I will be arming in my cabin. Call me when we are twenty cables away.'

'Aye, Captain. And the prisoner?'

De la Vallerie didn't even glance back. 'Punishment to continue after this little interruption. Leave him where he hangs.'

Before they needed all their wind to row, there was a brief clamour on the benches.

'Mershiful Chrisht!' wailed Da Costa. 'Three to one and he'sh attacking? Big Noshe hash gone mad.'

'Not only that, old man.' There was an edge to Januc's voice that made Jean look at him. 'They're all galleys.'

'Then we're losht. We might ash well give up now.' Despite this, the Portuguese still rose with the rest of them and fell back onto the bench at the whistle's blast, pulling the big oar through the water, sending the *Perseus* scudding across the calm surface of the sea.

'Why?' yelled Jean. 'What does it matter that they are galleys?'

The old man just groaned, already losing his breath, so

Januc continued for him. 'Double the men over a galliot, double the oars. It's a bigger boat and we could outrun them, especially with a following wind.' They rose and fell. 'But they've stretched their mouth too wide.'

Again Jean heard the tone, the excitement in it.

Rising, falling, sweat already cascading off them all.

'I don't much care.' Haakon grinned, a fire in his wild blue eyes. 'I've never been in a sea fight. This should be fun.'

'Fun?' was all Jean got out before the crack of a whip across the Norwegian's shoulders silenced him.

Corbeau stood above them, and he had swapped his nine-thonged weapon for a bullwhip. In a fight, he knew you needed greater powers of coercion, especially for the Muslims. 'Save your breath, you dogs!' he cried. 'Row harder, unless you want to end up prisoners of Allah.' He moved further up the gangway, lashing out all the way.

'Just one chance,' muttered Haakon, staring after his persecutor. 'Just one.'

Januc needed no such cattle-hide encouragement; he was rowing as hard as he could. *Two years I've waited for this*, he thought. *Two years for the corsairs once more to challenge the navies of Europe.* He knew that he could drown, be killed by an Arab arrow or a Christian bullet, but he also knew that should he survive the inevitable corsair victory would see him free again. Free to return to the life he loved, to harry the enemy for the glory of his master, Barbarossa, and his own profit; to set up a base like he'd had in Tunis, with beautiful women to tend him, another oasis of blue tiles and flowing water under a desert sun. And if this lunatic captain wanted him to rush towards that fate, he was only too happy to help him. Former comrades awaited, he felt sure, under those curving sails, men who would know and honour the name of Januc. So he rose and fell and pulled as if the strength of his arms alone could deliver him to this glory.

The lunatic in question returned from his cabin and made his way down the gangway to the forward deck. He was dressed in full armour of gleaming black, purchased in Milan at the cost of all the prize money from a particularly profitable voyage. It was light, he could dance and leap in it, and he could certainly wield the Turkish bow he held and the heavy rapier that dangled at his side. The armour was made of a series of alternating planes that would deflect all the arrows sent at him. He knew how the Turks and their pirate allies still preferred the old ways of saturation archery over firearms, imagining that, of the thousand arrows they sent at their Christian enemies, one would find a chink in their armour. He also knew why you paid for the best – no chinks.

When he reached the foredeck, de la Vallerie had no need of his glass, for the three corsairs stood no more than half a league away and the distance was closing rapidly. He could make out their preparations for battle, the archers massing on the decks and in the rigging, lightly armoured swordsmen preparing the ramps, boarding nets and grappling hooks they'd need to latch on to this Christian prize seeming to slide so happily into their clutches. The middle ship of the three was where their captain was. De la Vallerie could just make out a white turbaned figure in black robes despatching men to prepare his own ship and signal to the others.

*He must be a happy man*, de la Vallerie thought. *A dainty little sardine, the* Perseus, *for him to snaffle up.*

The enemy was coming within range of their gun, which was called 'No More Words' for its actions spoke for itself. The master gunner, Ganton, was a surly Breton, a terrible drunkard in port but a sober expert of his trade at sea. He had been with Louis for ten years now, and though his manner was usually less than respectful his skill had saved them in many a desperate scrap. Louis felt sure it would save them now. He called down to him on the gun platform at the prow of the ship.

'Ganton, the range, if you please.'

'And about time, Captain. I've been lining that scum up for a while.'

He bellowed his orders, sighted along the barrel, made some alterations to the elevation gears and touched a flaming taper to the hole. There was an immediate roar, and the solid shot he'd loaded sailed over the middle ship, clearing it by a mast's height.

The whole of the *Perseus* acted as the gun platform, and Jean felt the recoil buck through the ship which seemed to rear up and plunge back into the water. A few oars went astray at the sudden violence, and it took Corbeau several moments of bellowing and lashing to get his men to return to the rhythm.

They were so close now they could hear the jeering of the corsairs' crews.

'Enough, Ganton?'

'Enough, Captain. Next time I'll take out their mast.'

De la Vallerie smiled and said, 'A mast it is, but not that one. Load with chain, and be ready for my command. Corbeau!' He called down to his one-eyed subordinate. 'Stop whipping that man and come up here!'

When the brute was beside him, and his pomander, now filled with pot-pourri, was raised to ward off the smell – he'd found it the most effective mixture against the scent of blood – de la Vallerie explained, from behind it, the manoeuvre he required, then added, 'As you know – stop twitching, man, and listen to me – as you know, the perfect galley should be as a young and charming girl in the dance whose every gesture reveals her gentility, her vivacity, her alertness, while preserving a becoming gravity. How much more so our delightful galliot *Perseus*. Well, she shall prove herself with one beautiful flourish. Then we shall see if all your training has paid off. And if it hasn't' – and here he lowered the pomander enough for Corbeau to see his smile – 'either I or the Arab shall strip your skin from your body.'

Having listened to further precise instructions and with a hasty glance at the example of the hanging and somehow still breathing Ake, Corbeau went cursing back to his station.

Most of the crew had been with him long enough to react instantly to his orders, but the captain now required a bare second of perfect timing. All their futures depended on it.

The enemy were close enough now for those on the *Perseus* to hear the words they sang to the blowing of their trumpets and the crash of cymbal and drum. At a signal from the captain, the *Perseus*'s own three musicians struck up, on trumpet, fife and tabor, and played a martial theme in reply.

'Now, Corbeau, now!' yelled de la Vallerie.

Corbeau bellowed above the noise: 'Triple time!' The drum pounded and with the extra surge the *Perseus* seemed to leap out of the water and take to the air. Three strokes, and he cried again, 'Ship starboard oars!'

All the oars on the right side of the ship were pulled in, while the port side rowed on. The *Perseus* slewed viciously to starboard, but maintained its hurtling speed.

As the bow came around, de la Vallerie said calmly, 'Now, Ganton, if you please.'

With a final spin of the adjusting gears, the master gunner put taper to hole. The sailcloth packets full of lengths of chain and shards of jagged metal hurtled at one hundred paces into the sails of the corsair galley to their right, shredding them, dropping mast, rope and rigging onto the Arab's deck.

'One stroke! Now ship oars!' Corbeau cried.

The port oars gave a final push that directed the ship almost directly down the throat of the Arab. Almost directly, for the manoeuvre had taken them just past and, with port oars shipped as well but with a strong wind still filling its sail, the wingless bird that was now the *Perseus* crashed at full speed along the length of the corsair, splintering its port oars, crushing those rowers not swift enough to dive beneath their benches.

Within seconds it was over. It had all happened so swiftly, the enemy so surprised that only a few arrows had been loosed to fall harmlessly on the deck or stick in the sail.

'Port and starboard oars out! Row, you bastards, row like you've never rowed before!'

As they passed the aft end of the Arab ship, the oar tips were hurled into the water and the men immediately took the strain, to a triple-time beat. The corsair they had crippled lurched in their wake, and open sea lay ahead, with wind in their sails and the two other enemy vessels struggling to come about.

'That will do, Corbeau,' the captain called down. 'They'll never catch us now.'

He was so nearly right. He would have been but for the one man on the crippled ship that had kept his wits in the suddenness of the assault.

John Hood was an Englishman and a former master gunner in King Henry's navy. By a series of misadventures, through battle, piracy and slavery, he had finally found himself working for a new master – a heathen, to be sure, but one who gave him a life of profit and luxury he could never have dreamt of in Kent. Now he saw his first chance of booty since their defeat at Tunis slipping away to aft. He may have risen to captain's rank but he was still a gunner at heart.

'I'm not bloody 'avin' that!' he said.

Swivelling the basilisk gun on the rear platform, a light weapon he usually used against infantry on a deck, he swiftly sighted along the barrel and fired it. The shot within, at that range a dense cluster of metal fragments, hit exactly what he was aiming at: the junction of mast and sail beam. It shattered, dropping the heavy wooden pole and the yards of cloth onto the deck and the crew of the *Perseus*.

'Under!' yelled Jean, and he, Haakon and Januc, with all the instincts of the battle-trained, dropped their oars and dived beneath their hard wooden benches, seconds before the collapsing rigging fell on top of them.

Many were not so quick or lucky. When they emerged from the rolls of sail cloth, a grim sight met them. Some men were squirming, pinned between bench and beam, limbs crushed.

Others lay still, heads split, already beyond the hardships of the oar. The screams were terrible.

One struggling figure, shrieking and crying, was trying to force itself from under the cloth. Jean pushed his hands into a rent and ripped a hole in it, enough for the yelling, toothless head of Da Costa to emerge.

'By Chrisht, ladsh,' he shouted, 'I thought I wash drowning there!'

Haakon put his arms under the old man's, but when he tried to pull him up the Portuguese let out a yell.

'No, shtop! Shomething'sh got my foot.'

Jean widened the hole a little to look. Da Costa's left leg was pinned by the main beam and, by its angle, he could see the foot was undoubtedly broken underneath it.

'Leave him, Haakon. We'll need some help.'

It was not long in coming for de la Vallerie was urging Corbeau to clear the mess. Only half his crew were rowing at the moment and he needed to put some distance between him and the galleys, which were already coming about.

Soldiers descended, lifting the debris out of the way, hurling what was obviously beyond repair over the side. Some of their number had been in the rigging and lay now among the dead and dying. The lookout would never have to face his punishment for it had come to him much quicker in a long fall to the deck.

As swiftly as they could work, the tangle of cloth, sail and heavy wood was cleared away. When they came to lift the beam off Da Costa it took ten soldiers plus the strength of Jean, Haakon and Januc to achieve it. The old man let out a scream and fainted. He was dumped on the central gangway along with eleven more of the crippled; the dead were simply tipped over the side. Spare oars were produced to replace those broken by the impact. Within minutes, the *Perseus* was once more pulling through the water.

They were ahead of the galleys by maybe a quarter of a league, but de la Vallerie could see that the enemy had now come about and the wind that had so favoured him in the recent manoeuvre was now fully behind the corsairs. He could also see that the two undamaged galleys were leaving their crippled sister in their wake.

*What mischance*, thought the captain, strangely calm. *My brilliance defeated by a lucky shot. With the wind behind us in our own sail we could have outrun them: without it* . . . In a short chase the light *Perseus* could easily beat the bulkier Arab galleys, just on oar power. But the enemy had double the men to replace tired oarsmen at their posts, and every soldier on their ship could also row. His own were too proud to have learnt and too inept to be taught now.

No, he sighed. This contest cannot last long.

As if to echo his thoughts there was a boom of the forward cannon on the smaller of the pursuing galleys. The shot dropped well short and drew ironic cheers from his crew, but he knew that the Arabs were merely checking the distance. They wouldn't fire their cannon unless necessary. They wouldn't want to damage their prize.

Down on the bench, Jean and Haakon were rowing hard, driven by the double beat of the drum and the crack and whistle of the bullwhip above them. But Januc, it seemed, was rowing hardest of all. Anyone who knew the lie of his 'Christianity' would have found his efforts hard to believe. Anyone who had overheard his nightly prayers or, like Jean, seen the light in his eyes when the corsairs were first sighted.

But all hope had turned to dust in his mouth, crushed as surely as Da Costa's foot. And it had taken just a moment, when he saw second banner flapping on the main galley's mast. Above it was the inevitable red and gold flag with the crescent of Islam, a sight to cheer any of the Prophet's faith; below, however, was an end to all hope, unless he could pull the *Perseus* out of range by his own efforts.

The second banner was the captain's personal one. It was a hissing serpent picked out in silver on a cloth of purple. It was

175

the emblem of Hakim i Sabbah, slave master, brutal killer, rapist, torturer – and Januc's sworn and most personal blood enemy. He had slain one of Hakim's swarm of brothers in a quarrel over a woman in Tunis five years before. There was no redemption for Januc under the banner of the silver serpent. Only an agonising death that would make Ake's, still swinging upside down at the aftdeck, look like charity.

On that deck, the captain was giving his orders. 'Corbeau, on my command, we're turning the ship around. We'll let them get close, close, and then hold them even closer. My guess is they'll try to sweep wide and catch us between them so, Ganton, take out the mast of the second galley, delay their joining of the fray. Augustin, get all your arquebusiers to save their volley till we are joined to the big ship. They will grapple us, but we will let them board and set up our killing ground here. Is that clear?'

The three men looked nervously at each other. Corbeau said, 'Captain, the odds—'

'Are four to one by my calculation. Reduced to two to one if we take and defeat the big ship before the other can join. Good Christian odds, for we have God on our side. Remember, we are fighting the heathen.'

A heathen shot plunged into the water not fifty yards aft, raising a plume of water.

'Nearly time. On my command, Corbeau.'

They were about to be dismissed when Augustin spoke, just controlling a voice near cracking. 'And the rowers?'

De la Vallerie raised the pomander to his nose, inhaled a waft of pot-pourri, and considered. The Muslims he could discount for obvious reasons, but that still left ten volunteers who could be armed and forty prisoners who might not wish to swap Christan chains for infidel ones. Starved, weakened and whipped as they had been, they could provide little more than a shield for his soldiers, a way to absorb the first volley of arrows. An armed shield could be useful, though. It changed the odds slightly in his favour.

Glancing back, he saw that he still had a few moments, so he said, 'I will speak to them. Corbeau, single time, if you please.'

He descended to the gangway as the rowers eased up on their oars. Immediately another plume of water was raised, this time to starboard. The heathen were now in range.

'Volunteers, you shall shortly be given weapons to aid in our glorious fight and certain victory. But I speak now to the prisoners, with your tufts of hair, you whose hideous crimes have condemned you to your just sentences. Would you like to make amends for your sinful acts? Do you wish to be slaves of Islam, or do you wish to bear arms in glorious crusade against Christ's enemies?'

A silence greeted these questions as each man considered the prospect. If they hid under their benches during the fight there was a good chance they would survive, for rowers were the commodity on which the galleys thrived, slaves the mainstay of trade. Whichever side won would need hands on oars.

It was Jean who gave voice to the obvious question. 'And what's in it for us?'

There were mutters of assent from up and down the benches. De la Vallerie tried to focus on the area where the voice had come from.

'You would not become slaves under the crescent. Is not that enough?'

Jean stood up. 'A slave is a slave, no matter the flag at the masthead and, from what I've been told, a Turkish oar feels no different to the hand than a Christian one.'

There were more murmurs of agreement. Yet another plume of water, this time to port, emphasised the necessity for speed in these negotiations. If there'd been time, de la Vallerie would have taken this man out and killed him on the spot for daring even to address a captain of France. Instead, he just smiled. He was thinking of the odds.

'But, dear countryman, didn't I say? Fight well, help us gain the inevitable victory, and you will be freed as soon as we return to a French port.'

Jean had heard the minor nobility of France cajole, whine, bargain and beg on scaffolds the length and breadth of the kingdom, just before he took their heads off their shoulders. He knew a lie when he heard one. He also knew that in a fight, if he was going to be a slave, he would rather be a slave in arms.

'In that case, dear countryman, I am at your service.'

A cheer echoed him, and de la Vallerie smiled, for he knew he had decreased the odds a little in his favour and at a cost he would never have to pay. Even if, by the mercy of God, they were victorious, most of this rabble would not survive. And a bargain with a slave was no bargain at all.

'Issue them weapons,' he said to Augustin as he made his way back to the foredeck. 'You will find more in my cabin.'

While the Muslims and Ake's tribesmen remained the sole and half-hearted means of propelling the ship, the others' chains were slipped and the armoury disgorged into their hands a variety of weaponry: swords, cudgels, cutlasses and halberds, rusted and misshapen in the main but which the prisoners and freemen still grabbed eagerly.

'By the balls of a bishop,' Jean sighed, and moved forward, reaching out his hand as if greeting an old friend. Which, in fact, he was. 'Mine, I think,' he said, and the man who had seized it looked just once into Jean's eyes and let go of the strange square-headed sword with a resentful curse.

The man who held Haakon's axe was not so prudent, but the dispute over ownership ended swiftly with the big Norwegian's hands on a Spanish throat and a quick squeeze.

'Ah, my beautiful, have you missed me?' Haakon was kissing the blade again and again. He turned to Jean, shaking it in the air. 'My friend, life is once more sweet.'

'Sweet, and probably very short. If the Fugger were here, I don't think he'd give us very good odds. Stay close, and we'll watch each other's backs.'

There was one other person he wanted beside him in what was to come, and he quickly sought Januc out. He found him slashing the air with a scimitar. Ducking, he said, 'Keep that away from my head. Once in a life is enough for a taste of the crescent cut.'

Januc laughed and lowered the curving blade.

'I need to ask you something, Januc.'

'Well?'

In a low voice, Jean continued. 'I know you were – are – a janissary.'

'So?'

'So our pursuers are of the same faith as you – no, don't deny it, I know why you have chosen to pretend otherwise. You told our captors you were a Croatian, stolen as a child, an unwilling convert to Mohammed. Am I right? You get the better rations and kept your hair.' He pointed at the tuft on the younger man's head.

Januc's gaze was steady. 'And you are wondering whose side in the fight I will be on.'

'Something like that. I told you, I do not relish another taste of the scimitar. Especially from behind me.'

Januc glanced back, saw how much closer the galleys had got. He sought out the figure swathed in black robes standing beneath the serpent's forked tongue. They were close enough now that he could see Hakim, waving, shouting, urging his rowers to greater effort for the glory of Allah. He smiled.

'I have prayed for rescue by my Muslim brethren, it is true. But the man who hates me more than any other in this world is the leader of those who pursue us. This is beyond faith. This is blood feud. And Allah has willed it that either he or I must die this day.'

It was the Frenchman's turn to smile. 'Then I think we veterans of Mohacz should stick together. I would be honoured to fight by your side.'

'And I by yours.'

As they gripped each other's forearms, Haakon ran up.

179

'Now then, my friends,' he said, 'you'll have to leave your lovemaking till later. In case you hadn't noticed, we've a fight on our hands.'

The huge Norseman was shaking with the excitement. He threw the axe high up in the air, clapped them both hard on the back, and caught the weapon as it fell.

'Haakon,' Jean spluttered, 'we will in all likelihood be dead before this day is out.'

'I know,' yelled the Viking. 'Isn't it wonderful? If only Fenrir were here.'

Further comment was cut off by the cry 'To oar! To oar!' Placing their weapons beside them, the three seized the huge oaken beam and, on command, began to row at triple time. Hated though Big Nose was, his earlier action had impressed them all. If he could give them any temporary advantage in the forthcoming battle, they would take it happily.

He was preparing to do just that. The enemy were a bare three hundred paces astern now, preparing to pass him on either side and trap him in the pincer between them. If they succeeded in that, the *Perseus*, and more importantly its captain, were doomed.

'Now is the time, Corbeau,' he called down.

'Port! Reverse oars. Starboard, row!'

It was a manoeuvre known as the Drowning Stop, because it could turn the boat on its side if executed wrongly. And the *Perseus*, lurching to a halt that caused all its timbers to shriek under the strain, spun around from its middle and seemed for one ghastly second to be about to roll all the port-side rowers, including Jean, Haakon and Januc, into the sea. The Norseman, closest to the gunwales, even dipped his hand into the liquid and splashed his face before the ship righted itself, the port side came up and they were facing the onrushing Arab galleys, the smaller of which seemed to be directly before them.

As Corbeau called again for triple time on both sides, Ganton needed no prompting from his captain. He yelled at his gun crew, 'Shift to port! Far enough, you dogs! Now back a foot! Enough!' He wrenched at the adjusting gear, uttered a swift prayer to the Virgin, and touched the taper to the hole.

Once more the *Perseus* bucked along its length from the recoil; once more the smoke rolled in a dense cloud across the deck. When it cleared, Jean was one of many to give a cheer for the shot had taken out the main mast of the smaller galley, its black crescent banner, rigging and spars even now falling on the oarsmen, causing the ship to slew to the side.

Above the cheering, all heard the renewed call to row. The Silver Serpent galley had straight away changed its course and was sweeping down upon them. The black robed figure could be heard now, shouting commands at his men, above the shrill war cries of North African trumpets. There were maybe two minutes before they would be joined.

'Musicians!' cried de la Vallerie, striding towards the foredeck. 'Strike me up galliard!'

And when the music of that dance, banned by half the royal courts of Europe for its scandalous sensuality, blared out across the deck of His Majesty's good ship *Perseus*, its captain put one hand to an armoured hip and began to caper.

'Oh, sweet Mother.' Haakon shook his head. 'He's mad as well as ugly.'

'But he can sail,' said Jean, for even as Big Nose executed his nimble steps it was not the only dance he was involved in. He was yelling commands at all around him, trying to take the enemy head-on, to hole the bigger galley at the waterline with his iron ram. Hakim i Sabbah, wanting the prize of the *Perseus* as much as the victory, was trying to take him side-on for the grapple. Like two wrestlers they bore warily down upon each other, trimming and shifting with oar and sail.

'Listen,' said Januc, turning urgently to his two companions as they rose and fell, 'there are three things you will need to know to have any chance of surviving a fight on a galley.'

Jean leant in. 'And they are?'

'One: as soon as we come alongside they will lay down a barrage of arrows on our decks. They are firing from above, but they know that the soldiers' armour will mostly protect them. As they will have seen us armed, they will be aiming for us. So until they board us, stay under the benches. And keep your arses tucked in.'

Haakon looked sceptically at the small bench. He was a big man.

'Two: wait till you hear our second volley before you come out. My guess is Big Nose will shoot half his soldiers on the grapple and half when the enemy board. You don't want to take an arquebus ball from your own side.'

'Good,' grunted Haakon. 'And the third?'

Januc's attention had been taken by something on the foredeck, clutched in the captain's hand.

'What?' he said, half-mindedly.

'Three. You said there were three things we would need to know.'

'Yes, that's right,' said the distracted janissary, 'three.'

And quite suddenly he abandoned the oar, dodged the flailing whip of a cursing Corbeau and ran for the foredeck. Arrows were already beginning to fly towards the *Perseus*, but the arquebusiers held their fire. Two rowers in front and one to the side of Jean leapt up, plucking at feathered shafts jutting from their necks.

They were maybe two hundred paces from the enemy and closing fast when Januc gained the captain's side. De la Vallerie had ceased his dance.

'Captain,' Januc said, pointing at the Turkish bow, 'let me try.'

De la Vallerie looked at the naked prisoner before him, at the tuft of jet-black hair on his scalp.

'It's mine, prisoner.' The nasal voice was petulant. 'Why should I give it to you?'

'Because I can kill their gunner. Isn't that what you are trying to do?'

It was. The bow of the janissary, however – animal sinew wound around a core of maple with a hand grip of bone – was not like the light weapons de la Vallerie had hunted with back in Bordeaux. Despite all his practice, despite the desire, he'd never mastered it. He'd already sent an arrow towards the rear of the galley where he saw the enemy gunner crouched over his basilisk, a cannon filled with deadly packets of small sharp metal that could devastate his soldiers at close range, and he had already witnessed their gunner's accuracy. If this one could be killed, it would certainly increase the odds in his favour.

De la Vallerie didn't like standing this close to prisoners and he raised the pomander to his face. Yet over it, something in the grey eyes, some certainty therein, held his own. Experience taught him that battles were won or lost on instinctive decisions. Instinct now made him hand over the bow. He then turned his attention back to the forthcoming collision.

They were a hundred and fifty paces away. At fifty, Januc would have to make his shot, and he would get just that one chance, for the gunner, having made his final calculations, would only raise his head again to fire. Januc swiftly unstrung the bow, re-tied the loop, placed it between his feet and pulled the shaft down to notch the string. *Much better*, he thought, testing the increased tension. They were maybe eighty yards apart when he selected the best of the arrows, with the smaller flight required for shorter distances and a narrow tapered head of iron. One to punch through a deer's head at fifty paces, as he had done so many times after hours of stalking in the hills around Izmir.

The cry to ship oars came first from the Arab deck, swiftly echoed by Corbeau. Both sea birds were wingless now, propelled by the last lung-busting pulls, hurtling towards each other. Hakim had won the battle of skills, for the collision was going to happen amidships, not head-on, and Ganton's crew had not managed to reload for a final shot in time. The old gunner sprinted for his own basilisk, primed and loaded on the aftdeck.

Seventy yards, and John Hood, late of King Henry's navy, latterly in the service of the Moor, came up from behind the gunwale to sight along his weapon, Mad Meg, named after a harridan wife long since abandoned in Dover. Hakim knew the value of the man, had stopped to collect him and his favourite gun from the crippled ship, and Hood knew why. He was responsible for snagging their prize with that wonderful shot to their mast. Now, if he could just rake the foredeck, kill most of the soldiers and especially that dancing fool of a captain . . . He raised the glowing taper above the hole.

Sixty paces, no more, and, ignoring the shower of arrows beginning to fall like hail onto the deck, shutting out the cries of stricken men, Januc pulled the bow back to full stretch. He had not felt the latent power within one for two years, but his muscles locked in the familiar way, his breathing slowed and he took his sighting. He saw the gunner's hand make a final adjustment, saw the head just up above the gun's end, even saw the gleam in an eye that reflected a burning taper. He sighted on that gleam, breathed out, leaving just a little air, and released the arrow.

John Hood was lowering the match when something punched him in the face. He had no time to wonder what as he was dead before he reached the deck.

The arrows had become a dense cloud, and Januc ducked down behind the wooden palisade of the foredeck. Above him, projectiles pinging off the angled plates of his armour, the captain raised his sword in a swift salute.

'Keep it,' he said when Januc offered up the bow, 'but I'll want it back later.'

And then, in a scream of twisting, snapping wood that seemed as human as any of the screams of the wounded and the dying on both decks, the two ships smashed together.

Jean and Haakon had done as they were told and lay in the

muck and filth under the bench. The war cries, ululation of tongue and throat, did not draw them out, and they heard a dozen arrows thump into the wood above them, one of them lodging itself an inch from Haakon's nose on the deck. Then a volley of bullets crashed above them as forty arquebusiers – half the *Perseus*'s complement of soldiers – fired at the first rank of turbaned, scimitar-waving pirates who came pouring over the side of the bigger ship. Many were hit, bodies plunging down to land on bench and deck. Many were unharmed and naked feet pounded along the benches above them.

When Haakon went for his axe, Jean yelled, 'The second volley! Remember what Januc said!'

So they waited, and in an instant there came another crash of gunpowder, more cries of pain and terror, and a flailing body fell beside the huddled Norwegian. His huge hands reached out to drown the struggling pirate in the mire.

'Now!' said Jean, and he and Haakon rolled out from beneath their bench to see the third wave of the enemy, unhampered by the soldiers struggling to reload, sweep down upon the deck. There was no time to calculate odds, to fear or to take stock. Now was the time for the battle mist to descend, as red as the blood that sprayed all around them.

A turbaned figure in white ran at him, shrieking, a spear held high, aimed at his chest. Jean side-stepped just in time, the point buried itself in the gunwale behind him and, swinging the sword level with the spear shaft, he took the man's head off, seeing the startled look on the face as it bounced onto the deck. Jerking the spear out, spinning it up in the air to reverse his grip on it, he hurled it a dozen paces to impale the man who had got behind and under Haakon's whirling axe, whose scimitar was poised for the death blow. Haakon noted the kindness with the eyes in the back of his head but had no time to acknowledge it, for three more of the enemy, one with a spear and two with swords, were upon him and Jean was unable to decrease those odds further, having three screaming opponents of his own.

Jean leapt up onto the gangway. Driving forward, his blade circling, he feinted high, caught the man on the left under his raised guard, slicing him across the chest, then took both the other blades in a square parry as they descended towards his head and, flicking his wrists in a tight circle, sent the scimitars flying out of their hands. One man leapt in fear onto the benches while the other reached for and whipped out another scimitar strapped to his back. Jean drove at him and he retreated, skilfully parrying Jean's assault, until he smashed up against the hanging body of Ake. The huge black man's blood had made that part of the deck slick, and when his opponent's foot went from under him Jean lunged full length and hit the man in the chest with the flat tip of his sword. It was the one disadvantage of the weapon, that it could not deliver a kill with its point, but the blow was enough to knock the man on his back and Jean, bringing his rear leg up, sharply lunged again with a downward cut, impaling his opponent on the deck.

His efforts had carried him to the steps of the aftdeck, and for a brief moment he found not an enemy before him. It was one of those curiously calm moments that always occurred in battle, or at the exact moment in an execution when the sword struck. The noise of it all faded, cries and deathblows were snatched away, the red mist pulled aside like a veil by some unseen hand. Such moments of clarity had saved his life more than once and it was to save a life now, because within the calm he heard a small voice beside him. He turned and looked at its source.

Not a hand's breadth from his own face was another, a huge black one, covered in sweat, contorted by pain, upside down. Brown eyes stared into his while a voice spoke words he could not understand, yet when accompanied by a look towards his sword told their meaning perfectly.

Ake was beseeching him for a swift and merciful death.

In the silence that still held him, Jean seemed to move so very slowly up to the hanging man's feet, as he slowly slashed the cords there. Taking the weight, he lowered Ake gently down to the gangway, placing his back against the base of the aftdeck. He then reached for the fallen enemy's scimitar and laid it in Ake's huge black hands, saying, 'Later is always a better time to die.'

The silence was suddenly swept away by a body knocking him backwards, covering him. He tasted blood, thought it unfamiliar, and struggled up from under the dead limbs to see Haakon, stark naked, awash with gore, laughing like a maniac above him.

'That's one for one,' he cried, 'for that dog was about to stick a spear up your arse. I wager I save you more than you save me. Loser buys the first butt of wine!'

And with that, whirling his axe through the air, he ran back into the thickest part of the fray.

Despite the returning roar of battle, Jean was still able to hear his name being called. He ran, dodging, halfway down the gangway. Janus was there.

'Can you get that Viking back here? I have a plan.'

The Frenchman laughed because the Croatian was so calm, despite an arrow branching out, rather obviously, from his shoulder. It didn't seem to be affecting his mind though.

'I'll fetch him.'

'Come to the foredeck,' Janus said. Pausing only to snap the arrow shaft near the head, he disappeared from view.

Being above the main deck had allowed him to get a better view of things. He hadn't been involved in as much fighting owing to the number of the *Perseus*'s soldiers up there with him, but he had been in enough sea fights to know which way this one was going. The Black Crescent galley, which Ganton had dismasted, had now righted itself, cleared its wrecked sails from the main deck and was even now circling around the combatants to join the fray on the *Perseus*'s other side.

Once that manoeuvre was completed, the superior numbers would mean a speedy end to the fight. And a certain and painful death for Januc, once Hakim saw him.

Big Nose was thinking along much the same tack. They had absorbed the early attacks and his soldiers were fighting better than he might have expected under Augustin's nervous command, but he too was aware of the reinforcements shortly to join his enemy, and the consequences of that.

As he was thinking, that damned bowman appeared at his side.

'Captain?'

'You again. What now? Have you another target for my bow?'

'A target, yes. But I think we need more than a well-placed arrow. I was at Tunis—'

De la Vallerie looked down his large nose at the man. 'What of it? So was I.'

It was not the time to exchange stories, though a French captain fighting for Spain was an oddity, Januc thought. More so even than a Croatian fighting for the Turk.

The captain seemed to sense the question. 'A man may serve many masters in his life for many reasons. As I'm sure you know.'

'True, my Captain. Now I only serve my own skin. And it will not be preserved if we lose this fight.'

Three more arrows glanced off de la Vallerie's armour, causing Januc to duck. The captain swatted at them irritably.

'I suggest you make your point, we are about to have more company. What about Tunis?'

'Barbarossa's escape.'

'Ah yes. Driving at the heart of the enemy. You would have me and my soldiers do that? With you left on my ship, no doubt.'

'With me and two other fighters beside you. These two,' Januc said as Jean and Haakon hurled themselves over the guard rail of the foredeck. The Norwegian had taken a small cut to the forearm and Jean was nicked in the thigh, but behind them five bodies lay silent on the gangway.

'Ah, my most recent purchases.'

De La Vallerie peered at the two men, clutching their strange weapons, then looked up to see the progress of the other galley. They had maybe five minutes. Five minutes for a miracle to happen. For him to make it happen.

'Augustin,' he called to his harried subordinate. 'First company to withdraw, load and fire on my command only. Second company, hand weapons.'

The main deck, now that Jean and Haakon had left it, had rapidly been taken over by the pirates. The only two points of resistance were the fore and aft raised decks. Ganton was back there with the third company of soldiers, about twenty in all, throwing off assaults, losing men in each one. He could not last long.

With his orders obeyed, the companies prepared, de la Vallerie thought about a speech but realised there wasn't time. With a brisk 'Forward the second company!' he hurled himself at the nets that had been dropped over the side of the Arab vessel to board the Perseus. Arrows bounced and pinged off him, but several of his soldiers, less protected, were less fortunate. When he was halfway up, he yelled, 'Now, Augustin!' and a ragged volley swept the railings momentarily clear of the enemy. De la Vallerie, with Jean, Haakon, Januc and the fifteen survivors of the first company, burst over the side of the Silver Serpent.

The force of the larger ship's assault had carried it halfway down the Perseus's length before they'd managed to grapple her. This meant the counter attack arrived near the aftdeck of the enemy, close to where Hakim was now positioned, urging his men forward.

'Most of them are on our ship!' Januc yelled. 'At them!' And with the janissary cry of 'Allah is great!' – startling to many of the enemy, who were yelling the same thing – he rushed, scimitar swirling, toward the aftdeck and the man in black screaming orders and waving his own scimitar under his serpent banner.

'For France!' cried de la Vallerie, a cry echoed by his men, his sword thrusting at his enemy.

'Hoch, Hoch!' Jean and Haakon let out the mercenaries' war cry, terror of the battlefields of Europe.

Though they were outnumbered, the suddenness of their appearance, the ferocity of their attack and the soldiers' heavier armour caused momentary panic in the pirate ranks. They scattered before them, and the assault carried them right to the steps of the raised deck that was their target.

A huge Arab in breastplate, helm and shield held the stairs. Two of the company were brushed away before de la Vallerie lunged up at him; but the man pushed his sword aside with his scimitar and used the flat of the blade to deal the captain's helmet a huge blow, knocking him off the stairs to crash at the feet of a swarm of pirates. He disappeared under a shower of sword blows, hammers on the anvil of his armour, while his soldiers rushed to his aid.

Haakon swept the stairway with his axe and the Arab warrior jumped over it, to land just in time for the Viking to crash his shoulder into him. They rolled off the stairs, two vast men locked together, hitting the deck with a huge thump. Jean charged for the gap, his sword cutting down the two who tried to take the big warrior's place. When he reached the deck there were just five men on it. When Januc joined him there were three. Jean hurled himself at the two white-clad bodyguards, driving them back in a flurry of strokes. That left Januc facing the man in the black robes.

'Hello Hakim,' he said. 'Remember me?'

A look of such astonishment appeared on the Arab's face that Januc could only tip back his head and laugh.

'That's right. Januc.' He bowed slightly. 'In case you've forgotten, I'm the man who speared your brother like a pig.'

Astonishment changed to malevolence. Hakim i Sabbah was feared throughout the Mediterranean for the purity of his hatred, the skill of his sword and the savagery with which he dealt with any and all of his enemies. Only one man had ever escaped his terrible vengeance. That man stood before him now.

'By the beard of the Prophet,' he bellowed, 'I am His most fortunate child to have you delivered again into my hands.'

'Not quite in them yet. I'm here, Hakim, the serpent who slithers on his belly away from any real fight. Slither over here and see what you will get.' And with that, Januc dropped into his fighting stance, left hand reaching forward, sword arm curled back.

In a riot of silver and black, Hakim i Sabbah drove at his most mortal foe. It was an attack fuelled by fury, vicious but unfocused. Januc parried and deflected the shower of blows, dodging to left and right, not attempting to strike back, letting the attack move him around the square aftdeck. One glance at Jean told him the stairs would be held; indeed, the Frenchman had already despatched the two warriors who had tried to join their leader. Below him, the soldiers of the *Perseus* had formed a solid rank of armour over their stricken captain. And in their midst, leaping over their heads to strike down with his axe on any foe foolish enough to draw near, as if from behind some ancient shield wall, was Haakon.

Hakim's assaults had tired him and exhausted his initial fury. He remembered now the prowess of the man he was facing, how he'd despatched Hakim's brother, a noted swordsman himself, with arrogant ease. Hakim also remembered that he was the captain of the Silver Serpent, and men would soon be rushing to his aid. Patience, and Allah's favour, would bring him more than Januc's mere death – a drawn-out agony, lasting days, while he destroyed all that made his enemy a man.

Januc noted the pause, the calculation, and hoped that Hakim's first attacks had been enough to weaken his sword arm a little – his left arm, which made the Croatian's preparations more complex, for left-handers were difficult to fight.

*Patience*, Januc thought, *remember the rule of the sword. It is not this attack, or the next, or even the one after that. Feint, retreat, lure his sword each time a little more out of true. And then . . .*

Januc launched a side cut at Hakim's forward knee. The Arab withdrew it sharply, sweeping down with force to encounter the slashing blade, but Januc had halted its sweep suddenly and pushed the curving weapon, with wrist reversed, upwards towards Hakim's groin. Once more the black robes swirled back, Hakim's sword cutting down before him. Once more it encountered air, for Januc jerked it swiftly backwards over his own head, gathered his rear leg up to his front heel and lunged with a scything downward chop. Hakim saw the blow aimed to split open his head, a final commitment that, countered, would leave his opponent stretched out and exposed.

*I have him*, Hakim i Sabbah thought exultantly, and stepped back, raising his scimitar with both hands to perfectly square-parry the blow, to catch the sharp of the blade on the sharp of his own, to sweep and throw the weapon aside to feel his own curved steel pressed so delightfully against his enemy's throat. *I'll take an ear now*, he thought, *the rest of him later, and in pieces*. Visions of languid days of torture rose before him even as his weapon rose, his wrist braced for the shock of a collision . . . that never arrived. For behind Januc's head, as he brought his sword over, as his back heel came up to lightly touch his front one, even as he lunged again, a turn of a supple wrist delivered the blade level with the ground, straight into the armpit of Hakim, arm raised and triumphing in the symmetry of his party.

The scimitar's keen blade bit deep into the flesh, severing all the power that sustained the beautiful parry in an instant. Like a marionette with its strings suddenly cut, Hakim dropped his weapon and crumpled onto the deck, wrapping himself around Januc's blade as if to prevent it from causing further damage. Januc followed him down, and only when the pirate lay propped against the mast did he withdraw the sword.

Hakim's eyes were glazed in surprise and pain, but open. Januc brought his face down level with his.

'Allah is kind,' he spoke softly, 'for He has given me a great victory.'

Hakim tried to say something vicious but he died before he could form the words.

Looking up, Januc saw Jean regarding him.

'Will you take his head, Jean? We could use it.'

Wordlessly, Jean did as he was asked, while Januc swiftly severed the ropes of the serpent flag. It plunged to the deck, tongue and scales enveloping and swallowing up the body of he whose symbol it was. There was a despairing cry when the war banner fell, but it was as nothing to the cry that greeted the raising of Hakim's decapitated, still turbaned head. Wailing and cheering was all that could be heard for the battle on both boats had ceased instantly, the pirates losing all their will to fight.

But they were not the only pirates still around. The crack of a cannon suddenly reminded them of the presence of more.

The other ship, the Black Crescent, had finally cleared its rigging and wreckage and had borne around. It was nearly as big as the Silver Serpent, which meant that it still had twice the number of men onboard that had started the fight on the *Perseus*. Januc had hoped that the execution of their leader might have taken their appetite for battle away, but if its captain, Tarrak ben Youseff, had not the mad courage of his former leader, he knew an advantage when he saw one. His cannon shot was aimed at the front of the *Perseus*, the high foredeck just protruding ahead of the Silver Serpent's aft. Fortunately for Ganton and his men the shot was high, but Youseff was not concerned. Once he'd swept around the front of his former commander's vessel and grappled the *Perseus* on the other side, the day would be his.

After the elation of his victory, this vision of imminent defeat was hard to bear for Januc. Suddenly very tired, he sank down upon one knee, rolling the head of his enemy like a ball across the deck where it buried itself in the serpent's silver mouth.

'By all the devils, Jean,' he sighed, 'we were so close.'

But the Frenchman was paying him no attention. Instead he was looking intently at the bow of their ship, before which the Black Crescent was soon to pass.

'Did you,' he said, turning suddenly to the prone janissary, 'hear this ship fire any shots at us?'

'No. The Black Crescent did, but Hakim wanted us undamaged. Why?'

But he received no reply, for Jean was racing away from him towards the bow of the ship, picking up Haakon in his wake, brushing through the weary victors and the less sullen defeated who now saw their salvation about to pass the front of their vessel.

Two men still stood on the gun platform, holding swords. Taking no chances, Haakon lifted his axe and butted them with the haft in their faces. Jean ran forward and looked down the cannon's mouth. As he suspected, a large ball lurked in its depths.

'Do you know anything about artillery?' he said to the Norwegian.

'Nothing. You?'

Jean shook his head. 'Can't be that difficult though, can it? We point this at something and light this.' He gestured at the firing pan, then squinted along the barrel. 'Seems to be aiming highish and we want it low. How do we lower it?'

'Those. What are they called? Those wheels raise and lower it.'

Jean looked out. The Black Crescent was just starting to pass before them.

'Not enough time.' He tried to lift the end. 'Jesu! Impossible.'

Haakon looked at him and laughed. 'Stand aside, little man.' He bent to the tip of the cannon's carriage, crouching down on his haunches, tucking his huge hands under the wood. He took a deep breath and lifted, every muscle and tendon bulging. For a brief moment nothing happened. Then, at first slowly, then quicker and quicker, the carriage end began to rise and the barrel end dip.

'Enough!' called Jean, and grabbing the powder chest, he pulled it under. Haakon lowered the tip of the cannon onto it. Sweat fountained off him, carving channels through the blood, smoke and gore which covered him.

Jean looked out, and the Black Crescent was exactly level with them. He grabbed the taper and plunged it into the pan, just remembering to yell 'Move!' to Haakon, hands on knees and breathing heavily at the carriage end.

Within the space of two heartbeats the two men leapt sideways. There was a fizzle in the pan followed by a huge roar and an eye-tormenting flash. The gun lurched backwards, snapping its stays, hurling itself off the powder box and skewing to the side. It narrowly missed crushing the prone Jean. He scrambled up and over the wheel and tried to make out anything through the smoke.

It cleared a little, and the Black Crescent was before him. The ship was just as he'd seen it before the cannon's blast. There was no mark or any damage visible on its side.

Haakon, coming up beside him, looked too and wearily reached for his axe. 'Come on,' he said, 'more fighting to be done. Today is as good a day to die as any, for I'll not work those oars again.'

Oars! It was the oars that made Jean realise what was wrong. The enemy had stopped rowing. The boat was stationary in the water. As the realisation came, so the sight before him changed: the Black Crescent suddenly leant over away from him revealing a huge gaping tear at its waterline. And the strange silence that had hung over everything, the silence that follows or precedes a scream, was suddenly shattered by hundreds of them as the crew of the stricken ship began to hurl themselves over its side.

Of the forty freemen and prisoners who had taken up arms on the *Perseus* only thirteen, including Jean, Haakon and Januc, remained standing. The eighty soldiers had been reduced to twenty-five upright and ten more with severe wounds. Ganton, the old gunner, and Augustin, the sergeant-at-arms, had been killed in the last Arab assault on the aftdeck. Corbeau, if he lived, would not be using a whip again, his right arm severed by a scimitar slash below the elbow. He lay, clutching a rag to the oozing stump, staring at his captain, trying to recognise him through the pain distorting his vision. There was something different about him.

Captain Louis St Mark de la Vallerie could not smell a thing. This was normally a source of joy to him, but not now, for the flat blade of the heavy sword that had knocked him off the stairs on the Silver Serpent had smashed in his visor and crushed his nose, breaking it and skewing it to the left side of his face where it rested now, swollen and bloodied. It quite took away from the joy of the victory, accomplished through his skill and force of arms.

Jean stood facing the transformed captain with Haakon resting on his axe behind him. He had asked the question twice and received no reply, just a snuffling from behind the huge kerchief. He had also noticed that in the time he had waited, the aftdeck had filled up with the remnants of the *Perseus*'s soldiery. Shifting his sword onto his other shoulder, he asked his question again.

'Monsieur, is it not time we sailed for France?'

De la Vallerie kept the kerchief at his face and said, in muffled tones, 'Our mission is to Valletta.'

'Monsieur, we had an agreement.'

'We may return to France after Malta, we may not. When we do, we may talk again. Until we do, you will take your place at the oars.'

Haakon growled behind him. Jean raised a calming hand.

'That is not acceptable.'

The captain glanced around, saw all his men in position.

'Acceptable?' he roared, sending a shudder of pain through his tortured face, doubling his fury. 'I decide what's acceptable on the foredeck of my ship! You put down your arms, pick up your oars and row like the gutter scum you are or I'll have you flayed, fucked and fed to the fish!'

'We'll fight you,' Jean said simply.

'Then you'll die,' replied de la Vallerie. 'There's barely ten of you left.' And he nodded at his new sergeant-at-arms to move forward.

As he approached, Jean and Haakon vaulted over the guard rail and landed on the deck below. The ten other freed prisoners nervously gathered around them. Then there was a twittering, as of a flock of starlings lifting from a field, and fifteen black shapes rose from the benches. They all clutched weapons taken in the confusion of the fight. In their midst was the huge shape of Ake, pink flesh gaping as a result of the cruel wounds of the flaying knife, the shive still buried in his chest. Yet he called out in a strong voice, 'They die, you die.' And fifteen pairs of bare feet hammered in unison on the deck, fifteen throats opened to unleash the same battle cry.

A shock ran through everyone, Muslim and Christian, prisoner and slave, soldier and pirate.

'Shoot them! Shoot them all!' bawled the captain.

Over the rustle of lowered firearms, a single voice was heard: 'I think not.'

The voice, though soft, had a commanding tone to it and everyone on both ships stopped and looked up. On the aftdeck of the Silver Serpent that still towered over the aftdeck of the *Perseus*, dressed now in the flowing black robes of his former mortal enemy, a white turban crowning his head, Januc was leaning on the basilisk that the late John Hood had been just about to fire when an arrow snuffed out the light in his eye. John Hood's taper burned in Januc's left hand.

'I think not,' he repeated, and swung the muzzle of the gun around and down until it pointed directly at the soldiers who had primed their weapons below.

The gesture was enough. The soldiers shifted uneasily; then, as one, they shouldered their arquebuses. They had seen enough of short-range flying metal for a lifetime.

With a small nod, Jean turned back and climbed up the stairs, Haakon still shadowing him. The soldiers gave way, and Jean found himself staring once again into the bloodied, furious face of the captain.

'I have just decided what we will do. We—'

De la Vallerie screamed, 'I do not negotiate with peasants!'

Jean smiled. 'One day, we peasants will be tearing down your pretty little chateau. But for both of us to survive to witness that glorious day, you will now shut up and listen to me. Or my friend up there will end this conversation forthwith.'

Januc waved the taper. The captain, attempting to snort, grimaced in pain.

Jean continued. 'We have two ships, and the two smaller vessels that were attached to the big galley. Shall we divide the spoils?'

'I am not leaving the *Perseus*,' came the snuffled reply.

'My dear Captain, who would deprive you of that? No, you keep the *Perseus*, we'll take the Silver Serpent, and part, if not friends, at least not as enemies.'

De la Vallerie glanced at his cowed and exhausted men, then up into the muzzle pointed down at them.

'It seems I have no choice,' he said sourly. 'Very well. I will keep my slaves to take us back to Toulon to re-equip. You can use the Arabs and blacks to row you to hell.'

Jean looked back towards the main deck. His eyes sought those of Ake. He was standing, despite the pain and loss of blood, proud and upright in the centre of his people.

'No,' said Jean, turning back. 'In my brief acquaintance with it, I find I do not like this slavery. All men who wish to come with me will be free to do so. Those who wish to return to France can go with you. Ake and his people can take one of the Arab small boats and go where they will.'

De la Vallerie was stunned by the whole idea. He could only blurt out, 'And the Arab defeated? It is my right as conqueror to chain them to my oars as they would have chained me!'

'Any Arab can take the other small boat. It will be crowded, but they can join their brothers on that crippled galley out there.'

The news passed swiftly, in a variety of tongues, up and down the two ships. The consensus in both Arab and Christian thought, was that the man was mad. But it was said in some way, in all their tongues, that madness can be a special gift from God. And this madness was going to lead to freedom. Once indulged, however, the fear in all was that the madness would be recognised and stopped, so as soon as they could slip their chains the pirates and the Negroes divided up and, taking what food and water they could easily carry, scrambled into the two dhows on the far side of the Silver Serpent.

Jean watched from the foredeck of the larger galley as Ake's men skilfully manned the oars. Freedom gave them a new zest for rowing, and the small sail was soon catching the wind. As it pulled away, Ake, standing up in the prow, his chest now bound in sailcloth, turned and caught Jean's eyes for a final time. A little bow, and he was gone.

Jean felt a movement beside him. Once everything had been decided, it was Januc, with a corsair's deck once more beneath his feet, who had organised it all. He stood now at Jean's side and said, 'Well, my friend, have you thought now where you want this galley to sail?'

He had. The way was clear. Again he felt the pull, gentle but insistent, of a six-fingered hand.

'Italy. As close to Siena as I can get.'

'Is there profit in it? You have a corsair to command and you and I and that big lout of a Norseman could make a fortune in these waters.'

'Profit?' Jean nodded. 'Of a sort. Redemption is a better word.'

'It sounds like a good story. You'll be able to beguile the journey with its telling.' And the Croatian turned away.

'Wait.' Jean had realised something. 'Why didn't you go with the other – forgive me – pirates? Doesn't your home lie that way?'

Januc looked back. 'One home. But men who fought us and lived will have recognised me. I am now a corsair captain who fights his own. Besides, Hakim i Sabbah is one of a dozen brothers, each as vicious as the other. After today, I would forever sleep with one eye open. So I will consider my options as I ferry you to Livorno. It's in Tuscany, maybe a day's ride from Siena. Will that suit?'

'Will it suit you?'

'Livorno is a free port, a rat's nest of thieves, prostitutes and murderers, where men and women would slit your throat for a sou and gamble their grandmothers on a roll of the dice.' He smiled. 'My kind of town.'

The *Perseus* had finally been untangled from the Silver Serpent and even as Januc spoke of their destination Jean watched the two ships suddenly part. Few rowers had elected to join de la Vallerie, preferring to follow Jean, and soldiers were manning most of the oars – and making a feeble attempt at it. Da Costa, who had wives in too many French ports to take up a pirate's life, lay on their gangway, his foot set in splints by Jean. They were still close enough to hear him declaim, to the other wounded around him, 'Sho I shays to my friend Januc, I shays: try to remember to ushe the bow ash I taught you . . .'

Jean watched de la Vallerie, the only officer left, pick up the whip Corbeau had dropped and begin lashing. Turning his back to the sight and to the setting sun, his thoughts went ahead to Tuscany and back to a vow.

'A little longer, my Lady Anne,' he murmured quietly. 'Just a little longer.'

Up on the foredeck, Januc was already ordering the running of his ship. A fresh wind was picking up and the evening star was giving him his first clue as to direction.

A huge shape loomed between him and it.

'Just tell me,' Haakon rumbled. 'It has been annoying me all day.'

'What has, Norseman?'

'You said there were three things we needed to survive a fight on a galley. You only told us two. Hide under the bench . . .'

'Yes.'

'. . . wait for the second volley . . .'

'That's right.'

'. . . and the third?'

'The third?' Januc clasped his hands to his face. 'You mean, I didn't tell you the third? But the third is the most important of all!'

'Yes,' exploded the Norwegian, 'you said! What is it?'

Januc winked. 'Don't get killed.'

# FOUR

# DUNGEON

It was faint and almost lost in all the other sounds of the dungeon – the constant drip of water running down the green seamed walls, the scurrying of rats amid the rancid straw, the muttering, weeping and snoring of his fellow inmates who spanned the range of sanity, alike only in their handless state. Despite it all, though, the sound of someone in torment carries to those who have an ear for it.

The Fugger had such an ear. He had listened to himself long enough and to those at his gibbet. Two of their company of seven handless men had disappeared through the cell door. Neither had returned and only the occasional bat-squeak of terror marked any sense of the hours passing, though he thought they had been there a night and part of a day. He hunched further into the corner, taking care not to lean on the raven still tucked into the small of his back. There was comfort in its warm body pressing there. A small comfort.

'What have I done, oh Daemon dear?' he whispered, the sound making a bundle of rags next to him start and shout some nonsense, then rejoin the others in sleep. A keg of wine had been left for them and they had emptied it between them, all save the Fugger. He wanted his wits about him. They were all he had.

*And much good may they do me*, he thought. *I have swapped a gibbet midden for a death cell, the furies in my head for ones of all too real, stinking flesh. What was I thinking, trying to be some hero in an ancient story? What can I do here except echo the screams of those who have gone before?*

A different kind of scream, the hinges of the door swinging open.

Heinrich von Solingen stood there, the flames of a reed torch silhouetting him in the doorway. The two Germans looked at each other. The Fugger had managed so far to control his reactions to this nightmare from his past; if he shook a little more now it suited the role he had adopted. Heinrich merely regarded him as another tool for his master.

'Seems you're next,' he said, and beckoned the Fugger to follow.

'Oh yes, Master, all too happy, all too happy.' He belched and laughed. 'Such a kind master. Such good wine.'

Along with the wine to warm them against the dungeon's chill, they'd each been issued with an old and stinking blanket. His was red, barely holding together, its wool unravelling. Clutching this around him, and keeping his head down, he shambled and staggered after his gaoler.

The broad back preceded him into a dank corridor, guttering torches throwing their shadows over the rough walls and the misshapen cell doors that studded them. The floor sloped down and the cold and the wet increased, a chill forcing itself into his bones, the threadbare blanket a useless ward against it. Then, strangely, it began to get warmer and the iron-banded door they approached seemed to glow.

Heinrich rapped upon it three times. Three bolts were pulled and a key inserted and twisted. When it swung open, the heat struck the Fugger like the slap of a huge hand. The light was intense; there were dozens of reed torches, three score of huge cathedral candles, a fire blazing in a brazier, near which stood a table of metal implements he didn't want to consider. The light was intensified by the glass vault at the centre of the room. It bounced and was magnified by hundreds of crystalline, many-coloured chambers that made up the dome.

To its right, movement drew his eyes. Two men were crouched over some sort of hole, a wooden lid propped up beside it. From it came the sound of fast-moving water. They were pushing something into the darkness there, and he caught a swift glimpse of what looked like a leg suddenly disappearing. As the men replaced the wooden cover, he noticed that beside the hole lay two tattered blankets.

A door appeared amid the shimmering glass, the shape and size of a coffin lid, opening straight up, sticking out at a right angle from the structure. There was even more intense light from within, a searing brightness that the Fugger, still standing behind von Solingen by the door, instinctively shielded his eyes from. But not before he'd recognised the man in flowing robes who emerged, yelling angrily at someone behind him, within.

Giancarlo Cibo, Archbishop of Siena, was furious. They had made two attempts to attach the hand of Anne Boleyn to his handless 'volunteers' and each had failed. No matter how drunk and insensible he rendered them – and he'd poured considerable amounts of grappa down each of their willing throats – the men would become instantly sober at the touch of the six-fingered hand. The hand itself did nothing. No one apart from Cibo himself had ever seen it move. It lay inert; yet as soon as stump was pressed to stump, the men shrieked as if burned by a white heat and flailed about the room. Two burly guards could barely hold the scarecrow victims still. To start with they'd tried to sew the hand and stump together using fishing line, but the thread seemed to dissolve in contact with the skin. Cibo eliminated the variable by getting rid of the 'volunteer', but he had no luck with the second either, who had just joined his fellow in the long water ride out. The next one, he'd decided, would not be sewn. He'd had another idea. And this was what had finally caused the always malleable Abraham to balk.

'We are metallurgists!' Cibo shouted over his shoulder at the Jew who sat at his table, his head resting on his arms. 'What is the point of all this equipment? What could make more sense?'

He saw Heinrich standing at the door. He barely glanced at the Fugger.

'Is he drunk?'

The Fugger gave a little giggle and belched extravagantly.

'As you see, my Lord.'

'Well, I want him more so. You two' – he called to the two guards who were replacing the cover on the water hole – 'feed this pawless dog more liquor. And you' – he turned back to von Solingen – 'make up another pipe for the Jew. Not too much. I need him awake.'

Then he returned to the chamber and began pulling pieces of equipment to the crucible at its centre.

The Fugger was taken to a corner of the stone hall. Even though much of it was obscured by smoke and heat haze, he could sense the immensity of it. And looking up, he saw the smoke funnelling away through some kind of hole.

The guards gave him a bottle filled with harsh brandy. He turned side-on to them, placed the neck of the bottle beside his face and allowed the liquid to slip slowly down his thumb and onto his shoulder. He gasped, spluttered and giggled until it was half empty, then feigned passing out. The guards caught the bottle and moved away, finishing it between them.

The Fugger reached behind him and pulled out the raven. Jet eyes reflected the flames of the chamber.

'It is time, O Daemon dear,' he whispered. 'You must go and bring help.'

*But how, oh how?* he thought. If there was a vent at the roof of this dark cave, Daemon might find it eventually. If the hole was big enough he might slip out. But then? Would he find Beck waiting outside? And what could the lad do, beyond knowing that there was another way in to the palace? A way he had sought for years and never found?

Despair threatened to overwhelm him, worse than anything he'd ever faced in the midden cave. There, at least, he was safe, his own master, however low and filthy and lost. Here . . . well, he had no doubt that he would soon be following his predecessors' corpses to watery doom. And that might come as a blessed relief after whatever was being prepared for him within the glass vault.

He wanted to release Daemon but somehow he couldn't bear to, knowing he would never see him again. He held him, wedging the warm body against his side, within the blanket. His one hand plucked at its red thread, unravelling row after row. It made him think of his mother, in the warmth of their kitchen in Munster, forcing her young son to sit still and hold his hands out so she could untangle the wool and render it into skeins for her knitting. He'd pretend that he hated to do it, to be so domestic when he should be out with his father learning the ways of men, of commerce and property. In reality, he loved the soft texture wrapping around his hands, his two good hands, his mother crooning some old song or lullaby as she wound the thread round and round.

A jangle of it lay before him. He looked into the lustrous eyes of his companion; then, pulling the bird up to his mouth, after a struggle with teeth and fingers he finally succeeded in tying the end of the wool tightly round the raven's left foot. He then frantically unwound more and more of the blanket, using his two feet like his mother had used her son's hands, until over half of the blanket lay in a circle of red before him.

The command 'Bring him' was issued from within the glass dome, and Heinrich von Solingen emerged and made towards him.

'Go with all my prayers,' the Fugger whispered. Then he released the raven, just as the big German bent over him.

With a screech, Daemon took off, causing Heinrich to reel back with a curse. *Foul creatures*, he thought, and swiped air as the bird flapped down at him once, twice and again before giving a last cry and heading for the ceiling. Heinrich had the

206

oddest feeling that the bird had a trail of red behind it, like an exhalation of smoke, but he knew it to be nothing more than a figment conjured by his still-throbbing head and the swirling haze of the chamber. He ordered the guards to pick up the bundle on the floor that the Fugger had become, hiding in feigned unconsciousness.

When they brought him within the kaleidoscopic room, Cibo looked up from his preparations and said, 'What was that noise?'

'A bird, my Lord. They sometimes creep in through the vent.'

'Well, what are you waiting for? Put him on the table. No, not that way, idiot. His stump up this end. Nearest the crucible.'

Even though he'd long since lost all feeling in the wrist, the Fugger could feel through it the intensity of heat emanating from the iron cauldron half buried in the floor. Opening his eyes to slits, he looked into a face that was a stranger's yet oddly familiar. Grey hair burst from beneath a skull cap straggling a sharp, haggard countenance. Dark eyes regarded him dully, and it was these he felt he had seen before.

'Well, Abraham, shall we begin?' said the Archbishop, coaxingly. 'And no more scruples, eh? A few may suffer, true, wretches who are all but dead anyway, but only so the many will gain. The Philosopher's Stone is within reach. We have its secret before us, in this witch's hand, in this handless man. Come, for life eternal.'

Abraham muttered a few words and looked away.

'You will see, my friend, you will see.' Cibo gestured to the guards. 'Place the stump on the crucible.'

The Fugger's arm was lifted and stretched towards the white heat. All pretence of sleep gone now, he struggled, vainly, to pull it away. An inch, a finger's breadth, already the pain intense.

'No!' he screamed, and there was a hammering on the

dungeon door and voices calling Cibo's name. The guards, at a gesture from their leader, released the Fugger's arm.

'Your Eminence?'

It was Giovanni, Cibo's manservant and master of his household.

'My Lord, the council is here. They await you above. The final arrangements for the Palio. We need your commands.'

Cibo looked down at the gibbering Fugger, then across at the glazed eyes of Abraham.

'Well,' he laughed, 'duty over pleasure, I suppose.'

At his signal, one of the guards swept the hand into its velvet bag, then slipped that into the saddle bags. Slinging them across his shoulders the guard came and stood behind Cibo, who said, 'Will you carry on without me?'

The other man finally spoke. 'There may be some tests I can conduct in your absence. Leave the one-handed subject with me.'

'Good.' At the door of the kaleidoscope Cibo stopped, then turned slowly. 'You know, Abraham, I think we may have been approaching this incorrectly. We are men of science, yes, but this, in here' – he tapped the leather bag – 'this belonged to nothing less than Hecate, a Queen of Witches – its uncorrupted flesh proves it to be diabolic in its very nature. Believe me, I have seen that to be true.' He shuddered. And then a little smile came to his lips, a glow into his eyes. He continued, 'Therefore, forces beyond science should be harnessed in our quest.' He turned to his bodyguard and his master of ceremonies. 'We will hold a Black Mass. Here, tonight. See to it, both of you. We'll need the usual participants. Tell my mistress. Oh, and find a virgin – if there are any left in Siena.'

He swept from the chamber, followed closely by Giovanni and the two guards.

Heinrich left more slowly, muttering curses. Thinking.

*I am no theologian, but a Black Mass? An abomination in God's eyes, surely? Yet God has ordained this Italian to be*

*His true rock, the bulwark of the One Church. To God and Cibo my oath of obedience is sworn. In all things. All!*

He had never attended a Black Mass; but he could not balk at it, he would have to play the part required of him by Christ's representative. Yet, as he left the chamber Heinrich began to cross himself repeatedly, for he had heard of dangerous things appearing at such rituals. Evil things. Things with more than a whiff of brimstone about them.

When the door slammed behind him, the Fugger once more opened his eyes. Abraham hadn't moved, continuing to regard him in that unfocused way. The two men looked at each other, the only sounds the hissing of molten metal in the crucible, a distant rumbling of flames, the steady drip of water.

The Fugger thought he knew where he had seen the old man's eyes before. If he was right . . . well, he had to take that chance.

'Master,' he said, 'I have come from your son.'

Abraham's expression did not change. He showed no hint that he had even heard words spoken.

'Your son, master. He waits outside this evil place. He is trying to free you.'

Abraham got up and shuffled towards the open doorway of the glass chamber. He was almost through it when the Fugger called again.

'It is true. Your son will rescue you.'

The haggard man didn't even turn around to say it. 'I have no son.'

For the raven that some humans called Daemon, it was an easy choice. Caverns were not places where he liked to hunt, and he'd got the faintest whiff of something freshly dead, up beyond the fug of the cave.

So when his creature had released him, he'd followed the scent up on the spirals of smoke and swiftly came to a hole beyond which lay the promise of prey. It was narrow, so he'd squeezed his wings tight about him and pushed through, into a passage that curved upwards.

Eventually Daemon saw light, and within a moment had bumped into a metal grate. Beyond it, through slats, lay the early-evening sky. On the grate lay a rat's body.

He was not concerned now that he could get no further. He was concerned with hunger. It was awkward but, clinging upside down, he was still able to pull a brown haunch through with a red-tagged talon, to plunge in his razor beak, to rend and tear. The more he did, the easier it became.

It was hunger that brought Beck reluctantly along the side of the palace, away from her vantage point before the main gates. The longer she waited, the greater her anxiety. She'd been a fool to let the Fugger take the risk he had denied her. Now she was both helpless and alone. Back watching the building she knew held her father prisoner within it. Back doing nothing, able to do nothing but watch and wait.

For what? She'd sat there for a year before and not a single chance had occurred in that time to get in, or to pursue the Archbishop outside. He was always too heavily guarded, or surrounded by people. Once she had nearly lost all patience and attempted an assault single-handedly, despite the odds, but had held off knowing that one chance was all she would have.

That chance had now come and gone, on the road to Toulon. It should have been just her, Cibo and the hulking bodyguard – good odds! The man should have died there, his seal of office hers with which to forge documents for her father's release. Instead, other men with other motives had got in her way. One man especially. She had hesitated then, and again in Toulon, distracted by feelings that had never affected her before. And now, with that man gone and probably dead, she was back where she seemed to have spent her life, waiting for another chance that might be years in the coming.

Despite this realisation, she was still reluctant to leave her post until hunger forced her to, her own and the growling Fenrir's at her feet. In the winding alleys beside the palace, foodsellers had already staked their pitches, for the Palio was due to take place the next day. Prices had already started to climb, and Beck reluctantly paid three scudi for a meagre loaf of bread and some cooked meat which she didn't consider too closely. Long gone were the days when she ate according to the dictates of her tribe. Life on the streets of Siena didn't allow such luxuries. And Fenrir didn't mind the gristly meat at all.

It was while they were returning down the side alley to the front of the building that Fenrir suddenly growled and jerked the length of rope from her hand. He ran to the palace wall and began to paw at something on the ground. She saw a rat's corpse and was about to pull the dog away when she noticed the rat move. Since it was obviously dead, she looked closer. Something was moving it from below, and it wasn't the steady stream of smoke she now noticed rising around the body.

She bent down. Expecting another rat, the glinting eyes that suddenly fastened on her, set within a crown of black feathers, gave her a shock, but that was nothing next to the shock of recognition.

'Daemon!' she cried.

The raven ceased gnawing only for the time it took to say, 'Hand.'

Beck put down her food and looked back. The grate was set within two buttresses. For the moment, no one was in sight in the alley. She bent down and tried to pull the grate up but it was wedged solidly, held down by years of filth and sediment.

'Don't move,' she said to the raven, which acknowledged her departure merely by taking a bigger bite.

Beck ran back to the stall keepers. Several were still in the process of setting up and some stalls were more elaborate than others, with sides and awnings. She spotted what she wanted beside one of them and, while the two men were distracted by the voluptuous female form of an orange seller passing by, she seized the crowbar and ran back.

Inserting it into the grate she pressed all her weight down upon it. For a long moment nothing seemed to happen, then there was a slight giving followed by a rush of movement as the grate tipped up at an angle and the rat's body disappeared down the hole. Daemon hopped out immediately and, putting his head to one side, looked up at her with a reproachful expression.

'Here, you can share mine,' she said, handing over some bread.

While the bird set to munching again, Beck regarded it with wonder. She coughed and waved a gust of smoke away from her face, then breathed in again more urgently. There was some familiar savour to it. Somewhere, she had smelt it before.

And then it came to her. The smoke carried a memory of the last time she had seen her father before he smuggled her out of the palace, sitting before his crucible, its white heat reducing iron to molten metal, an acrid cloud enveloping him with its scent.

This scent. The scent in her nostrils now.

She blew her nose to the side of the hole before her. Looking down, she saw the thread trailing away into the darkness. What is that? She reached down and Daemon leapt up onto her outstretched hand. Running her fingers down the wool, Beck tugged it lightly, feeling the resistance.

'Clever Fugger,' she said.

She fought down the instinct to throw herself into the hole, to immediately trace the red line to its source, which she knew now must also be the source of the smoke. She had a vision of her father sitting in a cloud of it and the desire to slither into the subterranean depths and into his arms was overpowering.

But she was a street fighter of old and knew that plans

launched in haste usually ended in bad blood. So she swiftly untied the thread from the bird's talons and attached it to the grate before replacing it. Then she went in search of what she would need. It wouldn't be much. Her knife and a good length of rope should do it. And her slingshot, of course.

Preceded by Fenrir and circled by a cawing Daemon, she set out for the riverbed to look for smooth stones and to await the full darkness of midnight.

# FIVE

# THE BLACK MASS

Far beneath the surface, in a room that saw no natural light, the preparations were nearly complete. The score of reed torches lining the walls of the outer chamber had been reduced to a quartet – north and south, east and west. Of the Cathedral candles, only nine now burned outside the glass vault, while another seven stood within on an altar erected opposite the door, set around a huge gold cross, inverted, its top driven into the centre of the wood. The cauldron within, still glowing red from its hidden fire, had been emptied of its molten contents, half-filled instead with a mixture of spices, grappa and wine.

The scent of the sweet-smelling liquor made the Fugger's eyes heavy; he had caught himself slipping twice into a desired sleep, until the reality of his situation brought him back. He watched as Giovanni brought in the items, alive and inanimate, that now lined the glass walls. Another time, everything might have filled him with the wonder of the curious student he had been. Now, things familiar or strange created nothing less than a sense of total dread.

Soon, all activity was over, and silence, broken only by the occasional chirrup of a bound and blinkered beast, settled over the dungeon and its kaleidoscopic centre. Abraham lay on a cot outside the glass walls, insensible, a scraggy arm thrown over his face. He had not spoken a word in the long hours since the Archbishop's departure, and the Fugger's further attempts to press him about Beck had met with nothing more than a curt denial.

How long they waited, the Fugger had no clue, for time was absent from these dark reaches. To stay awake, he paced out the limits of his large cell, seeking some little hope in the near darkness. But the walls that funnelled up in smoke were clammy and sheer, the water that surged beneath the wooden stopper – he had dared to prise it open and look – was a maelstrom, terror for a strong swimmer, death to one such as he.

The only way out was the way in. He paused before the door for the fiftieth time, scanning its strong oak beams, iron bands and studs. *The only hope is beyond*, he thought, and as he thought it he heard a noise and such little hope as there was ended with it, for the noise developed into a chant that he recognised. It was the Latin Mass. Yet the words were a corruption of that tongue, and within its deep repetitions he heard the high, shrill note of desperate weeping.

A scraping of a key in the lock and the door moved slowly inwards, the chanting surged and he knew what was wrong with it. He was still scholar enough to understand what they were doing, these eight cowled figures who moved steadily, two by two, into the chamber, swinging censers filled with burning sandalwood. As they swung they chanted, and they were indeed reciting the High Mass. But they were reciting it backwards.

He reeled away from the cortège and fled to the side to press himself into the rock as if it could be made to melt and he to disappear through it. Yet he could only slip down the walls and curl up, press hand and stump to his ears, try not to hear.

The Devil was abroad in the world, everyone knew. All had to be vigilant against him. Had not even his own beloved Luther been confronted by him, hurled a Bible at him back in Augsburg? And these men were now inviting the Devil to join them in this chamber. The Fugger had heard how such invitations were issued and now the preparations began to make an awful sense, more so as the rest of the procession entered the room.

A woman followed the cowled, chanting figures, as naked and open as they were covered and hid. Only the flimsiest of silk loincloths adorned her, her full breasts rising and falling as she matched the monks' steady pace, now hidden, now revealed by the unbridled tresses of her hair. The swaying of her ample figure betrayed, it seemed to the Fugger, her voluptuous nature, disclosed again in the secret smile beneath a leather eye mask. She reminded him instantly of the statue at the Fonte Gaia. He was drawn by the memory, repelled by it, could not look away. She entered the glass chamber on bare feet, gliding through the two lines the monks had made, and took her place before the altar.

The female form that followed her could not have provided more of a contrast. She was covered neck to foot in linen of purest and unsullied white, gold sandals on her feet, her hair held in a wreath of blue and yellow corn-flowers. Even with the concealing robe, the Fugger could see she was barely a woman – a thin girl's body, a pale and freckled face, smirched by tears flowing ceaselessly, the desperation of her weeping increasing as she saw into what place she entered.

A man in black armour held her in his arms, marching at the funereal pace the chanting dictated. Faceless, a visor of the same dark sheen, the slits in it the bars of a cage within a cage. The stride remorseless, the blows of the girl's hands the weak flutterings of a moth against lamp glass. He too marched into the kaleidoscope and straight up to the altar where he laid the girl before the inverted cross. Out of his arms, she seemed suddenly calmer, until the Fugger recog-nised a new aspect to her demeanour, one so familiar to him – an animal in a trap, paralysed by fear.

The armoured man moved from the glass dome to pick up Abraham from his cot, depositing him on the floor inside.

Then he emerged again and raised one gauntleted hand to beckon the Fugger. He knew who summoned him. He had seen, staring through the slits in the visor, the eyes of Heinrich von Solingen. If there had been anywhere to flee, he might have made the attempt. But there was no escape, only this inevitability. Rising, he passed the black armoured sentinel and found that his pace was matching the rhythm of the chants, which seemed to rise in a crescendo as he entered, then ceased altogether when the glass door lowered, entombing them all.

*Thirteen*, he thought, counting the occupants. *Dear God, thirteen. Holy Father, protect thy servant.*

Silence, untainted even by the girl's whimpering, stretched for several heartbeats, broken finally by a cowled figure at the front who lowered the censer he'd been wielding to the ground, picked up a hazel wand as tall as himself and rapped its iron-shod tip three times upon the floor.

'Corpus Hermeticum,' a silky voice said from within the folds of cloth. 'Let us seek the wisdom of Hermes. Let us speak the true words of Thoth.'

As he spoke, Giancarlo Cibo threw off his monkish robes. He was naked but for a shift of silk wrapped round his thin waist. Turning to face his followers, he cried out, 'Let malefaction reign!'

'Malefaction!' came the roared echo as seven more robes were discarded and the monks, clad even as their master, began to gather items from around the walls. When each was ready they formed a circle around the cauldron, the naked shape of the mistress at their centre, Cibo to her right. Only the girl, immobile in terror on the altar, von Solingen in his blank black armour, the unseeing Abraham and the unwilling Fugger now remained beyond their ring.

The circle slowly started to move widdershins, against the clock. When the naked woman reached the central place before the altar again, she raised a bundle over the cauldron, a sack bound in twine that twisted and wriggled in the rising heat. Despite the desperate jerking, she held the bag there, leading the circle around. Then she began to chant.

> Toad and the stool
> Which he cowers under,
> Brain of bat
> With head split asunder

And she dropped the wriggling bag into the cauldron.

The bag sparked and flashed, what was within twisted and shrieked as it landed in the bubbling liquid. Then everyone joined her in the next words.

> Stir it into
> Satan's broth,
> Sacrifice
> To conjure Thoth

The next participant reached the apex of the circle, a jowly, tonsured monk who cried, as he threw his bundle,

> Hemlock and henbane,
> Belladonna, nightshade,
> Opium for dreams
> God has not made

And the cry, in unison:

> Stir it into
> Satan's broth,
> Sacrifice
> To conjure Thoth

The next man stepped up, chanted, threw.

> Mandrake shaped
> Like the nub of man,
> Shroud from a plague pit,
> Courtesan's fan

A chorus, another verse, the speaking coming faster:

> *Tooth of tiger,*
> *Silver adder's tongue,*
> *Entrails of she-wolf*
> *That never had young*

Faster now, the circle speeding around. The stench coming from the cauldron, flesh and plants of power combined, was piercing, acrid fumes making the Fugger's eyes run, his nostrils stream. The whirling made him nauseous and he rested his head, tried to block out the words, managed not to listen to all the verses. But when that familiar silky voice spoke out, he couldn't help but be drawn out again into the spell.

> *Blood from baby*
> *Torn from Mother's hug,*
> *Churchyard earth*
> *From grave new dug*

The circle was spinning so fast now that people were beginning to cry out, in fear, in exhilaration. On Cibo's last words, when his clod of soaked earth hit the pot, there was a unanimous cry, the last chorus seeming to come from one voice:

> *Stir it into*
> *Satan's broth,*
> *Sacrifice*
> *To conjure THOTH!*

A giant flame shot from the cauldron. The circle crashed to a halt, bodies falling outwards. One maddened monk barrelled into the silent, black armoured figure and bounced off. The Fugger buried his head again as another monk fell on him.

Only one man was still moving, his left hand spilling coloured sand in a large circle on the floor. He quickly filled the circle with the lines of a five-pointed star. Within that pentangle he wrote, with the falling, gore-red sand, the words 'suproc tse coh'.

Something was shaken out of a velvet bag to fall into the centre of the star of sand, onto the reversed words.

'Suproc tse coh!' cried the Archbishop of Siena. 'Hoc est corpus!'

And, gazing down upon the six-fingered hand of Anne Boleyn, the coven set about the raising of the dead.

High above them, yet already far below the surface, something moved slowly through a tunnel of infinite dark. At points, the chimney was so narrow that the blindworm creature was forced to dig its face into the earth, to hold its breath and push its head through tiny gaps, propelled by scrabbling feet and the clawing fingers of just one hand, trying never to release the woollen thread stretching out into the blackness.

Twice Beck had let it go when forced to pull with the strength of both hands to wriggle through a near-impossible opening. Once, when briefly climbing upwards again, she had snagged and split the thread, just at a fork in the tunnel. She'd struggled up the left channel for a dozen pulls of her body before deciding to go back and take the right channel where, after much panicky groping in the complete darkness, she recovered the thread. Thereafter, it remained locked in her grasp, making the way slower, but surer.

There was little air, and what there was of it was tainted with sulphurous smoke. Beck coughed, choked, spat mud but crept ever downward. Time passed but made no sense. There was only this blackness, the twistings of rock and clay, an occasional cave where she could sense space above her, where she could straighten for a moment and stretch her bunched limbs. Then, inevitably, the thread would lead her down again to a narrow hole and, with a last shrug and shift, she would thrust her head into it, squeeze her shoulders through, renew the painful scrabbling descent.

As a ward against the terror that constantly threatened to engulf her, she began to talk. At first it was nothing – childhood rhymes, snatches of psalms, the song of Solomon. Gradually, these words adapted themselves to her surroundings as if her life had only ever been this space, merging with the earth and mud, the foul air and the things she carried with her, her destiny dangling at the end of a red thread. 'Lord, though I crawl through the valley of dark death, yet I have my weapons clutched to my side. Though I breathe the poison of the air, yet am I strong. Knife and stone, slingshot and string. Follow the trail wherever it leads. To my father. To my father. To my father.'

The tunnel widened a little and, raising her face, Beck inhaled something different, redolent of both sweetness and corruption. It made her suddenly, fiercely hungry, yet at the same time nauseated, as if her hunger could only be sated by something foul and unnatural. She breathed again deeply, both drawn and disgusted, eyes closed to this breeze. Then something hit her in the face. A body. It ran into her, was repelled, then ran into her shoulders, scrambled up and over them. She cried out then and thrust her face into the mud before her, burying her scream, as wave upon wave of furred bodies, large and small, ran into the top of her head and on over her, tiny feet scampering down her back, running down her legs, hundreds, thousands of them.

It went on for what seemed like an age and then they were gone. She dared to raise her head, to suck in deep that repellent air, to thank her loving God for meeting them there and not ten paces further back when she was wedged in the narrowest gap. Then she took the thread again into her hand and pushed herself forward through the sickly-sweet smoke, towards a horror even the rats had fled.

Within the kaleidoscope of light, a kaleidoscope of sound. Shrieks, garbled pleading, maniacal laughter suddenly cut off, replaced by a desperate sobbing. The grunts of the lustful, the insatiable, cries of orgasmic delight, of rapine torment, prayers uttered as curses, curses as prayers. No relief for those who suffered, no satiation for those who craved. The endlessness of desire, the prolonging of sweet and terrible pain.

Nowhere to look; everywhere the horrors, the pleasures, the two so enmeshed it was impossible to see where one ended and the other began. One moment the Fugger was weeping with a depth of desolation he'd never known, even in the darkest nights of the midden, the next he was laughing as if his jaws would split from his face, as if some howling dog would burst from them, dragged out by the imps sat atop his cheekbones dangling fish hooks in his lips, pulling them back to speed the passage of this demon he was giving birth to. And above him no respite, just the revolving chambers of glass spinning now in frenzy, vomiting forth roses that grew and withered in an instant, amulets and eye sockets exploding in rainbow shades, dissolving and re-forming into the legions of the damned.

And everywhere the bodies. Joined on the floor, perched on the ends of the altar; men grappled with men while the naked woman took one after another, yelling her encouragement, her mockery, urging them on to greater acts of sweaty degradation either side of the white-clad virgin whose only movement was the endless flow of her tears. These soaked a handkerchief laid there for the purpose. Someone would wring this out regularly into a jewelled chalice beside her on the altar. It was already half full.

And the Fugger knew, somewhere in the small part of him that still could think, that all this was a result of the awful cauldron's contents, which had been stirred and heated and chanted over until it was ready to be painted onto the naked bodies, at armpit, nostril and groin. His struggles had meant that maybe his skin absorbed less of the thick liquid than some of the others who had willingly, joyfully daubed themselves. But he also knew that whatever was inside him was not diminishing in force but building, that the small part of him that still could reason was dissipating to nothing.

'What will I do when even that little is gone?' he cried out, his voice drowned in the shrieking. Then he realised he did know, and so he clutched that thought to him, his only hope of salvation.

Just when he thought the rock walls of the dungeon would burst apart, a command was called from the altar and all in the room froze, in mid-ecstasy or anguish, to look up. A stag-headed man stood there, antlers splayed and swaying, pointing over the crowd. And that small, thinking part of the Fugger remembered now that this stag, this Archbishop of Siena, was one of the small group who had not partaken of the foul broth, along with Abraham, the still-weeping virgin and the armoured Heinrich von Solingen.

'Prince of Darkness! Come to us now!' The voice emerging from the mouth of the stag was silky, low-pitched. 'Prince of this world, Father of lies, of the Other Truths, Diabolus, Ahiram, you who have a name and no name in all the tongues of the earth, descend to be with us, your servants.'

The heavy breathing of the disciples, the drip of water and of tears, the turning of the chambers, all noise was sucked away then, leaving a silence that yearned to be filled. As if somewhere someone had laid a hand against a door that would open upon them.

No, not a hand, the Fugger realised. A cloven hoof.

He heard a faint scratching, all heard it, and all looked up to the glass roof. Shadows, separate shapes, were moving together, forming into one dark cloud stretching over them. When all was obscure, when the shadow was upon them and they could feel its terrible weight, it paused there as if waiting for more.

The silky voice issued again from the stag's head. 'What do you wish, dread Lord? Name it and it is thine. Life act or death stroke, it is thine. Any abomination, corruption, degradation, it is thine. Show us how to do thy work, to honour thee. Help us summon the spirit of this dead queen, this she-hag, this Hecate who once did thy command with her six fingers and can again, with thy favour. Help us join witch's hand to beggar's stump. Name thy price and it shall be paid. It is thine! Thine! Thine!'

The scratching, faint at first, like a mouse running across a glass roof, grew louder with these words, seeming to come now from here, now from there, the upraised faces following the scurryings, some in terror, some in expectant joy. Soon it became a drumming, a steady beating upon the ceiling – thump! thump! thump! – and the glass began to bow, to bulge and push against its leaded restraints, forced inwards by claw, by finger, by palm of hairy hand.

A terrible scream, and all looked now as the girl in virginal white, previously so still, began to writhe and groan. Her body was in the grip of unseen hands, twisted and pulled, her legs spread wide, the movements of her hips lascivious, inviting, while her face, blanched in pure terror, showed her desperation, her terrible struggle to control what was no longer under her command.

'A sign! You have spoken! Thy will be done!' Cibo raised both arms in invocation, then pointed at the girl and turned to the Black Knight. 'Hold her! Hold her here for me!'

Heinrich von Solingen began to march forward, his gait steady and slow. On the altar, the stag-headed Archbishop began to loosen the silk at his waist.

It was then that the Fugger, unable to watch, looked down and saw a sight of more wonder than any yet paraded before him. There were two hands in his lap, and they were both his. He raised up the miracle. His new hand was the same to the touch, yet different, for he saw again the scars where the dog had bitten him as a child, the burn when he had been too eager to reach inside his mother's cooking pot. He bunched the fingers, stretched them out, delighting in forgotten sensations. He was complete, and a strength and a courage he'd not felt in seven years filled him.

It was at that moment he heard the voice.

'Look at me.'

A woman was standing within the pentangle, long dark hair, a horse's mane of it, flowing down over bare shoulders, a simple circlet of gold on her brow, another of sapphires encircling a long and graceful neck. Her eyes were pools of depthless black. He gazed into them, saw the flaw within one, the question and the answer in the pair. And when she raised a hand from within her gown of immaculate white, he saw it had six fingers.

'I cannot hold them long,' Anne Boleyn said. 'Their summons is strong, for they have a sacred part of me.'

The Fugger looked up and saw that everyone else was frozen: the black knight halted in mid-stride, the stag with arms spread wide, the virgin on the altar, her terror plain now that her writhings had ceased, every monk caught in their leers, all held as if in a painting by a troubled master. Only the candles still flickered.

She spoke again. 'Fight them. For help is closer than you think.'

The pentangle was between the cauldron and altar. Without stepping beyond the five-pointed boundary, she leant over and dipped her hand into the broth. Steam rose as she withdrew it and followed her as she stretched out to the altar. A drop fell from the little finger into the chalice there, where they had so carefully saved the young girl's tears.

'Remember this. Remember the power of tears.'

The faint scratching returned. He saw a slight movement from those around him, as if they were breathing in. Anne Boleyn shivered, and the edges of her gown, the jewels at head and neck, began to blur. In a voice suddenly strained, she said, 'Tell Jean, I do not doubt that he will come for me.' She then seemed to melt, dissolving and descending to the chamber floor, leaving only a faint trace of light and a six-fingered hand within a star of sand.

He looked down. His new hand had gone, but something

of the courage he'd felt remained. As the nightmare of the chamber returned in screaming ecstasy and pain, as a suit of black armour marched towards a girl in pure white, the Fugger knew what he must do. For he remembered the power of tears.

Moving to the altar, he picked up the chalice there and dashed the contents through the slits of the black helmet.

Heinrich von Solingen felt the liquid hit him. He had been burnt once before, with boiling oil at the siege of Novara. He still had the scars. This pain was a hundred times worse. It seared him, ate his flesh, filled his still unhealed head wound with molten fire. Bellowing in agony, he crashed backwards onto the sand star where a hand seemed to reach through his armour and wrap six icy fingers around his heart.

The scratching on the panes stopped in an instant. Echoing von Solingen's shrieks, the monks threw themselves as far from the writhing figure as they could, cowering against the glass.

The Fugger felt a blade at his throat, a soft voice slithering into his ear.

'Who are you, that you come between me and my will?'

He was turned around by the stiletto point of the weapon, gouging the flesh under his jawbone. Yet when he looked up into the furious eyes of the Archbishop of Siena, though he saw his death in them, he remembered the offset black eyes of a moment before and his courage held.

'We have met before, Giancarlo Cibo. For I used to keep a gibbet in France.'

And then the Archbishop of Siena remembered the moonlit crossroads, the tiny detail of a gibbet keeper who perhaps had heard his name.

'Well,' he said simply, 'you've come a long way to die.'

As he pulled back the knife to strike, a moment of wonder stayed the weapon in the air, and it was in that moment that a stone crashed through the back wall of the kaleidoscope chamber and struck Cibo on the shoulder. As he fell over the

Fugger to the floor, both heard the furious voice from beyond the shattered panes.

'Fuck! Missed his head!'

A demon, besmeared with mud from crown to toe, eyes and bared teeth the only gleam of white, stood outside the kaleidoscope whirling something above its head. Then a second stone smashed the remaining pane of glass behind the altar, and the demon stepped through the wreckage.

'Fugger!' Beck shouted. 'Where's my father?'

Glancing around, her question was answered. She went and knelt by the old man, hesitatingly reaching out a hand to his shoulder. Abraham's vacant eyes, though open, stared past her.

'Papa. Oh, Papa,' she whispered. 'What has he done to you?'

The sudden stillness brought on by the shattering of glass was just as suddenly ended as Cibo leapt to his feet.

'Guards! Guards!' he shouted as he ran from the kaleidoscope, heading for the dungeon's door.

Then everyone was screaming. Beck whirled to her feet, put stone to slingshot and was already aiming at the fleeing back.

'Fugger! This time I won't miss! Down!' she shouted, but he was too slow, and Cibo had made the portal and turned the key before she had a clear target. As the door swung open the first man to rush in took a stone in the face, falling backwards and crashing into the two men following him, bringing them all to the floor.

'Grab my father!' Beck cried. 'We must get out of here!'

Beck filled the leather with another stone as she ran. Cibo just managed to duck as it smashed into the lintel beside the doorway.

'Get them, fools!' He was pulling and slapping at the guards as they tried to extricate themselves from their wounded comrade.

'How?' the Fugger shouted at Beck. He was bent over the

old man, forcing him to his feet. 'There is no way out except the way in. And however you got in.'

Beck loosed another stone. A fourth guard who had tried to pass the heap on the floor fell back. Five more crowded the corridor behind him. She had lost half her stones in the dark passageways above. She only had three left.

'Not possible,' she called over her shoulder. The chimney entrance she'd come through was at the top of the long rope she'd brought and tied there. She'd find the climb difficult, but for her father and a one-handed Fugger it would be impossible. And she wasn't leaving this chamber without them.

She threw. Heard another cry. *Two left*, she thought.

Then the Fugger remembered, and the memory filled him with instant hope, even as it drowned him in terror.

'The water! Over there, behind the kaleidoscope.'

Beck ran, threw back the heavy wooden cover, looked into the maelstrom of foam. She whirled, fired a stone straight through the middle of the glass chamber, heard a cry.

'Bring my father!'

The Fugger scooped the man up, supporting him under his arm. He rose without objection, allowed himself to be pushed around the altar and through the shattered panes towards his daughter. Then the Fugger looked back. Under the still-writhing armoured form he saw the hand. He stepped back into the chamber and reached for it.

It was then that Heinrich von Solingen managed to wrench off the helmet. The face that appeared was a mask, a gargoyle, burnt and pitted and still smoking, skin peeling off forehead and cheek, eyebrows gone, eyelashes dissolved, one eye sealed shut. Through the other, a fierce blue gleam fixed upon the Fugger, and a mailed fist clamped down on his handless wrist. A voice emerged from the wreckage of the face.

'I will find you. Wherever you go, I will be there. In the end, you will beg me for your death.'

The Fugger felt the metal grip begin to crush. He cried out in dreadful pain. Then it seemed that the hand beneath the armour, the hand of a dead queen, opened, and with a howl of agony von Solingen fell back on it, clutching at his heart.

As Beck screamed 'Now, Fugger, come!' three guards finally burst through the doorway of the dungeon. He picked up the stiletto Cibo had dropped and made to step around the altar.

'Please.' The whisper came from right beside him. 'Please don't leave me here.'

The Fugger looked at the girl lying there in her virgin white linen robe, saw her freckled face, the desperation in the weeping brown eyes. He reached out his one hand to her.

'Come then,' he said gently, helping her climb down and move around the altar as if they had all the hours in the day, stepping carefully over the coloured shards at the back of the kaleidoscope, just as the first armed man came through its entrance.

A stone sailed over their heads, striking the guard full in the face.

'That's it! None left. Let's go!'

The Fugger stared into the foam. For a second there was only the roaring, the terrible churning of its surge.

'It's our only chance!' Beck had manoeuvred her father over the hole. She had swiftly tied the slingshot around their waists, binding them together. 'Go on!'

With the barest of glances back at the armed men now running out of the glass chamber, and with only a little scream of terror, the girl leapt and in an instant was sucked away.

'I'll stay.' The Fugger turned, dagger in hand, to face the enemy. He suddenly felt that this was a fine place to die. A dry one, anyway.

Beck didn't hesitate. 'You won't,' she said and, giving the Fugger a hard shove, she and her father followed him into the water.

The Fugger managed, 'But I can't sw—' but the last word was lost in the torrent.

Cibo gazed down into the water.

'After them!' he said, and when none of his men moved, he screamed, 'Obey me, fools!'

The guards looked at each other, looked away, looked anywhere to avoid their master's raging eyes.

'Very well,' he said, softly now. 'Then bring me Gianluca.'

The wounded guard, the first who had come through the door, was dropped at Cibo's feet.

'We need a marker.' The velvet voice was quiet, reasonable. 'We have to know where they come up. You're volunteered.'

He reached down and, with a strength surprising in an older man, tipped the soldier into the water.

A flailing arm waved from the foam as if in farewell and was gone.

'Search the river banks, all the secret pools. And remember this: I want them alive!'

With that, the Archbishop of Siena returned to the centre of his ruined kaleidoscope. He reached under von Solingen and, eyes averted, plucked the hand from the centre of the scattered sand pentangle. Dropping it into the velvet bag, he threw it onto the altar, then gazed at the gibbering monks, his growling mistress and his groaning bodyguard writhing among the shards of broken glass.

'Oh yes,' Giancarlo Cibo said to no one in particular, 'I want them very much alive.'

# SIX

# MIRACLES

Like most criminals she knew, Lucrezia was very religious.
And like many from the street, once she was done in the
church reciting the paternoster, the creed and three aves, once
the candles were lit and the foot of the Virgin kissed the
requisite nine and ninety times, she had begun on other
measures. She was the one people usually came to in such
circumstances, for she was the cunning woman of the
Scorpion *contrada* and she knew just what these measures
should be.

'Fetch them,' she had said.

The two young men she most suspected of abducting her
daughter had been seized by three of her burly brothers and
brought before her. They had pleaded innocence, as they
would. Nonetheless, she had made them lay their fingers
upon the shears she stuck in the edge of a sieve; yet it had not
turned to accuse either, but pointed resolutely to a third,
unknown party. A neighbour's son of eight, an albino in
whose strange eyes the future could often be discerned by one
who had the far sight, as she did, again did not accuse the two
– no vision of them had appeared to cloud his orange-tinged
orbs. And so, even though she knew how they had lusted after
her sweet Maria-Theresa, she had let the young men go.

The word had then been put out through all the clans of
Siena, and even though this was a busy time and one of great
rivalry between them, being the very eve of the Palio, a

missing child was a missing child; also, many had had dealings with Lucrezia, for she could make stolen goods disappear quicker, and for more money, than anyone in Tuscany. So information and sightings had come in gradually all day. One rumour said the girl had fallen in love with a boy from the Viper *contrada*, they'd been married in secret and were enjoying their nuptials even now. Lucrezia had dismissed that report because she knew her Maria-Theresa. She had raised her to be as innocent and pure as she, her mother, was worldly and corrupt.

Another report had been more disturbing. A girl had been seen by a guard at the Archbishop's palace entering the secret side gate just before midnight. This guard had told his cousin. Many girls entered the palace, for their holy Archbishop was renowned for his appetites, but most girls did so willingly, for the rewards therein. This girl, said the guard to his cousin, had wept piteously but hopelessly before the German, Cibo's shadow, who had dragged her inside.

The more she had thought about the palace, the more distressed Lucrezia had become. She rarely slept the night before the Palio anyway, but now, sickened by worry, she only had to close her eyes for a vision of evil to overwhelm her.

Lying there beside her fireplace, going over and over the steps she had taken and the few that were left to try, Lucrezia realised where she must go. There was only one place in Siena where this answer could be sought. It was holier even than the Oratory of her *contrada* in the Via Camollia.

She set off through the dark, near-silent streets, thinking of her destination. It was where her beloved Vittorio had proposed to her, and where he had died in her arms. She had not visited the Fountain of the Willows since that day ten years before. She had been planning on bringing her Maria-Theresa there, now that she was coming to womanhood. There were secrets that they had to share.

It lay just within the north wall of the city, on slopes too rocky for dwellings and thus unspoilt by humanity. The stream that gushed out of the rock was renowned for the purity of its water, its healing strength a miniature waterfall falling twenty feet down into a small pool. The pool was shaded, almost concealed, by three willows. It was deep, but no one had ever explored its depths; for it was said a siren lived down there who would drown any who violated her domain.

Lucrezia pushed through the drooping branches. A moon, three days from full, pierced the canopy with light, falling on the ancient statue, an armless maiden in a toga with hair bound up in the Roman style, moss- and creeper-covered. Lucrezia knew this was what many saw as the spirit of the pool, but not her. The nymph she prayed to and had often seen from the corner of her eye was naked, a girl barely come to womanhood, who ran across the water's surface as lightly as the Lord Jesus had upon the sea of Galilee. She had heard many prayers and granted not a few. She was the only one who could help Lucrezia now.

She sat at the water's edge and crumbled the bread she'd brought, throwing it out in an arc towards the middle of the pond. Large carp with fat, burnished bellies floated to the surface, snatching at the offering, dragging it below in flashes of gold. Then for the first time she took off the ring her beloved Vittorio, second husband but first love, had placed on her finger at this very place; she took it, kissed it, then threw it into the centre of the water. As the ripples coursed back towards her, she began to pray in a tongue long since vanished from the land but kept in the hearts of those who had the far sight, the tongue of the people who first lived by this pool and the one the nymph, young as a girl, ancient as the earth, must surely speak.

In the pool's moonlit surface, Lucrezia saw her face change to what it had been twenty years before, when she was as young as her Maria-Theresa. She asked, in that original tongue, for the chance to teach her only daughter the wisdom of this sacred space.

She was puzzled when the waterfall that flowed for ever, even if just as a trickle in the worst of droughts, suddenly stopped. Yet there was no time to marvel for in five beats of her heart water exploded again from the rock and with it a body. It crashed into the water before her, showering her in spray, and she leapt back with an oath of terror. For a face was once more staring from the mirror of the rippling pond, the face of herself as she had been twenty years before, yet different. The face of Maria-Theresa.

The miracle in the water spat at her and she heard her daughter cry, 'Mama.' She swiftly had her arms under the flailing body and pulled it from the pool, to flop upon her like a tickled carp.

It was just in time. The space vacated was immediately filled by another falling shape, screaming and corkscrewing as it came. It hit the water flat, arms spread wide, straight onto its belly.

'Holy God in Heaven!' screamed the Fugger. 'That hurt! Help me or I drown!'

Mother and daughter reached down together and dragged him to the pond's edge where he managed to claw his way onto the bank. He rested there, sobbing.

'Never again,' he gasped. 'I will grow old and dirty and happy. No more swimming.'

It was then that the water stopped once more, for several seconds this time, until an eight-limbed creature shot out of the wall above them like a ball from a cannon, soaking them all. Beck was pinned under the unconscious weight of her father, but hands loosened the slingshot ties binding them together, pulling them clear just as she was beginning to enjoy the feeling of no air in her body.

Beck fell back, gasping until she became aware that her shirt, and the bindings underneath, loosened in the pell-mell water descent, had flopped open. As she struggled to readjust her clothing, she looked up and saw the eyes of the Fugger, staring in shock at the folds she had closed too late.

It didn't take long for the last body to come through, and though he was grappled onto the bank to lie beside the others, Cibo's guard was undoubtedly dead, his skull stoved in by one of the collisions in the rocky passages above that the others had miraculously avoided. Yet he was no more speechless than the rest of them, for the normally loquacious Lucrezia could only stare at her daughter and sob, while Maria-Theresa did the same back. The shaking terrors went on for several minutes, during which time Abraham awoke, to a similar speechless sense of wonder.

Finally, Maria-Theresa managed to say, 'Mama, these people saved my life. But I think they are in great danger now.'

Lucrezia Asti loved nothing more than a purpose in life.

'Come.'

Clutching her miracle to her side, she led them out through the willow branches. She held them aside for the others to stagger through, then glanced back once to the waterfall, bowing her head in gratitude. As the green curtain fell she heard, within the swish of foliage, the faint but unmistakable sound of a girlish laugh.

'No!' screamed the Archbishop, backhanding his manservant, getting momentary relief from his frustration at the sound of the blow. 'I do not want to hear about the difficulties. I know it is the day of the Palio. Do you think I am dressing like this for my pleasure?'

He gestured for the other man in the room, the tailor, to approach again, and the old man did, nervously eyeing Cibo's jewel-laden fingers. Very carefully, he continued to affix the ceremonial ermine to the collar. It required stitching, and the Archbishop was always fidgety with a sharp point near his throat.

The tunic was of Cathay silk, the robes over it of finest Anatolian lambswool, dyed with the livid purples only found in certain muds in the streams of the high Atlas. The needlework had taken the Sisters of St Matilda two weeks to complete, the pearls mounted in a complex pattern denoting the astrological alignment that prefigured His Holiness' birth. Woven into the gold cross that stretched from neck to waist and across the chest were tiny filigree patterns of a deeper reddish-gold. Only the most sharp-sighted would be able to see they were in the shape of a series of fighting cocks, engaged in the very act of the contest, wickedly curved spurs glinting at their heels, combs raised in the attitude of combat. As the Archbishop of Siena, he was above the rivalries that rent the city this one day of the year. As a Sienese of the Rooster *contrada*, he was as passionate as any of his tribe.

The servant, hand raised to his throbbing cheek, spoke again, making sure he stayed out of the range of his master's fists.

'The word has gone out, Your Holiness. Your spies stroll the streets, the criers declare your generous reward in the taverns. Descriptions have been circulated.'

The servant felt it unwise to mention the joke he'd heard that morning, already doing the rounds, based on the fugitives' descriptions. It involved the sexual permutations wrought from a one-handed fool, a virgin and a Jew. He did not think the Archbishop would appreciate the humour.

'And my brother?'

'Your brother, Eminence?'

Cibo flapped the tailor away and moved towards the servant, who backed off, hands raised nervously to ward off a blow.

'My brother, yes, my brother, returned to the city last night. Sent for these five hours since.' The voice was calm again, silky. 'Why does the Duke di Linari not come?'

'Eminence' – the servant bumped into a pillar, was pinned there, his eyes seeking to avoid his master's – 'he sends word that he will attend when he can.'

'When he . . . can?'

'He is preparing, my Lord. You know, for the Palio?'

The servant smiled, which was foolish. He had nowhere to retreat, and the blows fell on him from every side. He covered his face as well as he could.

'The Palio! The Palio! Will you never cease squawking? On and on. I ask for my brother to come to me and you obviously failed to convey the importance of immediate response. Idiot! Dolt! Where is my whip? I will lash you to a bloodied mess. My whip, I say!'

'Here,' someone growled from the doorway, 'you can use mine.'

Cibo turned at the familiar voice to an unfamiliar and bizarre sight. A giant rooster stood there, crimson and emerald feathers across a vault of a chest, wings of chestnut brown, a black, silver and red coxcomb cresting a mask from whose centre protruded the sharp blade of a beak. The long neck of the bird was covered in white feathers, but in the middle were two slits. Behind them, something twinkled.

Hand raised to strike again, Cibo paused. 'Franchetto?' he said. 'What in hell's jaws are you wearing?'

'My colours.'

The rooster strode stiff-legged into the room. The stockings were black and wound about with red and gold straps. At his groin, a monstrous codpiece proclaimed a cockerel's chief function. At his heels, two curving Arab blades glinted. The bird stopped in front of the two men. The long neck bent down to inspect the Archbishop's chest, the head on an angle, as if considering a tasty piece of food.

'You have to hide your cock, being the impartial Archbishop, while I' – and here he preened, displaying his leg, thrusting out at chest and groin – 'I am free to display all the finery of my allegiance.'

He turned, walked a few paces back. Flapping his wings, stretching them wide, he let out a huge crow.

'Have you seen my latest trick? It's better than a whip. Stand back and watch this. That's right, another pace.'

The rooster whirled into the air, leaping from one foot to

the other, spinning round in a circle, heels high. The servant cowered against the pillar, his hands still raised to ward off a blow. The blade at the cockerel's left ankle sliced his little finger off.

'Cock a doodle dee,' crowed the bird, 'another victory to me!'

As the servant stumbled from the room gushing blood, Cibo laughed. 'Always so good to see you, brother.'

'And you,' said the bird, reaching up to pull off the head-dress and mask in one piece. 'Let me kiss you.'

It was a moment Cibo dreaded; but, as a sibling and a Churchman, he could hardly refuse the embrace. It was a relief then to see that the face emerging from the feathers was less ravaged than usual, the high forehead under its dark thatch ruddy, that plug of a Roman nose, and the jowly cheeks unspotted by canker. He would never be the Adonis of his youth, dissipation had seen to that. But the new cure for the French disease appeared to be working, at least temporarily, and he wondered if it had had any effect elsewhere. The skin was clearer, but what of the mind? Cibo, in his studies, had often noted the link between the rotting faces of the syphilitic and the blinding insanity that also seemed to afflict most of its victims. But, of course, with Franchetto any progression was hard to calculate, for he had been mad from birth.

*And yet*, Cibo considered, *this has not stopped him becoming the most powerful man in Siena. After me. And it hasn't been any evenness of mind that has got him there. Indeed, with the amount of blood Franchetto has had to spill to achieve power, the madness has been an advantage.*

*The Cibo brothers*, the Archbishop continued to reflect as the younger brother embraced the elder, *together again. The power restored to Siena, the twin pillars of society, Church and state. Giancarlo running the holy, Franchetto the secular, just as our father planned.*

Whenever he hadn't seen his younger sibling for a while,

Cibo always marvelled at their physical difference. Down to the mothers, of course, which accounted for his own refined features and the peasant, big-boned coarseness of the Duke.

Saying a little prayer in the hope that Papa, the late Pope Alexander, was enjoying some special torment in hell, the Archbishop hugged his brother back.

'Big brother.' Franchetto nuzzled into the other's neck then turned to plant a kiss and whisper into his ear, 'I have missed you. I have so much to tell you.'

'And I you, little brother.' Cibo disengaged himself from the large man's embrace and turned to the tailor. 'Leave us. Return an hour before the race.'

When the man had retreated from the room, Cibo shrugged off the heavy wool cloak and went to fill two crystal goblets from the decanter. He took them on a tray back to the chair his brother had sprawled over, his huge legs straddling one arm, swinging restlessly. The Churchman knew he could not keep Franchetto's attention long, especially on the day of the Palio.

'Your choice,' he said. Franchetto smiled and chose the left one. It was a game they always played, but it was a game with a serious history. Their father had died shrieking, poisoned by a brother. Not even a half brother.

Sipping, Franchetto said, 'And your travels? They were successful?'

'Up to a point. I ran into certain difficulties. But I got what I was after.'

'Oh yes?' Franchetto's tone betrayed his boredom. 'And what was that? You never told me.'

In answer, Cibo threw the velvet bag into his brother's lap and went to stand by the tall windows of the dressing chamber. On the street beneath the palace walls, costumed figures darted around on the personal errands of the Palio.

'It's a hand.'

'Yes.'

'You journeyed to England for some criminal's hand? My

gaolers take half a dozen every week. You could have had one of them.'

'Do you notice anything special about it?'

Franchetto turned it over and over. At last, with some triumph, he said, 'It's a woman's hand.'

'Very good. Anything else?'

It took a while longer, but when the oaths came they were loud and vehement.

'Yes! Six fingers!' Cibo continued staring down at the street. 'They used to fidget in the lap of Henry's queen, Anne Boleyn.'

'The witch? The whore majesty?' Franchetto was animated now. 'They say she knew tricks even my Cecilia is ignorant of. Which doesn't leave much out.' He placed it on top of his codpiece with a sigh. 'If only the dead could awaken, eh?'

The Archbishop turned from the window. 'That is exactly the point.'

Franchetto was puzzled. 'But you've been gone the best part of two months. What have you kept this in?' He sniffed it. 'It doesn't smell of brandy. Smells of . . . flowers.'

'I haven't kept it in anything.'

'Then . . . Holy Christ! Holy Christ!'

'And that is my other point. Look, pick it up off the floor and put it back in the bag, will you? I can't touch it. I can't even look at it. I'll explain why.'

And to a now attentive Franchetto he briefly retold the story of his journey, the triumph and the setbacks, ending in the events of the night before in the chamber deep below them. His brother was suitably impressed with the tales, up to the last, when his humour got the better of him.

'Oh, Giancarlo, big brother!' He wiped tears from his eyes. 'In the heart of your palace? In the middle of an orgy? You with that stag's head? How frustrated you must be! But you still have the hand. You can try again. I'll find you another virgin, it'll be my pleasure. What more do you need?'

The Archbishop kept his temper. Franchetto was the only

person he had to do that with, and it gave him a pain in his stomach.

'I need Abraham. Without him I cannot hope to free the essence of humanity latent in this hand. Which will make me – and you, dear brother – the most powerful men in Italy. No, in the world.'

He went to look once more down into the street.

'Make no mistake, brother,' he continued, 'it is vital we find both the Jew and these dogs who rescued him. For once the secrets of this hand are revealed, we will be in control of nothing less than the quintessence of life itself.'

# SEVEN

# THE PALIO

It was a fine day for a horse race. The sun shone from a cornflower-blue sky, unblemished by cloud, yet the heat was tempered by one of those breezes the Sienese called 'the breath of the Virgin', fragrant with almond blossom, borne down from the Tuscan hills. In addition, the fountains had been scattered with rose petals and filled with the distillations of rosehip, so the sweet smell of that flower pervaded the city too. It was those scents, mingling with the musk of the chosen horses, one for each *contrada*, that created the particular savour all in the city adored. The citizens' nostrils filled with it – that and the equally strong scent of money to be had. For on this one day of the year money flowed around the city like water from the thousand fountains, passing from the purses of rich and poor alike to the sellers of meat and wine, to the whores and the pickpockets, the fire-eaters and the stiltwalkers, to the men who gave odds on the race and those who sought to change those odds with bribes to jockey, trainer and groom. Fortunes won and lost, reputations shattered and made, lives ended in tavern brawls and alley assassinations and life begun in the same locations as the lust for money transformed to the lust for flesh. It was the day to put aside one's identity and don another with a mask, to revel in the freedom granted by a disguise.

It was the day of the Palio.

But in the stable of Lucrezia's house, the heart of the

Scorpion *contrada*, people were not thinking of fortunes, they were thinking of survival. The stallion on whom the hopes of so many rested stood unattended in his stall, for one of Lucrezia's brothers was its trainer and her nephew its jockey, and they too were crouched down on the stable floor hearing of a night of horror beneath a palace.

When she finished telling her tale, the tears flowed again down the cheeks of Maria-Theresa. She wiped them away with her one free hand, the other holding on tightly to the only hand of her saviour, as it had almost from the moment they emerged from the pool. The Fugger was unspeakably content with this and made no effort to free himself. In his life, he had never held the hand of a woman other than his mother. And she had never caused such strange and complex stirrings within him. The life he observed in this girl, who was also a woman – the innocence, the purity yet power of her feelings – was of such a force it made him feel like a page of new paper with nothing written upon it, no years of degradation, no tales of endless nights scrabbling for survival in a gibbet midden. It made him feel alive. He was conscious of the glances that came his way from her family, but they were not hostile, just curious. The only thing distracting him from the way Maria-Theresa's hand moved in his was the mirror sight opposite where his comrade Beck clutched at the old man's hand.

He looked, and remembered the woman's body swiftly hidden again under the man's clothing. He'd kept silent, knowing that if someone felt they had to go to that trouble to conceal who they were there must be good reason. He knew about concealed identities. He would wait to know . . . hers.

As Beck looked away briefly from the father she had not seen in ten years, she met the Fugger's eyes and she too remembered. It troubled her, yet she'd only donned the disguise to achieve what she had now achieved, to hold her father again in her arms. In a whispered conversation she'd begged Abraham also to keep her secret for a while, yet she wasn't sure why. Except that now was perhaps not the time to be herself again. For as she listened to Lucrezia, she knew danger was far from past.

'I have been out on the streets. There's a prince's ransom offered for the capture, alive, of this gentleman' – she indicated Abraham with her hand – 'and not much less for the rest of you. The gates are all shut and heavily guarded. The spies of Church and state are spreading throughout the city. I myself was asked if I knew a woman who was looking for a kidnapped virgin. It is only a matter of time before someone takes the gold and talks.'

Maria-Theresa spoke. 'We cannot give them up, Mother. I would have died. I will die before I let them go.'

'No one is speaking of giving them up, child. But how do we save them?'

Beck said, '*All* the gates are locked?'

'All save the Porta Pispini. And men with good descriptions search anyone trying to leave.' Lucrezia moved to the stallion in its stall, stroked its neck. 'What if we split you up? Wait till the revelry tonight. Even the guards will be drunk then.'

'We will not be split up,' said the Fugger, and looked at Beck who nodded, held his eye for a moment, blushed and looked away. 'We must go to Montepulciano. We are to meet our comrade there, and in the meantime his friend there will shelter us at his inn.'

'Montepulciano is still beyond the city walls. The hills there are said to be the source of many of the springs that fill Siena with water. The source—' Lucrezia broke off. 'The cisterns, Giuseppe. What do you think?'

Her brother rubbed his grey stubble. 'It is possible. I have not been down them for many years.'

'I have.' Maria-Theresa leant forward excitedly. 'Giovanni took me there last year to play.' Giuseppe gave his son the jockey a clout around the ears.

'Cisterns?' said the Fugger.

244

'The rich in this city, about two hundred years ago during a plague, wanted their own water supply that could not be contaminated by us peasants.' Lucrezia spat on the floor. 'They built these chambers, tunnels, underground channels to bring it to them. Then more water was discovered and they fell into disrepair. The passage you came down to the pool was probably one of them. Some lead out, it is said, in the direction of Montepulciano.'

The Fugger leant forward. 'It is said?'

'No one to my knowledge has ever followed them all the way out. But water still flows from them. And what comes in . . .'

'. . . Must lead out.' Beck stood. 'We will take them. I will not stay here to be caught like a weasel in a trap.'

'Now wait!' The Fugger rose too. 'I made a promise to myself. You all heard me. Not three hours ago. No more water. Ever. And you want me to go to a world of it?'

'But I will be there.' Maria-Theresa's eyes shone up at him. 'I will lead you through them. There are many walkways. You won't have to swim much.'

'It's that "much" that concerns me.'

But the squeezing of the girl's hand did a little to calm him. A fragile calm that was immediately broken by her next words.

'The problem is the way into them. Giovanni and I only know of the one. It's a hidden entrance. But it is in a corner of a public place.'

'And where is that?'

It was Lucrezia who answered. 'The Piazza del Campo.'

The Fugger choked. 'But isn't that where they hold this thing, this Palio?'

Lucrezia smiled. 'It's where "this thing" starts and finishes. The bullfight was last night, the fist fight this morning. At noon the horses will be loosed through the city streets from there.'

'Good.' Beck was on her feet now, tying the slingshot

around her. 'The Campo is where we need to go anyway. I left Fenrir and our sacks with a stall holder there.'

'Are you all mad?' cried the Fugger. 'It's right beside Cibo's palace! He – all of them – will be there!'

Lucrezia's smile never faded. 'In a lifetime of doing it,' she said, 'I've discovered there is no better place to hide than in plain sight.'

Giuseppe was backing the stallion out of the stall, bridling him. Lucrezia left and returned with masks and costumes. Handing them over, she said, 'Welcome to the best team in Siena – the Scorpions!'

Humming a hymn of battle, the party flung open the doors of the stable and marched out to the street where the rest of the *contrada*'s members, numbering some hundred and fifty, were already gathered under the crimson banner with its black and menacing emblem, its wicked sting curving above them.

The Fugger barely had time to mutter, 'I thought I was the mad one,' before a young woman's hand was once more thrust into his and he was dragged into the middle of the parade. A clash of drums and cymbals, a chorus from a dozen trumpets, a shout of 'Scorpio!' and the procession lurched off.

Reports came in to Heinrich and Franchetto from spies cast like a fisherman's net over the city. There were many sightings, but always something wrong in the detail. The Jew was monstrous, as Jews often were, with gold teeth and a hump. The young man was a Biblical warrior with a curved sword, the madman missed a leg as well as a hand, while the virgin had turned whore and plied her trade in a house near the Palazzo Marescotti. The fugitives were said to lurk under the banner of the Wolf, the Snail or the Scorpion, bound to their *contrada* by an oath of death.

On any other day, time would yield them up. It was not that big a city, and the reward was enormous. But time, Heinrich knew, was what the pursuers didn't have. Many of those attending the Palio came from beyond the city walls. They would be drunk and happy for the first few hours after the race, then drunk and quarrelsome, finally drunk and morose and wanting to go home. To try to funnel them through the one gate while Heinrich observed each face would be to provoke a riot that not even Franchetto and his men, in the full flow of their brutality, could control.

With a hunter's sense, Heinrich put himself in the position of the hunted. They would know of the beaters, the armed gangs who swept through every neighbourhood offering inducements to betrayal, both violent and financial. Only the sick or the guilty remained behind on this one day, and quarry would be too easily flushed out. Within the thousands on the street, then, lay the security of the herd. The wolf pack could snap at the edges, but most would remain safe within the centre of the drove. It was like the retreat from a battlefield. Keep together, present a solid block, you had a better shot at survival. Flee on your own, and you would be chased down and butchered.

*They are here, or will be soon*, he thought as another passer-by paused to acclaim the horrific wonder of his 'mask', then realised his error and moved swiftly on. Heinrich had looked in a mirror just once and knew what it was people saw. His face was one vivid wound, a scarlet gash from brow to chin, raw and weeping. He could still see, now that the fused lashes had been prised apart, but the missing eyebrows gave him the look of a skull.

*All the more reason to find them*, he thought. *They will also pay for this.*

He was standing with his back to the Palazzo Pubblico, the opposite end to the tower, looking across the Campo as the crowds swept in, each *contrada* preceded by its banner and its huge war cart constructed to resemble the individual symbols. A giant Swan nuzzled at a Scorpion, a Caterpillar duelled with a Unicorn, each entrance to the square greeted by mighty cheers and equally raucous boos, swelling as each cart was taken from the overcrowded square. Already at least twenty banners waved above their yelling partisans, which left at least ten more *contrade* to go, though where such numbers would fit he could not see. Huge numbers crammed the central space, held in a ring of fences and armoured troops; others packed every terrace, balcony and colonnade opposite them. Between, an outer ring was kept clear for the main reason everyone was there: the race.

With a burst of crowing, the Rooster *contrada* entered the Campo, at its head the tall, strutting figure of the Duke Franchetto, resplendent in his brown, crimson and emerald feathers. Heinrich decided to note where he settled. Then he would join him so they could co-ordinate the search of the square from within.

A sudden explosion of greater noise within the hubbub, screams of panic and abuse. Just to Heinrich's left, a baker's cart burst out of a side alley, sending vast wheels of bread rolling in all directions, pastries flying through the air, tarts sliding underfoot. Once collapsed, though, the cart did not stay still, for something was moving under its fallen awning and the whole structure was advancing steadily across the ground in a crush of flour, sweetmeat fillings and splintered wood, scattering people on every side. The baker ran along beside it, a switch in his hand, raining blows down on the moving bulge, a curse for every strike.

'Bastard! Assassin!'

The stick rose and fell but did nothing to halt the cart's progress. The awning got caught on another cart, skewing it, slipping gradually off, and from under it a huge, snarling animal appeared, more wolf than dog, its grey-white pelt bespeckled with flour. It paused to catch the switch in its vast jaws, wrench it from the baker's hands and snap it to kindling. Triumphant, it let out a long howl. Then it resumed its relentless march forward, pushing through the outer rim of spectators and across the race track, seeking to enter into the heart of the central crowd itself, dragging the cart with it.

Heinrich had heard that howl before. *Where had it been?* A sudden throbbing at his temple made him reach up and touch the swollen skin there. Then the memory came. The ambush in the hills outside Toulon had been preceded by the same howl.

'The dog! Grab the dog!' he yelled at the half dozen men-at-arms beside him. Two got themselves bitten in their enthusiasm to obey the order while a third, more sensibly, gathered up the awning and threw it again onto the animal. It took the unbitten four to hold it down, but eventually there were no more stirrings from beneath.

'A young man, no more than a boy really.' The vendor was shivering under Heinrich's questions. 'He left that cur with me, said he'd be back later, gave me two scudi for my trouble. Two scudi! Look at what it's cost me. Three nights' baking, a month of living at the least. Holy Mary!'

'You! Get a stick and collar on it. Now!' Heinrich ordered.

It was a struggle, and one man was badly mauled, but finally the hound had a rope round its neck and a long stick wedged in, attached through a loop and twisted tight, allowing the men to keep the dog thrust before them. They forced it to the ground, waiting for orders.

Heinrich looked across the crowd and saw that the main entrance to the Campo was closed off, that all the *contrade* were in position inside, the horses already being led to the starting point up to the right of the Palazzo Pubblico.

'Now.' He bent down until his eyes were level with the strange, rectangular, maddened ones of the dog. 'Let's just see who it was you were trying to find.'

Gathering his six armoured men behind him, he signalled the two who held the stick tight to loosen their grip. The dog immediately rose and plunged, snarling, into the central crowd, causing the impenetrable barrier of humankind to give way, opening a channel that the soldiers quickly widened to a breach. Heinrich, taller by a head than most of the Italians round him, immediately saw the direction in which they were moving and it puzzled him. They were making for the huge black, red and gold Rooster, the richest flag in the square. Towards Franchetto Cibo. But when his banner started waving back and forth, Heinrich saw another revealed behind it. On it a black creature of scales, claws and hideous fangs dripping poison.

The dog was making straight for the sign of the Scorpion.

Years of lonely vigil at a gibbet had left the Fugger unprepared for the Palio crowd. The heat, the panic of being trapped by walls of bodies, the close confines of the heavy leather Scorpion mask meant that he was soaked in sweat long before he entered the square. And the sight of so many armed men engaged in an obvious search did nothing to calm him. What was worse was the knowledge that many in masks were also thus engaged, that a hundred spies or more moved among the crowd. Every mask that loomed towards them could conceal an enemy. Only Maria-Theresa soothed him a little, never relinquishing his hand.

Beck was faring better, mainly because her concern was so focused on her father. Abraham was frail and here, pushed and buffeted by the crowd, he was beginning to sway alarmingly. His forehead was heated and slick, his tongue swollen, he complained of cramps. He said he lacked the medicine he depended on from the kaleidoscope.

There was nothing for them to do but wait as Lùcrezia had decreed. Once the race was over, mayhem would be loosed upon the streets, and under the cover of that revelry the fugitives would be able to disappear underground. That was her firm belief and nothing, not even the appearance by their side of the Cibos' Rooster *contrada*, would change it.

'Soon, soon!' she shouted into the Fugger's ear above the noise. 'It is a huge build-up, then the event is over in a moment. A little like my first husband!'

A bigger roar, and all faces turned to the balcony of the palace as the Archbishop emerged, preceded by his guard of twenty wielding their halberds. The horses, in the colours and symbols of their respective *contrade*, the jockeys in bright coats and caps, bare-backed and struggling to contain their spirited mounts, were gathered below to be blessed. The Scorpions, like all the others, surged forward, pushing the crowds up against the barriers and soldiers that marked off the race track. The Fugger, Beck, Abraham and everyone else found themselves picked up and swept along, their feet dangling under them. And the Fugger, perhaps half a head taller than those around him, saw through the slit-eyes of his mask another mask more grotesque than any in the crowd around him, all the more horrific for being made, not of leather and cloth, but of flesh and hair. Heinrich von Solingen was moving towards them, against the tide of the crowd, with a force of armed soldiers behind him. He was not thirty paces away.

'Beck! Beck!' The Fugger struggled to make himself heard above the tumult, but in vain. Lowering his head, he whispered fiercely to the girl beside him, 'He comes! The enemy! Somehow he knows us!'

For Maria-Theresa, there was no hesitation, no politeness. Sharp elbows in ribs opened a channel to her mother, who listened and spoke quickly to those about them. A little passage was forced through the human wall and Beck, the Fugger and Abraham were pushed into it, heading away at an angle from their pursuers, up towards the tower. They were halfway from the crowd's periphery when they heard a sound within the greater noise that caused their step to stutter. A long, hunter's howl.

Beck's and the Fugger's eyes met.

'Fenrir!' they both said, and as they did the Fugger saw von Solingen turn towards them again, leading his phalanx of men unerringly to where they were.

Urging Lucrezia and Giuseppe to redouble their efforts to get them through the crowd, Beck and the Fugger thrust as hard as any. But they did not have the force of a wolf before and armoured men behind, and the gap between them narrowed.

It was hard to detect little shifts in such a crowd, but Heinrich had fought so many battles where noting the slightest change, the merest gap opening, was the key to winning. And here, even in the sea of shapes and colours, he saw a group move from the protection of the Scorpion banner and cut away at a different angle from the rest of the surge, away from the focus of the race. It was odd, and oddity was what he was looking for in this uniformity.

But his were not the only experienced eyes looking for shifts in the crowd. Franchetto Cibo too had seen his brother's bodyguard moving towards them. He too had seen the movement within his Scorpion rivals' ranks.

'Follow me,' he called to his lieutenant, and with ten men at his back and his short whip rising and falling brutally, he began to march steadily to intercept.

Before the Palazzo Pubblico, the blessing was concluded and the horses led off to the starting point under the tower. The Archbishop leant out over the balustrade. Stretched across the front of the balcony was the ancient, tattered relic, the prize for all this, the cloak that was the Palio itself. A remnant of it rested on top, and all in the square were focused on that, for when it fluttered from Giancarlo Cibo's hand, the race was on. Reaching the top of the little flight of three steps, he carefully picked up the fraying square cloth. As Archbishop, he was impartial to the rival factions. As a loyal son of the Roosters, he had worked out a little signal, a slight hesitation before he let the cloth fly. It would not be much, but in the crazed five-minute sprint through the streets that was the Palio, a second's forewarning could make all the difference.

*I've got them.* Heinrich had seen the three figures, different somehow from the rest. The way the small one tried to hurry another limping one along, the way one kept looking back, his strange shuffling gait interrupted by his constant turning.

*Got you.* Ten paces away now, the hound before him, breath heaving between bared fangs, almost pulling his men off their feet in its eagerness. His mind was already turning to the ingenious tortures available to him within the Archbishop's dungeon. He didn't like a lot of what these Italians did, but they were masters of cruelty, he had to admit that.

One of those Italian masters, Franchetto, moving in from a different angle, could see the German a little closer to the prize than he was himself. National pride required him to redouble his efforts, and he laid the whip about him even more enthusiastically. Pride, and the thought of his coffers filling with his brother's gold. He would be first. He had to be first.

A little square of cobalt-blue cloth was raised above the crowd. A slight hesitation and a horse surged forward, hitting its stride just before the cloth fluttered free, just before the rope dropped across the track. Fifty paces along the first stretch, the fleeing Scorpions pressed themselves against the race track's wooden barriers.

'Got you!' yelled Heinrich and Franchetto simultaneously, hands descending just as the cloth fell and the Rooster jockey, cruelly spurring his horse's flanks, stole his lead. Just as Beck yelled 'Under!' and half-dragged, half-pushed her father beneath the wooden rail. Just as Fenrir, delighted at the sight of his friends, burst free of the men who held his leash. Just as the Fugger wriggled out of the cape that Heinrich had grabbed and followed his companions. Just as Maria-Theresa, Lucrezia, Giuseppe and three others from the Scorpion *contrada* also burst through onto the race track.

The screams of those who watched them dash almost under the hooves were lost in the noise of the race. The Fugger saw the massive animals bearing down on him but panic spurred him on, and he even managed to push Abraham none too gently in the back. The horses were all blinkered, but two scented the dog at their feet and reared back, ending the hopes of the followers of Snail and Broadsword. Somehow the group made it across, just as the bulk of the horses crashed by them. One of Franchetto's guards was foolish enough to follow and had his brains dashed out by flying hoofs. The rest had to wait, furious, for the horses to pass.

Sprawled breathless against the opposite barrier with the race still crashing by, it was Beck, pulling her father after her, who urged them on. 'Through! Through!' She was up and pushing at the spectators before her who, stunned, opened up a slight gap through which they fled.

The crowd was thinner here, for most were trying to push towards the finish line on the other end of the Campo, where the horses would re-enter. The Scorpions found a channel and surged through it, but not before the Fugger, glancing back, saw the last of the horses pass, revealing the tortured face of von Solingen and a huge man garbed as a rooster. Both now urged their men across the track.

Maria-Theresa struggled to Beck's side, the Fugger's hand once more held in hers.

'The entrance. It's up that alley beside the palace. Come!'

They had gained maybe fifty paces on their enemy who even now, united in a band of some twenty men, were ducking under the barrier. The scattering crowd would not hold them up for long. Three of the *contrada* had picked Abraham up and were running with him, the old man almost unconscious, urged on by Beck, Fenrir at her side. Maria-Theresa alternated between pulling and being pulled by the Fugger. Lucrezia and Giuseppe ranged ahead trying to clear a path with shouts and blows.

'This way!' yelled the Scorpion leader, her voice carrying above the crowd. 'It's a few paces down the Via di Salicotto!'

They entered the alley at the palazzo's side, only for Maria-Theresa to let out a wail of anger. 'The storm drain! The entrance to the cisterns, it's under that!' A huge cart in the shape of a giant goose was straddling the lane, blocking all progress beyond or down.

'Shift it!' barked Lucrezia, and the Scorpions put their shoulders to the cart and heaved. It gave slowly. Too slowly.

Fenrir bared his teeth and let out a long, low growl.

'Well, well, well,' said Heinrich von Solingen, breathing heavily. 'It looks like this hunt is over. I win the prize.'

At the centre of his men, Franchetto Cibo pulled the Rooster mask from his face and said, 'But I win the money. Know that, German.'

Heinrich nodded, and whispered through burnt lips twisted into a parody of a smile, 'Just as long as their bodies are mine.'

He took a pace forward. A sound, naggingly familiar, made him stop, twitch and instinctively duck.

'Remember me?' Beck stood under the whirling rope of her slingshot. 'This time I really won't miss.'

Two of Franchetto's men raised crossbows.

'If he fires at me,' commanded Heinrich, 'kill the old man.'

The guards began to move down the alley. Long stiletto daggers appeared in the hands of the Scorpions. Even Maria-Theresa had a blade. Like the others, she knew it was hopeless, but she was not going to subject herself to this man's attentions again. She would die there. It was better than the alternative.

'You know,' said a voice familiar to some of the people in the alley, 'I didn't think it was possible for you to get any uglier, German. But it seems I was mistaken.'

Everyone turned. At the alley's end, their backs to the Campo, three Unicorns stood, white surplices flowing to the ground beneath masks that had both mane and horn. One of the unicorns held a bow in his hand. The biggest one, an axe. And the man who had spoken had an unusual square-tipped sword, its wide, flat blade balanced lightly on his shoulder.

'You!' Heinrich spluttered as all three removed their masks and dropped them on the ground. 'Are you a cat? How many lives do you have?'

'More than you,' said Jean Rombaud easily, bringing his

sword down before him and moving forward. 'At least one more than you.'

Both a stone and an arrow flew, and two crossbowmen fell.

'Claim your money, my Lord. Grab the old man and the girl,' said Heinrich, unsheathing his sword. 'I'll deal with this scum.'

Jean swiftly calculated the battle odds. He hadn't come this far to see his friends murdered at the end of an alley.

'Januc, I think they need you down there more than we do.'

'You can handle this many?'

Haakon laughed. The sound went with the battle lust in his eye and two of the enemy broke step when they heard it. 'There are only seven of them. Didn't you see me on the galley?'

'Six,' corrected the janissary, his bow a blur, a feathered shaft appearing as if from thin air in the neck of one of the advancing men. 'Now you might just have a chance.'

With that, he leapt up and caught a flagpole thrust out over them. He spun his legs over, balanced on it, then stepped onto the narrow ledge that ran the length of this side of the palazzo. With a brief salute, he ran down it and leapt off to land lightly between Franchetto Cibo and his quarry, a curved sword suddenly in his hand.

'That man,' said Jean, 'is a show-off.'

Heinrich yelled, 'Get the big brute, leave the French runt to me!'

Haakon looked at Jean. 'Brute?' he said. 'I'm deeply offended.'

'*You're* offended? He called me a runt.'

Then they turned back to the enemy and, as one voice, let out the old mercenary cry.

'Hoch! Hoch!'

They closed, Haakon's axe swung at shoulder height causing five soldiers to leap back. Heinrich side-stepped it to come straight at Jean, his heavy-bladed broadsword chopping down. Sparks flew as finely forged steel met its match, and intensified as Jean changed the square parry over his head to a slope that the German slid down, the force of his charge taking him through and past. A guard to his left, seeing a clear opening, lunged at Jean's exposed chest. Twisting his body sharply round, the sword slid down the front of him, slicing through the Unicorn tunic to the flesh beneath, the force of the lunge bringing his opponent close. Jean dropped his raised hands, the pommel of the sword crashing down onto the guard's knuckles. His scream of pain was swiftly cut off when Jean elbowed him hard in the mouth, knocking him backwards.

Just in time, for Heinrich had recovered from his charge and had borne around swiftly. He thrust at Jean's open back and the Frenchman just had time to drop the sword point square to the ground to parry, the broadsword's blade snickering under his armpit. For a moment they were locked there, looking into each other's eyes over a metal crucifix of Toledo steel, two swordsmen awaiting each other's move.

Their stalemate ended when a body crashed into them both, blood streaming from an axe wound to his shoulder.

'Five!' shouted Haakon exultantly, his triumph ending in another yell as four swords thrust at the stomach he'd exposed after his last killing cut. Three he caught on the haft of the axe, the fourth bit into his hip before he spun it away.

'Bastard!' he yelled at his assailant. 'I hate to bleed!'

And with that he pulled the axe over his head and, chopping down as if splitting kindling, split the man's head in two.

Jean spun away from the impact of the body. Heinrich took it full force, and it pinned him momentarily. Jean had time to look up the alley.

Two men had fallen to Januc's scimitar, two more were engaged with him now. Three Scorpions lay dead, a soldier sprawled across them, while another hacked in blood frenzy at their bodies. The remaining four were driving Beck, the Fugger, an old man, another man and two women Jean didn't know back against the cart, urged on by a screaming man in the plumage of a fighting cock. It was a matter of seconds before they were pinned against the wood by the brutal swords, captured or slaughtered.

'Haakon!' he called. 'To me!'

The Norseman's axe swung in a circle upwards, gathering blades. He swept them up and away, and the enemy, to keep hold, had to follow them. A gap opened and he leapt through it. Jean took a final swipe at Heinrich, whose leg was still pinned by his fallen soldier. He ducked under the square tip, which missed him by a finger's width.

Jean and Haakon arrived just in time. Beck had managed to slash the hand of one man, disarming him, but the other three's flailing weapons had the rest pinned. Januc had wounded another but had taken a cut himself to his forehead and blood was flowing into his eyes. He seemed to be parrying the two weapons that still danced at him – for Franchetto had joined the fray with his rapier, now that the odds were more favourable – by blind instinct.

Jean crashed into the side of one guardsman, Haakon into another, and then they were shoulder to shoulder before the alley end, their companions in the temporary shelter of their weapons. Januc, through his veil of blood, saw that he was isolated and, slipping under the wild swings and lunges of the Duke, joined Haakon on the other side.

'What kept you?' He grinned at them through a veil of blood.

The three were soon four, as a snarling wolf hound ran to his master's side.

'Fenrir! By the grace of the gods!' Haakon bent down and swiftly removed the rope and dragging stick, to be rewarded by frantic licking and whimpers. The Norseman smiled. 'Now I know we will triumph!'

There was a silence for a moment, punctuated by a huge cheer from the square.

'Ah!' Lucrezia gasped. 'Someone has won the Palio.'

Jean, Haakon and Januc levelled their weapons out before them, to counter the ten now levelled at them – for Heinrich had come forward with his remaining men. For a moment there was only the intense deep breaths coming from them all as they waited for someone to make the first move. Jean had seen the way Haakon had limped, he could see Januc reaching up to wipe away blood every few seconds. His own side pained him badly now he had time to feel it. The enemy were far from unscathed, but they were still double their numbers.

Heinrich knew it too.

'It is over. Surrender now, and maybe some of you will be spared. The women, anyway. They at least have their uses.'

His men laughed and leered. Behind him, Jean heard Beck curse.

'Fuck you! I'll have your balls on this pick before you have anything from me!'

Which Jean, even with his mind elsewhere, thought was odd coming from a boy. Then he was distracted by the sound of a cough and a voice, low and silky. It instantly brought back to him the nightmare of the gibbet cage.

'Really, Heinrich. When you can take what you want, why do you bargain?' The Archbishop of Siena stood with his back to the Campo. Behind him were his twenty bodyguards. He smiled again as his men moved forward. 'So let us finish what you have started. No bargaining is required. They either throw down their weapons or they die on the spot.'

'One question, Most Holy Father, before we face our most holy punishment.' Lucrezia's voice was thick with contempt. 'Who won the Palio?'

'Ah, my daughter, I regret to have to inform you, and my dear brother, that we cannot crow in triumph today. We – the Rooster *contrada*, that is – came second.'

'Mother of God!' stormed Franchetto. 'Who has dared defeat us?'

'It's a sting in the tail to be sure,' said his brother. 'For the first time in half a century, it is the year of the Scorpion.'

The cheer of 'Scorpio!' that broke from mother, daughter and uncle resounded down the alley. The Fugger looked wonderingly at the girl, then mutely gestured to the advancing swords.

'I know,' said Maria-Theresa, eyes bright, 'but don't you understand? This is really important. This is the Palio.'

Lucrezia stretched out her knife before her. 'I have lived long enough,' she sighed. 'This is a good day to die. Scorpio!'

To the ranks of men halting before this defiance, this cry seemed to echo for ever down the little alley. Then all became aware that it was not an echo at all, but a chant taken up by scores of voices growing rapidly nearer. Within moments, the banner with its scaly, carapaced creature, poison dripping from its fangs, was waving at the alley's entrance. Under it were a hundred and fifty celebrating Scorpions.

'Father!' yelled Giovanni from beneath the flag, oblivious in his joy to the scene between them. 'Aunt! We won! We won!'

'Yes, nephew,' yelled back Lucrezia, 'but unless you speed to us, like our Mephisto to the finishing line, we will have lost!'

And thinking of no faster way to bring them she leapt forward and stabbed the nearest guardsman in the chest.

The Scorpions drew their stilettos and rushed forward under their banner. Jean, Januc and Haakon whirled and struck out before them and the combination of assaults, in front and behind, caused the bodyguard rank to implode. In vain did Heinrich, Franchetto and the Archbishop cry for order. The alley dissolved into a mass of flailing bodies in which the heavier arms of the soldiers were of no advantage. It was as if a tide had rushed into a sea cavern, all order flung apart like jetsam.

While the warriors kept at bay any soldier thrown out from the riot, Maria-Theresa and her uncle managed to crawl under the cart and prise off the drain cover.

'Quickly!' Lucrezia shouted in Jean's ear. 'This way!'

The girl went first, guiding Abraham down, to be followed by Beck. Januc slipped in after, and he just managed to grab the back of Haakon's breeches before the Viking tore off into the centre of the fray. 'I was just starting to enjoy myself!' he moaned, allowing them to pull him through the narrow grating, Fenrir dragged as reluctantly behind him.

The Fugger hesitated at the edge of the hole. 'Reminds me of the midden,' he said to no one in particular. Then he leapt back out from under the cart screaming, 'Daemon! Daemon!'

How he hoped to be heard above the noise of combat not even he knew. But *Corvus corax* is a mighty bird, and hunts more by sound than by scent. In a rush of feathers, a blur of black descended onto his shoulder and cawed loudly in his ear. Clutching the bird to him, the Fugger leapt into the hole.

Jean looked back at the mêlée. He could make out the taller figures of Heinrich and Franchetto striking out at all around them, friend or foe. For an instant, the German's reddened eyes found him, and Jean saw the frustration and the fury there. Drawing a finger across his own throat, Jean smiled, and was rewarded by the sight of the hideous face contracting itself still more as Heinrich struggled to fight his way through to him and failed.

Jean half descended into the hole, then turned back to Lucrezia. 'How can we leave you and your brother?'

'Do not be concerned about us. We will sting them a little, then melt like water into the desert sands. It's what scorpions do.'

A man-at-arms was thrown from the crowd near her. She reached down and cut a hunk out of his ear with her stiletto. He howled before being sucked up again into the throng.

'They'll never follow you down there. It's a labyrinth, and my daughter has the only thread. We'll bring you news in Montepulciano. Where will you be?'

'On the road in from Radda, at the sign of the Comet, just outside the city walls.'

Jean felt a rope being tied around his waist.

'Go with God,' said Lucrezia, and with a cry of 'Scorpio!' she rejoined the fight.

'I have torches hidden further down,' Maria-Theresa was saying as she knotted the rope around him. 'Till then we are mole blind.' She ran to the front of the file. 'Ready?'

Careless of reply, she headed down the passage. The rope tightened and each in turn was jerked forward into the darkness. The sounds of violence faded behind them and soon all that could be heard was the dripping – of water and of blood. They would have to wait for the promised torch-light to see either.

# EIGHT

# At the Sign of
# the Comet

Mathias van Frew sat in the crook of an old olive tree, resting a rusty arquebus across his knees. From this vantage, he had a view both down the road to Siena and up the steep hill to the walls of Montepulciano. Though the crests of the battlements were shrouded now in the early-morning mists, they could not conceal the immensity of the fortress-town beneath.

From his perch, he could also see the front door of his inn and the comet emblazoned across its oak panels. As he regarded that flaming symbol, Mathias sighed and uttered his usual little prayer of thanks to Santa Catherina. Though his eyes were focused on the task he'd set himself, his mind could not help but contemplate what was his. Especially as the man who had made it all possible was once more resting under his red tiled roof.

The inn was back from the road, a long driveway shaded by ancient cypresses leading to the large courtyard, the house set within crumbling outer walls of vivid umber. He knew it had once been the summer residence, and plague retreat, of a rich Sienese family, abandoned for nearly two decades before Mathias van Frew, soldier of fortune, stopped to have his wounds tended in the grounds and decided never to leave. The finest grapes in Tuscany grew all around, the wine presses were coaxed back into life, and the sun shone nearly all year round, drawing the pain from his many wounds, banishing the memory of the rain mist he'd grown up in, these rolling hills studded in vine, olive and chestnut the landscape of the mind he'd always desired, that he'd only dreamt of in the flat waterlands of his native Holland.

He owed the discovery to Jean Rombaud, who had carried him there after an ambush had gone badly wrong, who had stayed with him until he could pull the musket ball out and Mathias' flesh had grown pink and healthy again, then left him with both their shares of the booty looted from the hill town they'd pillaged. The gold had set up the Comet, and Mathias, in the ten years since Jean had left vowing to return some day, had changed from a reed-thin Dutch boy to a fat and contented Tuscan, host of the most prosperous country inn of the region of Montepulciano.

The chance to repay some of this debt was a delight to him, despite the disapproval of Laura, the local girl he'd married, grown fat with and had five children by. Her word was usually law. But when Jean and his band of wounded, filthy stragglers appeared two nights after the Palio, it was Mathias' word that, for once, ruled. He put them in a section of the sprawling house he'd recently renovated but hadn't yet opened. Endless food, the best of his wine, new blankets and fresh bedding – anything they could desire was immediately provided for them. And Mathias himself cleaned and stitched the wound in Jean's side, just as Jean had done for him ten years before.

'Still in the same trade then, Jean?' he'd said, as the gash was gradually pulled together by the thread.

'In a way, old friend,' came the enigmatic reply, 'though I am working more for myself these days.'

And then Jean slept with his strange crew beside him in a row. A giant with a giant dog, a bandaged, dark head appearing from another blanket, a one-handed man wrapping that one hand round a young woman, an old man shivering in three blankets despite the heat of the fire.

Between him and Jean, a small young man with dark, tightly curled hair.

Mathias had blown out the candles and looked back at the room, lit only by firelight. A strange crew indeed. But Jean had always attracted interesting companions. He should know. He had been one himself.

He had closed the door softly and gone to watch outside. Jean had not spoken of pursuit, but that could have been an oversight due to tiredness. His friend was in his care. Shouldering an arquebus that he only used now for the occasional quail, he had taken up his position in the olive tree.

The morning star still winked, despite the glow on the horizon. It was his favourite time, this hour before dawn, and today the sun would rise on a particularly fine day. Jean Rombaud had returned and there were debts to be paid.

For the next few days all they did was eat and rest. The summer had arrived in full force and a searing sun beat down on the ochre earth of the Tuscan hills, drawing from it the fruits of the field and the vine. In the private courtyard that served their wing of the rambling house, a huge chestnut spread its flower-laden boughs, scenting the air, while water flowed from a giant stone fish into a conch-shaped bath. Here there was a delicious coolness and shelter from the intense heat, sheepskins and blankets were scattered on the floor of umber tiles and a table was never empty of the delights of the region. Huge clay amphorae were filled with cool young wine that caused laughter and eventual sleep, with no ill results; vast cured hams hung from the branches, recently brought down from the Apennine snows where they had seasoned: goats' cheeses wrapped in vine leaves, crushed on wheels of rough, dense bread; brochettes of kidneys and sweetbreads roasted over an open fire – a suckling pig revolved there one night, a whole sheep the next; fava beans mashed with first-press olive oil and wild garlic, eggplant fried with savoury, hard cheese. Figs from the previous year's supply steeped in grappa, along with Laura's pancakes stuffed with chestnut and ricotta, sated whatever pangs of hunger remained.

In the drowsy warmth of the evenings came the stories. There was much to catch up on since the parting in Toulon. Haakon and Januc told the tale of the taking of the corsairs, the huge, fair Norwegian discovering that he had indeed inherited the bardic lyricism of his father; while the smaller, dark janissary crouched by the cooking fire, as if in a desert oasis, drawing his audience in. They counterpointed each other so well that the tale was demanded again the following evening, and again on the third, by which time the enemy fleet had increased to twenty strong and Jean had lost track of how many dozens he had personally slain with his square-tipped sword.

The tale of the dungeon was told once, on the third night, and left everyone silent save for the tears that flowed again from Maria-Theresa. It was told by the Fugger, whose nervousness at the telling was dispelled by the steady pressure of the girl's hand on his handless arm, her fingers returning from the wiping of tears to gently stroke his wrist.

Beck spoke little, filling in such detail as was necessary but no more. She was unused to company, having only ever had one objective in her life and having decided that a solitary life was best to pursue it. Now that it had been achieved, and Abraham was beside her and beginning to show signs of recovery – Januc, who knew something of the matter, had undertaken to wean him off his craving for Cibo's 'medicine' – she could not decide if she could or should remain a 'he'. Something in her longed once again to be her father's loving daughter, helping him with his work, providing him with the home and comfort he needed. But something else was work-ing within her too. She likened herself to one of those feral cats that haunted the same alleys she had as a member of the street gang, the Sicarii, in Venice. She had been in the wild, fighting for survival, too long. She was not sure she could return to the domestic.

And then there was Jean. Another reason she seldom spoke was that she was convinced he would know her secret if she did, and she was both thrilled and horrified at that idea. There was a quality to his watchfulness, a way he had of taking in all detail around him. She had the feeling he had not always been this way, that the mission he'd undertaken – which the Fugger had told her about, this vow made to a dead English queen – had changed him. He laughed sometimes and his face was transformed; Beck thought of a waterfall suddenly stumbled upon in a forest. Mostly he watched and listened. He seemed to be waiting for something, gathering strength with every breath of air.

She knew what he was doing. He was waiting to leave.

While she watched him, he watched the boy with the slingshot. His feelings were confused, because sometimes he thought of Beck as a comrade, sometimes as the son he'd never had, even though any son Lysette and he could have produced would have been more than half the age of the dark-haired youth opposite. But then those feelings would go and be replaced by something unsettling, as he studied the dark eyes beneath the curly hair, the sudden shy smile or laugh triggered by some interaction between Haakon and Januc. When Beck laughed, inevitably the boy would glance over to where he sat, their eyes would meet for a moment and then they would both look away. It happened more often than just by chance, and Jean found himself waiting for it, enjoying it, even the confusion of it.

As if he did not have enough to be confused about. While he both needed and enjoyed the peace and the healing, the laughter, good food and wine, he was never fully able to rest because in his mind's eye he still saw, wherever he looked, the shadow of a six-fingered hand. The tale from the dungeon had only increased his anxiety for now he knew that Cibo was planning nothing less than the conjuration of the dead, had even partly succeeded, for Anne *had* come in a vision to the Fugger. What had she said? 'Their summons is strong'? Even without Abraham, his enemy was sure still to be attempting unspeakable acts. Jean knew that as soon as he was recovered he would have to return to Siena to fulfil his vow. That was never in question, and if he'd ever wavered, the story of Anne's appearance in the midst of the Black Mass and her final words, which the Fugger had told him quietly in private, would have prompted him. His Queen did not doubt that he would come for her. He could not doubt it either.

Yet he was also aware of the truth of what his enemy, Heinrich von Solingen, had said during the fight at the Palio. He might have all the lives of a cat, but he had used up five before he ever saw Anne Boleyn, and at least another three since.

So Jean watched and waited and gathered his strength. News would be brought to him as soon as anything occurred – Lucrezia had promised her daughter's rescuers that. But he also knew that if something didn't happen soon, he would have to make it happen.

It was on the fifth night that Haakon and Januc, praised for their storytelling, full of relived bravado and, in Haakon's case, too much young wine, decided to go off to the modest brothel that Montepulciano possessed.

'The girls are delightful, inexperienced really, not like those army sluts you're used to.' Mathias was enjoying old mercenary company. Then he added hastily, on seeing his wife enter with another tray of sweetmeats, 'Or so I've been told.'

'I just hope there are many.' Januc's dark eyes glowed. 'I have been two years before the mast. And I had three wives before that. Three! All at the same time.'

'And what about you, young David-with-a-slingshot?' Haakon bent down. 'Got something other than stones in your pouch?'

Januc and Mathias laughed while Beck blushed furiously and tried to cover it up with a deeper than normal voice.

'Please, gentlemen, my father!' She smiled slyly and winked. 'Maybe when he falls asleep later I'll sneak out. Save some for me, eh?'

'Can't guarantee that, but as you wish, young master. Ah Jean,' Haakon called as the Frenchman came back into the courtyard, 'we're off to see the ladies of the night. Will you accompany us?'

Jean stopped in the doorway. His first thought was of safety, but Franchetto's soldiers, who had scoured the town, had departed the day before. It was probably fine to venture out. It had also been a long time. Jean had had his share of every aspect of life while campaigning and he was as much a man as any other. But since the plague had taken his wife, he had known only two women, brief moments to relieve his loneliness more than anything.

It was then he saw Beck looking at him intently. There was something in the look, the same mystery he'd seen before, some question being asked. He also felt a surge in his groin when he looked at the boy, and that disturbed him still more. He was a soldier and he'd lived most of his life with men, but his inclination was, and always had been, towards women. He didn't know what this feeling was, and to dispel it he said, his voice suddenly thick, 'Sure. Why not?'

There was a great roar from Haakon and Januc who slapped him on his back and immediately started gathering some food and wine to take as presents.

'Well, that's nice, isn't it?' The voice, suddenly gruff with native Yorkshire vowels, was also full of venom. 'Taking yourself off to a brothel? No wonder a queen entrusted you with her hand. So noble a knight! So . . .'

Beck turned and stormed out of the courtyard.

'Well, Jean!' Januc's grey eyes were alive with mirth. 'Can you recognise jealousy when you see it?'

The Frenchman shifted uncomfortably. 'Jealousy?'

'Of course. And you know what the Greeks say: "A woman for love, but a boy for pleasure."' He gave a lascivious wink. 'An all-too-willing boy from the way he looks at you.'

'You are mistaken, janissary.' There was a harder edge to Jean's voice now. 'There's something ailing him, that's all.'

'There is.' The Fugger rose from one of the sheepskins, carefully removing his arm from under the sleeping head of Maria-Theresa. 'A word, Jean?'

Later, having watched Januc and Haakon noisily depart, Jean went to find Beck, who was crouched over a sleeping, fevered Abraham, bathing his temples with cool water. Beck rose at Jean's signal and preceded him outside, leading him away from the house and down to a crumbled part of the outer wall. A gibbous half moon hung over the fields, etching the vines and olive trees in silver. Below them, Haakon and Januc could be heard noisily shooshing each other as they marched towards town.

'You'd better hurry if you're going to catch them up.' Beck's stance was closed off and hostile.

Jean came up to the unforgiving back. 'I changed my mind,' he murmured, then added as he put his arms around Beck, 'besides, my tastes have always run another way.'

Beck elbowed Jean hard in the stomach and slipped forward, instantly filled with contradictory thoughts and emotions. *He wants me, he loves me, he thinks I'm a boy, oh God, he's a lover of boys* were just a few she went through before she turned and dropped into a fighting stance. It was then the laugh came, the one she heard so rarely and liked so well when she did. He was standing just a few feet away, clutching his belly in both pain and mirth.

'Oh, I deserved that. But I just couldn't resist.'

He took a step towards her and she took one back.

'The Fugger. He told me. He saw you, after you came out of the water. Just for a moment. Long enough to . . . to know you.'

He broke off and the laughter left him. He took another step towards her, then another, and this time she stayed where she was. When he was before her, he placed his hands on her shoulders and turned her until the moon was reflected in the darkness of her eyes.

'No one knows me. No one ever has.' She looked away, because she couldn't think of anything else to say.

'I will,' he said, and bent to kiss her.

When their mouths came together, there was a release in both of them, and later, on a bed of pine boughs he swiftly made, there was another, and a third when her tears came, springing from a source so deep inside her that it had never been tapped in the long age since her father was taken away. He held her while she cried, soothing her with his hands, his kisses, his murmured words. Soon, he felt the tears change from sadness to something else, to a kind of fierce joy: feeling it, he wrapped her even tighter in his arms, felt hers return the pressure. They held each other until they both slept, and long after into the night.

'You are a crow, a barking dog, three times a fool!'

The blows fell on the helpless servant, twice as hard because Franchetto wanted to direct them at the other man present but didn't dare. He hated not being able to hit whom he pleased, whenever he wanted, but in the week since the Palio, the German bodyguard's eyes had developed a fanatic's gleam, a fire that shone from the ruin of his face and made him the very stuff of nightmares. He was certainly not a man to strike, however insolent his monosyllabic replies, his endless silences.

So Franchetto repeatedly struck the messenger bringing the latest tidings of gloom. It was not new news. It was no news at all. The Viper might fight with the Bear, the Broadsword loathe the Panther, but every *contrada* hated authority. The riot the Scorpions had begun had become general and had taken a day and a night to quell. The Cibo brothers had been manhandled by the mob, peasant hands actually laid on noble flesh. In the aftermath, a few too drunk or too infirm to run away had been hanged before the Palazzo Pubblico. But the real culprits, the Scorpions, had vanished under the rocks whence they'd come, spiriting the fugitives with them. And the law of *omertà*, silence, seemed to bind the town together despite the lure of fortunes and the threats of death. Spies went everywhere and returned with the same story – nothing.

So while Franchetto Cibo vented his temper on the latest of them, kicking him around the room, Giancarlo Cibo drew Heinrich aside.

'My brother is ensuring that the only information we receive will be happy and thus useless. We will achieve nothing here.'

'I am beginning to think the same.'

The Archbishop moved over to the window and looked down into the Campo, where five bodies swayed on the scaffold.

'You hunt, do you not?'

'Anything and everything, my Lord.'

'Like me. And there are different tactics for different game, haven't you found?'

His bodyguard nodded.

'If you cannot run something down you draw it to you. You bait a trap, do you not? And we still have the bait our quarry most desires. I have seen the look in that Frenchman's eyes. He will not give up.'

'He will when I pull his guts through his mouth.'

'Indeed. But you have failed, on several occasions, to do so. I think I have to make it easier for you somehow.'

Franchetto had finished his beating and was now noisily drinking some wine. His brother regarded him with ill-disguised disdain. Then he snapped his fingers.

'We will not draw him here, to a fortress. But we know how he favours the open road, the ambush on the way. So let him stalk us while we stalk him. Franchetto,' he called, 'is the Pope still beseeching us to join the Emperor to deal with Luther's schism?'

The bigger brother spat on the floor. 'That stinking Farnese dog! Trying more of his tricks.'

'He wants us out of Italy for a while so he can work his intrigues, isn't that right?'

'Yes. And we will not fall for that.'

'Oh, but we will.' Giancarlo smiled. 'We will go to Germany immediately, for three reasons. One, we will have the ear of the Emperor, which has been listening too long to the demands of our Farnese enemies. Two, we will draw out the scum who escaped us and deal with them appropriately. And three . . .' He paused. 'Three, I have forgotten.'

But he hadn't, and both the other men knew he hadn't. The Archbishop forgot nothing. He just didn't think they needed to know, for the moment, the strongest reason for going north. Apollonius. The Emperor's own alchemist and one of the greatest of the age. Greater even, some said, than Abraham the Hebrew and Paracelsus at Basle. If Cibo couldn't lure his Jew back – and there seemed to be a risk of that – he would consult Apollonius. The German sage would be more than excited by the sight of the six-fingered hand. He would recognise it for what it was as Cibo had: the key to the door of immortality.

'Yes, to Germany, I think. And let our preparations be secret. That should ensure everyone knows our destination before the week is out.'

Lucrezia arrived with the news the next night.

'My sister, that sweet young whore, God preserve the instrument of her good fortune, had it from the Archbishop's manservant himself. They go to join the Emperor in Germany, and in haste, for they set out tomorrow. They are talking of it like a crusade. The Cibo brothers will end the Protestant heresy single-handed. No offence, Fugger.' She had been eyeing the closeness of her daughter and the German since her arrival with mixed feelings.

'Offence to my heresy or to my single hand?' said the Fugger. 'Either way, none taken. And where is the Emperor now?'

'Wittenberg, they say.'

'Wittenberg?' It was Abraham who spoke now. His fever had broken the night before, and though he was still weak, the worst of his cravings seemed to have passed. He'd allowed his daughter, whom he'd agreed, on her urging, to regard for the moment as his son, to feed him vegetable soup at the meeting. Now he pushed the spoon aside and with some excitement said, 'Wittenberg is where Apollonius makes his experiments. It is the centre of alchemy in the world. Cibo will not care about any crusade other than that one, his own. He goes to consult the master, to get him to do what I could not.' He began to cough, recovered, and his eyes shone. 'He never realised that by dulling my resistance with that drug he also dulled my abilities. But he is right in one thing. That hand could hold the very destiny of life.'

Jean, crouching on the far side of the courtyard, carefully put down the wine he was drinking. 'That hand's destiny,' he said quietly, 'is in the fulfilment of a vow, nothing more.'

He rose and went to stand by the cooking fire, newly prepared for the night and already fierce, and stared into its searing red depths, the miniature worlds existing in the heart of the flame – here a cave of white intensity collapsing in on itself, there a channel of powdered ash stirred by that collapse. He was lost for a moment in that movement, its heavenly beauty, its hellish depths. A familiar hand on his arm drew him back to thoughts he was trying to avoid. He spoke softly for only Beck to hear.

'And my destiny lies there. Consigned to the fires, waiting for hell to suck me down. Because I will fail in my vow. Who am I to fulfil a quest for a queen? The knight in some ancient lay? The hero of one of Haakon's sagas? No. I am a peasant, a

274

soldier, a headsman. Nothing more. Who am I to challenge archbishops, princes and dukes?'

Beck drew him around. 'A peasant who has taken heads off all of them,' she said. 'A headsman whom a queen of England saw fit to trust with all she had left. And as for the Devil . . . if he wanted you, he's had plenty of chances to claim you before now.'

Jean looked at her again, and marvelled at her again, as he had in the moonlight the night before. The way she said his name made him feel whole, in a way he hadn't felt in a long age, and he suddenly, desperately wanted to stop there, just stay with his good friend Mathias, make wine, hunt in the fields, have children with the woman who made him feel like that.

'And what if I choose to . . . turn away? To stay here with you?'

For a moment she looked, as he had done, into the flames. 'And begin our life together in a betrayal? I would always think I had stolen you. She would always be between us and her hand would pull us apart.'

He knew she was right, even as he wanted her to be wrong more than he'd ever wanted anything; knew that all would turn to ash, that he would keep no promise, to Beck or anyone, and fulfil no dreams unless and until he fulfilled his vow.

He was suddenly aware that all were looking at them, waiting for his words before giving their own. He so wanted to be the man he'd always been, not a leader, just one free to do as he chose. And because he wanted that, he had to offer it to those who followed him. He stepped back into the middle of the courtyard.

'I made a vow that I can't break. Until I have found what I lost, there is no peace for me in this world. So I have to go to Germany.' He looked at them each in turn. 'But you – Fugger, Haakon, Januc, Beck – you have come with me this far and I have led you into terrible danger. I go towards more of it.

You made no binding vows to me or anyone else. As a friend, I would give you some advice: do not follow a madman on a mad quest.'

Haakon rose up immediately, putting down a haunch of meat to say, most seriously, 'Where you go, so do I. The runes have told me that much. Besides in my country, my mother used to say: "If you are mad as a springtime stoat you are still sane for the sowing."'

Januc smiled at him, then quickly hid his amusement. He had learnt that the big Norwegian took both his runes and pronouncements from his mother very seriously.

'And what does that mean, my friend?'

Haakon scratched his head. 'I don't know. But I do know that there is madness and then there is madness. Madness for me was getting fat and lazy in a brothel in Tours. But is it madness to fight, to journey, to dare? Besides' – and here a gleam came into his sea-blue eyes – 'think of the stories we have yet to make!' With a brief nod he sat down again and resumed his eating.

'Well.' Januc rose, tugging at his thin, oiled moustache. Of all of them, his dark hair had grown back the quickest, was nearly a match for Beck's. 'I am loath to break up the company, and I have rarely met men I so enjoyed fighting beside. Is there gold, Jean, where we are going?'

'I do not know. I find I have lost my appetite for gold.'

The Croatian whistled. 'Then you definitely need me along. To look after your financial interests. And I cannot go back to my homeland empty-handed, for I was not created to farm. So it looks like I will come too. For a while, at least.'

The Fugger tried to get up, but Maria-Theresa was clinging on to him. Gently, he disengaged her hands.

'You know that I will come.'

As the girl started crying, reaching up and tugging at the Fugger's arm, Jean said, 'Fugger, it is I that owe you a debt, not the other way around. You freed me from the gibbet. And you have found some peace here. Why not take it?'

The Fugger smiled, and stroked the girl's hair for a moment.

'I think the peace will remain here for a while. Maria-Theresa is young' – he could see Lucrezia nodding emphatically at that – 'and very grateful. I do not want to presume on that. If I go and come back, maybe we will understand this more, both of us? And anyway, you need me. Germany is where I am from.'

He bent down to console the weeping girl.

Finally, Jean turned to Beck. She had gone to rejoin her father and was feeding him soup again. She didn't look up, just said, 'I must take my father to Venice, to our family, where he will be cared for.' Then she raised her eyes to add, 'And after he is safe I will come to you, wherever you may be. No power on earth will hinder me.'

The strength of these quiet words made even Haakon stop eating. Yet no one apart from Jean and perhaps the Fugger understood the force underlying them. Abraham, suspecting something, gazed at her for a long moment. Jean held her eyes then looked away, back to the red glow of the cooking fire, to the collapsing world and a heaven and a hell that beckoned there.

'It is settled then,' he said. 'We leave tomorrow.'

Later, after preparations had been made for the dawn departure, with Mathias filling saddle bags for several horses, they gathered for the last time in the warm courtyard, the sky overhead a scattering of rich and shining gems. The morrow was forgotten in a feast eclipsing any that had gone before, in contentment, laughter and song. The lay of the galleys was once more recounted to loud acclaim. The Fugger traced the constellations for all, telling the myths, mainly for his Maria-Theresa, while her two hands never left his one. Jean sat near Beck, not touching, not even looking, both a little shy suddenly yet both feeling the heat build, knowing they would steal away again once her father was asleep. Abraham was lively though, as if he'd slept for a thousand years and now had just awakened.

Haakon had told several runecasts in the preceding nights, commenting on the past, envisaging the future. A life full of love and contentment for Maria-Theresa, a second, unprecedented win for the Scorpions at the next Palio, a vizier's hat for Januc back in Istanbul. Lucrezia, who had only just arrived, was intrigued as she herself was a reader of palms and cards. She had learnt in the stones that there was a night of love ahead of her with a tall, fair stranger, and there was little doubt in her, or Haakon's, mind that the prophecy would be fulfilled promptly.

Only Jean's future was undecided, but now, with the wine working within him and his love untouchable an arm's length away, he decided he needed the distraction.

'Come, Haakon, let us peer into the murkiness of my fate.'

The Norseman tumbled the runestones out again upon the green cloth laid on the tiles, turning them face down, swirling them, then getting Jean to do the same.

'Now,' said the Norseman in the serious voice he seemed to adopt for this purpose – nasal, over-pronounced – that had everyone fighting to control their laughter, 'focus on your question, keep it silent and strong in your heart, and pick out three stones. Lay them down before you as you think they should be.'

Jean thought of love, then obeyed. Haakon had him turn them over, one by one, analysing each stone as it appeared.

'RAD. Upright. I would say you are going on a journey, and you—'

Laughter interrupted him. 'It needs no revelation from the spirits to tell us that, Norseman. Otherwise I have been stuffing those saddle bags with food for no purpose!' yelled Mathias.

Haakon continued with an injured air. 'If you please. This is a rune associated with the god Odin. Mercury here in Italy. The raven in some cultures. It could mean trickery.'

'You hear that, Daemon?' the Fugger called up to the preening bird in the chestnut tree above. 'Even the stones do not trust you!'

Struggling over the laughter, Haakon continued. 'A journey is indicated, anything could happen. But the runes that follow will tell us the outcome. Next, please.'

Smiling himself, Jean turned the middle stone.

'It looks like an arrow flying towards you, Jean. Better duck! Especially if I shot it.'

Januc laughed until he saw Haakon's face. The big Norwegian had gone a little pale, and when he spoke, his voice had lost its pompous tone.

'TIR. Reversed. The god of war. See, I wear this rune around my neck.' He briefly showed them the metal arrow hanging on a thong under his jerkin. 'Upright, like this, it is a rune of power, of courage, even madness, in battle. The berserker's sign.' He was silent a moment, contemplating.

'And reversed?' Beck asked, coming to join the circle.

Haakon said nothing, except, 'Turn over the last one, Jean.'

When he had, all saw what seemed to be an open mouth trying to swallow the other stones. Only Jean was swift enough to see the shadow form in the Norseman's eyes. Form and disappear before the others looked up.

'PEORTH. Reversed. That's all right then. Looks like your wish will be granted.'

Haakon flicked all three stones over and melded them with the others. The suddenness of the move surprised them all but Haakon dismissed any questions, saying the runecast was ambiguous, and refused to read any more. He launched instead into a boisterous and epic tale from his homeland to do with clever farm boys, troll kings and beautiful maidens with cow tails hidden down their dresses. Soon all were laughing again.

Later, as the Fugger and Maria-Theresa slept chastely in each other's arms, when Abraham had finally exhausted his

words for the night and slumbered and Januc had disappeared in the direction of the town, Jean watched Lucrezia head
into the house with a meaningful glance backwards at
Haakon, who slowly rose to follow. He was just in the
entrance when Jean caught up with him. He took his arm.

'What did you see, Haakon?'

Haakon shrugged. 'Nothing. It doesn't matter. We were
just playing. You should never do that with runes. My mother
used to say—'

He stopped when he saw the steadiness of Jean's gaze.

'What did you see?' Jean repeated, softly.

Haakon met his eyes. 'All right, I'll tell you. It doesn't
matter what you thought your question was. Your real
question was underneath it. PEORTH is a dice cup. A
gamble. Reversed is twice as dangerous, twice the risk. It's
tied to RAD, to the journey, what you are trying to do. To
your quest.'

'And that arrow? Aimed at me? Reversed too, right?'

Haakon looked past Jean at Beck, disengaging her arm
from under her father.

'Yes,' he said quickly. 'The god of war, reversed. Hardship,
struggle, great odds.'

'We've always known that.'

'It means something else too when joined to the trickery of
RAD, of Mercury.'

'And that is?'

Beck had started to move towards them. Haakon's voice
had become a whisper. 'Betrayal. Someone close. Very close.'

'Very close?'

'Yes. If I were to hazard . . . someone here tonight will
betray you.'

Jean watched his friend disappear into the house. A hand
was laid on his shoulder. Jean turned, but for a moment did
not see the eyes he had grown to love. All he saw was an
arrow flying towards him from the red flames of a fireplace.
An arrow of betrayal.

PART THREE

# THE RECKONING

# ONE

# HELLFIRE

It was Fenrir who first told them something was wrong.

He had been ranging, as usual, far ahead. Every day of their journey he had preceded them, warning of brigands in the mountain passes, of wolves, of villages hidden in forests. His keen nose and ear at night allowed the party to sleep without fear for he would not wake them without reason. They had learnt, a dozen times, to trust his instincts.

So when he ran back to them, ears flattened against his skull, the hair on his neck and along his spine raised as if by a brush, when he crouched behind his master's horse and gave out a continuous low growl, everyone shifted in their saddles and reached out to feel the comfort of their weapons.

'Hedge knights, you think?' Jean said softly to the man beside him.

The Fugger touched his fingers to his stump. The very naming of that particularly German variety of highwayman made it ache in memory.

'It's possible. We crossed the border into Bavaria about six hours back, by my reckoning. We are within the territory.'

'My Fenrir is not frightened of a bunch of disinherited noblemen.' Haakon had descended to comfort his dog. 'Look at him. Something he's seen or sensed has terrified him.'

Fenrir stood, growling still, hackles raised, despite his master's strokes.

'What lies ahead, Fugger, do you know?' Januc had taken the precaution of stringing his bow.

'If my memory serves, a small town called Marsheim. It has a famous abbey, and an abbot equally famous for his love of vice. The sort of man who gave the Catholics such a bad name here in Germany, who prompted our holy monk Luther to his holy rebellion.'

As soon as he had crossed the border of a German state, the Fugger had begun to feel like a Protestant again.

'The sort of place our Archbishop could well desire to rest for the night,' observed Jean.

'What do you think?' Haakon was scratching Fenrir behind the ears. 'Shall we heed my hound's warning? Set up camp here, go in and scout at dawn, as usual?'

Jean felt their eyes upon him; another decision expected. With each one taken it had become a little easier. Advice he always heeded, even from the dog; but, after debate, the final choice was his. He'd insisted they wait when they had first caught up with Cibo's party a week before in an Austrian forest, not go charging in at dead of night as Haakon, especially, desired. Three weeks struggling in high mountain passes summer seemed not to have reached, forcing their way through snow drifts at times, had exhausted them all. He had even let their quarry gain a few days' lead again, when Januc was struck with an ailment of the guts and could not ride. The enemy had at least fifty men-at-arms and he needed all his comrades. Also, as strong as the pull of the hand was, Jean was aware just how lucky he had been so far. He had survived a gibbet and a galley. To rush into an armed camp, even while most of them slept, was challenging fate too far. Besides, he had the distinct feeling it was exactly what Cibo wanted.

He had another reason to keep his skin in one piece: Beck had promised to kiss every inch of it when she met them at the rendezvous in Munster, the Fugger's family town. As long as it was unblemished by wound.

His thoughts were interrupted by an agitated cawing.

Daemon, who had been resting quietly on his master's shoulders, suddenly rose up into the air, flapped twice and flew swiftly ahead.

'Carrion,' murmured the Fugger. 'My Daemon has a nose for things that are dead.'

Jean's mind was made up. 'We'll heed the animals, yet proceed a little further. Maybe what has so upset our Fenrir and lured our raven will become clear to us too.'

The party moved on, down the long avenue of beech trees sheltering the road. The sun was sinking into the west, giving them ample light to see the ruts made by the Archbishop's carriage the day before.

'There's a ridge up ahead,' said the Fugger. 'I think it overlooks the abbey, and beyond that lies the town.'

Before they gained the viewpoint, three things happened to halt them.

Firstly, the wind change Daemon had first noticed now gusted down upon them from the direction in which they were headed. It brought with it, faintly but unmistakably, the sound of screaming. Secondly, a bell began to ring, but not in the regular way of summons or warning. It struck once, then once again, then three times quickly. There followed a silence. Then from a different bell, one single toll.

'A curious way they have with bells, these Bavarians,' said Januc. 'What—'

He never got to ask his question because at that moment the third thing happened and it ended all conversation for a while.

A cat, a big, brindled tom, appeared on the road ahead. Fenrir growled but needed no restraint from Haakon to hold back. The cat was moving strangely, dragging its hips along the ground as if its back were broken – which it wasn't, for it then leapt up, skittered a few feet forward on four paws, then flopped and resumed its sideways slide, mewing all the while.

Behind it came a black and white dog, a town cur. It seemed to be in pursuit of the wounded cat but then ran past it and towards their horses. It halted just before them, and this time Fenrir needed to be restrained from launching an attack; but then, ignoring them completely, the dog ran to the side and began to assault a rock there. Snarling in frenzy, it hurled itself onto it, attempting to bite it, to prise it from its position with scrabbling paws. The dog's mouth filled with blood, teeth were spat out, claws ripped off; still it continued with an overwhelming ferocity. Finally, it threw back its bloodied muzzle and howled, then ran, slipping onto its side twice before disappearing into the woods.

The cat, meanwhile, had just laid down.

'Dead.' Haakon had descended to pick up the body. 'Poor thing.'

Fenrir whined and nuzzled at his master's hand.

'Do we go on, Jean?' the Fugger said, hoping for a no.

'I think we must.' Jean dismounted. 'But slowly. Let's take a look from your ridge.'

It was up there they found their second body. Human, this time.

Daemon's caws drew their eyes to it; he was quarrelling with a crow in a linden tree. The corpse was wedged between two branches, on the rise just off the road. The man, it seemed, had tried to climb higher and had fallen back, because an undershirt flapped a dozen feet above him. At the base of the tree, a monk's cassock lay, torn in half. The body was naked, and cruelly marked with gouges. Januc climbed up to have a closer look.

'There's flesh under all his nails and his hands are covered in blood,' he called down. 'The fall probably killed him for his back looks broken. But . . .' He hesitated. 'But it might have been a blessed release. I think . . . I think he was trying to rip his own skin off.'

'Holy Father,' whispered the Fugger, 'what madness is this?'

Jean pushed his way through the knee-high bracken of the ridge, the others following. When they reached the point where the slope began to descend and they could see into the valley, they gathered to look down. The foliage did not completely obscure the view.

'My eyes are not so good for distance.' Jean turned to his companions. 'Does anyone have the long sight?'

Haakon put a foot on the low branches of an oak. 'I grew up eating little but fish. Fish is good for the eyes, my mother always said.' He hoisted himself swiftly up the tree, agile despite his size, gazed down, ducking this way and that around the branches. 'I see a walled enclosure, gardens within it, a big stone house at the centre.'

'That would be the monastery,' the Fugger called up. 'Are the monks there?'

'I do not see . . . wait, there is some movement. Some men moving around a garden. They seem . . . they seem to be dancing. And there's some smoke rising further on.'

The wind eddied around the ridge. They each caught a faint trace of laughter borne on it. There was an odd quality to it, as if it lacked all humour.

'The town is beyond, is it not, Fugger?' Jean asked.

'It is.'

'Haakon, come down. If the town's afire too we may not have much time. Let us go and see what is happening there.'

With some dread, they mounted and began the descent. But if they were reluctant, Fenrir nearly refused to move. Only a stern command from Haakon got the beast going, and even then it slunk along at the rear of its master's horse, hair standing up, whimpering.

The light rain that had pattered intermittently upon them most of the day turned heavy as they approached the monastery. From a distance it seemed the gates were open; but drawing near they saw that one of the huge, iron-studded panels lay flat on the ground and the other hung off just one hinge. Under the end that reached the ground lay a man, squirming, naked, his hands pinned as if he had tried to catch the gate as it fell.

Jean, Januc and Haakon together just managed to raise the gate long enough for the Fugger to drag the weeping monk clear. They cut some strips from a nearby cassock and bound his mangled hands. While they did this he gradually ceased weeping, his eyes searching the sky.

When they were done, he leant towards the Fugger and whispered, 'Beware, Brother. The Devil has loosed his flames upon the world. St Anthony's Fire has come, and now is Doomsday near. Unless I shut them out.'

With that the monk rose up and tried to put his crushed fingers once more under the hanging gate, and nothing that the Fugger attempted to say or do could draw his attention away from the task.

Jean, on hearing these words, had stood a little apart. He had gone so pale that Haakon came to him and touched his arm.

'What is it?'

'St Anthony's Fire.'

'Do not take the words of a madman seriously. He is possessed of an ogre, a demon, that is all.'

Jean looked up at the other man. 'It is not all. He will only be one of many. When St Anthony's Fire takes a town, all are taken, all possessed. It happened to the next village to ours, when I was a child. It destroyed the place. Half the people died. The other half went mad. Barely one in three was exorcised.'

'Wait.' The Fugger joined them. 'I too have heard of this. Whole villages deranged, cursed with visions of hell, perishing in flames only they can see. Yet people coming from outside the village are not caught up by it. They can only witness the effect of the curse, not share the horror.'

Januc had left the bandaging to the others and had been looking within the walls. He came out just in time to hear the Fugger's words.

'That is not entirely true,' he said. 'In parts of Turkey there have been similar massings of Djinn, the Screaming Demons.

288

They speak of flames and other horrors. It is said the demons enter the body through the mouth, from the air, from bread or water. So, my friends, keep your mouths shut tight. Wrap a cloth about your face, breathe through your noses only. But do not eat or drink while we are here. And talk as little as you can.' He watched each of them as they cut further strips from the cassock and placed them around their faces, then added, 'Follow me. There are other things you must see.'

Pulling weapons from their sheaths, they entered the enclosure. Inside the gate, the Archbishop's carriage they had seen from certain vantage points along the way stood abandoned. One of the leather straps that had suspended the litter above the chassis to lessen jolting had been cut, and it leant over at a strange angle. Someone had tried to hitch up the horses and failed, for two waited half-tied in the traces while two more stood in a nearby carrot patch, munching. Beyond, the gardens were laid out in huge beds sweeping back to the main house, a stone island in the vegetable sea. Bodies were dotted around each one, some naked, some clothed; in one, the three monks Haakon had first seen from the ridge were still dancing, trampling their seedlings into the earth. Laughter mingled with the sounds of weeping. Smoke rose from the outlying buildings to greet the rain, but none from the monastery itself which, as they approached its entrance-way, was silent.

'This is as far as I came,' Januc said. 'It doesn't smell right beyond here. Smell!'

All four raised their masked faces.

'Ugh!' Haakon turned away and spat. 'What is that?'

'It smells of . . . of mice,' said Jean.

'Mice, certainly. And – stale piss.' The Fugger shuddered. 'And you think we should enter here?'

'Jesu save me, for I burn!'

This cry of anguish burst from the silence of the darkened hallway. Immediately, a score of other voices began to shriek, as if the first voice had been their cue.

'Shall we descend into Hades, my lords?' Januc's grey eyes twinkled above the brown cloth over his mouth.

'Cibo's carriage lies abandoned. He's either in the village or in here,' Jean replied, raising his voice above the wailing. 'So I'm going in.'

His sword poised before him, Jean entered, the others close behind. The hallway was low-ceilinged and dark, the murky light of a day's end dissipating into the stone-flagged floor and the oak panelling of the walls. A staircase ran ahead of them up into the gloom. On either side were doors, one open, one closed. Beyond the shut one to the left could be heard a steady repetition, as of someone counting. Through the gap of the half-opened door the screams poured.

Using the square end of his sword, Jean pushed the door wide. At first, the gloom intensified, then shapes could be discerned, moving around as if in a mist. Suddenly, one ran at them, gibbering. Jean ducked the heavy gold censer the monk was swinging like a mace at the end of its chain. It crashed into the wall beside him, exploding in a cloud of sweetness, of sandalwood and frankincense, temporarily overpowering the stench of mice and urine that was thickest in this chamber. Jean stepped to the side and, as the monk, screaming, tried to raise the wrecked censer, slapped him hard on the side of his head with the flat of the blade. He collapsed at Jean's feet.

The wailing in the chamber doubled. Peering in, the company was able to make out – on every surface, thrust into corners, hovering by the fireplace – men, garbed and un-garbed, beating themselves and each other with bare hands, tearing out chunks of hair. All in the room were tonsured, and thus in monk's orders. Of the party of Siena there was no trace.

Closing the door behind them diminished the wailing, and Jean led the party to the other side of the hallway. Beyond that closed door they could still hear the regular chanting of a single voice. As they hesitated before this door, they could make out the same words being repeated over and over: 'Here I stand, King of the Jews. I can do no other, King of the Jews.'

'Blasphemy upon blasphemy,' muttered the Fugger. 'Christ and Luther both.'

'If blasphemy is the worst awaiting us beyond this door, Fugger' – Haakon was crossing himself as he spoke – 'I myself will be well pleased.'

Then he raised his huge foot and kicked the door in.

This room was as light as the other was gloomy, for candles glimmered on every surface. Hundreds filled the room with their glow, balanced on the fire guard, hanging from the ceiling in wire frames, thrust into rough holes scored into the walls, covering the long refectory table, scores of them set out a small hand's breadth from each other. Only one area of the table was uncovered by dancing flame, and such was the brightness after the gloom for a moment none could see why that was. The shadow was in the form of a body, that was clear. When their eyes had accustomed themselves they could make out the substance of a body as well, and see what the candles finally illuminated so well: a man crucified on the table.

He was small in height but large in girth, his distended belly thrusting up his brown cassock. Three stilettos pinned him in place, one for each hand, and one through crossed ankles. Blood had pooled all around him, flowing in streams down the table, diverted here and there by the endless candles like log jams in a river. He had lost a lot of it.

While the Fugger turned away, unable to contemplate the sight, Jean, Haakon and Januc went to each of the cruel daggers and, at a signal from Jean, pulled them sharply out. The delirium that had caused the man to chant was swept away in a howl of pain, to be replaced by the oblivion of the faint.

Januc raised his stiletto. 'Italian?'

'Sienese. Look at the base of the blade.'

There, lodged just above the grip, was a familiar symbol – the fighting cock of the Rooster *contrada*.

'Seems we share a common enemy with this man.' Jean threw the dagger at the door. It lodged there, quivering.

While Januc and Haakon went, candelabras in hand, to search the upper levels of the monastery, Jean and the Fugger set about staunching the bleeding and dressing the man's stigmatic wounds. It was when they had wrapped the limbs in bandages torn from a table cloth and were moving him to a chair beside the fireplace that he woke with a shriek.

'Am I in heaven? Have I joined my Saviour?'

'You are still of this earth, Brother,' said the Fugger.

'Then who are you, behind your masks? Are you with that accursed Cibo and his hellhounds? If you are, then better to have left me to die in poor imitation of our Lord, for you have brought damnation to His sanctuary.'

Jean put a hand on the man's shoulder. 'We seek the Archbishop but we do not wish him well. He is our enemy, as he seems to be yours.'

'Double damned be he who comes with the kiss of a friend and is my foe.'

'Amen. What has happened here, Brother?'

The man looked at the Fugger and smiled, despite the pain, as the one-handed man clumsily adjusted his legs for him.

'I have not been called "Brother" since I took charge of this house of God. It is quite refreshing.'

'You are the Abbot of Marsheim?' Jean asked.

'I am. Would that I were just a simple brother still, and had not witnessed this day's events.'

'What happened, Father?'

'My son, I could not find words in any of the five languages I speak that could come close to describing this day. But tell me – my flock, my monks, how are they?'

Haakon and Januc entered then, shaking their heads at Jean's look, indicating that all above was as it was below – another circle of hell.

'Something . . . possesses them,' Jean said.

'It is the demons that Cibo unleashed, for there were none before he arrived.'

'Tell us, Father.'

The Abbot told of the Italian's arrival, how he arrogantly demanded lodging for the night. He had expected another sort of stay, for the monastery had a reputation for an excellent cellar and a lax attitude to morals.

'Much like he was used to in Italy, no doubt. But there are those of us here in Germany who, even though we may not like the havoc wrought by Luther, appreciate much of what he has done. God's house was corrupt, and I a too-willing participant in that corruption. No more! I set my house in order, returned to the simple virtues of my vows. I myself began a fast and have eaten no bread or flesh for a week. I can afford the abstinence, as you can see.' That gentle smile again, swiftly fled. 'That did not suit His Eminence or his mad brother. They took over the house, encouraged the monks in their former ways, brought food from the village, wine, bread, even women.'

He winced, in memory and pain.

'I knew the Devil was abroad once more. I still held to my fast, but everyone else began to gorge like pigs at a trough, most of my monks joining in. But, something . . . something happened. A door was opened and the Beast unleashed into the world. This morning, Brother Andreas threw himself from the tower, screaming that the fires of hell were gaping for him. His legs shattered, yet he got up and ran through the gates. And he was just the first. Soon everyone had a demon inside them – my monks, the Italians, all. And because I did not, and tried to cast theirs out, they descended on me and perpetrated this sacrilege.'

He raised his bandaged hands and stared at them in horror.

Jean leant in. 'And where have they gone, Father?'

'To the village, I think. Most of their men-at-arms were

lodged there. They shouted that they needed an army to defend them.'

A scratching at the door had them turning with weapons raised. The terrified face of a monk appeared and he was seized before he could bolt.

'Do not harm him!' called the Abbot. 'He is my confessor, Brother Anselm.'

The frightened young man was brought into the room. He wept when he saw the Abbot's wounds.

'My son, my son,' said the Abbot fondly, a tear running down his face. 'Anselm joined me in my quest for purification. He fasted and prayed too. The only one. The only one.'

Jean led his men outside, leaving the weeping men to their reunion.

'Did you hear? The only men not possessed of the demons are ones who did not eat or drink,' said Januc.

'They are also the only ones actively seeking God in this accursed place. I don't see how you can blame the food. The Devil strikes where he will,' argued the Fugger.

Jean interrupted before Haakon could speak. 'Food or fiend, we do not want to stay here. What we seek is in the town, in the midst of the madness. It will be dangerous enough. But while Cibo's bodyguard are fighting the Devil's legions, we could not ask for a greater distraction.'

'Let us make use of it while we can,' the Norwegian agreed, lifting his axe onto his shoulder, 'and get free of this terrible place.'

Mounting their horses, each calling for the protection of their own god in their own way, the four men rode into the heart of St Anthony's Fire.

'Giancarlo.'

*What a lovely voice. Like an altar boy's, that innocent.*

'Go back, Giancarlo. Holiness. Giancarlo Cibo. Back to the inn.'

*But I just came from there.*

He tried to locate the angelic face, but it moved, a shadow slipping round to his other side.

'It is different there now. Order. Is restored. Love. Is restored. Friends are there, a brother flesh of your flesh blood of your . . .'

*Blood.*

Now he remembered. Blood had driven him from that smoke-filled room in the first place. His own, coughed up in unimaginable quantities, until he would have drowned had he not found some air. Then other people's blood, he'd forgotten whose. Big men with weapons had become very scared. Frightened animals fled or fought. Fleeing had brought them to the town, from the slaughter at the monastery. But demons could not be escaped in such a manner. Demons had preceded them.

'But they've gone.' The sweet voice came from above him now, as if along a sunbeam. 'Didn't I tell you? Go see for yourself. After all, there's nothing for you in this stable, is there, Giancarlo?'

There wasn't, not now. Not now he'd learnt the truth that changed everything.

Hell wasn't buried deep. Its roof was a finger's push through the crumbly crust of skin and old bones that made up the stable floor. Hell was directly beneath his feet. No, it wasn't quite true. The chambers were there; if he stamped the sufferers would hear him again and renew their terrible wailing. But hell had burst its petty bindings. Hell was loose in the world.

'Yes, Giancarlo, yes! Hell is everywhere. Except at the inn. Where your friends are.'

*No one who speaks so sweetly can tell lies*, he thought.

He was wrong.

He pushed the inn door open and found no friends inside, no brothers. Wild dogs snarled at each other, teeth drawn back in a rictus of terror. They had human bodies, but that was all. He always knew his brother's lycanthropic tendencies. For the sake of good government he had restrained them. Now, Franchetto stood on a window ledge, naked, baying at a moon only he could see, lodged just next to the fireball sun. Beneath him a pack of what used to be called his men snapped at another man before them. They had weapons drawn, but none such as Cibo had seen before. Spade-headed rats wriggled together in the hands of one, like a furred whip. A chair leg was crested by a scythe's blade, a pot had daggers thrust through it. All were levelled in defence of their master; for this other man, cloaked and helmeted, was trying to approach the howling Duke, his intent clear – to wrestle the werewolf to the floor and throttle it.

Something about this figure seemed familiar. The Archbishop tried to speak, to command, but his voice came out too slowly, distorted and deep. All other sounds seemed normal compared to it: the howling from the streets, the baying on the ledge, the wailing of the damned a finger's thrust below his feet. Finally, he got a word out.

'Heineeriich.'

The figure heard. The figure started to turn, as slowly as the Archbishop's speech had come.

At the first glimpse of scarred flesh, Giancarlo Cibo began to scream. Like the words before it, the scream emerged into a world run down, where time had ceased its normal function. Nevertheless, sound continued to emerge, matching in pace the revelation of flesh.

Heinrich von Solingen had never been a handsome man and a virgin's tears had destroyed most of what had made his face human. But now, Cibo saw a sight that finally brought his screams into alignment with time. For as Heinrich's eyes swivelled round to fix on his master's, a long snake slithered from the cave of one socket and slipped, so slowly, into the other.

Cibo did not stop running until his back was pressed against the town well. Ice had replaced flame on every surface of the main square of Marsheim. The cold reached down inside him like frozen knives plunging within his body, stopping his breath and forcing icicles of blood from his throat.

Something moved at his breast. He tried to lower his eyes, but it took such an effort. *What might be down there*, he thought, *held within the folds of my cloak? I have a pocket there, no, a pouch or . . . that's it, a bag! There's something in it.*

He forced his eyes down. On his chest was a pouch. It was made of purple velvet yet it was somehow also completely transparent, for he could see within it, pointing up at him, a hand with six fingers. As soon as he saw it, the hand formed into a fist and began to beat at his chest. He knew the pounding would not stop until his heart shattered into a thousand icy shards.

'Jesu, mercy!' he cried as agony spread across his body.

A rent appeared in the skin of the earth, hell slowly opening for him, every blow of the Witch of England driving him down into it. He could do nothing to stop his own fall. There was only the pounding, and a heat so white his skin began to dissolve.

'Jesus!' he called again, knowing it would be the last word he would ever speak. He looked in farewell to the road south, the one that led past the abbey and on over the mountains to his homeland.

Four horsemen rode into the square. This, at least, was a vision he had expected – the Four Horsemen of the Apocalypse, there to usher in the destruction of the world. They were to be welcomed, for it meant plenty of company in the descent to Hades. Enough, perhaps, for the Devil to be too busy to deal with a lowly archbishop for a while. Yet, even here, there was something wrong with the vision. He did not expect consistency, not in Marsheim. But of the four horsemen, only two were meant to be bringers of war. And all four here had weapons in their hands.

'Where is plague? Where famine?' he shouted at them, then

realised it was a mistake. They hadn't noticed him before. Now they had.

There was something familiar about the man who dismounted. Cibo knew he had seen him before. And when the man reached down and picked Anne Boleyn's hand off his chest, Cibo remembered where. He even knew his name.

'Rombaud. Jean Rombaud,' he croaked.

The executioner gave no sign he had heard, just kept staring down into the velvet bag. He didn't even look at Cibo when he got up and moved away. This annoyed the Archbishop. He deserved more than that. He had left this man in a gibbet cage to rot. Was he not worthy of revenge?

'Kill me.' The words came clear in his new-found tongue. 'You cannot leave me here. Kill me.'

The executioner didn't look back until he was in his saddle again. Finally, he said something Cibo couldn't quite hear. Then the four horsemen rode from the square. Hell opened once more and Giancarlo Cibo's further pleas were lost in the wailing of the damned.

Jean had said, 'You are in hell. Why should I set you free?'

To Januc and Haakon, it was incomprehensible. To have a mortal enemy at your mercy – why would any man let that opportunity pass?

Jean could not explain it. The moment he saw Cibo, slouched against the town well, covered in vomit and blood, Jean had thought, *It ends here. I will use my sword, perhaps for the last time, to take the head of our enemy.* But it was Anne herself who stopped him. Not by appearing in a flash of celestial light, nor even by gently whispering within his mind. It was the memory of a word he had spoken to her, sworn his oath by, recalled now by the touch of that hand, even though he felt it through the velvet of the bag. The hand he had kissed, been shocked by, heard her laugh about. The hand he had sworn, by that word, to save from the forces of hate embodied within the man at his feet.

The word was 'love'. Remembering it, Jean suddenly saw that to bathe the hand in blood now, however justified the shedding, however prudent the action, went against the spirit of what he'd pledged to do. He had enough stains on his own hands in trying to gain hers back. Now he had reclaimed it, so effortlessly compared to all he had been through, now the quest was nearly over, he wanted to return to the feeling of the oath, to the core of it, to that one word. To love.

He could not explain that to his friends. He was not a man of words and they were, like him, warriors unaccustomed to such sentiments. But then a thought came, and it made him smile as they rode from a town still burning with St Anthony's Fire. One of the benefits of leadership was that he didn't have to explain anything.

# TWO

# SIEGE

'Do you not know a safer way, Fugger?' Jean had asked.

Three days they had been on the main road north from Marsheim. Three days and they had barely crossed the border out of Bavaria, and that only because Jean and Haakon had remembered some of their Catholic prayers – enough, anyway, to convince a large party of hedge knights they were not heretical Lutherans.

Across the border into Württemberg – same day, different faith. It was the Fugger who was called upon to declaim the Little Monk's teachings to dour and doubtful apprentices in a small town square.

'Watch the road north,' one of the interrogators, a little friendlier than the rest, had warned, tapping a grimy finger to his large nose. 'The Brotherhood of the Shoe lies in wait for parties the size of yours.'

The Fugger had later explained about the peasant rebellion of twenty-four and twenty-five, fought under the symbol of the worker's wooden clog.

'Most of them were slaughtered at the war's end by their former masters,' he'd said, 'but some still must lurk in the passes.'

'Maybe I can pacify them with words from the Koran.' Januc had felt left out in all the religious declarations.

Then Jean asked his question about a safer way.

'I know some paths through the woods that few tread,' the

Fugger had offered. 'But the forest roads are strange and the going slow.'

'No one travels slower than the dead,' Jean had said. 'So we'll take your strange ways.'

All too soon, Jean was regretting his choice. On the main route, at least the enemy was in plain sight, armed and demanding. In the dark woods, spectres lurked in every shadow, behind the moss-encrusted humps of dead trees, in the tendrils spread across the rotted-leaf floor. The path was mostly too narrow to ride so they led their horses, stumbling over the roots of trees whose branches folded upon them, pressing down; the sky, when glimpsed, was black and louring. Rain thudded ceaselessly onto the roof of the canopy, never seeming to penetrate to the forest floor. The light changed from grey to greyer and the little fires they lit at night only drew the darkness closer.

Everyone folded into themselves. Barely a few words were snapped at each other, no stories were told to brighten the camp fire's gloom. All suffered, but for Haakon it was worst.

On the fifth day out of Marsheim, he started developing 'tree fever', muttering to himself at his horse's head. On the seventh he was seeing trolls behind every other tree. On the eighth he seized his axe and ran into the forest to chop at a small, gnarled oak that had insulted his mother. To a man used to the horizons of the sea, the confinement was intolerable.

That night, with Haakon halfway up an alder in an effort to see the heavens, the faithful Fenrir whimpering at the foot of the tree, Jean took the Fugger aside.

'How much more of this?'

'Not much,' said the Fugger. 'Oh no, no, no, not much at all, isn't that right, O Daemon dear?'

The raven let out a strangled caw, not even bothering to lift its beak from under its wing.

' "Not much" is not the answer I seek.' Jean was suddenly annoyed, as if the endless forest were the one-handed man's fault. 'And why have you started to babble to that bird again? I thought you'd stopped all that.' He grabbed the dancing figure by the collar and held him. Only the Fugger's feet still scuffed a bit on the ground and his eyes moved here and there. Jean tried to speak more gently. 'Is it just the forest, Fugger, or what lies beyond it? Come, man, we all know how hard it can be to go home. That's why many of us never do.'

But the Fugger was not hearing sympathy, nor was it a friend's concerned grip on his collar. And he was not looking down into sympathetic eyes but up into ones hard as slate, set in a jowled, mottled face, the voice like jagged shards from the same stone.

*What have you done, Albrecht? Where have you been these seven years?*

*I lost my hand, father. And then your gold. And then . . .*

'Fugger? Fugger?' A hand was shaking him. 'How much longer in the forest? How many days before we reach Munster?'

'Another day, and one more night in the forest. We will be there near noon the day after.'

'Good.' Jean released the Fugger, patted him on the shoulder, then went to help Januc persuade Haakon down from his tree.

The Fugger sank down beside a silver birch, pressing his face into the moss spread like a rug around its base.

Munster! It had been his suggestion as a rendezvous, when Beck had insisted she would join them in Germany as soon as Abraham was safe, even though Jean had argued she should wait for him in Venice. It was the Fugger who had finally come up with the solution of his birthplace. He said there would be a welcome there, coin for the road ahead, fresh horses. Yet only he knew the true reason why he had suggested it.

It was the only way he could go home.

*Look, father. See what I have achieved? See who are my companions? Hear them testify to my worth, my courage*

*along the hard ways we have travelled together. I am part of a*
*glorious quest – and all for a Protestant queen.*

No! It would not do. Such an explanation could merit only one response. No matter that the Fugger was a grown man, had been to university, could speak five languages and read the Bible in Greek. He had lost the family gold. He had betrayed the family trust. And Cornelius Fugger would still reach up into the roof, as he had always done, to the beam where there was a gap between wood and loam. He would pull down the hazel switch that rested there. He would raise it up on high . . .

It was as the Fugger said. By noon on the tenth day out of Marsheim, the forest had thinned until even Haakon was satisfied, gulping down the sight of a horizon like a near-drowned man gulps air. Soon they were into cultivated fields, and vineyards that reminded Jean of the Loire. The way they had followed through the darkness merged with a bigger route; even the rain ceased, the late August sun once more warming the land.

They were riding to the top of what the Fugger had promised was the last hill, from whose crest the majesty of his city would be revealed. Before they reached it, though, they all heard a dull thump that had the other three reining in.

'What? What was that?' said the Fugger, who had ridden past, oblivious.

'What would you say, Januc?' Haakon turned to the Croatian. 'Culverin or saker?'

The janissary shook his head. 'Sounded more like a bombard to me. But they tend to haunt me. Three months, night after night, while your Emperor besieged Tunis. Thud, thud, thud. It was all I could do to keep my wives satisfied.'

'Culverins? Bombards? What are you talking about?' The Fugger brought his horse back level with them.

'Well, wood sprite' – Haakon had become convinced, one night in the forest, that their guide was a demon leading them to a green doom – 'unless your reformed Munsterites have had news of your arrival and are attempting to salute you, yonder is the sound of a city under attack by cannon. And that,' he added, tipping an ear in the direction of a new sound, 'is musketry.'

The crackling, interspersed with another three booms, accompanied them the final hundred paces to the hill's crest. Once there, they gazed down upon a sight familiar to all three warriors.

The city was spread over three hills, its walls undulating up and down the slopes, encircling it entirely. There was a ditch before them and two hundred paces before the ditch a set of earthworks paralleled the walls all around, though these were not continuously linked, more a series of extended bastions and emplacements. It was, beyond doubt, a siege.

Jean turned to the Fugger, whose twitching had been shocked into stillness by the sight. 'There was a disadvantage coming by the back ways to your city. We had no news of this. Who would be attacking Munster?'

The Fugger squinted at the besieger's lines. 'I can't think, Jean, unless . . . there do seem to be a lot of white and blue banners outside the city. With gold crosses.'

'So?'

'It is the sign of . . . wait! Of course! The Bishop of Munster! He who would suppress the Reformation. Of course!' He clutched at Jean. 'Suppression! The town was one of the first to declare for Luther. The Catholic Bishop is trying to get it back.'

'Oh good, just what we need,' Jean sighed, 'another war.'

'Holy war!' said the Fugger, suddenly bright-eyed.

'Is there any other kind?' Januc's smile never reached his eyes.

Jean walked his horse a little apart and cursed fluently and continuously for a full minute. All hopes of a swift reunion with Beck, a swift departure for France with fresh horses and fresh Fugger gold, were gone. It was possible that she had not made the city yet, that she was even now approaching from the south. But they had left Montepulciano a month and a half ago and not only had they travelled at the slow pace of the Archbishop's carriage, they had also contended with the endless forest. Beck had promised speed once she'd settled her father in Venice. So travelling alone and fast by the main routes, she had to have arrived by now, and would have had to make this same decision about whether or not to enter the city, to go to the Fugger's family house. If they missed each other here, they could chase across Europe for years, they could pass at a dozen paces in the night and never meet.

Rendezvous, however difficult, had to be kept. *Really*, he thought, *there is no choice.*

Turning back to the others, he said, 'All we can do is descend and find out what this war is about. We won't be able to attempt the city till nightfall.'

The Fugger was aghast. 'Attempt the city? What do you mean, "attempt the city"? How will you get through the siege lines?'

Jean looked at Haakon and Januc and smiled grimly. 'Oh, there are always ways through those. As Beck might already have found out. Shall we go and look for some old comrades?'

It was Haakon who found Johannes. Or rather the other way around, for the old Swiss musketeer caught sight of the huge Norwegian as Jean's party was stopped and questioned for the fifth time since entering the besieging lines. Jean was explaining again how they were there to volunteer when a voice roared out from a group of wounded lying on the ground.

'Now I know the Devil comes for me, boys, because his bastard whelp stands over there!'

'Johannes Brauman!' Haakon threw back his head and laughed. 'Haven't you given up this game yet? You must be a hundred!'

Haakon picked a path through the moaning bodies until he reached a man leaning against a cart axle. The others followed, including the officer who had been questioning Jean.

'You know these people, Johannes?' he asked.

'I know this big lout. Nearly broke my back outside Bologna, falling off a bridge. Are these others friends of yours, Hawk?'

'They are.'

'Then they obviously lack any judgement. Do they follow the trade?'

'They do.'

'Stupid as well, then, if they are here to offer themselves in this Godforsaken war.' The old man tried to spit, but began to cough instead, blood flecking his lips. When he had regained his breath he said to the officer, 'It's all right, Piet, I can vouch for them. Haakon here wouldn't know an Ana-baptist from His Eminence's arsehole.'

The officer nodded, and moved back to his post.

Johannes gestured to the ground beside him. 'Make yourself comfortable, friends. I'd take you to my tent, but I have to await the attentions of that butcher-surgeon.' He nodded to a tent from which some heavy moaning had been coming steadily. It quickly built to a shriek, instantly cut off. 'God have mercy on my body, then my soul.'

Jean looked at the old man. He was a big Switzer with hardly a hair on his head – except in his ears, where it grew in a profuse disorder of mottled white. His face was as lined as if someone had taken a knife and cut a score of furrows from the back of his head over to his chin, with gashes left and right level with his nose. Thick wattles of pallid flesh hung at his neck. His left eye was a cloud, the other red-streaked and gummed. His breathing was raspy and he clutched to his side a filthy piece of crimson-stained cloth. Jean didn't think he'd ever seen an older man in any company he'd served in. It wasn't a profession that encouraged length of service.

'Would you like me to take a look?'

Johannes one-eyed Jean with suspicion until, at a nod from Haakon, he slowly peeled away the makeshift bandage. A gush of blood followed the revealing of a soaked undershirt. Jean, probing with his fingertips, felt the hard lump of metal wedged between two ribs under the skin. There was no bubbling of foam around the wound, so Jean knew it had not pierced the lungs.

'Musket ball?'

'I doubt it. Those scum in Munster don't have many of those left. Ayee! Careful, will you? No, it'll be a bit of rusted bucket, or a coin perhaps. They don't believe in money, see, so they've been firing them at us for weeks now.'

The Fugger laughed. 'Don't believe in money? The people of this city are renowned for their desire never to let a single thaler go.'

The old man squinted up, wincing, as Jean continued to probe. 'How long since you have been here, sonny? They have overthrown the Church in there and set up what they call "the New Jerusalem". Though the money lenders weren't driven out, they were strung up by their balls and burnt to death. Christ, man, what are you about down there?'

Without replying, Jean went to his saddle bags and returned with his barber's kit. He said, 'You can wait for the butcher, or you can let me work.'

Januc, who had had an arrow head removed by Jean on the *Perseus*, said, 'He is good, old man.'

With a nod, Johannes turned his face away. Jean had worked the edges of the metal piece free and now grasped the end of it with his pliers. At a glance from him, Haakon and Januc held the old man down. When they had him, Jean jerked the fragment free and swiftly stemmed the flow of blood with a cleaner cloth. Johannes fainted, but a swig from Haakon's flask – grappa from Montepulciano – revived him. Jean handed him the bloody piece of metal he'd removed.

'Pah!' spat the old man. 'Looks like a piece of a comb. Not even a little profit in being hurt.'

Jean used more grappa to cleanse the wound, stitched it, then wrapped an unstained cloth round and round the big chest. At the end of the procedure Johannes was pale but still awake.

'I think you will be all right. But do not remove the bandage for at least a week.'

The Switzer painfully leant over towards his pack. 'I do not have much money to pay you with, surgeon. Can you wait? We are on a bonus when we take the town and as much loot as we can carry away. You can have your share then.'

'Keep it, old man. I'll swap my skill for some information – if you feel up to talking.'

'If you help me back to my tent, there's food and wine for you there. I'll tell you anything you want to know.'

Johannes's 'tent' turned out to be a hut of reasonable size. Smoke from the cooking hearth filled it, and a begrimed servant hurried about to provide a meal for his master and his new friends.

Once settled on his large truckle bed, a mug of hot beer in his hand, Johannes listened to Haakon's shortened version of why they were there.

'Sure I can help you get in. You've both served in sieges, I take it? There are always ways in and out. But why you'd want to enter that hell hole . . .' Johannes spat. 'They're all madmen in there. And mad bitches too. They don't fight for money like all the other good Germans I know. They fight for God. It's so unreasonable.'

The Fugger's eyes gleamed. 'Unreasonable? The city reforms according to the word of Luther and the law of God, and you call it unreasonable?'

'Luther?' Johannes laughed, then began to cough, clutching his side in pain. When he had recovered, he continued. 'Most men who attack the city fight under the Protestant banner.'

'But I have seen the flag of the Papist Bishop of Munster!'

'And flying right next to it is the Eagle banner of Philip of Hesse.'

The Fugger stuttered in shock. 'The . . . the Landgrave of Hesse? But he is the temporal leader of the Protestant cause. Luther's protector!'

'Aye, queer bedfellows, you might say. Catholics and Lutherans combined. But the madmen in the city threaten both orders. So they ally to cut out the disease before the contagion spreads. Speaking of which, what did you stitch me with, you butcher, cat gut? It feels like a dozen of them are scratching down there.'

Jean poured the old man some more of the beer and said, 'Explain it to us, Johannes. We need to know what goes on in there. What disease do you speak of?'

'They call themselves "Anabaptists". Say that only adults who know the word of God can receive the blessing of the water. Then they are baptised again.'

The Fugger said, 'It's an extreme position but a debatable one. Why would they be so persecuted for holding it?'

'Because of what goes with it. They believe they alone are God's Chosen. So they have set up his Holy Kingdom, the New Jerusalem, to await the final reckoning. All will be destroyed and only they, the true believers, will survive. Lunatics from all over Germany, from Holland, France, even England, have flocked here to the call.'

'And this second baptism is so bad that Lutherans will ally with Catholics to crush it?' The Fugger was hopping about the room now in agitation.

Johannes laughed. 'I don't think most men would give a whore's cuss for their bathing habits. It's what goes with it.' He leant in. 'They have done away with money, I told you. But marriage too. A man can have as many wives as he likes. It's because there are so many unfrocked nuns. Raving with lust, they are – cast off their habits and, uh, picked up new, nasty ones. The women are the most vicious fighters. They eat any prisoner taken. Having first ravished him!' The one eye gleamed. 'The Black Widow's death, they are calling it.'

'But—'

Jean silenced the Fugger's next outburst, pulling him down.

'I'll tell you this,' Johannes continued, 'whatever they believe gives them the power of fanatics. They don't fight reasonably at all! They don't seem to care if they die. How can you take a city like that? You kill five lunatics, another five take their place, just as happy to die! Sixteen lousy months we have been here. Sixteen! But the pay's almost regular and there are no more civilised wars to go to, more's the pity.'

'So Jean,' Januc said. 'You still want to enter this place of djinns? Beck's tough. He can fend for himself.'

Jean stood up and walked to the hut's entrance. It was starting to get dark, and a gibbous moon was rising above the trees, a moon equal in his memory to the one in whose beams he had lain with Beck at the Comet.

'The Fugger and I will go in. I made the boy a promise. Besides, we need some help now and the Fugger can get us some gold, can you not?'

'Of course. My family will do anything to help my friends.'

But the Fugger didn't know how he felt about the decision. There was his mother, his sister. There was also his father, and a city he loved in the grip of some madness. Different from the madness he had seen at Marsheim. Maybe as bad.

Jean continued, 'We will say we are mercenaries, come to offer our services.'

Johannes guffawed. 'They will hang you in an instant. No soldiers of fortune fight for them. Only soldiers of Christ.'

'Then we will have to say we are some of those. I'll let the Fugger do the talking.'

It was swiftly arranged. Johannes headed a company whose task for the next three nights was to probe the defences for weaknesses under cover of darkness. They had spotted a broken area of wall where the Bishop's ineffective artillery had actually scored a success. The Switzer sent for his second in command, a runt-faced Hessian called Franck. Franck agreed to take the wall section and hold it for the time necessary to slip the men inside.

The assault was set for midnight. They ate and drank and talked little. The Fugger's agitation had changed to a strange stillness, only his eyes alive and darting. Haakon and Januc were silent too, still disapproving.

When it was close to his time, Jean spoke. 'Watch the tower, to the left of where we go in, every midnight. We will signal from there any time from the third night on. If you see a white cloth waved, we will be coming out and we will be coming out fast. Be ready.'

'We will,' Haakon grumbled. 'I still think this is madness, Frenchman.'

'And you are right to think so. But I have no choice.'

'I don't see why I can't come too.' Haakon's voice was surly.

Jean smiled. 'Because, from the sound of it, the people in this town have been slowly starving for ten months. We might be able to mix unnoticed. You . . .'

'Are you saying I'm fat?' Haakon stood and glowered down at Jean.

'Not at all. You are a warrior in his prime. People cannot help but notice your magnificence. They would flock to you as to a god. And it sounds as though there are enough of them in there already.'

Even the Fugger turned away to hide a smile.

'Besides,' Jean continued, 'wherever you go your monstrous wolf will follow you. And this is a city under siege. Do you want to be dining on Fenrir stew tonight?'

As the dog growled at the mention of his name, Franck stuck his head inside the hut doorway. 'It's time,' he said shortly, then ducked out again.

'Very well,' the Norseman growled, 'but you will leave the hand?'

Jean strapped on his sword, picked up a saddle bag of provisions, and finally the velvet bag. He looked at it for a long moment, then began to wind it within a bandage he had cut and wrapped the bandage around his stomach, until the hand rested snug against the small of his back.

'I will not. Only I can fulfil my vow. No, Haakon, no arguments. I will return, in three nights, with the hand, and Beck, and Fugger gold to see us on our way to France and the Loire to finish what we started. In a month we can be back in Montepulciano, if we choose. There we can all grow fat.'

They went to the emplacement from where the assault would be launched. Fifty men stood in the pale moonlight, checking weapons and harness. Franck moved up and down, speaking in a low voice to the company leaders. After a moment he signalled to Jean that he was ready.

'I'll see you in three nights.' Haakon nodded, then he and Januc went to stand on an earthwork step where they would have a better view.

'Allah guard and protect you both,' said Januc as he went, then added with a wink, 'and watch out for black widows!'

The word was whispered down the line and the company stood to, Jean and the Fugger taking up their positions in the rear of them. The German spent his last minutes talking incessantly to Daemon, whom he then released. The bird flew up to perch on the edge of a gabion. A superstitious soldier threw a stone at him so the bird flew up and away with a disdainful caw.

'Now,' called Franck softly, then led the way over the barricades.

They were twenty paces away from the wall when a cry broke the stillness of the night.

'To arms, to arms! The enemy is upon us!'

Three arquebusiers fired before the assailants reached the

ditch. Wooden ladders were swiftly thrown up against the wall, and though newly awakened men were pouring onto the ramparts, they were a scattering compared to the concentrated thrust of the mercenaries. Armed with short pikes, double-handed swords and entrenching tools, the Swiss and German warriors swiftly cleared all resistance from the crest of the weakened wall. Franck had run down the rubble the other side and, with a strength that belied his stature, was laying about him strongly with his huge double-handed sword. In a moment the company had poured through the gap and their arquebusiers had set up a firing position. A ragged volley swept aside the first who rushed at them, and for a moment the only guns firing were their own.

'Now is the time!' Franck was at the top of the wall again, calling down to its base where Jean and the Fugger crouched. They scrambled over the rocks and debris and knelt beside him. 'I have seen all I need. Your best chance is over there. Good luck!'

The mercenary captain had pointed along the wall, where a fall of masonry led down to street level. Houses lay half-gutted there, most of the roofs torn down to prevent the structures within the walls catching fire in an assault, a fire which might spread to the town. They looked unoccupied, and Jean immediately led the way down the shifting rubble, under cover of another volley.

They ran, dodging from shadow to darker shadow, until they made the nearest house. Its walls were so battered that anyone peering in from outside would see any movement within. So, when the distraction of Franck's withdrawal was at its noisiest, they ran to the next house. Here, a ruin of furniture greeted them, and they swiftly made a nest out of the items to conceal themselves from within. Jean peered carefully over the top of a table to observe the final retreat, and the reinforced defenders' re-taking of the wall. When the last crackle of gunpowder had faded into the night, and the moment of silence that followed had been broken by the jeering of the Munsterites, Jean flopped down, put his back to the table and chewed upon a piece of dried meat.

'We'll move at daybreak. When there are some people about,' he said.

The Fugger did not act as if he had heard. He lay with his head buried in his arms, eyes closed, tortured by images as bad as any conjured in his midden. This was his city, yet what had his city become in the seven years of his absence? He couldn't believe the stories! A realm of fanatics and flesh eaters? Could his family have become like that? His gentle mother, his giggling sister? Even his unbending, morally upright father? Only tomorrow will tell, he told himself.

He was wrong. He didn't have to wait nearly so long.

The voice came from above them, from among the rafters of the long-destroyed second floor. It was a hymn, to an old familiar tune, though more of a croak than a clear utterance; yet the words, if slurred, were instantly understandable.

> *Some in heavy chains have lain*
> *And rotting there have stayed,*
> *Some upon the trees were slain,*
> *Choked and hacked and flayed,*
> *Drownings by stealth and drownings plain*
> *For matron and for maid.*
> *Fearlessly the truth they spoke*
> *And they were not ashamed:*
> *Christ is the way and Christ the life*
> *Was the word proclaimed.*

From the darkness above them, there was a snickering laugh. A score of rat-like eyes glittered in the moonlight.

'Welcome, Brothers. Welcome to the New Jerusalem.'

# THREE

# MUNSTER

The sound of the blow caused the two other women in the house to pause, breath held, hands suspended from activity, waiting for the silence of the inhalation to end and the wailing to begin. Each hoped the sound of the crying would put an end to it. The master of the house didn't have as much strength these days, after all.

It came, Alice's high-pitched, juddery squeal. Since she had always been the favourite, Alice normally received the least of the beatings. Not this morning, though. Her mother, and Marlena, the old nurse, winced at each of the three blows and again at the roaring that followed.

'Get out! Get out! You slut! Would you drive me mad?'

The door of the master's room flew open and a squealing Alice was pitched out. She fell, all sharp bones and shuddering breaths, at the feet of her mother, who stooped to comfort and enfold her, to bend her own frail body over this, her youngest, her only remaining child.

Glancing up, avoiding his eyes, Gerta pleaded. 'Cornelius, dearest, what stupidity has Alice committed now? Oh, you bad, bad girl!' The voice chastised, but the way she rocked her child comforted. Her husband was terribly short-sighted, after all.

He stood in the doorframe that once he would have filled. He may have lost a third of his bodyweight during the privations of the siege but he had lost none of his swift anger. Rather the reverse.

'That slut we have raised,' he shouted, 'speaks to me again about marriage. About becoming the third strumpet to be kept by that buffoon, Thaddeus. A Fugger marrying a tanner is ridiculous enough. Becoming nothing better than a whore is another thing altogether.'

Alice, the indulged child in whom Cornelius's temper most often manifested itself, spoke angrily through her tears. 'But he is one of the Twelve! He has the King's ear! If he does not protect me, the King may marry me off to any old butcher!'

Her mother's arms were inadequate protection from Cornelius's blows.

'Jezebel! How dare you speak to me of a king? That . . . tailor! I will keep you safe, I, Cornelius Albrecht Fugger. You are mine to dispose of. Mine, do you hear? And when this madness is over, and order restored, I will marry you to the ugliest, oldest butcher I please! As long as he has some gold left to pay for you!'

The effort had exhausted him, and he stepped back, bent down to rest his hands on his knees.

'Now, get her out of my sight. Get her out!'

Mother and daughter scurried off to the safety of the kitchen, where Marlena applied damp cloths and soothing words. It failed to stem the weeping for quite a while.

'Why can't he see?' Alice sobbed. 'Look at me! I am becoming ugly, old. My teeth are rotting, my hair falling out. No one will want me. I don't care if I am Thaddeus's third wife, or his fifth, at least I will have a husband. Before it's too late. Ohhhh!'

Cornelius had slammed the door to his room, but because so much of the interior wood had been stripped out for fires and fortifications he could still hear the sobbing. His hands itched to reach up to the beam, get down the hazel switch he kept there and beat and beat until there were no sounds but the beating. But he knew he didn't have the strength for it. He was getting old, and the disasters of recent years had made him age quickly, what with the starvation and his turn on the battlements. They actually expected him to fight! He, Cornelius Fugger, the man most lacking in violence in the whole city!

His family, that was all he cared about, and they treated him in this manner? First his son running off with two years' worth of profit, now his daughter wanting to marry . . . a tanner? Well, he had taken better care of them than they had of him; it would all be proved eventually, when the lunatics were overthrown and order was restored. Oh, he had taken great care.

He went to the fireplace, with its long-dead ashes, and carefully shifted a stone from the wall, placing it on the ground beside him. Raising a candle, even his poor eyes could see the glimmer of the gold coins piled up in the niche. Three years' worth of trading before the madness began. Ready for the restoration of the illustrious name of Fugger to its rightful place in Munster.

A scratching at the door had him hastily replacing the stone. He turned and barked, 'Go away!'

His wife's voice came timidly. 'But Cornelius, dear husband, the meeting.'

He had forgotten. Another cursed gathering of the Elect, the so-called 'Tribes of Israel', in the square. More apocalyptic lunacy! His contempt for it knew no bounds. But no one could stay away. No one who wanted to live.

'All right, I am coming,' he said. 'And tell that slattern daughter of mine to wear her oldest dress. She will not flirt with the whoremasters who run our city!'

There was only one good thing about the meetings – the punishments. Everything seemed to be a crime these days, punishable by death or maiming at the least: lewd conduct, blasphemy, hoarding. Even scolding one's parents.

Cornelius chuckled. *Maybe that's what I should do. Testify to Alice's shameful behaviour this morning, her disrespect. See how much Thaddeus the tanner will want her when they've chopped off her nose!*

There was another benefit to these meetings in the square. If the punishments continued at the present rate there would be no one left able-bodied enough to man the walls, and deliverance, by the Bishop and the Prince, would be assured.

In the great square of Munster, beneath the eaves of St Lambert's, under the sightless gaze of the dozen latest traitors to the Word whose heads adorned its crenellations, the twelve tribes of Israel Reborn had gathered to greet their king.

Jean and the Fugger waited with the rest, surrounded by their captors, two dozen beggars who lived in the rafters of ruins no one else would consider. They had seized the two men and bound them swiftly. They had taken their weapons and searched their bags. Yet they had not touched one mouthful of their food.

'All belongs to everyone, and everyone shall partake of all,' the scab-faced leader had told him when the Fugger tried to bribe him to let them go with a promise of more food. 'We will bring it to the meeting.'

And as they waited, their captors paraded them with pride, explaining to the curious how they, beggars though they were, had played such a part in the defence of the city.

'Snuck over in the attack last night, Brother,' one explained to an onlooker. 'Spies come to bring us to ruin. But the Lord set us to watch in that place and he has delivered our enemies into our hands!'

'I keep trying to tell you, er, Brother.' The Fugger attempted again to speak. 'We come to offer our help. This man is a great warrior . . . ach!'

The leader pulled back his hand to strike again. 'I told you to keep quiet! Our King will decide. He has a powerful way of sorting the lies from the truth.'

Before the Fugger could risk another blow, trumpets blasted from the entrance of the church and the crowd swept forward to the raised platform, bearing the two prisoners in their midst. As the first trumpet blasts faded, twelve figures emerged from the church to the slow beat of a solitary drum. Each wore the robes that all had seen in frescoes on the walls of churches and cathedrals of the land, the robes of the elders of Israel: long, of glorious hues, purple and gold, sweeping to the ground. Each one's head was covered in a shroud of pure white linen, each clutched a shepherd's stave in one hand and a corn flail in the other. They fanned out, six to each side, and stood at the front of the platform.

As the last of them parted, behind them was revealed a person who made all gasp and begin to whisper each to the other. She was in a simple shift that covered her to her bare feet. Her long hair was piled up in a bundle on her head and her eyes were cast down, seeming to focus only on the hands tied before her.

*She is beautiful.* A vision of Anne Boleyn came to Jean, walking as slowly to her fate on Tower Green. *And she too is bound for execution.*

Voices murmured excitedly all around. 'The Queen, the Queen!'

The murmurs were lost in the roar that followed as another man walked out onto the platform, alone, and moved slowly towards the crowd, without looking at the bound woman, who reached out to him as he passed. The roar filled the square, reverberated around the town, carried even to the besiegers' lines outside.

'David! David! David! David! DAVID!'

Jean had noted the rich apparel of the Twelve, but this man's clothes were sumptuous, studded with jewels that glittered in the bright sunshine, a crown upon his head of plain gold yet with an emerald the size of a gull's egg in the middle. The face under it was ten years younger than the face of the youngest of the elders. A clear, unwrinkled brow, a straight nose, dark, heavily lashed eyes. As he raised his arms, bracelets of silver flashed from them.

The movement instantly silenced the crowd. Then a voice that seemed to be made not of sound but of some exotic essence, rich as burning sandalwood, smooth as honey, reached out to caress every ear in the square.

'My people,' the voice spoke gently, yet clearly, as if it were weighed down by a sorrow too great to name. 'Oh, my people.'

The arms were lowered and the cry 'David!' echoed again from the arches of the cathedral. The arms were raised once more, silver and gold flashing. The voice came again, a hardness building within it.

'And Jeremiah spake thus, chapter thirty-three, verse five: "Behold the days are coming, says the Lord, when I will raise up for David a righteous branch, and he shall reign as King and deal wisely and shall execute justice and righteousness in the land."'

Here he paused, and seemed to look out at each individual in the crowd before continuing.

'Am not I your David?'

'Yes, Lord.'

'Am not I your David?'

'Yes, Lord, yes,' came the reply from every hoarse throat.

'And what shall become of the Jezebel who has betrayed me, who has been denounced by my own Elijah?'

The Elder on the extreme left raised his stave and pointed it at the bound woman. At the gesture, her legs gave way and she sank to the floor.

The crowd spoke just two words in one voice: 'Hang her!'

Bejewelled hands rose again, commanding instant silence.

'No, my people, not the noose. For is it not written in Amos nine, verse ten: "All the sinners of my people shall die by the sword"? Is it not said that the beauteous Anne, Queen of England, martyr to the cause of reform, died thus?'

It was as if Jean had been struck. He gasped. He could almost feel the hand bunch at his back as if summoned.

The crowd roared, their King raised his arms again, raised his voice, pointed at the woman and cried, 'I, King Jan of Munster, will be as generous as my sovereign brother Henry of England to my Queen. Let the justice of the Lord be swift and merciful.'

He stepped aside, making way for a masked man holding a sword, almost identical to the one Jean's captors clutched beside him. The weeping woman was raised up on her knees. Jean saw the executioner was experienced in his craft, for he used an old trick. Jabbing one point of the square blade into the base of the victim's back, the head jerked up because of the sudden pain and was off in an instant, to bounce and roll at the feet of her former husband.

And then this King-God did an extraordinary thing. He picked up the head, kissed it full on the lips, then threw it in a high arc out into the crowd, who went crazy with delight. Then their David went to the body, slumped in a fast-expanding pool of blood, and began to jump up and down on it.

Jean Rombaud had witnessed all manner of barbarity in his life with the sword, and participated in much of it. But at this he turned away. Turned away and closed his eyes, reaching inside himself for some sight that would banish what he had just seen. In that instant he knew his career as an executioner was over.

Beside him, the scab-faced man was cheering as loudly as any.

'Who . . . who was that unfortunate woman?' the Fugger was saying to him.

A cackle came. 'Unfortunate woman? That was one of the queens, King Jan's second wife. Had too nagging a tongue on her, so they say. Hey, throw the head over here!'

'Fugger,' whispered Jean, for their faces were suddenly close together in the push of the crowd, 'there was more sanity in your midden.'

The Fugger was weeping openly. 'My family is here somewhere. We must get them out.'

Once more a trumpet blast stilled the noise. The battered body was gone, no doubt to decorate some battlement as a warning to others. The bangled arms were raised again, and Jan Bockelson, King of Munster, in a voice somewhat hoarser than before, called out again.

'And now, my children, your father only has three wives. It is written that four is the number of the handmaidens of David. Who will take the place of this Jezebel, to be joined to me in a ceremony tomorrow night? Who desires that highest of honours?'

If Jean thought the example of the former Queen's end would deter others he was wrong, for he was swept up in the surge of women rushing towards the platform, shouting out, 'Pick me! Pick me!' The jostling allowed Jean to work again at the ropes binding him, for his guards were as distracted as any. Now, in this frenzy, he broke the last of his bonds. The beggar's leader saw his prisoner's hands come free and made to raise the alarm, but an elbow in the throat silenced him. Jean caught his sword as the man fell, and swiftly sliced through the Fugger's knots. A dozen people separated them from their bags, so Jean reluctantly abandoned them and turned to try to force his way through the crowd.

The Fugger made no effort to follow, allowing himself to be borne wherever the crowd willed, transfixed by what he was seeing. A woman, no more than a girl really, had been selected. As Jean turned back to tug at him, she was being lifted out from the crowd, her hand placed in the hand of the King.

'Come, Fugger! Quickly, man! Do you not wish to look for your family?'

'No need.' The one-handed man waved his stump at the platform. 'I have found them.'

It had been seven years, and she had been a bud of a girl then, all apple cheeks and fair, coiled hair. She was thinner now, but she hadn't changed that much. The girl being hailed as the next Queen of Munster was undoubtedly his sister Alice.

'Fugger!' yelled Jean, to no avail, for the man was moving

as if in a trance towards the stage. Jean could only allow the momentum of the crowd to carry him in the Fugger's wake.

Nearer the front, the crowd began to thin as disappointed suitors made their way back. Some stayed to watch and jeer, because the girl's father had now crawled up onto the dais and was pleading with those who held his daughter.

'Lord! King of Kings!' he implored. 'She is the only child we have left. The only hope of her parents' old age is a good marriage for her.'

The beautiful face of Bockelson smiled down upon Cornelius.

'Why, dearest brother and soon-to-be father' – his voice was nectar, causing Alice to sigh – 'can you think of a better future than to be one of the wives of the Lord's anointed? To stand at his right hand at the day of judgement? Besides' – and here he bent down until his face was closer, while the tone lost a little of its sweetness – 'you talk as if you are trapped in the old days before the revelation of the Word. There are no good or bad marriages. There is only union under the Law of God.'

'My only beloved son was taken from this world.' Gerta had joined her husband on her knees, tears streaming down her cheeks. 'Do not let me lose my daughter. Not yet. She is not ready.'

'Silence!' roared Jan Bockelson, raising his arms above the two prostrate figures. 'Silence, and hear the word of your David!'

It was just then that the Fugger reached the platform. Two guards with halberds stopped his progress, but he was a mere few paces away from where his parents knelt, and he had heard their last declarations. Into the silence that awaited the King's word, the Fugger's voice exploded.

'Mother!' he cried. 'Father! It's me, Albrecht! He is not lost. He has returned!'

There was the sound of breath being expelled and held. No

one ever spoke when the King was about to pronounce. All had witnessed the terrible mutilations awaiting those who did.

His parents, turning at his cry, saw the familiar yet alien figure who struggled with the guards. His mother looked, looked away, closed her eyes, opened them, looked again. His father stared, unbelieving. It was little Alice, clinging to King Jan's raised arm, who broke the silence again.

'Albrecht? Oh, Sire, Lazarus has risen! The lost have been found!'

'Let him up here,' bellowed the King. 'The prodigal! The prodigal returns! Praise be to the Lord, for this is His Miracle!'

The halberdiers parted and the Fugger fell onto the stage. His mother clutched his shoulders and both wept, while Cornelius looked on, eyes narrowed, hands twitching. Before he could speak, there was a further eruption before the stage as the last three of his would-be captors fell on Jean, and fell rapidly off again, clutching faces and sides.

'Sire,' yelled their leader through bleeding gums, 'we caught these two sneaking into the city last night. They are spies, our prisoners, brought before you for your justice.'

'Seize him!' commanded Bockelson, and the halberdiers and some of the elders fell upon Jean. Once more his sword was taken and this time handed to the King.

'Well, well.' He turned the weapon over in his hands. 'I've seen one of these before. Is it true? Are you spies, Philistine assassins come to slay me?'

The Fugger, until then gripped by the power of once more holding his family to him, suddenly realised the danger he had put himself and Jean in.

'Most Mighty!' he cried, prostrating himself. 'We had heard of your glory. One of the prophets you sent out came to where we rested and spoke the Good Word. I then knew I must return to the land of my birth, delivered by you from degradation. And my friend here is a mighty warrior who saw that your enemies were his enemies and comes to offer you the tribute of this, his sword.'

Jan, who himself spoke in the language of apocalypse, liked it when others did the same.

'Is this true, swordsman? Have you come to swear fealty to me?'

Jean, who had fewer words and fewer ways with them, simply looked at him and said, 'I have.'

'And I can testify to his skill with that sword' – the voice came from the back of the stage, pronouncing the words in heavily accented German – 'for I have seen him wield it often enough.'

'Uriah Makepeace,' Jean said as the masked man came forward, pulling off his leather disguise.

'The very same.' The removal of the shroud revealed a bearded face, a nose long ago broken and badly reset, a head bald from nape to crown. He continued, in English. 'Don't worry about me revealing my face, they all know who I am. 'is lunatic-ness 'ere just likes the costumes. Oh,' he continued with a smile, 'and none of 'em speaks any English. Bit useful, that.'

Impatiently, King Jan cut in, in German. 'Is he English, this fellow?'

'French, your Holiness,' Makepeace replied in the same language, 'and a famed executioner. It was he who cut the head off your precious English martyr what you was referring to earlier.' Then he added, in English, 'A contract that should have been mine, you poxy French scavenger. Oh and 'e's a little obsessed with 'er "martyrdom", as 'e calls it, 'is March-hare-ness is.'

'You! You are to be honoured among men! You will come tonight and tell me of her beauty, of her sacrifice.' The King's handsome face was coursed with wonder and Jean, more and more confused, just nodded.

'Enough!' cried King Jan, as the tumult from the bleeding captors, reunited Fuggers, and a restless crowd built. He spread his arms over them all and a silence fell immediately. 'Lo, are the sundered joined once again. Lo, the miracle of man and wife will soon be consummated. Lo, are new recruits gathered from all countries to fight for His righteousness. Now, as it is written, in Jeremiah, chapter thirty-one, verse four: "Again I will build you, and you shall be built, O virgin Israel. Again you shall adorn yourself with timbrels and shall go forth in the dance of merrymakers."'

And speaking thus, the King of Munster began to spin his bride-to-be around and around. The trumpets played again and all the Elders, all the townspeople joined in, leaping to the music.

Makepeace leant into Jean. 'What I tell you? Mad, the lot of 'em. Why don't you come with me, Rombaud? Unless you desire a dance?'

Jean called to a still-weeping Fugger clutching his mother, his father a stiff and forlorn sight beside them. 'Leave word where I can find you.'

On receiving a nod, Jean followed the English executioner off the dais, filled now with whirling figures in Biblical robes. Around and around they danced, slipping in the patches of fresh blood that coated the wood. None of them seemed to care.

# FOUR

# THE JUDAS KISS

The joy of the reunion lasted only until they crossed the threshold of the house.

'My room,' Cornelius ordered, disappearing into it.

'I know you have had a terrible time, Albrecht,' his mother whispered, stroking, for the hundredth time, his savaged wrist, 'but so has he.' She kissed him again, then let him go.

As the Fugger entered the room with its terrible memories, he ducked far lower than the lintel required, seeming to become smaller, to shrink back in size to the boy who had wept so often within those panelled walls. He couldn't help but look up. There it was, as it had always been and would be until Doomsday – the hazel switch, thrust into the gap where the beam and the loam of the ceiling failed to meet.

'Well?' His father had his back to him, standing before the heatless fireplace.

The Fugger knew what his father wanted and it was as if seven years were snatched away in a moment. He had just lost the family's gold at a roadside tavern in Bavaria. His stump began to throb as if newly sliced.

'I was attacked, Father. Robbed. My hand . . .' He held the stump up to the rigid back. 'There were too many of them. There was nothing . . .'

He faltered. The silence, the quality of the listening made him falter. It was like the moment after lightning, just before the thunder.

'Nothing?'

His father turned, his face blotched and purple, muscles twisted in the frenzy the Fugger had recalled almost every night of those seven years. He recoiled, shrank still further into himself, forming a barrier with his own body as he had against the fierce rains and scorching heat when crouched beneath the gibbet.

'Nothing? Seven years gone, a family near ruined by your stupidity, and you say "nothing"?' Cornelius was moving around the room now, his limbs shaking with rage. 'All the problems that beset us, all, commenced at the time you lost us our gold. If we had had it safe in Augsburg with my cousin, I would not have had to remain in Munster, I could have got out sooner when the madness began. Now, we have lost almost everything.'

He began to scrabble at the rock inside the fireplace. The Fugger looked up to see the stone come away and the light of the candle flicker on the bright metal inside.

'Look! By my skill I have built up our fortunes again, double, treble what you threw away. But I cannot get it out of this city, and soon the forces of our liberators will take this town and wreak a terrible vengeance. They will not distinguish between the fanatic and men like myself. They will kill me and take my gold. And the only child worth anything to me will have been plundered by a lunatic. If she survives she'll be worthless!'

The Fugger stuttered, 'Father, they may spare the women—'

'Spare? I care nothing about spare! She will be a broken vessel. I cannot sell the virginity she no longer has. She is livestock. Once she has Jan Bockelson, she may as well have a platoon of mercenaries, one after the other!' He looked down at his cowering son. 'And you! This all began with you, all of our misfortunes. You are as worthless as she will shortly be!'

In the depths of the gibbet midden the Fugger had heard his father say all this before, a thousand, thousand times, had bent under the storm, wept into the dungheap, cried his unworthiness to the raven and the rats who were his only companions.

But that was before he met Jean Rombaud.

'No, Father,' he cried, 'I have done such things! The man I came to Munster with? Jean Rombaud? He is the man who took the head of England's queen. He is my friend.'

'A butcher for a friend? This is your achievement?'

His father had to see! Yes, his son had fallen as low as man can fall. But he had risen again. He was part of a noble quest. He had entered the realm of the Devil and snatched the Devil's prey. He had spoken to the shade of Anne Boleyn herself. His son was the knight errant of a Protestant queen. Surely Cornelius Fugger only had to hear to understand?

'No, Father,' he said again, and poured out the glorious tale.

At first the older man interjected with insults and comments on his sanity. Gradually, though, he quietened, listening with mouth half-opened to the scarcely believable events. And when the Fugger returned to the subject of what had brought him back to Munster, his father reached into the cavern where his gold was hidden, pulled out a golden thaler and began to toss the coin back and forth.

'And this hand' – his voice was soft now – 'he has it with him still? Here in Munster?'

'Yes, Father. We have escaped from terrible situations, and when we escape from here, we will fulfil Jean's vow. We will journey back to . . . to the place where we met, and we will bury it there. And our Queen can at last rest in peace.'

'A queen, eh?'

The gold coin went back and forth between his father's hands, catching the candlelight. The Fugger, now his tale was done, felt suddenly very tired, the sparkle of the coin making his eyes droop.

His father went on, 'I am thinking of another queen. At least one who would be thus . . . honoured. Ah, Albrecht.'

The hand that came down upon his shoulder made him wince, but it settled there and did a strange thing. It began to caress. 'Albrecht, my dear son, don't you see? You have the chance to redeem yourself to me. To save your sister, your mother and the honour of the Fugger name.'

'How, Father?' The Fugger's voice had risen a few notes. He couldn't stop staring at the hand on his shoulder. 'I would give anything to do that.'

'Of course you would. You are the son I raised you to be, a man of honour.' Cornelius leant in, his voice low. 'Jan Bockelson thinks that this Anne Boleyn was a martyr to the cause of the new religion. Do not ask me how. You saw how excited he became when he found out who your friend was. How much more so were he actually to possess a part of her?'

A hand on his shoulder. A gold coin still held up, catching the candlelight. The Fugger didn't understand.

'A part of her, Father?'

'Yes, my boy. Give him this witch's hand. He thinks he is God on earth, a new Messiah performing miracles. The only one he hasn't tried is the raising of the dead. It will stop him marrying your sister. He'll be saving himself for Anne Boleyn.'

Suddenly the Fugger knew what his father meant. 'You want me to betray my friend?'

'You would rather betray your family? As you did before? When one act on your behalf could save them?'

'Oh Father!' Of all the horrors he had experienced in this room, this realisation was the worst. 'No! I can't. I can't!'

'You can, and you will.' The tenderness had vanished. The purple blotches were back, the fury returned to the eyes. 'For if you do not, you will have betrayed us all again, consigned your sister to hell, your mother to rape and murder, your family name to the devil. You will be punished in hell for that. Oh, and on earth too. Oh yes, punished on earth most keenly.'

The Fugger watched his father reach up to the roof where

a hazel switch lay in a gap between loam and beam. He closed his eyes, seeing only the deep blackness of a midden. The blows that had fallen upon him there in his nightmares, just punishment for his innumerable sins, fell upon him now.

'Another week, ten days at most, I reckon,' said Uriah Makepeace. 'They're good fighters, for non-professionals, but it's the food that'll wear 'em down. Always the same in sieges, right? King Jan's going to let all the women and children leave soon, and the women are the best fighters. The men won't last long after they've gone. Someone will betray the city.' He leant forward. 'Speaking of food, can I tempt you with another bowl of rat stew? I know a lot of people complain of it, but I've always been partial to a bit of rat. Just as well, really.'

It was the second day Jean had spent with the Englishman and he had been a useful guide to the defences, enabling Jean to spot some alternative routes out of the city, should they be necessary. He could confirm what his former comrade had told him. The defence was near to final collapse.

He declined the rat, pushed his chair away from the table. 'You don't seem to be suffering too much, Uriah. Not compared to the scarecrows I've seen around the city.'

'Ah.' Makepeace helped himself to another ladleful. 'That's because I'm 'is Majesty's military adviser and Lord 'igh Executioner in one. The favoured rarely starve. As you shall see at the wedding feast tonight.'

Jean stood, and went to look out into the street. He was still hoping the Fugger would come and find him. He had left word at his house with his mother, but she had said he was involved in family business and would come if he could. If not, it was vital Jean came that evening to the palace, to the wedding. Jean hoped it would be their last evening in that hellish place.

'Can this Bockelson really take a fourth wife?' he asked.

Uriah laughed."e can do what 'e wants. Actually four is quite moderate. Since 'e made polygamy legal, some of 'is followers took as many as twelve. 'ad three myself, but once the novelty wore off, they were just a load of nagging women, so I got rid of 'em all.'

'So his word is the law, is it?'

'Oh yes. Quite the piece of work is our good King Jan. 'e used to be a tailor, did you know? In Leiden. Still makes all the costumes you see 'imself. And 'e used to perform in all the Passion plays and suchlike. Got the word of God direct, so it seems, and 'e can rant for days, all that Biblical stuff. Very effective. Coupled with 'is good looks – and you know how that impresses the ladies – well, 'e just took power. Did quite well 'ere for a while, 'ad other Anabaptists flocking from all over.' He sighed. 'A few thousand tried to break through, relieve the siege, but those Germans and Swiss out there slaughtered 'em in the fields. So it's just us now. And unless this apocalypse 'e keeps on about comes soon, it'll be finished in a matter of days.'

Jean came back to the table. 'And what about you, Makepeace? Are you going to fight till the last?'

The Lord High Executioner guffawed. 'Oh yeah. You know me. I'm a mercenary like you. I've only stayed this long because the wages are better 'ere than out there. They don't believe in money, see. Just leave it lying around, or stuff it in their cannon. So I've picked up a tidy amount. I'll make my move in a few days, probably. Want to come? I could use an extra sword to guard my booty.'

Jean shook his head. 'I aim to be gone soon, maybe even tonight. Friends on the outside are waiting for me.'

'And your friend, the one you came looking for? Do you believe me now? I 'ear about anyone who gets in or out. Trust me, no one of that description's climbed over in the last couple of weeks. Everyone's trying to go the other way.'

Jean nodded. He hoped Beck had already found Haakon and Januc in the siege lines, that she would be there when he emerged. If not, there was no point awaiting her in a doomed city. He would have to think of something else.

'Well,' said the Englishman, stretching. 'Got to be seen doing my job. For a few more days at any rate. Time for a stroll around the defences before the ceremony. Want to come?'

Jean grabbed his sword, picked up his saddle bag. He could still feel the weight of the hand nestled into his back. 'Why not?'

One last look for Beck, just in case. Check the tower where they had entered was still the best place to leave. Then visit a madman's palace, and hope the Fugger was as ready to go as he was. He suspected he would be. That father of his did not look like someone you wanted to be around for too long.

Cornelius was not a member of the most successful banking family in the Holy Roman Empire for nothing. His negotiating skills were sharply honed and he could smell desire in all its forms, whether for power, money or the caresses of a woman. And he had learnt, in the three years since his city had been transformed by the beliefs of the radical Christians, that the promise of an apocalyptic salvation was, for many, the most powerful desire of all.

He had played King Jan like a lute. Flattering him for honouring his family in the choice of their daughter, caressing him with honeyed words of how he had the ear of the Emperor himself, how he would fetch Jan's fellow monarch to negotiate the besiegers' surrender personally. He had had an astrological chart commissioned that pointed to the imminent apocalypse, the laying waste of the King's enemies by a divine queen, risen up to aid the ascension of Jan and his elect to the highest realm of God's infinite majesty. Above all, he tempted him with hints of what he would reveal to him that night. A special dowry for his daughter.

'For you see, Almighty,' he declared before the huge throne that Jan straddled, 'this very night will I present the means to that ascension. For is it not written in Ezekiel, "Take the dried bones of Israel and the bodies come together in resurrection"?'

Jan chewed upon the not-so-dry bone of a freshly roasted dog. 'Chapter eleven, verse ten.' He sucked noisily at the marrow. 'I keep telling them all – I await the last power to perform the ultimate miracle. The raising of the dead. Then shall all who have died in our cause be raised up. For as that verse goes on, "So I prophesied as he commanded me, and the breath came into them, and they lived, and stood upon their feet, an exceedingly great host." That's why they all fight for me and die in joy. They know I will find the power to raise them up again.'

'And you will find that power tonight, Most Holy. All I ask is that you place your guards and that they look to me for a sign.'

The former tailor's eyes shone with a fanatic's desire. 'They are yours to command. Provide me with this and you and your family will sit at my right hand when I ascend to my kingdom above.'

Then he turned to whisper something in Alice Fugger's ear, something that caused her to blush furiously, giggle and fix on her father a most impudent stare.

Cornelius backed away, fake joy on his face, bowing before the throne. Near the door, he spoke to the leader of the palace guards. When he got to where his son stood, he snarled, 'Where is this so-called friend of yours? If he doesn't come soon, your sister will be wed and our family's name destroyed.'

The Fugger's eyes were shut tight and he murmured words over and over to himself. When his father pinched him hard, he opened one eye and said, 'He will be here, oh yes he will. Jean Rombaud keeps his word, even if his friends do not.'

'And he will have this hand on him? You are certain?'

The Fugger nodded a few times, jerkily, then shut his eyes again and returned to his chanting.

He did not chant for long. The door to the chamber was opened again, and the two executioners strode in.

'Ah, my most excellent general Makepeace.' The King had risen on his dais and his court automatically did the same. 'And his equally illustrious friend. You must sit by me and tell me about the martyrdom of my cousin Anne Boleyn. Did you not know we were related? Oh yes, the Astrologer General has drawn up a hereditary chart. We are both of the house of David. Like our saviour, Jesus!'

Jean stayed bowed low in emulation of Makepeace. The last thing he wanted was to be trapped in a mad conversation about his Queen. Fortunately, another would-be queen was upset that her King was not paying enough attention to her. Alice distracted Jan with a tongue in his ear, and Makepeace and Jean were able to back away.

With a pillar behind him, Jean looked over the room. It resembled one of those masques the nobility were so fond of, or the feast of fools, where outlandish costumes were donned to match outlandish behaviour. Here the robes were all of a Biblical nature, and white-bearded desert prophets stood in groups conversing with women in shawls and headdresses, sandals on their feet. Heavily armed men in curved helmets, like metal turbans, stood around the walls. Reed torches burnt in holders every dozen paces, sending monstrous shadows across tables that, if they did not sink under the weight of food, would drive to a delirium of joy the scarecrow bands Jean had seen that day at their posts defending the city walls. It was always the same in any army, royal or peasant. The leaders ate while their followers starved.

*If I can just find the Fugger we can be gone. I'd rather be hungry at that tower while we wait for midnight than stay here and partake of a madman's wedding feast.*

He spotted his companion across the room. He was standing next to his father in a curious pose, his head sunk into his shoulders. Jean could just see Cornelius whispering furiously to his son from the side of his mouth. There seemed to be something wrong with the Fugger, in the way he was standing, as if something was broken in him. And he was shuffling again, just as he had under the gibbet.

*All the more reason to be gone*, Jean thought, and he began to push through the crowd. As he moved, there seemed to be another movement within the room, of soldiers and prophets shifting position, and he had a vague sense he was part of a galliard, even the centre of that dance, that his steps were causing others to react and counter his moves. He tried to shrug the thought away, blame it on the city, the madness of it, the madness he had seen in so many desperate eyes that day. Nonetheless, as he walked across the room it seemed time was slowing down somehow, as if in anticipation of some event. Even his own motion appeared slow to him and it seemed an age before he was standing before the Fuggers, father and son.

His friend's eyes were fast shut, but with a sharp elbow from his father in the ribs they jerked open to dart wildly around, seeing Jean, refusing to settle on him, flitting from torch, to crown, to dais and back, hovering finally somewhere above Jean's head.

'My friend,' said Jean, 'what is wrong?'

'Friend.' The Fugger's eyes at last fixed on the Frenchman, filling with tears as they did. Stepping forward, raising his one hand to Jean's neck, he kissed him on his left cheek. 'I am sorry.' The one hand dropped away, and Jean stepped back.

'Sorry?' The words came out so slowly, as if slurred. 'For what?'

As he said it, something in him already knew the answer and he turned, but not quickly enough, for burly men in Biblical helms were there to stop the arm that reached for his sword, to seize the other, to subdue him quickly through weight and numbers. As he fell under them, all he could see, in the eye of his mind, was Haakon's last rune, turned over on the stone floor in Montepulciano. TIR reversed, the arrow aimed at him. The rune of betrayal.

Held tight, he was dragged to the centre of a room suddenly clear, for everyone had scattered to the walls at the disturbance. King Jan was standing before his throne on the raised dais, a phalanx of armed men before him.

'What does this mean? Why do you treat my guest in this way?' He broke off, and his voice leapt a few notes in pitch. 'Or is he an assassin sent by my enemies?'

Makepeace strode forward. 'Most mighty, I know this man. He is a believer, like us, he means you no harm. He is here to help. He—'

'I think not.' Cornelius had come up beside the Englishman and now stepped before him. 'What would you call a man, O Holy One, who knows your greatest desire and withholds it from you?'

The Holy One snapped, 'I would call such a man a vile traitor, because he denies to God's Prophet the means to do his will.'

'Even so.' Cornelius now reached out and put his hand on Jean's shoulder. 'And such a traitor is he. For he conceals that which you most need to lead us to our ascension.' Stepping back, he barked, 'Search him!'

Jean's clothes were torn from him and he was powerless to stop it. He stood naked before the throne, the only covering on his body the bandage he'd wrapped around himself before entering the city.

'Oh, Fugger,' he called, 'what have you done?'

The end of the bandage was seized and his guards released their grip on Jean long enough to spin him out of it. Round and round he went, in the now silent room, and when he stood there finally and completely naked, a velvet bag lay at his feet.

There were gasps, and Jan Bockelson cried out, 'What does he have there? Is it a weapon?'

Cornelius snatched up the bag and raised it high in the air.

'A weapon for your use, Majesty. A weapon sent from God. Behold the legacy of our beloved martyr, Anne Boleyn!'

And with a flourish that would befit a street conjuror, Cornelius Fugger drew a six-fingered hand out into the torchlight.

There was mayhem. People surged forward. Jean pulled his left arm free, hit the man who had held it in the face, tried to twist away, but another guard seized him and all subdued him with kicks and blows.

Anne's hand was borne to the dais, and there the King snatched it up with a screech of joy.

'It is true! Six fingers! By heaven, six! And untainted, untouched, fresh as if taken only today. A miracle! The Lord has delivered unto us a sign. For is it not said in Ezekiel, chapter thirty-seven, verse eleven: "And you shall know that I am the Lord when I open your graves and raise you from your graves." ' He raised the hand high into the air. 'Behold! He has opened the graves. He has raised us from our graves. The kingdom of heaven is upon us!'

A universal shout, cries of 'Alleluia!' and 'Hosanna!' filled the room.

'Look ye, O my people, the hand of the Lord is upon us!'

'Amen!' came the reply.

'A queen's hand is with us, to raise the sword and deliver us from our enemies.' Jan stood now upon his throne, towering above them all, messianic fire in his eyes. 'I have found my fourth queen, as written in the scriptures. Today I marry Anne Boleyn.'

Only one voice cried out in fury at this, but Alice was struggling against impossible acclaim. When the hubbub had died a little, his daughter delivered into the arms of his wife, Cornelius once more stood forward, pointed at Jean and shouted, 'And what of this traitor?'

'He who would withhold the very key to heaven?' Jan Bockelson waved a hand towards the naked executioner. 'I will devise brave punishments. Bind him. Take him to my dungeons.'

Arms pinned, ropes cutting into his wrists, Jean was

dragged off through the jeering throng to a curtained doorway behind the throne. He had managed to glance up once and met the eyes of Makepeace who shook his head in despair. But the last face he saw in the room was the Fugger's, who had come forward and was weeping as Jean was bundled past him.

'Forgive me,' he was saying through tears, 'please, please, forgive me.'

Jean's tongue could form no words for his mouth was filled with his own blood, his throat choked once again with despair. But it was not the blows of the guards to his body nor the ropes' cruel binding at the wrist that hurt him now. It was his left cheek where the pain was greatest, for it was there that a man he called his friend had placed a Judas kiss.

# FIVE

# OLD ENEMIES

'Is it surrender?' Haakon peered at the main gates where the first of the townsfolk were beginning to emerge.

'I think not. Look at who's coming out.' Januc climbed down from the gunpowder keg he'd been standing on. 'Let us go and get a better look.'

The third morning since Jean and the Fugger had entered the city had dawned cold, the grass lightly frosted, summer just beginning its slow fade into a memory of warmth. They had alternated the watch, shivering and in vain, all night before the tower but there had been no signal from their companions within.

'Perhaps they will be among these?' Haakon knew the hope was false as he said it.

'The old, the young, and the women. This siege is nearly over.'

The scarecrows who straggled from the gates were empty-handed, bones thrust out from barely clinging rags. They limped into a gauntlet of jeering mercenaries who vented their frustrations at the hardship of the siege on their skeletal bodies.

Turning away in disgust, leaving the Norwegian to scan the crowd in faint hope, Januc watched a large party of mounted men ride into the camp, preceding and following an elaborately carved and decorated carriage. *Reinforcements*, Januc thought, until something about the carriage, the way the body of it sat on leather straps, stirred his memory. He looked again at the head of the column where a huge man was studying the crowd before him, seeking a passage through to the banners of Munster and Hesse. The man turned back and called an order, and Januc was able to get a look at his face. It was a wreck, a deathmask on a walking corpse, and he had seen it once before, and briefly in a street fight in Siena.

The janissary turned and pulled Haakon swiftly away to crouch behind a pile of fascines stacked ready to reinforce the nearby earthworks. The horsemen and carriage passed within a few paces of them.

'And what, in the name of all our unlucky stars, has drawn that devil to this place?' asked Haakon.

He had glanced over the fascines as the carriage went by, had seen the face that peered out of the window. He had last seen it beside a well in a town ablaze with St Anthony's Fire, and he had hoped never to see it again.

Giancarlo Cibo was sure he had had a reason for this journey when setting out. But everything after Marsheim had become a blur of blood and confusion. Firm decisions dissolved in doubt, accompanied by a constant red disgorging through his lips. He found it hard to concentrate, to give directions. For the first time ever in his life, he allowed another to take control.

A spasm seized him, a handkerchief raised too late. Drops falling to join the stain that had spread across the chest of his travelling cloak. Cibo threw himself back against the padded seats of his carriage and dabbed, yet again, at his mouth. Beside him, Franchetto stirred and muttered. *The man would sleep in his armour at the battle's crest*, the Archbishop thought. But at least sleep dulled his brother's pain, for his personal legacy from Marsheim was to be bent almost double, his bones locked, every muscle strained. A gradual uncurling had taken place during the journey to Munster, accompanied by an agony of burning in every one of his limbs, but he had some way to go before he could stand straight. When he walked, he looked like a crow prowling for scraps. Only when he slept was there some respite from his constant moans.

And his brother had been one of the luckier ones. They both had. A dozen of his men had died at each other's, or their own, hands. Died screaming, beset by demons, different for all yet the same in the richness of their horror. A sword plunged repeatedly into a chest might have been the actual reason for his departure from life, but no one who saw this leave-taking could miss the pitchfork that ripped the man's soul from the flesh that housed it. All had been left with some impairment in body or mind. Another half a dozen men had deserted that first night to crawl back to their homes. Those that remained were a bent and twisted lot, clinging together in fear. The one man who appeared unchanged was the man leading the column now.

Cibo knew differently, for he saw that Heinrich von Solingen had taken embers from St Anthony's Fire and placed them behind his eyes. He had gained a mind to match the wreckage of his face.

It was Heinrich who had organised them after the worst of the nightmares had faded, who had led the search for the hand and convinced his master that the executioner's appearance and the taking of the hand was more than hallucination – a deduction the Abbot had confirmed, just before Heinrich killed both him and his young confessor. The pretence of holy crusade that had brought the Cibos to Germany had to be maintained. The crucifixion of a fellow prelate, if it got out, was unlikely to help in that.

Cibo appreciated the discretion of his bodyguard. This pretence had brought the party to Munster, for the Papal emissary, Petro Paolo Vergerio, had been embarrassed by their unexpected arrival in Frankfurt and had urged them on. The situation was delicate, he had explained, with the

Emperor and Pope trying to convene a general council at Mantua that all sides, Catholic and Protestant, would attend. He did not want the eminent Archbishop upsetting any of the waverers.

'Why not go to Munster, where Catholic and Protestant are united against the peasant Anabaptists?' he had said. 'It is a sign that we may resolve our differences. Offer your "crusading" skills there.'

Cibo had heard the tone in those words, had made a promise to himself that one day he would delight in humbling the pompous fool. But he had nowhere else to go while his spies criss-crossed the German states in the hope of hearing news of the hand. Some Bavarian hedge knights of Heinrich's acquaintance had questioned a party matching the description of their quarry near the borders of their state. Some scowling Lutheran apprentices had admitted the same across those borders. Then . . . nothing. They had disappeared. So Munster seemed as good a place as any to wait for further news. He could be seen to pursue the Holy Church's cause while he pursued his own.

Now, his coughing subsided, Cibo was drawn forward by the sound of cheering. Seeing that they were only a few hundred paces from the banners of fellow noblemen, he called Heinrich to a halt.

'I must change into my holy robes before I greet those I have come to aid.'

'And your brother?'

Cibo glanced across at the still muttering Franchetto.

'Leave him where he is. We will have enough explaining to do. Go and announce me.'

In clean vestments, and with an honour guard of the dozen soldiers who could still walk upright, the Archbishop was led to the pavilion of the Bishop of Munster. He expected more formality in his entrance, the usual rituals of greeting between princes of Church and state. But the Bishop's small tent was crowded and the Bishop himself too excited to remember the courtesies. Cibo had met him a few times, at the conferences that had punctuated the early years of the Lutheran schism. He was excitable, and common, overly familiar, as so many of the Germans were, and time had not changed that. It had merely added several jowls to a face that had never lacked excess flesh.

'Ah, dear fellow, so good of you to come,' Munster said, as if the Italian were there for supper. 'I am sorry that we cannot receive you with more pomp, but your arrival coincides with a great day. The first signs that the enemy is about to break. They have sent out their women and children for lack of food. Soon, soon, I will have my city back. Have you met the Landgrave?'

A tall man, dressed in full armour, a helm clutched under his arm, a staff of office in his hand, looked up from a map in annoyance at the Bishop's interruption. Philip of Hesse's grey beard spilled over his gorget, and matching grey eyes stared out from a weather-lined face. He made no effort to bow and kiss Cibo's ring, merely nodded stiffly, muttered something in German and returned to hearing reports from the soldiers around him.

'Not one of us, I'm afraid,' the Bishop whispered, his greasy face uncomfortably close to Cibo's, exhaling an odour of stale cabbage. 'Ah well, a new world. And he will help deliver my city to me again.'

Cibo endured a seemingly endless diatribe against the Anabaptists until a disturbance at the flap of the tent interrupted the Bishop and a soldier bearing his colours rushed up to whisper in his ear, handing him a small scroll of paper. Munster read it, clapped his hands together and called once more to the Landgrave.

'My dear Prince, we must clear the tent. Only our most trusted officers must stay. I have news from within the city. News that will deliver it to us perhaps!'

Philip scowled at this loud demand for secrecy but gestures to various officers ensured the Bishop's desires were swiftly obeyed. His meaningful look at Cibo brought the Bishop to his fellow Catholic's defence.

'He is here, with fresh men, to help us. He wants our enemies laid low as we do. He must stay.'

With ill grace, the Landgrave nodded briefly, then again to his guard at the tent's entrance.

A flap was thrown back and two Fuggers, Gerta and Alice, were ushered in.

Januc had asked the Norseman, 'How good are you at skulking?'

'I never skulk,' had been the proud reply.

So he'd said, 'That's what I thought. Which is exactly why I go alone. For whatever is happening within that tent, we must hear it.'

Thus Januc found himself wedged between two wine casks under the eaves of the Bishop of Munster's pavilion. Rain gushed off its sloped canvas roof and sought out every crack of his clothing. Yet he was grateful, for the downpour meant that the guards, who might have patrolled round the tent, were now huddled into whatever shelter they could find nearby. Though he was well concealed, observant eyes might still have discovered him. The rain made listening hard, but fortunately agitated people always speak loudly.

'I know this woman,' the Bishop said. 'She is the wife of Cornelius Fugger, a generous benefactor of the Church in Munster. He is a member of the great banking family. I'm sure you all know them?'

The Landgrave, like every German prince, did indeed know them; nearly all were severely indebted to the family. Nearly all hated them for that reason.

'A Catholic and a Fugger? I thought they were all Jews.' Philip of Hesse's insult drew a sycophantic laugh from the half dozen of his commanders who stood around him. 'The Emperor made a gross error in allowing Christians to practise usury. Does this Fugger want to sell us his city? We will take it for free, woman. And we will do it for him with "interest" added.'

There was more laughter, but if Gerta was scared of her august listeners, she was more terrified of her husband's eventual wrath should she fail in her mission. That terror made her bold enough to speak.

'My Lords, the Bishop here knows my husband to be a good son of Munster. And he would see his city saved from the evil that has consumed it.'

'As it will be soon. The city is within days of falling,' said the Landgrave.

'My Lord, would that were true.'

'It is true. You women coming out proves it. You have no more food in there.'

Gerta's voice quavered. 'My husband fears that, food or not, there will not remain a city for you to relieve. King Jan dreams of the final apocalypse, of Armageddon. That here and now the prophecies will be fulfilled.'

The Bishop snorted. 'The fantasies of a madman!' He turned to Philip. 'You see what happened when your Luther translated the Bible into German? Lunatics chose to interpret God's word directly.'

Before the Landgrave could counter the argument, the woman's restraint broke and a wail burst from her.

'But he is a lunatic who will burn my home rather than surrender! All our homes! And he has just been given the weapon he needs to hasten the flames!'

'What weapon?' Philip snapped at her. 'No weapons have entered the city.'

'He thinks it is a sign from the Saviour himself.'

'A sign? What babbling is this? More Anabaptist nonsense?' The Bishop's patience had reached its limits.

Gerta continued through her tears. 'A man was captured in the city yesterday. A Frenchman who had snuck over the walls with . . . with someone else. Concealed on him was this weapon. Their deliverance, they are all saying. It is . . . it is a severed hand.' The tears overcame her.

'A hand, you stupid woman?' Philip of Hesse could pretend politeness no longer. 'What use is a hand from some criminal's corpse?'

'They are saying it belonged to that English queen they executed in the spring. Anne . . . something. The hand, it . . . it . . .'

'It has six fingers. It is a witch's hand. The Devil's work, for it does not rot nor wither!' Alice finished her mother's news in a burst.

Giancarlo Cibo had been standing quietly to the side, his mind separated from the conversation around him, coughing blood quietly into a handkerchief. When these last words reached him, he thought he was hearing them in another time, when the news first came to him in Siena that Anne was to be executed. Ever since Marsheim time had been strangely dislocated, the past forever pushing into the present. But when Heinrich beside him stiffened and actually dared to grasp the Archbishop's arm, he realised the words had been spoken here and now and God or the Devil had guided him to this place. He didn't much care which.

'My Lords.' He spoke quietly, but the timbre of his voice was as seductive as ever and the other men leant in to listen. 'My Lords, I know something of this hand. I have seen the power it has to ravage men's minds. If this madman possesses it, he may have found what he needs to wreak his apocalypse. He may leave you nothing but a city of ashes to recover.'

The words, so softly spoken, seemed to still Gerta's tears and concentrate the minds of the princes of Church and state.

'And so, woman, do you bring nothing but this bad news?' the Landgrave barked at her.

Gerta swallowed nervously. 'I also bring a way into the city, my Lord. If you will be so good as to take it. A secret way, that only my family know of. My husband awaits you on the other side of this passage, and servants will guide you to the city gates to throw them open to your army.'

The Bishop said, 'And he will be blessed for this, in this kingdom and in the kingdom to come.'

Gerta seemed to have spent her store of courage; but Alice had always been a saucy girl, and her brief flirtation with royalty had added a boldness unseemly to her years and supposed station. Seeing her mother's little resolve die away, she continued for her.

'My Lords, my father wants something else to seal the bargain. He fears some of your soldiers, in the heat of the sack, might be . . . indiscriminate in choosing their victims.'

The Landgrave had been raised to at least aspire to a chivalric code. Here was a woman, and a not unattractive one, pleading for protection.

'I will assign one of my officers here to guard you and yours from abuse.'

'I thank my Lord.' Alice curtseyed prettily and fixed the older man with the sort of look that had first caught the eye, and weakened the knee, of an aspirant king. 'But my father would feel safer if a party of soldiers were sent to convey certain, uh, possessions we have, back out the same way he lets you in. With your guarantee of their safety.'

Everyone present knew what was being discussed here. The Fugger family's wealth was legendary. And Philip sensed a way to reduce some of his own heavy debts to them.

'My Lady' – he inclined his head towards her – 'I am delighted to offer you my personal guarantees. Men will be assigned. Honest men,' he added with a glance around at his officers. Holding their eyes, he continued, 'But which of you, my brave officers, will have the honour of being our Menelaus, the first Greek to enter this Troy and throw open its gates to us?'

The eyes swiftly found other things to look at. All knew those in the vanguard of such an attack would be the most vulnerable, and they had all come to respect and fear the viciousness of these visionary defenders.

'My Lords' – the soft voice of the Archbishop commanded attention again – 'we have come here to help in the crushing of God's enemies. May I offer the services of my most trusted officer, a good German and defender of the faith? This is work for Heinrich von Solingen, who, I believe, you may know.'

Most men there had hesitated to regard Heinrich fully in the livid scar that was his face, but Philip of Hesse swallowed and did it now.

'I have heard of you,' he said. 'Were you not one of Frundsberg's officers?'

'I was.' The cobalt eyes were fixed at a point in the tent's roof, above the Landgrave's head.

'And will you do this for us?'

'I will.'

Marsheim had concentrated Heinrich's mind on one objective: to kill the men responsible for his transformation. He would take Jean Rombaud alive, because his master required it, required from him information about the English queen which Heinrich would be delighted to extract. Once they had it, the last of the Frenchman's cat-lives was promised to him. But the Archbishop had said that the gibbet keeper, the one who had thrown the burning liquid in the dungeon, could be slaughtered immediately – but that didn't mean it had to be quick.

*God wants me to do this*, he thought. *He has brought me to this place where the witch's hand is. For where it is, there are my enemies. God's enemies too, one and the same.*

Januc stayed while the details of the assault were worked out. He heard enough through the rain to know that a diversionary attack would be made that night on the far side of the city at eleven bells, and that four hundred men would follow Heinrich down the secret passage one hour later. He would use his own soldiers, but the majority would be volunteers. Officers might avoid first assaults but men often craved them. The danger was the greatest there, but so was the opportunity for loot. And loot was the only enticement available now that the women had left the city.

As the meeting broke up, he slipped from his concealment and made his way to where Haakon and Fenrir crouched in the scant shelter of a supply wagon.

'We will volunteer then,' said the Norseman. 'Join the assault and so be there to protect Jean when that devil reaches him.'

'How many times have you fought von Solingen?' Januc was looking down, scratching Fenrir's ears.

'Uh, a few. There was the ambush, that back street in Toulon and, uh, Siena. Well, you know that, you were there.'

'I was there. But that was a blur of a fight, and he would only have seen me for a moment. Besides' – he ran his hand over his dark head – 'my hair is back, my moustache too. I don't think he'll recognise me, under the right helmet. Whereas you . . .'

Haakon thrust his chin out. 'Do you think I'm going to let you go and rescue Jean by yourself? He needs me.'

'He needs you alive. Think, man. That djinn will know you instantly and what help will you be to Jean with your head rolling on the ground?' He put his hand on the other man's huge forearm. 'I will go in. Then Jean, the Fugger, Beck, if he's in there, and I will all come out and come out fast. That's when we will need you, you and your axe and our horses to get us away.'

Haakon was silent for a while, scratching at his golden beard. One day in a siege camp and he'd already picked up lice!

'Very well,' he said finally. 'We will wait for you, Fenrir and I. But if you are not out by dawn, we will come in and drag you out by your heels.'

'I shall pad my breeches in anticipation,' Januc called over his shoulder as he went back to their horses and baggage to prepare.

A while later Haakon rejoined him. 'I have been thinking,' he said.

'Allah protect us!' laughed the janissary, but stopped when he saw his friend's unsmiling face.

'I know why I follow the Frenchman, Januc. I have sworn an oath to be loyal to him until our quest is fulfilled. But why are you still with us? Why do you risk your life in this cause?'

It was a question that had already occurred to the Croatian.

'Allah wills it. Without him I would not have escaped the galley. So I am bound to him somehow. For now.'

'For now?'

'Nothing is for ever, Norseman, as we both know. Causes are lost, loyalties change. It is the mercenary way. For now, my loyalty is to my comrades. I will not betray you.'

'Good enough.' The big man smiled briefly. 'For now!'

As he watched the huge back moving away from him, Januc let the question play within him for a while. The future, despite what these Protestants said, was not predestined, that Januc truly believed. It was a sheet of parchment awaiting the imprint of the scribe's quill. What was written for now was that he would do his utmost to help Jean escape from the madness that was Munster. But, finally, he would also help himself. He had often heard the Fugger boast of his family's wealth. It was obvious some of that wealth would be coming out of the city this night.

'Allah guide me,' he muttered. 'Maybe there is a way to serve friendship and profit too.'

# SIX

# THE TAKING OF
# MUNSTER

Jean Rombaud shivered in the corner of the empty wine cellar which served as the earthly gaol of King Jan's heavenly kingdom. Makepeace had accompanied the guards that hurled Jean down the stairs, barking insults and commands, as befitted his position; but at the cell door he had managed to whisper of his return later before throwing Jean some rags to cover his nakedness. They did barely that, and little to stop the creeping chill – a match for the coldness gathered about the Frenchman's heart.

He sat in a position dictated by the bonds that had rapidly followed the rags, hands down by his ankles, head resting on his knees. Yet it wasn't the constriction that caused him to groan aloud, nor the injuries he had sustained, for the men who had beaten him were apprentices to the Painmasters' Guild, the hurt they inflicted superficial. It was the knowledge that Anne's hand was again in the grasp of an enemy, once more the focus and subject of a madman's fantasies.

Far away, he heard a faint rumble which could only be the thunder the day had long threatened. Letting his head sink upon his knees, he gave into his despair in a way he had not since he first awoke in the gibbet cage. All the joy he'd experienced in the past months, the companionship of the Fugger – how the thought of him now twisted in his heart! –

of Haakon and Januc, even the love he'd discovered in Beck, all this now appeared as a distraction from his true task.

*No one else should have been involved*, he thought. *I should have gone after Cibo alone. Letting people join me? Leading them? It was cowardice. Worse, it was a betrayal of the only thing I found to be true and alive in a lifetime of lies and death.*

Despairing, the only sounds the distant roll of the storm and the steady drip of water down the rough walls, Jean was unaware of time. A torch flared on the wall outside the cell, flickering light through the bars of the small window set in the door. But he had seen all he required. Death cells, he had long since discovered, needed little study. Each one was more or less the same.

He was sure he had not slept overnight, but Makepeace said it was near midday when he returned.

'You've stirred the ants' nest, my friend, and no mistaking.' Makepeace had dismissed the guards, loosened Jean's bonds and laid out some mouldy hard biscuit and a flagon of brackish water. While Jean ate and drank Makepeace continued. 'I've not seen 'em all so enthusiastic since the siege began. The 'ymns, the 'allelujahs, the ecstatic visions. 'is Madness-ty 'as got 'em all convinced it's the sign of deliverance, 'er 'and is.'

Jean kept on eating, giving no comment, so Makepeace hunkered down beside him, pulling some dried meat from his doublet pocket.

'Last of me rat.' He gnawed furiously. 'Difficult to get at any price now. Which means if the rats 'ave gone, time is very nearly up for this place, despite all the 'osannas and such. Means I'm on me way out, tonight probably.'

He chewed hard for a few moments, looking at Jean, spitting out pieces of gristle. Finally he said, 'Look, you gotta tell me, Rombaud. I've known some strange souvenirs in our trade. There was that Flemish bloke – Wilkens, Jilkens, something like that. 'e liked to take an ear from each of 'is clients. 'ad a bagful of 'em and could remember every name that went with the 'ead they was formerly attached to. Said 'e was going to stick them on 'is wall when 'e retired. But 'er 'and? Anne Boleyn's 'and? Only probably the best known appendage in the world! What was you thinking of?'

Jean put down the biscuit he'd been trying to eat.

'It is not something I can explain to you. But it is vital that I get the hand back. Will you help me to do that?'

Makepeace whistled between his few teeth. 'I'd like to, friend. Brotherhood of the sword, and all that. But I'm risking enough just talking to you 'ere. You know 'ow tyrants get. They think everyone's plotting against 'em. I plan to lie low, and make my escape tonight. Look.' He lifted his ragged shirt. Under it was a leather undershirt and sewn all round it were gold coins. 'Most expensive armour I ever owned.' He laughed. 'Two 'undred and six gold thaler. Should buy me a nice little tavern back in Southwark.' His laughter ceased. 'So, sorry and all. But I've too much to lose. You understand?'

Jean nodded. It was best that he was alone anyway.

'You could tell me what he has planned. This King of yours.'

'That I can do.' The Englishman tucked in his shirt. 'Some sort of ceremony to restore life to Anne's bones, raise 'er up from the dead, complete with fiery sword to rain brimstone on 'er enemies and 'asten Armageddon.' He smiled. 'You see? I've been 'ere too long. I've picked up their way of talking.'

'And when will this happen?'

'Midnight, of course. Best time for conjurations, so 'is astrologers tell 'im.'

'And me? Do I have a role in this pageant?'

For the first time, Makepeace looked uneasy. 'Yes, well.' He scratched his chin. ''e's very, uh, Old Testament in his beliefs, is our King Jan. 'e'll see your execution as a kind of sacrifice. Doesn't want me to do it, I thank God. Though maybe you won't. 'E's, uh, planning something else.'

'But it will be part of the ceremony?'

'I think so, yes.' The uneasy look stayed on the Englishman's face and he leant in closer. 'Look, I could . . . I could say you attacked me, you'd got a weapon and . . . I 'ad to, uh . . .' He pulled a dagger from his sheath. 'Spare you the pain. Which there will be. You saw what 'e did to 'is wife.'

Jean stretched his still-cramped limbs. Was it only three and a half months before that the Fugger had offered him the same swift despatch from a different prison, the gibbet cage? It was as tempting now as it had been then. And yet, had he taken that offer, his enemies would already have wreaked what harm they could with the hand of Anne Boleyn. His refusal then had led to this much delay, at the least. And it had given him a glimpse of another kind of love he'd forgotten could exist in this world.

'Thank you, but no. I have breath and thus hope.'

'Not much, I'm afraid.'

'A little more with that dagger hanging at your side.'

Makepeace glanced down and shook his head. 'You wouldn't keep it for a moment. Too big, see.' The long blade caught a little of the dim torchlight. 'But . . . I wonder?' He reached his hand inside his doublet to the small of his back. 'You might, just might, get away with this. If we was clever.'

In the palm of his hand, reaching from the callused base of his fingers to the middle of his wrist, rested a slim shaft of dark metal.

'Ever seen one of these? It's called a pistole. From Pistoia, you know, near Florence? "City of assassins" they call it. Well named too. Everyone carries one of these.' He flicked it up into the air, caught it. 'You can throw it. It's deadly sharp and so well forged, you can even bend it nearly in 'alf, then bend it back. It's a little favourite of mine, 'elped me out a dozen times.' His eyes glistened with a memory of slayings. 'Still, can't be sentimental about a weapon, eh? Tell you what, I'll trade you it for your sword.'

'My sword?'

'Aye. I saved it in the madness up above. I've taken my last 'ead, me. This gold will buy me a new career – innkeeper. And I can't think of a better memento to 'ave above my bar than the sword what took the 'ead of a queen.'

Jean only needed a brief consideration. The Englishman was right: it was wrong to be sentimental about a weapon. And he was offering Jean a chance.

'Agreed, then. Now, where could we . . .'

The chest wound he'd received in Siena had part-opened in the struggle with Bockelson's guards. It drew Makepeace's attention and oozed when he squeezed it, causing Jean to groan.

'It might just . . .'

Whistling again, the Englishman used the little knife to slice off a few longer strips from his own cape. These he daubed in the blood, then, bending the pistole so it lay flush to Jean's skull, he deftly tied the other strips around his head, tucking the fabric under Jean's black and now reddened tufts.

'Not bad,' Makepeace said, standing back. 'You look bloody enough to act 'urt. Keep clutching your 'ead, put more blood on when you can. Long as they don't rub you there, you might get away with it.'

'It's a chance, anyway. And I thank you for it.'

Gratitude made Makepeace uncomfortable and he mumbled his way to the door.

'A last favour?' Jean stopped the Englishman before he could call to the gaoler outside. 'When you make it to the camp outside, can you find a friend of mine? Haakon is his name, a huge Norse axeman. He'll probably have a wolf beside him. Tell him . . . tell him what has happened. And tell him that while I am alive I will not give up hope.'

'Then long may you remain alive. And I 'ope to see you again, Jean Rombaud. If only to get my pistole back.'

His feet tramped up the stone stairs. Jean settled once more into his position to wait, a time made more bearable by the fact that Makepeace had loosened his bonds and by the touch of a thin strip of steel, wrapped in cloth, against his skull. A strange thing, for it was uncomfortable yet it gave him the only comfort he had.

*The Fugger would call that a paradox*, Jean thought. *A word, an idea – yet another thing I would not have discovered if I'd taken the quick way out in the gibbet.*

The thought of the shuffling German with all his tricks and tics and strange sayings made Jean smile for the fraction of time before he remembered why he was lying there.

'Why? Why?' the Fugger cried, and then realised that he had cried it out loud, that he had once more failed to contain his misery. He knew this by the looks of the three scarecrow men his father had gathered from their various posts on the wall to work for their former master. He knew it by his father's curse and his return from the far side of the room where he had been crouched over the trapdoor, listening.

'Quiet, fool! Do you want to bring a patrol down on us?'

Cornelius stood for a moment above his son, eyes afire, furious. The Fugger could see the big hands twitching, as if they longed to strike and had to be desperately restrained. Blows would have fallen were it not for the servants.

Frustrated, the older man went back to his post and the Fugger to his thoughts of despair. To the punctuation of the cannon booming on the far side of the city, his mind whirled with images from the past months, of escapades and assaults, weapons clashing, monks chanting, naked bodies plunging in heat. Vision after vision, none staying, all bleeding into each other: an executioner with a wolf's head, a slingshot hurling skulls, a crucified raven. Faces raced at him, only to grimace and gibber and race away. Two lingered longer than the rest: Jean, with his eyes that had seen too much, with no anger in them, with something much worse, the terrible hurt of trust betrayed. And beyond even this image, another kept returning: the hideous mask from the dungeon in Siena that was no mask at all, mouthing words.

*I will find you. Wherever you go, I will be there. In the end, you will beg me for your death.*

His father signalling silence, calling the servants over to take the rope's end, barely interrupted the thoughts in his son's head.

*He is coming for me, that I know, and the only man who could save me from him I have betrayed.*

His thoughts were as jumbled as anything he'd experienced lying in the stinking warmth of the gibbet midden. But they were worse here, because here the nightmare was incarnate in his father, tensing himself to pull on the rope that ran through the large iron ring on the floor. The trap led to the old passage that emerged in a dry riverbed beyond the walls. His grandfather had used it, years before, as a way of bringing in goods he did not want the city or his competitors to know of. But little Albrecht Fugger had never seen it as a way in, for he had never been entrusted with its portal beyond the walls. In his imagination, the passage only went one way – out, to freedom, to a world beyond beatings, a world where his failures weren't manifest, his fate still his own to decide.

Now he knew he had always been wrong, that the leaders of reform, Luther and the others, his father too, were right. All *was* predestined. There was no escaping one's fate and the passage only led in.

Thus it was no real surprise, when the trapdoor was pulled up, that the first head to appear had no face. It was a ruin, a pitted, near featureless landscape that flinched backwards at the torch thrust downwards by Cornelius, eager to greet his rescuers.

'Put it out, fool,' growled Heinrich von Solingen.

It was no surprise, but the horror of the image in his head melding with the horror emerging from the trapdoor had the Fugger up on his feet in an instant.

'No!' he cried from a throat suddenly thickened by the ghost of a mailed fist clamped upon it. 'You shall not have me!'

The Fugger fled into the midnight city, running swiftly towards the sound of the guns.

As the torch was lowered and Heinrich's eyes refocused, all he saw, for an instant, was the back of a man bursting away from him through a door. Yet even in that instant he caught a whiff of things familiar. He could not dwell on it, because the fury it raised was diverted by the fool with the unguarded torch, who was again waving it upwards in a parody of welcome, babbling the while.

Von Solingen grabbed the torch, dropped it on the floor and stamped it out. The room darkened suddenly, but the gated lantern he carried revealed all he needed to see. So he took the old idiot by the throat and squeezed until all noise, even breathing, stilled.

'Silence,' he said. Allowing the man to slip from his grasp and fall to the floor, he leant down into the underground passage and whispered, 'Bring them all out. First men to secure the doorway. Quietly. Now' – he turned back to a spluttering Cornelius Fugger – 'which way to the gates?'

They had waited for a seeming age in the complete darkness of the tunnel the Fugger girl had led them to, breathing in each other's rank breath, sensing each other's fear. Men yawned, but not from tiredness. All knew the risks of such a night-time assault, knew that many of their number would never see a day's light again.

At last, the shuffling forward began, and Januc, who had worked his way forward into the vanguard, right behind von Solingen's own troops, concentrated on the only plan he had – to stick as close to the ugly German as he could and, if they found Jean alive, be ready to bury his blade right between Heinrich von Solingen's huge shoulders.

Januc saw them ahead as he emerged into the gloom of the warehouse. The companies were already assembling and crowding out the space.

'All right, first company with me. Let's secure the street.

And you' – Januc saw him turn to a quivering townsman – 'I never want you to leave my side.'

'But my . . . goods. These bags here,' Cornelius was jabbering. 'I have the Landgrave's word.'

'I will leave men here. But only after you lead me to the gates will you earn the wages of your betrayal.'

'But my servants can show you—'

'No!' Once more a mailed hand choked off the sound of pleading. 'Forward!'

Heinrich's men moved out behind their leader, Januc close behind. Three townsfolk trying to raise the alarm were swiftly silenced, but Januc didn't even draw his blade. He would fight to defend himself, that was all. His weapon sought only one victim this night.

The voice, so impressively controlled, so marvellously deep and full, poured over the ecstatic crowd.

'And it is written in Ezekiel: "So I prophesied as he commanded me, and the breath came into them, and they lived, and stood upon their feet, an exceedingly great host." ' King Jan paused, and looked down on his followers from his dais. 'And I say unto you, that time has come. See what God has sent his chosen people. See the symbol of his love for us. See the hand of Anne Boleyn!'

Jean didn't want to look. He was more concerned with rubbing the ropes that tied him to one pillar of the Great Hall – like Samson, he'd been told, mockingly – up and down against a rough patch he'd found on the stonework. But the power of those six fingers was great, they drew him now as they had from the first moment he'd seen them. Strangely, as he looked, he heard, through all the gasps and acclamation of an ecstatic crowd, a deep laugh, the laugh of a queen, just as he'd first heard it months ago on Tower Green. He knew it was a trick of memory, but for a moment it made him smile. He redoubled his efforts on the ropes.

'Behold!' Jan raised the hand to cries of 'Hosanna!' and

'Hallelujah!' 'See how it is unblemished, though the body died so long ago. Died, but shall be resurrected this night.'

To a universal shout, trumpets blared in welcome, drums were beaten, the staves of the Elders were rhythmically thumped on the wooden stage. The noise quickly settled into a steady beat, those who were without percussion clapping in time or chanting the words 'She is risen! She is come!' over and over. The King began to dance, a series of sinuous steps. Anne's hand held out before him, her fingers in his, as if she were his partner in a galliard. As the pace of the drumming, stamping and chanting built, as sweat bloomed on faces, Divara, First Queen of Munster, gave a rapturous cry and started to swirl, arms straight out, head thrown back, eyes half-shut, lips apart in a steady exhalation of pleasure held in the single word 'Come!' Others began to spin and cry out as their King stepped into the centre of what became a circle of seven dancing women, moving left. Around them another circle of Elders moved right, and around them the guards and remaining members of the court joined hands and took the opposite route, paralleling the women. It was not just flesh joining them in these concentric rings. They pulled around and around, the pace building along with the one cry, the one word, the invitation.

'Come! Come! Come!'

Jean remembered something Makepeace had told him, that before his elevation to royalty, in the days of his tailoring in Leiden, Jan Bockelson had been an enthusiastic participant in the local Passion plays. He had been a notable John the Baptist, it was said, and had created some of the more spectacular effects.

Jean could believe it. The way Jan held the hand was perfect, the weight and angle finely judged, the movements so counterpointed that even Jean could believe there was a whole person spreading beyond those six fingers. King Jan's followers certainly believed, saw the illusion as fact, expected the immediate and corporeal appearance of their saviour: Anne Boleyn, Queen of the Apocalypse.

'Come!' was still the one cry of the whirling circles.

The pace was building, the air filled with an energy that crackled around their heads. It was like the moment in a storm before the lightning and Jean did not know what would happen when it struck. Would Anne Boleyn appear? The Fugger had told him that she had done so before in the dungeon, at a moment just like this, a moment of great need and evil men's desire.

*I did not fear my death except in this, the harm I could do after I passed over were this vow not spoken.*

That is what she had said. And he had failed in that vow.

Jean concentrated on the bonds and the patch of rough stone. One rope had already snapped, the other was fraying. And pressed against the back of his head was a thin strip of steel which gave him hope. If he could reach it in time.

He soon found himself chanting with the rest.

'Come! Come! Come!'

The element of surprise had not been as great as the attackers had hoped. One screaming man running through the town had woken those who had managed to sleep through the diversionary barrage. The townsmen, many of whom slept near the main gates, had poured out of their barracks, and though many had been cut down in the mercenaries' first assault, accurate firing from the walls had broken that attack and allowed many defenders to take up positions behind barricades. The gates were held and with each moment that passed more Munsterites were arriving. The gates had to be taken, and taken fast.

Januc, crouched with the others in a conquered storehouse, knew it. He knew von Solingen did as well – and there lay Januc's problem. He would be content to lurk in this building and let others carry out the vital assault. He had no cause here, except Jean Rombaud. But in this maze of a town, with fanatics defending every street, the only way to get to Jean would be right behind the big German. If Heinrich was a normal commander he would order his men forward, stay in safety, and claim the glory later. But he was not normal. His eyes were filled with a vision of blood and the cross that Januc had seen on the battlefields of the world. Heinrich would lead the assault himself, and Januc would have to follow him. Follow him and keep him alive – for the moment.

Januc noticed two wagons standing to one side, big oak carriages of the kind used to transport goods. The wheels looked intact. He approached his leader, who was intent on organising reluctant men into assault waves. Clutching his newly purchased broadsword – he'd felt that Heinrich might just remember a scimitar – he went up and pulled at Heinrich's sleeve.

'Captain, these wagons. We could push them before us, give us some cover.'

Von Solingen, who had been about to berate one from the ranks who had dared to interrupt him, instantly recognised the wisdom of the interruption.

'See to it then. Lead one of the wagons yourself.'

The wagons were quickly pulled into position before the barrack doors, a few men placed before them to scatter, draw fire, the biggest men standing behind, ready to heave.

'Now!' Heinrich yelled.

The gates were flung back and the front men burst out, most of them cut down in the first seconds. The others heaved on the wagons and, after a moment, they both lurched forward. Their appearance through the gates called down more fire – the defenders were staggering their volleys like trained musketeers – and a saker's blast exploded into the centre of the left wagon. It ripped apart some panels, metal and splintered wood causing men to reel aside, dead or dying. But the cannon was loaded for flesh, with small fragments, not the heavy ball that could have broken a wheel. The shuddering carriage rolled on, picking up speed as fresh men replaced the fallen.

Twenty paces to go now, the fire from above and ahead slackening as defenders put down arquebus and musket to seize sword, stone and pickaxe. Fifteen, and the wagons, catching the gradient of a downward slope, began to fly away from the hands that pushed. They nearly slewed together, then split apart and smashed into the barrels and gabions that made up the inner barricade. It was designed to meet resistance from the front should the gates fall to direct attack, so its rear aspect was weak and it imploded like kindling under the adze.

'Hoch! Hoch!' cried von Solingen, his mercenaries taking up the battle cry, following him from behind the wagons and over the crumpled barricade. Bodies trapped there were crushed under heavy boots, while those who had escaped the shattering now flung themselves onto the assailants. They lacked armour but not ferocity, and the combat was brutal.

A pitchfork thrust at his chest caused Januc to spin and block with his sword upright, the force of the attacker's charge bringing his face level with the Croatian's. For a moment, Januc gazed into the face of a cobbler or a wheelwright, not a soldier, with eyes fired by fear, lit by a fanaticism that now powered the swing of the pitchfork at Januc's head. He ducked it easily, stepped close and snapped his knee into the other's stomach, once, twice, taking away his breath. He raised his sword, and the man who was not a soldier looked up at death descending from his hometown sky. With a sudden twist of his wrist, Januc brought the pommel of the sword straight down, hitting the crouched and winded man just above the temple. He fell, like a beast in an abattoir, neck turned up for the killing stroke to follow. But Januc had moved on. He was there to kill, but only one man, and only when that man had led him to his comrade. The cobbler or wheelwright would wake up later and then have to take his chances in the sack of his town.

Ahead, he saw the enemy whose life he had to preserve, in the thickest part of the defenders' final resistance. Somehow he had got separated from the bulk of his men. Heinrich von Solingen was standing there, feet spread wide apart, his giant double-handed sword carving a figure eight in the air before him, leaving a cleared space between him and five snarling assailants who darted towards him on every angle the huge blade did not cover. A sixth joined and the lance he carried altered the balance, the thrust of it forcing the German to parry. Air no longer filled by his scything metal was filled now by the other five, their weapons rushing at the exposed stomach.

Januc was there, taking three of the thrusts on his own sword, a fourth on his breastplate, a fifth led away by a swing of his hip. There was no time for consideration then, no time to care if these were soldiers or civilians. They were men with swords and they were trying to kill him, and in a few seconds they were all dead, falling to the long and the short blade of the two mercenaries.

The mask was before him, words moving on the half-lips. 'I owe you.'

'And you will pay me,' whispered Januc as the other turned away.

The gates were twenty paces beyond the carnage of the barricade and the heavily armoured mercenaries gained them easily, a wake of bodies marking the progress of men who had not Januc's restraint. The early, too eager ones died screaming in a shower of boiling liquid that fell like molten rain. Von Solingen was not that far gone in blood that he had forgotten the lessons of a siege. He had not stood under the deadly shower, but was back a pace, deploying his few crossbowmen to keep down the heads of the assailants above.

'The beam!' he shouted, and the dozen strongest men, recovered from their exertions on the wagons, now stooped below the giant bar of oak that rested between the metal supports at either end of the gates. 'Lift!'

The bar seemed frozen for a moment, then slowly, so slowly, it rose. A man dropped, caught by a rock flung from above, the flinger himself reeling back, plucking at the feathered bolt that sprouted from his neck. Heinrich took the man's place and, at his joining, the bar flew from its supports. The men raised it high above their heads and ran to hurl it against the walls beside the gates. Another group ran forward to pull them open and, after an initial groaning reluctance, the gates of Munster swung wide for the first time in sixteen months, and the men who had waited so impatiently for their opening began to pour in.

As the first of the reinforcements entered, Heinrich rallied what was left of his own men. 'Now,' he said, 'we'll let these Swiss bastards do most of the work. But we will move around the defence to the palace. For the palace is where our prize lies, according to that scum who led us here. Bring him to me!'

A quivering Cornelius was dragged from the barracks by his guard.

'I have done all you require of me. I have a bargain with the Landgrave!' he bleated at them.

The men laughed and Heinrich leant over him. 'The Landgrave is breaking wind in his tent. He will not enter the city or honour any bargains until this heretic rabble is dealt with. So you' – and here he jabbed the elder Fugger in the chest – 'are going to lead us by back ways to the palace.'

'But my . . . my possessions?'

'Your gold is safe, banker!' He spat out the last word like an insult. 'I left men to guard it. Once you have led us to our destination you can go to it or to the Devil.'

Cornelius sagged in the guard's grip. He knew he had no choice. 'Very well. I know a route that will be little guarded.'

Screams were filling the streets. The Swiss were spreading out and beginning the slaughter of the men who had so viciously opposed them for sixteen long months.

'The defences will not last long.' Heinrich pushed Cornelius before him. 'Lead us to the palace.'

Januc took his place a few men behind their leader.

*Rombaud,* he thought, sending his silent words out into the savaged night, *if you are still alive, stay that way a little longer.*

His last bond snapped as the whirling reached a peak and bodies started to plummet off the dais into the rest of the swaying crowd; first the guards, then the Elders, finally the inner core of women. All fell, save one, kneeling alone in the centre of the platform, head bowed, arm raised, hand joined to another hand that seemed to be the only thing holding him up.

'Behold!' cried King Jan, his strong voice ending the cries of the last of the falling dancers. 'Behold she who has come to save us all, to drown our enemies in her holy fire. Cry welcome to the Queen!'

At the end of Jan's hand it seemed a flickering light was coalescing, his fingertips passing sparks into those he held, receiving them back; and within the flames crackling above both hands a greater shape was growing, an arm beyond the hand, a body beyond the arm.

As one the crowd cried 'Welcome!' and Jean, still standing at the pillar, looked too, could almost believe he saw the damask dress, a square collar, the first hint of a long neck.

'No!' he screamed, and as he did the doors of the great hall burst open and a soldier, his brow split by a wound gushing blood, fell through them.

'The gates are broken! The enemy are here!'

Crying thus, the soldier fell and died in the doorway.

The silence that followed was absolute, as if a hole had opened in the air and sucked all noise within it. All heat too, for the flames that had danced up the arms of a dead queen had vanished as she had. A tailor from Leiden was left kneeling on a stage, clutching the remains of a corpse. Magic and majesty swept away by the simplicity of death entering a room.

As complete as the silence was the noise that followed it. The doors were slammed shut and screams, commands, prayers exploded, the crack of Jean Rombaud head-butting the first of the guards indistinguishable amid the babble. The second managed at least to cry out before a forearm to the throat choked off the sound, but Jean was moving through the crowd before the guard's body reached the floor.

The people, in their panic, had rushed to where their leader still knelt, Anne's hand still loosely clutched in his. Jean managed to squeeze right up to the front of the stage before he was noticed.

An Elder in title, a youngish man in reality, saw him and cried, 'The prisoner is loose!'

Fear opened a slight gap in the crowd and, ducking under the frantic grasp of the crier, Jean scrambled up onto the platform, rolling beyond the outstretched arms. He came up onto his knees and found himself face to face with Jan Bockelson.

'Help me, brothers!' the King of Munster managed to get out before Jean's arm went around his throat.

Standing in the same movement, Jean brought his victim up with him, his hand rising to the back of his head just as the first of the Elders tried to climb up onto the stage. And just as Jan Bockelson had silenced the crowd with the raising of Anne's hand, so did Jean Rombaud now with the raising of his. For in it was Makepeace's pistole, a small enough object it was true, yet vivid when pressed against the neck of their Messiah.

'No, no,' said Jean clearly. 'If you want your king to live, you will stay where you are.'

Silence again in the hall. Beyond it the unmistakable sounds of battle drawing ever closer. Pressure within and pressure without and the pressure of a blade against King Jan's throat allowed his words to squeeze through.

'Please don't hurt me!' he whimpered. 'Please!'

'Then do, very slowly, what I tell you to do. Place the hand within the folds of my doublet here. No, not *your* hand, the *other* one.'

Just as the movements of the hand before had been followed so closely, so they were now by the same eyes. The attention was absolute until the doors were flung open again and another man, less bloodied than his predecessor but equally terrified, ran into the room, yelling, 'The enemy have reached the great square!'

There was silence no more. One of the Elders, a head taller than the rest who Jean remembered Makepeace had named as Knipperdolling, the Court Viceroy, stepped up to the dais. Jean's blade bit into flesh and a trickle of blood appeared at the throat of his captive.

'You may murder our leader,' cried Knipperdolling, 'but if I do not go to the aid of my flock we will all be murdered.'

'Then go. I do not seek anyone's death here. Your city will see enough of that tonight. I will leave with what I came with, that is all, and take my own chances on the streets.'

'Lower your weapon and use it in our cause,' pleaded Knipperdolling. 'Expunge your sins, take up Christ's love. You may yet find salvation among us.'

'I think not,' said Jean. 'Mine lies elsewhere. But I would not stop you hastening yours.'

'What are you doing? Don't leave me with him!' screamed the would-be Messiah as Knipperdolling and the rest of the Elders made to leave, seizing weapons stacked at the door. 'There is no salvation without my word! Come back! I command it!'

Knipperdolling paused in the entranceway. 'For once, and only now do I realise it, the word of God and the word of Bockelson are not one and the same. At the last, I choose God.'

He and all the other men ran from the room. Jean knew, by the volume of the sounds coming from the streets, that they would not have far to go to find the swiftest route to their salvation.

'No!' screamed King Jan, straining against the blade so that Jean had to loosen his grip slightly to prevent him slitting his own throat. The relaxation was enough for Jan to twist free and he fell out of Jean's grasp and onto the forefront of the stage. There he was grabbed by the women of the court.

'Fuck,' Jean said, remembering Beck.

In the midst of his harem, the King regained a little of his courage.

'Seize him!' he screamed. 'There is yet time to raise Anne Boleyn and bring destruction on our enemies. The hand. We need the hand!'

Makepeace had said that the women were the fiercest fighters in the town. And these seven, headed by the large Divara, looked as fierce as any Jean had ever seen. Enflamed with devotion to their leader-lover, knives bigger than his had suddenly appeared from within their flowing gowns. The way the women held them, he knew they had used them before.

They surrounded the stage. As each attempted to leap up onto it, Jean cut the air before her. He was fast, but they were clever and the stage too wide for him to cover in a single leap. One would make it soon, and he would have to kill her. In the act of killing, more would make the stage, more would die and, very likely and soon, so would he.

The torchlight flickering off his pistole flashed brighter off the women's blades. He was tiring, and the cut he had inflicted on the first woman to get her knees up onto the platform hadn't stopped her trying again. As Divara herself made the leap, Jean's knife poised for the first of what would be many killing strokes, the doors the Elders had closed behind them burst open for the third time that night.

If Jean had any hope that the conquerors of Munster would be so concerned with murder and rape that they would afford him a chance to escape, that hope left when he saw Heinrich von Solingen in the doorway.

*This is the moment*, Januc, standing behind Heinrich, thought. *I strike, I bury my sword up to its hilt in this devil's back. Without their leader, maybe the rest will lose heart. We might, just might, prevail.*

He even raised his sword, but then Heinrich turned to him and said, 'You! Take that traitor to his gold. Get them out of the town. It is my gift to you, for saving my life. We are even.'

And the moment was gone, the back that could have held his sword moving away through a crowd of scattering, shrieking women. Heinrich, cuffing aside a weeping man dressed as an Old Testament king, leapt onto the raised platform where Jean had already killed the first two men who had come for him but had gone down under the attentions of three more. Twenty men were surrounding him when Januc, still hesitating at the door, saw something raised in triumph above the throng. It looked like a hand.

He turned to Cornelius Fugger cowering at his side and said, 'Take me to your gold. Take me now.'

*Strange*, thought Jean as he writhed on the floor of the dais, blows from feet and fists falling on him. A gap had briefly opened between the flailing legs and for the merest instant he could see all the way to the doors. *Strange how familiar that man in the helmet looks, the way he holds himself, the way he grips Cornelius Fugger by the arm and leads him out.*

Then the gap closed. Another opened almost immediately and he was swept into a cloud. He was grateful for its red warmth because it took him away from the blows and the pain and away, finally, from the cries of doom spreading through New Jerusalem.

# SEVEN

# THE SCATTERING OF THE QUEST

Haakon wasn't sure if it was the first shaft of dawn or merely the glow from the dozen fires that had sprung up within the city, but he took the light as the harbinger of the day and made his preparations accordingly. His axe he had honed beyond the point of sharpness, until he felt he would only have to level it at someone to cut them in two. He had gone into the camp and purchased breastplate, mail undercoat and helm, as well as a small but powerful bow and a quiver of arrows. He had even managed to find a leather collar for Fenrir, with razored barbs thrust through at angles that would cost the hand of any who dared try to seize the wolf-dog. With both of them prepared, and with the excuse of any light in the sky, he was ready to go in.

Haakon had watched the city gates crumple inwards and the waves of Switzers pour unopposed through this breach. But the many casualties that had come back through showed the opposition beyond was still fierce, and reports from the wounded told of how the townspeople had absorbed the initial thrusts and were now mounting a heavy counter-attack.

He stood before the gates, uncertain. The most direct way forward was through them, but as Munster was a town he did not know, he would have to follow the assault aimed at the heart of the city. No matter how much he avoided it, he would have to fight most of the way, with all the risk that entailed. He would also have to keep pace with the advance and his friends might need him sooner than that. Indeed, every moment that passed increased their peril. There was the alternative of the Fugger passage into the city but then he would be in a strange town walking alone into Christ only knew what opposition.

He had positioned himself to the side of the road, a hundred paces before the gates. Wounded men limped or were helped past him and he scanned all of them, half-hoping to recognise a bloodied but living comrade. One man, a short and stocky warrior, seemed to have shed more blood than most, indeed more than any human could spare and still be walking. Head to feet in gore, his face almost obliterated by clots, the man trailed a sword on the ground behind him which ploughed a furrow in the dust. He was a few paces past when Haakon noticed the shape of that furrow. It was square. The sword making it belonged to an executioner.

'Hey!' Haakon called and caught up with the warrior. 'Hey, you, you! Where did you get that—'

He would have finished the sentence if the half-dead, bent-over man had not driven into the Norseman's stomach with a shoulder and suddenly straightened up. The action took both of them off the roadway and onto the verge, the man on top, Haakon on his back, winded and greatly surprised, for there were not many men who could lift him and those that could were generally not anywhere close to death. Such was the shock that he lay there silently, staring up at the bloodied mess of a face not a hand's breadth from his own, until a voice emerged from the face speaking in a tongue Haakon had learnt when fighting with an English company in Flanders.

'Easy, matey, easy. No need for you and me to 'ave a quarrel.'

Uriah Makepeace's dagger made its presence felt just where

373

the mail undershirt was weakest, under the armpit. It prevented the Norwegian's first impulse to rise because, though he was sure he could best this bloody apparition, he did not need an arm-weakening wound to take with him into the tasks that lay ahead.

So instead he said, one word: 'Fenrir.'

The growl made the eyes within the gore widen. They shifted to the side, saw the dog crouched there, hair rising around the razored collar, fangs bared, its rectangular eyes agleam and murderous.

'Shit!' the Englishman pronounced carefully, not moving. 'I 'ate dogs. Except when they're roasted.' Then a light came into his eyes. 'Wait! A dog. A big man. You're not . . . oh, what was the name? 'awkman? Something like that?'

'Haakon. Why would you know that?'

'Because I have a message for you from Jean Rombaud. Tell you what, you call off your 'ound, I'll take this little knife away, and we'll talk, all right?'

A little later, crouched in the lee of an earthwork, Makepeace told Haakon what he knew.

'And 'e said to be sure to let you know 'e will never give up,' he concluded. 'While 'e's alive there's 'ope, 'e said.'

'And do you think he is still alive?' Haakon watched as a cloth wiped away the blood from the face. The Englishman had assured him earlier that none of it was his.

'Dunno. But 'e's got more lives than a cat, that one.'

'So it is said. I must find out if he has one left.' Haakon rose.

'Not that way, friend.' A hand delayed him. 'The lunatics are fighting for every inch of the main road in.'

'Then I know of another way, a tunnel into the city. But I will not know where I am when I come out the other end.'

Makepeace looked back whence he had come, at the steady stream of soldiers entering and leaving the main gate. 'Look,' he sighed, 'I want to be on me way. But if you take me to this tunnel, I'll give you a route from the other side to follow to the palace. Can't do more than that.'

Men and dog skirted the earthworks, Haakon detouring briefly to collect the horses. Leading them down the old riverbed Haakon had last taken to see Januc off, he tied them to a stump and, after a little groping, found the entrance behind the thorn bushes, the metal grille swinging on rusted hinges.

'All right,' said Makepeace, 'I know where we are. This must come out somewhere among the old warehouses. There'll be this small square just beyond 'em, and three roads leading off. Take the—'

The growl halted him. Something or someone was moving just inside the tunnel.

A hand lifted to lips, an axe and square-headed sword raised either side of the entrance, a dog crouched among the thorns. Whatever it was moved slowly and with effort, the breathing heavy; a sound of some object, a body perhaps, being dragged. Makepeace indicated that he would strike first and Haakon shook his head, mouthing clearly, 'Mine.'

So when the shape emerged from the gloom of the entrance into the murk of the new day, it was the Norwegian who threw himself onto it, the axe haft coming down in a blow designed to stun. But the target of the blow sensed or heard the wind of the strike through the air. Something was raised, and wood thunked into sackcloth filled with metal, a dead sound replaced by that of a sword ripped from a scabbard. Makepeace brought his weapon down now, a killing stroke, but a blade met it and deflected it into the grille with a clang that shattered the stillness of the dawn. The shape rolled away under the triangle made by sword and gateway and on into the thorn bushes ahead. The snarl which greeted this intrusion caused a cry of sudden fear and anger, in it a tone that Haakon recognised.

'Fenrir! Off!' he yelled and, raising his arm to halt the Englishman's next attack, called into the bush, 'Januc?'

There was a moment of silence, then the Croatian's voice.

'Haakon? A fine greeting you give me, my friend. I'll be plucking thorns out of my arse till Doomsday.' He emerged from the bush, his sword still raised before him. 'Who is that with you, Norseman?'

'Uriah Makepeace, at your service.' The Englishman stepped forward, carefully.

Introductions were brief, explanations not much longer.

'You left him there?' Suspicion filled the Norse eyes that Januc avoided.

'He is dead, my friend. It was time to look to myself.'

'Is that what these are about?' Haakon nudged at the two bags of gold coin Januc had pulled from the tunnel. The blow of the axe haft had split one and Januc was picking up the coins that had spilt out.

'I told you this time would come. The time when Jean was beyond hope.'

'You saw him die? Actually saw his life bleed away?'

'As good as, Norseman. I saw him at the palace falling beneath a dozen swords. I saw him in the power of that German. His life was a short breath from its end and so would mine have been had I stayed.'

Haakon spat. 'If you did not see his body, janissary, then I will not believe he is gone. And I am going to find out for certain. Will you come with me?'

Januc raised his eyes. 'I will not. Only a madman pursues death for no purpose.'

'And you have found your purpose in this gold?'

'*Our* gold, if you will help me. It is hard to carry and the way ahead dangerous. There is enough here for both of us to die rich men. Die in our beds.'

Haakon hefted his axe to his shoulder. 'I can think of nothing worse. Find yourself another porter.' He turned and walked into the tunnel.

'Haakon!' Januc half rose, calling after him, but the gloom had swallowed the man and his shadow of grey wolf. 'May Allah protect you,' he added softly, in his own tongue.

'Now me,' said Uriah Makepeace. 'I'm always willing to earn a little extra. No such thing as too much gold. Where do you want these carried?'

'This way.' Januc lifted one of the bags. 'And while we carry, you can tell me the story of how you got that sword.'

Without a lantern, Haakon held to the fur of Fenrir's neck and allowed the better-sighted dog to guide him through the darkness. Despite a few stumbles they emerged swiftly into the murk of a big storehouse, its ruined roof pierced by the light of the new day.

It shone on three bodies. The two soldiers were obviously dead, crumpled in unnatural poses, one thrown back over a barrel, the other half sat on the remains of a table. The third man, however, was alive, bound to a wooden pillar and whimpering through a rag stuffed into his mouth. There was something about the face, twisted as it was in intense fear, that seemed familiar to Haakon.

'Spare me! Please, take pity on an old man,' Cornelius Fugger screeched as the rag was pulled out. 'They have taken everything from me. My money, my family. I am not worth hurting.'

Haakon swiftly stripped the bonds from him and pulled the shaking man to his feet. 'You will not be harmed, as long as you do exactly what I say. You will lead me to the palace.'

Complete horror twisted the captive's face. 'To . . . to the palace? Not again!' he wailed. Then indignation briefly replaced the terror. 'Does no one know their way around this damned town any more?'

Through his sobs, Haakon heard another sound and went to the entranceway to listen. It was one with which he was familiar, a sound that had brought him much joy in stormed cities across the years. It was a trumpet blast and its refrain spelt out a simple message: Victory! Munster had fallen.

'Come on.' Haakon hoisted the man to his feet. 'The main square, and as fast as possible.'

The streets bore confirmation of the trumpet's message, for looting had begun in earnest and mercenaries were carrying any object worth the effort from the houses, slaughtering any displaying the slightest desire to oppose them, and many who did not.

Haakon, a weeping Cornelius preceding him, moved through the devastation. It was not far to the square, and their arrival coincided with the triumphal entrance of Philip of Hesse and the Bishop of Munster.

Just behind them rode the Cibo brothers.

Franchetto was in full armour but still hunched forward, Giancarlo upright in the red robes of his office. They were moving towards the platform where only recently the King of Munster had received the acclamation of his people. He was there now, but all vestiges of majesty had been stripped away, leaving a naked man in a cage, his body blue with bruises, blood coagulating in patches around his many wounds, eyes downcast and glazed. Those townsfolk who had survived the assault, the many who had always hated and feared him, jeered him now, and there was a continuous barrage of muck that coated him.

As the mounted leaders reached the stage, Haakon scanned the scene for any sign of Jean and his nemesis, von Solingen. The German was a hard man to miss, and Haakon's eyes found him soon enough, surrounded by his guards. Looking closer, he made out a sack-like thing at their feet, and only after staring through the shifting figures of the crowd was he able to see it was made not of cloth but of flesh, trussed like a chicken. That thought took him for a moment back to a hot day in Tours, to an abattoir and a competition with this unmoving, bound figure. At least it meant one thing: Jean Rombaud *was* alive. There was no point in binding a corpse.

He was too far away to hear the exchanges on the platform. The cage containing Jan Bockelson was hoisted up onto the façade of St Lambert's church to much derision and acclaim. First Philip, then the Bishop, made speeches, the latter calling over the Cibo brothers at one point and obviously praising them for the conduct of their men, for Giancarlo then made a speech himself and at its end signalled Heinrich to follow them back out of the square. A pole was placed through the bonds on Jean's ankles and hands and he was carried, hanging like the trophy of the day's hunt, through the square towards the main gates.

Haakon, abandoning his weeping guide, made his way down through the people to intercept the convoy, with no plans as to what he would do there, just needing to see Jean closer to. Fenrir went before him, the dog's growls opening a gap swifter than any pushing would have done. Soon they were standing at a rank of soldiers, the Landgrave's personal guard, who lined the route in and out.

He reached it just as the brothers were passing. Ten paces behind them was the battered figure of his comrade, dangling from the pole. His breathing was shallow and he was obviously not in this world, which was as well for him. Haakon watched, all other sounds fading, his huge hands clasping and unclasping on the haft of his axe. He wanted to lift it up and fling it with all his great strength, take the heads off the brothers, follow up with his short sword, his snarling warrior dog, somehow reach Jean and free him, steal horses, ride triumphantly away. It was a majestic vision, and the gap between desire and reality brought tears.

It was when the last of the procession had passed that Haakon finally felt the hand tugging at his shoulder. He shrugged it off, but it returned and tugged harder, and this time a voice went with the insistent pull.

'Fuck! Tell me what has happened here, Norseman.'

He turned, and Beck was standing before him, hands at hips, one clenching and unclenching on the pommel of a sword. The look was a mixture of distress and fury, the latter directed straight up into Haakon's eyes.

This had been her fear, that she would come as fast as she

could and it would still be too late. Watching her beloved's body carted like dead game through the street, Beck's mind went back to each delay on the road, searching for that moment when she could have moved quicker, ridden harder, been here just a day, an hour, one bell's ring sooner to prevent this atrocity.

Too late! Because it had taken too long to join their relations in Venice. Her father's weakness had made travelling slow work, and when they arrived they discovered the Jewish ghetto had been sealed off on some Christian suspicion. No one went in for a week. Once inside, she had finally found Abraham's cousins and their husbands, who were more than willing to welcome the relation they'd never met, for he was reputed to be the best jeweller of the scattered family and the trade was thriving with the exquisite gold from the New World. They were less willing to let Beck go.

At first things had been friendly. They'd persuaded her to stay the one extra night to attend a feast of welcome. But she had been too long out in the world, in the freedom her male attire had given her, to enjoy being segregated with the other women, wearing a borrowed gown. Unwisely, she had opened her mouth to complain of the restrictions, to tell of how she would need to be away the next day to pursue her 'mission'. To the women of a people whose mission was simply survival in a Christian and malevolent world, this was incomprehensible. To the men, it was a threat to the order that allowed them to survive in that world.

Too late. For the next day the door had been bolted and only opened to bring her to where the men met. Abraham was there, better by the day, once again becoming the strong father she had loved, but also the strong father who now demanded obedience. He had told the others of their adventures, of the escape from Siena and of the mystery of his child's 'mission'. He had observed his daughter and at least some of her relations with the Gentile.

'The days in the wilderness are over now, Rebecca,' he had

said. 'We are back where we belong. And, at last, I will have the joy of seeing you married to a good man, in the faith of our people.'

It had been said gently, but there was no mistaking the command within the wish. It was to be. Seeing the resolution of those around her, Beck had managed to bite back on the words that would tell of the good man she had already met, the man she had to join. Common sense now told her to seek silence and plot escape.

Too late. For it took a week, a week of dutiful womanhood, of ceremony, family life, forgotten skills with a needle retaught to hands that craved not thread but a slingshot's cords. Within days, the women had told her that a husband had already been found, that her father was making the arrangements. She'd smile and bow her head while pressing the needle into her finger, using the pain to hold back a scream.

They hadn't trusted her. All remembered how 'she' had once been 'he', for it was when Abraham had first smuggled her out of Siena that she'd adopted the guise of Beck and had maintained it for a year in Venice. They remembered how 'he' had joined 'his' cousin Daniel's street gang, the Sicarii, Jews who fought back against the Christian oppressor with slingshot and knife. Her relations would not be fooled again.

But at the Shabat feast, she had put on a display of such contentedness that even the most suspicious were convinced. She was the best dancer there and led everyone time and again onto the floor. And when the men had drunk enough sweet wine, when the last aching limb was lowered onto mattresses, she had slipped from under the arm of a snoring cousin, reclaimed the boy's clothes waiting for use as cleaning rags, quietly picked the lock of the back door. The Sicarii had used the canals as their roadways; a stolen skiff and a dozing Venetian guard had seen her clear of the ghetto walls. A jeweller's house had yielded up a gold chain that was turned into coin for the road, more clothes, the first horse, and the materials to make a slingshot. Armed, anxious, barely sleeping, buying a new horse when one tired, she had at last made fast progress to Munster, the on-the-road rumours of that town's siege driving her even faster.

But it was too late. For now she stood there, all her hopes black ash in her mouth, watching her love hung like a deer's carcass, the prize of some hunt. While the man who was his friend stood uselessly by.

She shrugged off Haakon's arm and said, 'Why are you leading me away? Didn't you just see him leave?'

'I am trying to think like Jean. I need time for that.'

'Time?' The fury in the raven eyes made him wince. It was aimed at him like a stone from a slingshot. 'The time it takes to watch him die on a pole? Are you his friend? Or are the wages not high enough, the risks too great . . . mercenary?'

Though this last word was spat at him with equal amounts of venom and phlegm, Haakon's temper held. 'Easy, boy. I love him as well as you.'

'Do you? And the others?'

'The Fugger went with him into the city and has not reappeared. Januc . . . Januc has taken to the mercenary road again. Come, the city gates will have been closed to keep in traitors. I know of another way out.'

On the way back to the warehouse, he told Beck all that had transpired as he knew it. On hearing that Jean had surrendered himself to the danger of the siege for her sake, delaying his sacred quest, she drew blood from her lip with gnawing teeth.

'Do not feel guilty in this,' Haakon said. 'He loves you, lad. I have seen the love he bestows on a true comrade. He could not let you down.'

'And you?' Beck tried to convert the cause of the tears that rushed to her eyes into anger at the only person there to be angry at. 'Will you let him down?'

'I will not. But Januc was right in this – the odds are too great now. But they want Jean alive, that is clear. Why, I don't know. So we must follow and wait for a chance, some sign, some weakness on their part. I think such a chance will come.'

They were silent in the tunnel, Fenrir once more leading them back, though occasionally the dog stopped to growl into the darkness from which they'd come.

'Do you think someone follows us?' Haakon had paused again to look back.

'I neither know nor care.' Beck could barely stop herself running through the gloom. When they got to the horses on the other side, she made a show of adjusting the harness while she wiped away the moisture from her face, the blood from her lips and the tears that had flowed only where there was no light to see them by. In a low voice she called, 'So, Norseman, shall we see if we can hasten our luck?'

Without waiting for a reply she was up and off. Haakon sighed and struggled onto his far less willing mount, recognising the instant, unwelcome strain in his thighs.

'Give me a deck under my feet any day,' he muttered. 'Yah!'

Dancing eyes finally settled on the departing horses, then moved back to the hand that was holding the thorn branch aside.

'Remarkable,' he said, looking at the sixth finger, nestled in beside the little one, just as easy to move. Yet a needle plucked by his teeth from the bush, reversed with his tongue and thrust into the new flesh drew no blood, caused no pain. That was not true of the finger next to it, nor the one beyond that. They bled, they hurt. He liked the sight of the one, the sensation of the other, so he kept pricking them for a while, until he wondered if phantom digits were not the beginning of a brave new phenomenon. If they were, anything could return. Anything. Hadn't he seen that in a dungeon somewhere?

It was not to be. Raising his other arm, he saw only the

same old stump at its end. Quickly he lifted it and began to suckle on the puckered skin.

*So, all hope is gone then*, he thought. *There is no resurrection of the flesh.*

He stumbled out into sunshine, pitilessly bright now the storm clouds were gone. It was not right, this daylight land. He raised his one hand to shade himself, and the gesture drew a response from a nearby tree.

'Hand! Hand!' came the harsh voice.

Looking up, he saw a large black bird. Its eyes flickered over him for a moment, then returned to the task of grooming that had been interrupted by his master's reappearance.

'Ah, Daemon, are you come?'

The Fugger began a little dance in greeting, and the raven swooped from his perch and circled just above the head of the shuffling man, cawing the while. Then the bird dropped onto his shoulder, head angled to the side, eyes fixed upon him.

For a moment, he was happy just to dance, until the sun intruded again, no real heat in it to oppose the chill early autumn wind. Yet somewhere, he knew, there had to be a place of both darkness and warmth, a burrow against the cold whose boundaries could be defined with one hand.

But not here, not in this place of sunshine and death where the mad were kings and fathers reached up into ceilings for instruments of pain.

'Shall we go, O Daemon dear?'

The raven, with a croak, flew away from the morning sun, settling into a tree fifty paces ahead, head turned back, body bent forward.

'Clever bird! You always know the way.'

Bending his face to the path, eyes slitted against the glare, the Fugger took the first step along it towards the darkness he craved.

# EIGHT

# SALOME

'The problem with these so-called Lutherans,' declared Giancarlo Cibo, 'is that they are so obsessed by sins they do not know how to commit any.'

Five days in Wittenberg and he was already intolerably bored.

'And this is the best our gold can buy?' Franchetto threw another damp log onto the meagre fireplace where it gave out more smoke and little heat. This was the most spacious room in a house that would have fitted comfortably into the Siena palazzo's stables. 'Do they not know who we are?'

'They know as much as they need to know, brother. Two scholars seeking knowledge. Catholic princes are not popular in these states, you might remember. This is the heart of the Reformation. This is where Luther began the schism, where he runs it from.'

'Luther!' Franchetto spat, and stretched his back. He was almost upright again. 'If we came to Germany to return it to the Church, what better way than to stick a knife into that fat chest?'

'As always, dear brother, I admire your unquenchable thirst for blood and despise your stupidity.' The elder Cibo leant forward so his whisper would be heard. 'Germany is lost to the Pope and the Emperor. Luther has survived every attempt to assassinate or dissuade him. He is beyond our

385

reach. And anyway, we are not here on crusade. We are here for this.'

Beside him, on the table, sat the hand, its fingers resting on their pads, the palm raised slightly. He reached out and touched it. It was strange how he'd been unable even to look at it before and now he needed it always within sight. Obviously, it was to do with how he felt. There was less blood around when he had it near, less coughing, and this alone told him it was the key all alchemists had been seeking. He just needed Apollonius to open the door with it. The door to life eternal.

Apollonius! His real name, Cibo remembered, was Hans Dreschler, a cobbler's son from Breslau. But somehow this child of ignorance had become one of the greatest authorities on the hermetic sciences. Even Abraham, with a mind un-opiated, could not rival him. And Wittenberg had long been the centre of esoteric knowledge. It was said that the ancient ways of power, lines of potent energy, met in that place as nowhere else on earth.

However, Apollonius was not a man to be rushed, and he exemplified the national characteristic of dourness. Though Cibo had been in touch with him over the years, exchanging knowledge and modes of experiment, his arrival and this new element he sought to introduce had not provoked the wonder and instant action he was expecting. Its six fingers, and the fact it had survived unblemished the death of the body, caused the German merely to shrug. That it had once graced the arm of an infamous queen simply made him nod, and then only once. He'd asked the exact time and place of death, and had then told Cibo he would do some astrological calcula-tions and speak to him when they were confirmed. As for Cibo's prisoner, he did not know what questions to ask him yet. Once again, he would contact him when necessary.

Giovanni, the brothers' steward, had failed to wile away the wait. He had gone into town and returned with the best whores the place had to offer – large, lumpen creatures of vast stupidity and no invention. Franchetto had had three, one after the other, and had not cared that they yawned continually as he bent to his task. The Archbishop had taken the smallest, who still had mountains of flesh he found distasteful in the extreme; but she knew nothing of pleasure or pain, had hurt without thrill for him and had not even been able to pretend she enjoyed being hurt back. He had longed for Donatella, his Sienese mistress, and her exquisite technique. And he had beaten Giovanni with no restraint to encourage him to do better next time.

The brothers awaited him now, shivering before the smoking, heat-free fireplace; so when the door opened they were disappointed to see a scrawny youth.

'A messenger from Apollonius,' announced Heinrich von Solingen.

The youth was pimply, no more than nineteen, with the thick, wheaten hair of the region. He stooped, had a slight lisp and an insolent look in the eye, and the Archbishop instantly understood why Apollonius had displayed no reaction to the remains of the famed seductress of England, Anne Boleyn.

'Hans . . . I mean my master, sends his respects, and this.'

He handed over a small scroll of parchment, then stood close to the fire, picking at his face.

Giancarlo Cibo unrolled the paper and glanced swiftly down the list of questions written there. They were all to do with the actual moments of the execution, those few vital seconds when death and life conjoined. Only one man could answer them.

'Thank your master. Will you take some wine with us?'

'Better not.' The youth swallowed a yawn. 'He doesn't like it when I am away too long.' He ambled to the door, turned back. 'Can I tell him when you might have the information?'

'Soon,' said the Archbishop, looking at Heinrich. 'Very soon, I think.'

'Oh, he will be pleased.' The boy smiled briefly and was gone with another yawn.

Cibo gestured to his bodyguard. 'These are the things we need to know.'

Heinrich read them, then grunted. 'He will not want to tell us.'

'How boring for all if he did.' Giancarlo smiled at the German. 'Break him, Heinrich. Break him, body and soul.'

'With pleasure.'

The German left the room. They could hear his footsteps fading away on the cellar stairs at a slow and even pace.

Jean also heard the footsteps, the steady, deliberate tread of them, and knew it was about to begin. In a strange way, he was glad. In the five days of waiting he'd had nothing but his regrets for company. These ate into his mind more than the cords did into his ankles and wrists, burnt his throat with a gall fouler than the soup they poured down it twice a day, chilled his heart more than the dankness of stone could his body. Now at last he would be out of limbo and into hell. No matter how much the priests had tormented his childhood with visions of the eternal flames reserved for sinners, he'd always felt they were preferable to the endless nothing set aside for those who had done nothing with their lives. At least he had something to atone for. Perhaps, in the way he dealt with the hours to come, he could seek that atonement.

There were voices beyond the thick oak, then the searching of a key in the lock. When the door swung open, Jean blinked and turned his head away, keeping his eyes open but down to take in the light a little at a time. In the complete darkness of his cell, even the small flicker the lantern gave out was sharp as sunshine reflected off the sea.

The lantern was set down and a brazier fetched from outside to place beside it. Within their now tolerable glow, Jean gazed up at his captors. There were the two who fed him every day, hefty, muscled brutes with the permanent half beard and broken-nosed look of the Tuscan. And there was Heinrich von Solingen. From the wound of his face, his eyes shone, as if he was about work he loved.

He set down the sack he was carrying and metal clanked on metal within it. He turned towards Jean, an approximation of a smile upon what used to be lips. A whisper slipped through them.

'I am going to destroy you, Frenchman.'

'You are going to try . . . Scarface.'

The word was added quietly, as an afterthought, almost a dismissal, with no hint of insult in the timbre to colour it. Its very simplicity produced the reaction. The German swung back his boot and kicked hard at Jean's face. Limited though his movements were, he was able to turn just enough to take the blow on the shoulder, on top of bruises from beatings at Munster, causing agony to rip through him. Yet with the agony he felt a sudden triumph. He now knew what sort of torturer Heinrich von Solingen would make. An angry one. Calm torturers were more effective, for anger was a weapon to be turned back at whoever felt it. As it was the only weapon to hand, Jean grasped it gratefully.

'Tie him to the wall!' cried the German, and his assistants grabbed Jean, slipping off the wrist straps and stretching his hands to rebind them to the two iron rings embedded in the stone, once used to hang sacks of provisions beyond the gnawing of rats. His feet were splayed, ropes lashed around his ankles, then around the two heavy barrels that were the only furnishings of this cell.

'Strip him,' came the guttural command, and the meagre cloth that had covered him since the dungeon in Munster was wrenched off.

'Shall we start below or above? Or in the middle? Any preference, Frenchman?' A slight quaver in the voice contradicted the studied calmness of the German's words.

*This is a man who finds it hard to master himself,* Jean

thought. But he did not reply. Words, he could see now, were blades he could cut with. And they would only stay sharp if he used them sparingly.

He did not know what they would ask him. He did not know much anyway. He only knew he would tell them nothing, for this little was all he could still do for Anne Boleyn. And he was discovering there were different ways not to tell something. The first way, Jean decided, was to stare above the man approaching him, above the glint of lantern light on metal. There, on the stone-flagged walls, he could see a courtyard in Montepulciano and the dark eyes of Beck looking up at him from beneath her close-cropped hair.

Her dark eyes flashed every time the door of the merchant's house opened. They did not really expect anything other than the Archbishop's servants. But there was always that little hope that they would try to move Jean. Anyway, every face noted was an enemy recognised. A youth had gone in two days before and Haakon had trailed him back to the university, more to stretch his legs than anything. The night before that, Giovanni, the Archbishop's steward, whom Beck had recognised from Siena, had taken in four laughing women who had emerged an hour later sombre and quiet, the smallest among them weeping inconsolably. The steward had soon developed a vivid black eye and his rare excursions had become increasingly agitated. Of the Cibo brothers, though, there was no sign.

Yet Beck did not blame them for not stirring out onto this street. Winter seemed to have bypassed autumn but the only effect here was the cold, because the roofs of the houses were so tightly linked above that no light or liquid penetrated. If any chill rain had fallen it might have done something to wash away the foul-smelling channel that clogged the road-way's centre, muck thrown out to join it from every window. They had been fortunate, though, for the last of her gold from Venice had bought them what passed for luxury in Wittenberg, a room just bigger than the plank bed into which she, Haakon and Fenrir squeezed together. Most importantly, its window gave a view of the doorway behind which they knew Jean was imprisoned.

It was Haakon who had managed to stop her first and every subsequent impulse to storm the place. Where he had learnt such sense, he was not sure. He would gladly throw himself into the thickest part of any fray, howling his Norse battle cries, and if it was just his own life he was risking he would not have hesitated. But his death would lead inevitably to the death of his friend. However glorious, such an end was mere vanity if, in the dying, he did not secure Jean's survival.

And the survival of this boy who, in a way he didn't understand, Jean loved.

'We wait, we watch, and we find another way,' he said gruffly each time the lad reached for slingshot and knife.

He kept them both occupied getting information. They would listen in on the conversations of those men-at-arms who were allowed out in twos and threes to inn and brothel, Haakon, familiar with that world, chatting to the whores, Beck pretending to doze over a mug of beer while the guards spoke in their native Tuscan which they thought no one else could understand.

Between them, they learnt of the cellar where the prisoner was kept, and of the thrice-daily visits paid by their commander, from which he would emerge, sometimes swiftly, sometimes less so, always his distorted face mottled further with rage. They learnt of the frustrations of the brothers, the ceaseless bickering, the anger deflected onto hapless servants. And they heard many tales of Giovanni, trying to conjure entertaining gold from the dross metal of Wittenberg life. It was a town centred on the learning of the university and Luther's steady construction of a new religion.

'You'll find more sin in a Neapolitan nunnery . . . and twice as good-looking whores!' wailed the steward that evening, drawing sympathetic laughs from the three soldiers at the table.

Beck had come downstairs to eavesdrop when she saw the Italians enter. Haakon was scouting the back of the merchant's house again, hoping he'd missed something there. Despite his restraining of her, she knew he was growing more agitated by the hour with their inaction. He was as desperate to find a way in as she was.

'If you don't mind whores with beards!' one of the soldiers declared.

'They all have beards,' said another. 'You've just got to look at the right face.'

More laughter, but Giovanni was not to be put off his whining so easily.

'I tell you, if the prisoner doesn't break soon' – nausea swept over Beck – 'then I will end up with no part of my body left to bruise. Did you see what that beast Franchetto did to me this morning?' He raised a sleeve to reveal the marks where fingers had gripped and squeezed. 'Entertain us, they say. Tease and entice us. But the dancers I find just clump, and the whores just yawn. In Siena, I have to turn away the entertainers, the standards are so high, the competition so fierce. Here, a drunken song is the best they can manage.'

The rest of the whining faded into the background hubbub of the inn's main room, for Beck's thoughts had suddenly been caught by something within all the complaining. Her mind whirling, her eyes fixed on the table before her, she nearly missed Giovanni's leaving. She sprang up and followed the Italian steward as he picked his way among the foul deposits of the street.

'Signore! Signore!' she called after him. Once he had stopped and let her catch up, she carried on in Italian. 'Excuse me, but I couldn't help overhearing you in the inn back there.'

'Jesu preserve me, a countryman!' Giovanni exclaimed, trying to scrape something off his shoe onto a doorstep. 'What ill wind blows you here, young master?'

'The same as you, I think. I serve another who has business here. Though by the sound of it, my master treats me a little better than yours treats you.'

This produced another wailing account of the miseries he had to endure. Beck listened, nodding in sympathy, then, when the steward finally paused for a second's breath between lamentations, cut in, 'But my master has not your problems. He brought his own entertainer with him from Bologna.'

'Ah!' cried Giovanni. 'God be praised for the sense of the Bolognese. And what does this entertainer do?'

Beck tucked her neck further into her collar, affecting embarrassment. 'Well, this entertainer is my sister, sir, and she is a . . . uh, dancer, I think, would be the best way of putting it.'

'A "uh, dancer"?' The Italian's eyes gleamed. 'And does she have a "uh, speciality"?'

'Oh yes, sir, most certainly. Her speciality is, is . . .'

Beck was gazing furiously above the head of the steward, into a memory. It was of a time when her father was just a colleague of Giancarlo Cibo's, before her flight to Venice. One of the Archbishop's maidservants had taken a liking to the young and lonely Jewish girl and had let her play in areas of the palace that she cleaned. One of them was a room where Cibo displayed the results of his patronage. The statues were mainly flowing Greek and Roman nudes, men and women locked in fleshy embrace. The paintings were similarly decadent. She remembered one especially because she was told that the subject of it was Jewish.

'My sister dances as Salome,' she said. 'Dances for Herod to win the head of John the Baptist.'

The Italian was hopping from foot to foot, the filth on his shoes forgotten. 'And does she ever perform this dance for anyone other than your master?'

'Well, not usually. But my master is out of the city at the moment. And she is easily bored. She could be per-suaded . . .'

A fee was rapidly agreed, an advance paid, the arrangements made for later that night. The sum was high. Both of them knew they were not speaking of mere dancing.

'You arranged what?' Haakon bellowed an hour later.

'Look, help me brush out this hair, will you? We haven't got much time.'

Beck had bought a small mirror in the shop next to the one where she had purchased the wigs. Between them they had spent most of the advance, but she hadn't needed much else. Just some silk. Seven veils were what she remembered from the painting. Seven, dropped around the room, draped over furniture, over the watching, leering King.

Such was Haakon's bemusement at the idea that he found the brush in his hand and had even pulled it through the thick tresses of the wig a few times before he realised. He threw it down, just as Beck jumped up and began fiddling with the strings of her doublet, her back towards him.

'Are you mad, boy? What happens when you are in there?'

'When *we're* in there. I've brought you a headsman's mask as well, try it on.'

He almost reached for it. 'No! I mean what happens when you start to dance. They'll see straight away, won't they?'

'See what?'

'See what? May the gods give me strength! That you're a boy!'

'Will they?'

Beck had unbuckled the doublet and now pulled the undershirt off, swiftly followed by the bindings of cloth wrapped round and round the chest.

'Of course they will,' Haakon sighed. 'You can't fool . . . leaping Christ!'

'What?' Beck was facing him now, hands on hips. 'You've never seen breasts before?'

'Not on a boy, no,' murmured a suddenly subdued Norseman. 'Never on a boy.'

It was strange. What was that word again? The one the Fugger used?

Paradox. Another paradox. This one concerned pain. Because the greater the agony he endured, the greater the reward when he awoke later from his faint, flesh still imprisoned, mind quite clear. His tormentors would be gone, and the others could then arrive.

They would all be there, sometimes together, as if they were sharing a meal again back in Tuscany, sometimes alone. Januc would speak of scrapes and scimitars, the infinite advantages of a curving blade. Haakon would tell him several of his mother's homilies, each more untranslatable than the last. The Fugger would dance and shuffle before him, avoiding his eyes.

When Beck came it was different. There were so many things he wanted to say to her, that he had been unable to say before, in their little time together. His strength had always lain in actions not words, and he regretted that now, because he was suddenly unsure if she knew how much he loved her, how much that sudden recognition had shifted a weight that had pressed down on him since his wife and child had died, like a stone rolled away from the entrance of a cave, letting in the light. Yet now she told him she understood without his words, let him know it was the same for her – that he had arrived in the mansion of her heart and painted every room there a different colour.

That morning, Cibo had joined his bodyguard, and his dispassion had been much more painful than the brutality of the German. As Jean awoke from his enforced sleep, he twisted in his bonds and agony took him again. As there was no one there, he allowed himself a scream.

The hand that touched him then was familiar and strange at the same time. He was comforted by its coolness, the way the fingers traced the bones of his face, bringing relief to the harm inflicted there.

She stood before him, that smile upon her face. The filigree of grey that had run through her hair back in the Tower was gone. It was all black now, except for the tones of red, like peonies scattered on some Loire hillside.

Anne Boleyn raised the hand again, let the six fingers move over him, feeling out his hurt, a balm where they touched. The arm they had broken was knit again, the leg also. When she joined his ribs, his breathing came clear for the first time in days, and he breathed deeply, inhaling her summer-tinged fragrance.

'They have wronged you, Jean,' she said, a deeper darkness in her eyes.

'Oh, my Lady,' he replied. 'That does not compare to the wrong I have done you.'

'What wrong?'

'My failure. Your enemies have taken what you entrusted to me, what I swore to defend. Your cause is lost.'

She leant into him, laid each of her hands on either side of his head, as she had done that night. 'Did you not say "while I am alive I will not give up hope"?'

He smiled at that, for hope had left him some days before, as he heard his body break.

Her smile matched his. 'This should tell you something, Jean Rombaud. It reminds you of *my* promise, the one I made you on the scaffold: "We two shall meet again." And not just in a dream.'

She was gone then, and the sunlight left with her. Chased away, perhaps, by the sound of footsteps on the stairs.

As well as the brazier, carried on metal poles by the Tuscans, two lanterns were brought in now. Heinrich held one, the Archbishop the other. When Jean saw him, his defiance wavered a little. The man knew too much about pain.

The cleric came up to him, raising the lantern to study the results of his last efforts.

'It's interesting.' The silky voice spread over him, a cough followed by the raising of a handkerchief to dab at lips. 'What one man can bear that another would have already died from. Thresholds, eh? An interesting word. Limits, and things to cross over, both. You and I have witnessed many cross the threshold between this life and the life to come, haven't we, Executioner? I can never experience that moment enough, can you?'

Jean was silent, giving his enemy nothing.

'How fitting that we will share it now. You will know more about it than me, alas for you. Though I am sure you crave release from this life, do you not? Are you ready to cross the threshold? Your journey from one hell to another is about to begin.'

Cibo's cough, the red marker on the cloth, gave Jean another weapon of words, his last perhaps. Through broken teeth, he chose each word with care.

'It is true I know something of death. I have seen it written on a thousand faces. Yet I have never seen it so clearly as it is written on the face before me now. I may precede you to the flames, but you will burn beside me soon enough.'

The Archbishop did not speak at first, and such little colour as he had vanished. He coughed, and a cloth raised too late failed to prevent the blood seeping down his chin. He turned away, mastered himself, turned back, a smile again in place.

'We don't need you any more, Executioner. Apollonius has decided he doesn't require your information after all. The secret, he believes, lies in the actual flesh of that accursed hand. I suspected as much, the way its touch so affected me. So we will treat it with mercury, slice it, open it up. Especially that extra finger. He believes the core of power lies there. Harnessed, and who knows? I may yet deprive you of your companion of the flames.'

Jean laughed. It was an absurd sound coming from a man hanging broken on a wall, and in a fury Cibo snapped, 'I made the mistake of letting you live once. I shall now take the greatest pleasure in watching you die.' Turning to his bodyguard, he added, 'Let's see how slowly we can make that happen, Heinrich.'

The German wrapped a cloth around his hand and picked up a knife that had been resting on the coals of the brazier.

'Shall I begin, my Lord?'

A nod, and the knife was borne forward. Instinctively, Jean shut his eyes, raised his head, tried to think of Tuscany, of Beck. He felt the heat approaching his flesh . . .

There was a tentative knocking at the door. The blade was removed a little, and Jean opened his eyes again to see Giovanni standing in the doorway. The steward gazed in fascination at the suspended, bloodied man, the words he'd come to speak lost.

'Well, fool?' Heinrich bellowed at him.

'The . . . the . . . the entertainer is here my . . . my Lord.'

'What entertainer? Ah, ah yes . . .' Cibo turned to his bodyguard. 'Giovanni thinks he has found some Italian whore to dance Salome of the Seven Veils for me, then satisfy me afterwards. Well, she'll have to wait. We will not be long, I think.' He paused as Giovanni turned reluctantly in the doorway and the blade once more approached. 'No, stop.' A smile came to the reddened lips. 'I am forgetting, Heinrich. Pleasure protracted is pleasure twice as keen. The same goes for pain, of course. Let us leave our friend here to anticipate his final mortification a little longer. His dying will be all the sweeter when I have had the – how shall I say it? – the little death this whore will give me. And since Franchetto has gone into the night with his men, I shall not even have to share her. Only if you care to, my dear Heinrich?'

The German stiffened and walked to replace the weapon on the coals.

'I will watch over you, my Lord, as always, and that is all.'

'Really, Heinrich. Will you never learn? Pleasure and pain, my friend. Pleasure and pain.'

They left the brazier, and its heat filled the little cell, the first Jean had felt in he knew not how long. He was grateful for it, and the light as well. It made shadows move against the walls and in them his companions seemed content to sit and wait for him to die.

Haakon couldn't help but stare. His vision was obstructed by the narrow eye slits of the mask, so he needed to turn his head from side to side to see all of her.

Her! This is what was so hard to accept. It was the same person he'd glanced at a thousand times. And it was not the same. How could he ever have thought Beck anything other than a woman? A lovely one too, small but well shaped at breast, a slim waist, and features of face which, when seen in the context of womanhood, were not unpleasing. Not that he could see them all now. A veil covered them, rosy-hued like the others draping her. They did not fully conceal, they hinted at a desired revelation. One at each breast, one for each leg, a partial skirt over the hips. Under that he could just make out the darker patch of cloth that lay at the source of the most womanly part of her, held there by a taut silken cord. The seventh veil.

He had to look away. The black hair of his wig spilled out from under his headsman's mask, making him itch wherever it touched. She said it concealed him in some way. It annoyed him in many. He scratched vigorously. They had made him leave his axe in the corridor outside the room, otherwise his hands would have been occupied.

'Stop it!' Beck hissed at him. 'You're like a bear in a beehive. You're meant to stay unnoticed. They won't watch me with you doing St Vitus' dance.'

'Well, your wig hasn't got fleas!' he hissed back, still scratching.

Beck sighed and struck a pose, leg out, a bare foot reaching from beneath the silk. It had been an offcut, but it had still cost her most of Giovanni's advance, yielding just enough material to make the costume. She was never sure about women's clothes, but Haakon's lascivious then embarrassed reaction showed it was probably all right. Yet now she was standing there in that small, cold room, the enthusiasm that had swept her forward was gone, replaced by doubt and fear.

She tried a move to the left, raising and banging down her timbrel on a knee, its taut skin drawn over a half-moon frame, the small metal links giving out the only music she would have, apart from the jingle of tiny bells at her ankles. The move was clumsy, awkward, not enticing in the least – and she had to entice beyond the fantasies of any man! Why did she ever think she could do this? Because she danced well the dances of her people? Those movements were restrained, eyes cast down, demure. They were not the movements of a Salome.

Voices came from outside the door, and when it opened all considerations of performance disappeared in the shock of being in the same room as her enemy. Her hands instinctively reached for a weapon that was not there, and she saw Haakon cease his scratching and slip a hand to his side, twitching for the reassurance of an axe.

*This is the moment,* she thought. *They will see through these thin veils, not to the woman but to the body of their foe. They will pierce the Norseman's disguise, call their guards, we will be overpowered, then subjected to the same horror they have been inflicting on Jean. This moment, now, as Giancarlo Cibo walks in, coughs, raises his handkerchief to his lips, sees . . .*

'Ah, Salome.' There was a trace of liquid in the voice. 'You I recognise, Princess. But who is your friend?'

She was not Rebecca, daughter of Abraham, nor Beck, the boy warrior. She was an Italian whore who enticed with a dance. She was Salome. She had lived with disguises all her life. And she had watched men watch women.

'Your Eminence.' In her low curtsey, she made sure the

loose-fitting veils around her breasts slipped forward. 'Every Salome needs an executioner. How else am I to take the reward for my dance – the head of John the Baptist?'

She sensed rather than saw Heinrich react to the words. Haakon was not moving a false hair under the German's scrutiny, but he was not a man who could look insignificant. She leapt up, clashing the timbrel above her head, striking an elaborate pose, drawing all attention to her. Under her arm, beneath her paint-thickened lashes, her eyes found and held the bodyguard's.

'Really, he's just here to make sure I get paid.' Her voice had slipped into the street accent of the Veneto. 'You'd be surprised how many try and cheat me, once they've had their . . . fun.'

Another pose, this time some flesh shown at the thigh, the timbrel shaken level with the ground, tinkling around to finally rest at her hip.

'I wouldn't be surprised at all, my dear.' The voice had a huskier quality to it now. 'Alas, there is so much evil in the world. And does your executioner watch all the "fun"?'

She raised the half-moon to her face, peered over the top of it, her eyes wide and blinking slowly.

'Oh no. Gunter is discretion itself. He hears nothing, says nothing, sees nothing. Unless the client requires anything different, of course. Anything is possible, for a price. Anything.'

She had reverted to the more refined accent of the dancer, with a hint of the knowing girl thrown in. Eyes downcast, she heard the cough again, and slippered feet moving away to the fireplace.

'Maybe later. Variations always interest me.' Cibo sat, while Heinrich stayed at the door. 'But for now, my dear, shall we see if Salome can earn her reward?'

She glanced at the Archbishop. He was leaning forward in his chair, his high forehead mottled by some internal heat, his fleshy, sensual lips damp and slightly parted. To his side, his arm stretched out towards an empty chair, seeming to rest on the table between them. To rest and not quite rest.

Suddenly Beck saw why his hand hovered just above the wooden surface. It was moving up and down another hand. Cibo's fingers were stroking the severed flesh of Anne Boleyn. As if she were there, and Archbishop and Queen held each other in anticipation of private entertainment. Beck saw the desire Cibo felt for her dance, but she also saw the far greater desire he felt for what was, and was not, beside him.

Shivering, she placed one foot slowly in front of the other, the tiny bells jangling her progress. The little courage she'd found had vanished. She felt lumpen, unskilled, unequal to the task she'd set herself. Getting through the door of the house had been her first concern. Everything else was an invention of the moment, single actions and reactions dragging her forward.

*Why am I here, in this strange room, nearly naked? What did I think I could achieve with a dance? Why didn't I listen to Haakon? What demon possessed me?*

She shivered again, to a tiny tinkle of bells. And then the answer rose before her in a name.

*Jean. I am here for Jean.*

They had watched Franchetto leave with ten of his men. That meant there were still twenty more somewhere in this house. They had no time to search against those odds. She had to make them bring her to Jean. Or bring Jean to her.

A vision of her love lying hurt so close by replaced her fear with anger. *Anger and love. Power to be harnessed for something else. For a dance, perhaps.*

It began with a gentle tapping of feet, a tucket of little bells, like a summons. An echo at the hand, the chiming of metal held in a wooden frame, that one hand raised swiftly to meet the other above the head, a sudden strike of the half-moon. Then a slow drumming of fingers, building up into a storm on a reed roof, hands lowered to pass before the veiled face, linger before the breasts, drift down over stomach, hip and thigh as if cool rain were flowing down in waves over too-hot flesh. Her head swaying now, rolling from side to side, and then all around, mouth open under the half-veil, eyelids nearly shut, the merest hint of light from the kohl-darkened eyes. A bare foot raised, toes pointing down, leading the leg out to the side. A slight spring onto that foot, the other raised behind, the timbrel running up the leg like a caress, a rhythmical fluttering now. A strike of the drum at the thigh and a piece of material freed, suddenly floating through the air, sailing like a silk javelin, to crumple and fold onto the sitting man's shoulder.

'One.'

Cibo smiled as he spoke, running the cloth through his fingers, draping it finally over the hand beside him, his eyes feasting on the flesh revealed. It was a strong thigh, muscles rippling under the golden skin, and he imagined his nails running along it, from the dimple of the knee and up. The thought brought on a cough and the rosy silk darkened when he snatched it up to his mouth.

The stamping now, a counterpoint to the drumming, bare feet resonating on the wooden floor. Another shot of rose through the air, the same target hit again, opposite shoulder.

'Two.'

Haakon heard Cibo speak but he didn't look, his eyes held by the other thigh now revealed. He didn't want to stare – this was his comrade, after all, Jean's love, as he now knew – but the dancing form before him, hidden by the veils, had also become something else unto itself, and the rhythm of feet and hand, the harmonious jangle of the bells, all fused in his senses in a way he could not help. And he sensed that the stiff form of Heinrich von Solingen beside him suddenly relaxed, then stiffened again, the quality of the attention transformed.

She was moving around the room, the percussion empha-sised on every fourth beat, her feet touching the floor to spring away again. She never quite looked at the man in the chair, but she never quite looked away either, completely aware of him, of his attention on her, of a promise held out then slowly withdrawn, only to be offered again.

They could not see the hesitation; she used it as a pause only between beats, but it gave her the time to slip one of the knots she'd tied at the back of her neck and one of the bindings there was loosed, held for matching moments of revelation and concealment before a breast was freed from its constraints and three men gasped for air in a room suddenly lacking it.

Through the sounds of bare feet slapping the wooden floor, the harmonious jangle of metal at wrist and ankle, two voices were heard: Beck's little groans as each silk flew free from her body, and the moan of 'three' that emerged from the Archbishop's mouth, then a whispered 'four'. The 'five' was mouthed only, yet seemed to echo round the room as power-ful as silent thought can be.

She stood before him now, only the face and the waist still covered, and that by the smallest of rose patches held in place by a silken cord. She had placed her hand before it, and the timbrel was held in front of her, not quite concealing, not quite revealing, her breasts, like a Botticelli maiden rising from a shell. Cibo's breathing was shallow, eyes trying to penetrate the last of the barriers.

'More?' she breathed. She was standing just before him, bent slightly over towards him. Peeling back the veil from her face, trailing it slowly into his lap, her voice emerged from behind it like oil. 'Do you want more?'

'More?' he whispered. 'Oh yes, much, much more.' Then, raising his voice, he said, 'Leave us. Leave us now.'

And then it came to her. She didn't think about it. She just spoke.

'But what of my reward?'

'Reward?' The word distracted him and he sought her eyes. 'What reward? You will be well paid. Afterwards.'

'Not money. That's for me, but what of Salome?' She raised her arms above her head, joining them in an arc of hands and timbrel. 'Salome wants her reward too. She wants a head.' She leant in closer so that her breath was in his ear.

'You don't mean . . .'

'Oh, but I do. My special treats work so much better if we play the scene for real. My . . . reward for you will be so much the greater. Surely, your servant here can go and drag some wretched cripple off the street? Or perhaps' . . . she paused. 'Perhaps in his own house, his Excellency has some lazy servant who has displeased him and deserves . . . punishment.' She almost let her tongue touch him. 'Pleasure *after* pain, don't you think?'

Cibo gasped at the familiar words. He had long given up the hope of any depravity shocking him. Yet this bewitching child had just done it! He smiled now, for Wittenberg had suddenly become the most interesting place he had ever visited.

'A cripple? Some servant?' He paused, clutching at the six fingers beside him. Then he laughed. 'No. Nothing so common for my Salome. Heinrich?'

'My Lord?'

'Fetch me the prisoner here.'

'The . . . prisoner, your Eminence?'

'The Frenchman, Heinrich. My Salome requires a head before she finishes her performance. Lucky for me that we have one to offer her. No! No discussion. Fetch him here.'

The German left and Beck gestured at Haakon. 'Gunter here is a fine taker of heads.'

'You have done this before?' Cibo was unable to take his eyes from hers.

'Oh, once or twice.' She dropped the timbrel another fraction. 'For very special clients.'

'My dear,' said the Archbishop of Siena, '*you* are the special one.'

Haakon went outside and returned with a block and his axe, the weapon's shape disguised in a piece of sacking. His mind whirled as much as his body shook. He had not thought it could come to this. Getting through the door had been the limit of his plotting, violence the only progression. What was going on now he didn't understand. He just knew he had to be ready.

Heinrich returned, alone.

'Where is he?' snapped his master.

'My Lord, they are bringing him. But—'

'Yes?'

'My Lord, you promised him to me.' The German did not try to keep the petulance out of his voice.

'Priorities, Heinrich. My Salome needs this gift more than you do. To bring her inspiration for the rest of her . . . performance. Is that not right, my child?'

Beck's eyes, which had been on the door since Heinrich's entrance, flicked back to Cibo's. She remembered just in time to flutter them.

'Yes, my Herod. One gift for another.'

'And here it is.'

Of all the play acting she had done that day, the hardest was to keep her face blank now, as Jean's naked body was dumped into the room by the two gaolers. There could not be any life in that mess of blood and shattered bone, burnt flesh, flayed skin. He lay like a marionette with strings severed, and the walk she had to make across to him was an agony of small, slow steps. She raised him gently by the clotted hair, and saw the blood at the mouth bubble with a little breath.

'Oh yes,' she said softly. 'This head will do. Better than any other.'

The block was placed in the centre of the room, and Haakon, a tear forcing its way out of one eye, laid Jean's head gently upon it. Cibo had come forward and was gazing down into the glazed eyes of the Frenchman. Cradled in his fingers, stroked as if it were a pet, was the hand of Anne Boleyn.

'How fitting, Jean Rombaud, that you should die now in this way. And for my pleasure.' He returned to his chair, laid

406

the Queen's hand down on the table, and said, 'Strike away, headsman!'

That final word woke Jean, as if someone were calling him, but he could not distinguish between this dream he was in and the one he'd left on the other side, for the people were much the same in both. He had been back in Montepulciano, his refuge, the full moon's beams playing upon the beauty of Beck's naked skin. Now, in this waking dream, she was above him again, nearly as naked, save for the thin cord around her waist. Her hair had grown though, and taken on a darker hue. Had so much time passed since he last saw her? Yet nothing could alter the quality of her loveliness.

In this vision, Haakon stood before him too; even though he wore an executioner's mask and black hair spilt from beneath it, it could only be the Norseman. Jean felt a momentary concern that Beck was naked in his presence, but then he saw the axe emerging from a sack and he knew his companion was there to end his pain at last. He began to look beyond the falling of the blade to a world where his dead awaited him.

It was the axe. Heinrich had thought his unease came from being cheated of his prize – his enemy's death at his hands alone. But when he saw the axe raised up he remembered immediately where he had seen it before. And he saw, through the slitted leather mask and the false black hair, to the Norse face beneath.

'No!'

Heinrich was standing on the other side of the room, behind his master's chair, but his move forward was blocked by his master rising in excitement. For the dancer, at that exact moment, was removing the seventh of her silk veils.

Beck pulled the cord free from her hips and found the gap she had created at one end for her fingers. She grasped the knot at the other end, then reached into the pocket of Haakon's smock and removed a stone. At the same moment, the axe began its descent and the slingshot rose. Three swings had it whirling above her.

'No!' cried Heinrich again, but this time he did not move forward but grabbed Cibo, trying to pull them both behind the chair. The stone took him in the wrist under the hand that held his master's struggling head, and he heard a bone snap there. They fell in a heap behind the inadequate shelter.

The axe that had seemed to be moving straight down towards the block and the exposed neck changed directions in a sudden shift of shoulder and wrist. The first gaoler's surprised look stayed on his face even as his head bounced onto the floor. The second managed a scream, but the back swing took him in the throat and cut it off.

*This is a wonderful dream*, Jean thought. *The best yet.*

While a second stone was retrieved from the pocket, in the small pause before rope and silk once again whirled in the air above them, Heinrich tipped the table over and increased their shelter by its width. He had managed to get his short sword out of its scabbard, despite the awkwardness of using the unfamiliar, unbroken hand. Cibo lay under him, racked by violent coughing, crimson running unchecked from his mouth.

'Haakon! Grab Jean!' Beck screamed.

'One moment.' The Norseman was striding towards the upturned table, axe held on high. 'Something to settle first.'

His journey across the room was interrupted by a new and not unfamiliar voice.

'Ah brother! What a night we have had!'

When Franchetto Cibo spoke these words from the doorway, he was looking back into the corridor and grinning at his bodyguard, Bruno-Luciano, who had surprised his master that night with a hitherto unrevealed depth of carnality. It was only after they were uttered that he turned back to enter, just as Heinrich bellowed, 'Help us!'

Franchetto only got the briefest glimpse of the strange scene before a naked woman stopped whirling something above her head and slammed the door on him. There was a key in the lock, rusted from disuse, and it took both her hands to turn it. It clicked just as someone crashed into the door and indistinct bellowing erupted from the other side.

'Haakon!' she yelled, and the Norseman now turned to her. 'No time! Grab Jean, for the love of God! This door will not hold for long!'

The Norseman could just see over the edge of the table. 'Another time then,' he said clearly, seeing the German's eyes narrow, the hate mirrored back.

Thrusting the shaft of his axe behind his back into the folds of his cloak positioned to act as a sling, he stooped and put his arms under the Frenchman's body. It did not hang right when he lifted it, and he could not believe how light it was. The lifting obviously sent pain shooting through him, for Jean's eyes suddenly opened and, in a distinct voice, he said, 'Have a care, you great ox!'

Haakon smiled down at him. 'Welcome back, little man.'

There were two crashings of wood then, one at the main door where a large body was hurled against it, one where another of Beck's stones hurtled into the table, a finger's width below where Heinrich had unwisely raised his head.

'The door is giving,' Beck called. 'Where now?'

There was one other door in the room, off to the left side of the fireplace. Haakon knew the back of the house lay in that direction and he could only hope all the hours of scouting there had not been in vain.

'This way!' he shouted with a confidence he did not feel, and threw the door open.

A murky passage was indeed revealed, leading he knew not where. He hesitated, but the splintering of the other frame left them no choice, and Beck ran to join them. Pausing for a second once more to raise the slingshot, she found her head was close to Jean's. She heard him whisper, 'The hand. We cannot leave it here.'

It had fallen to the floor when Heinrich had jerked back the table, and lay now an arm's length from it, resting on its fingertips, as if waiting.

Heinrich's cry of 'To me!' brought yet another crash, and the door shuddered inwards. It would not last much longer.

Beck hesitated.

'Please,' Jean whispered. 'All is lost without it.'

She said sharply, 'Take him! Go!' and as Haakon set off down the passage the main door burst open and two men fell through it to sprawl on the floor. A third brandishing a sword leapt over them and it was he who died, Beck's stone taking him between the eyes. He was dead before he began to fall backwards, and an outflung hand struck Franchetto in the face as he tried to enter. He clutched his nose with a cry, temporarily blocking the doorway.

Beck dived for the hand, aware as she did so that a shape was rising from behind the table. Something sliced down through the air towards her. She twisted, folding in on herself, landing at the same time as Heinrich's sword bit into the floor an inch from her head. Her right hand snatched up that of Anne Boleyn as she fell over it, and she used the motion of the roll to keep going and end up on her feet.

Franchetto stood in the doorway, clutching his face, screaming. Two men started to push past him. Heinrich was between Beck and her only means of escape but he was bent over his sword, his back slightly to her, trying to pull it from the floor where the force of his wrong-handed death blow had lodged it.

Stepping forward on her left foot, she lifted her right back and kicked him hard between the legs. He crumpled, and she leapt over his falling body, running down the passage into the darkness, the two men just behind her. She ran into something in the dark, was picked up, placed to the side. There was the sound of two blows. In the entrance to the passage another man had appeared. There was no width in the passage to use her slingshot so she merely pitched the last of her stones at the shape. There was a yelp of agony.

In the gloom, she could just make out Haakon stooping to pick up the prone Jean.

'Come on!' he cried, setting off. 'I think this way is out.'

Another door opened on to the small courtyard, full of barrels and sacks, that Haakon had observed on his night missions. Five hunting dogs snarled and snapped, straining at their short chains. A dozen paces across, a gate gave on to a lane. Their horses were there.

'Here, take him!' Haakon passed the body to Beck and it was her turn to be surprised at the weight.

She looked into the ravaged face, whispered, 'Oh, my love! What have they done to you?'

'Come!' the Norseman yelled, stacking the last of the heavy barrels against the door just as the first shoulder hit it from the other side. He took Jean back and they ran for the lane, where a familiar growl greeted them.

'Fenrir! Foe!' Haakon shouted, and the dog followed the pointed finger and ran into the yard they'd just fled. A sound of crashing followed by a confusion of snarling and yelling erupted there.

Beck was in the saddle, Jean passed up to be cradled before her. Haakon was on the other horse in a trice, and pausing only to cry 'Fenrir!' he kicked first the side of Beck's mount, then his own. They sped down the darkling lane as the first bloodied man ran shouting from the yard.

The night gatekeeper at Wittenberg's main portal later tried to excuse his failure to keep it shut by telling of the strangeness of the vision, as well as the suddenness and force of the vision's appearance. But the Hochmeister did not believe his tale of a naked Valkyrie bearing a dead warrior in her arms, accompanied by a huge headsman and a giant wolf. It sounded like the product of a wine-clouded mind, and since the gatekeeper already had a reputation for drunkenness, he was brutally flogged before being dismissed from his post.

The Hochmeister was so hasty in his anger he did not even hear of the other group, some thirty armed men who had again forced the gate and, preceded by baying hounds, disappeared urgently into the night.

# NINE
# THE HEALER

They rode hard through the rain-driven night, but dawn revealed their lead to be much diminished, for the hunters were riding only one man to a horse. Judging from the howling of their dogs, they were now less than a league behind.

So Beck had plunged into the woods, up a path that had rapidly become little more than a deer track. Haakon had followed, cursing all the way, his wood madness from the road to Munster returning almost instantly. Only his love for Jean kept him going, his need to get his broken friend away from the fiends who had broken him. But after an hour's galloping deeper and deeper into the dense foliage it was not his madness that told him that they could not go on much further, it was his sense. Their horses were breathing spasmodically, their flanks bedaubed with the continuous foam of exhaustion. Behind them, the hounds' barks drew ever nearer.

Beck was following Fenrir. It was all she was capable of doing. They had stopped just long enough for her to put on her boy's clothes and to swathe Jean in a blanket, neither covering seeming to have the least resistance to the never-ending rain. The only sign that Jean was alive were the groans he would let out when her horse lurched over, round or through some obstacle. Then his eyes would start open and a shudder would rack him, until the next merciful faint carried him away again. His pallor was deathly, the only colour provided by the blood oozing steadily from between ragged lips. She felt sure that at any moment she would look down and he would be gone, and the bitterness of that, after all they had gone through to free him, made her colder than even the water and wind. So she tended not to look down but focused as far as she could on the tail of the wolf dog ahead of her.

Fenrir was driven by the instincts of the hunt, as both chaser and chased. The forest floor was criss-crossed by little pathways, mainly for the use of small animals. Somehow, he always picked one that could accommodate a horse as well, his muzzle lifted to the wind, discerning the different scents.

His last turns had led them upwards, climbing a large hill within a grove of silver birch. The horses' heads began to droop, more foam appearing on chest and shuddering flank. Fenrir gave them a very brief respite at the next slight crossroads. He stopped at the junction and began to whine. He seemed to want to go straight ahead, but something kept forcing him back onto the other path, the one that looked wider and went downhill.

Haakon pushed his exhausted horse up beside Beck's and called down, 'Which way, Fenrir? Come, we must choose!'

'I do not think it matters now, Norseman. Listen!'

The baying was close. The pursuers had arrived at the last crossroads and chosen the uphill route.

'How long, do you think?' She was almost too exhausted to speak. Jean slumped against her as if dead already.

'Not long.' Haakon gazed at her for a moment. 'We may have to make other plans. Fighting plans.'

'There are thirty of them at least! How do we fight?'

'The same way as if there were three or three hundred. Fight as if you do not care whether you live or die.'

'But I do care.' She was looking into Jean's face when she said it.

Fenrir, who had made several more attempts to run up the path ahead, suddenly sneezed ferociously three times, gave a little yelp and leapt onto it, almost as if he had broken through some invisible door. Instantly, he was bounding along it, his barks beckoning them on.

'Well, maybe he thinks the same as me,' muttered Haakon. 'The top of a hill is a better place to die than the base.'

Two more minutes of riding and they reached a clearing, backed by a rocky outcrop. The hut was so carefully blended into the foliage they could not see it at first. Only a plume of smoke gave away its position, and that could almost have been mist clearing from the boughs of the oak and linden that had been bent together to provide the roof of the structure. Walls woven out of coppiced branches spread between the trunks of both trees, and on closer viewing were seen to perch on top of a platform suspended off the forest floor. It was as if the structure hung from the trees, like a massive fruit.

'What is this?' said Beck, shaken from her torpor.

'A good place to die.'

Haakon had dismounted and was moving forward, stringing his bow. The barks had got that much closer. Their enemy would be at the last junction all too soon.

'Is that what you have come here to do?' The woman's gentle voice seemed to come not from within the structure but from the very trees themselves.

Beck and Haakon looked at each other, then Beck stepped forward to the base of the oak and said, 'We'd prefer to live. But others may not give us the choice. Can you shelter us?'

'It seems I cannot even shelter myself, since you have found me. It's hard for wolf or dog to find the way up here, but yours did. Its need must be great.'

'All our needs are. Those that pursue us would slaughter us without mercy. They have already nearly killed one of us, by slow and foul means.'

Beck walked back to where she had laid Jean on the ground. She gently lifted his head and poured the last of the water from her flask between the ruins of his lips, watched as most of it ran down the side of his mouth.

A shadow fell across her. She had heard no sound of her approach, but a tall woman in a simple brown woollen shift, iron-grey hair woven in a single tress reaching to the backs of her knees, stood above her now. Her face was heavily lined, but full, strong teeth gleamed from a mouth that was wide and looked well used to smiling. She had none of the bent-back brokenness of most older women after a lifetime of care, and her soft brown eyes were kind.

The dogs' yelping was so close now. Maybe they had reached the grove of silver birch.

'Will your dog follow me, if I bid him?' The woman spoke to Haakon.

'He will obey no one but me. What would you have him do?' Haakon was standing at the head of the little path they had just come up, an arrow notched. 'No, old woman, do not get too near him, he's . . .'

But she had already gone over to Fenrir. The dog stiffened at her approach, his head still pointed down the path. He showed his teeth, gave a little growl in his throat, but then it changed into something like a whimper as she bent to him and began whispering in his large velvet ears. When she arose, a little flask hung from the hound's studded collar. A single drop of some viscous liquid oozed from the neck onto the forest floor.

'Take him down to where the two paths cross, where he was first reluctant to come up. This liquid was there in large measure and dogs hate that. This little' – she pointed to the leaking flask – 'they love. Send him along the other path and they will follow him. He will come back to you?'

'He will always find me, but—'

'Then take him now. Or they will find us.'

Haakon looked at the two women and down at the slumped body of his friend. This clearing was the only place in the forest where he did not feel the madness descend. It was not a place to die after all. It was a place to live.

Without another word he led the dog, who was trying

but failing to dislodge the flask at its neck, back down the path.

'Now, my dear. My name is Hanna.' She spoke softly, touching Beck's arm. 'Shall we get this poor man into my house?'

Inside, the structure was much larger than it appeared from the outside. It was a single room, but spacious; in one corner, a fireplace and chimney were built into the rock face of the hilltop. There was a table, benches, some chairs, all woven of the same coppiced wood that made up the walls. Flowers and plants were everywhere, fresh in bundles, dried in wreaths and posies. Beck immediately saw the arrangement of glass over the fireplace, and a little shiver shook her. Something similar had stood in the centre of the kaleidoscope that had become her father's prison. But this gave off no acrid metallic gas, rather the fragrance of ripe berries.

'Juniper,' said Hanna, looking up briefly from the examination she'd begun of Jean, and noticing Beck's curiosity. 'It was a little early to start on them, I had not finished all the gathering. But my stocks were low and something told me I might need some.' She raised Jean's left arm and felt along the bone. 'Broken. As well as the right leg. Several ribs, most of the fingers and toes. Then there are the wounds. So, essence of juniper to cleanse those, then a nettle poultice. Marshmallow and comfrey for the breaks and . . . cypress for all the bruising.'

There were several tubs of flowered rainwater in the hut, adding to the sweet profusion of smells. Hanna dragged one over beside the bloodied body and fetched down a bolt of white linen from the eaves that she quickly cut into pieces. Dipping one into a tub, she began carefully to daub at the blood caked over Jean's body.

'I will help,' said Beck, reaching for a cloth, only to mistake the distance and fall forward slightly.

'You will sleep, child.'

'But he is my . . . my friend. I must see him well.'

'And the best way to do that is to let me explore him in my own way.' Hanna rose to lead Beck over to a truckle bed, laying her down upon it. 'Drink this,' she added, holding up a cup of cool liquid so refreshing that Beck was suddenly joyously awake and the next second the complete opposite.

'What is it?' she murmured, her coldness dissolving under the blankets that were being tucked around her. She was snoring lightly before she could hear a reply.

Hanna had worked her way halfway down Jean's body, gently cleaning away the caked-on blood, wincing at the depth and multiplicity of cut and burn, when she reached what she thought was a blood-sodden bandage. Unwinding this, she realised that it was a container; in it lay a six-fingered hand. Though surprised, she felt no revulsion. She nodded at it, to it, before briefly wiping the little traces of Jean's blood from its rosy whiteness. Placing it to one side, she returned to the task of trying to save a life.

When Haakon returned an hour later, having watched Franchetto, Heinrich and thirty horsemen ride past and having followed them for a short distance to make sure they were well and truly sidetracked, he found both his comrades unconscious. Beck looked like a boy of twelve, wedged into a mountain of skins and blankets, an actual smile transforming the usually scowling features. Jean, though scarred and bruised in the face, such of it that could be seen, could at last be recognised again. He lay on a bed of soft fir boughs, his body wrapped from toe to top of head in strips of white cloth. Haakon saw that each glistened with moisture and when he touched them they were warm.

'Augh! What is that smell?'

Hanna laughed. 'By themselves, each plant has a lovely scent. They seem to combine . . . unfortunately. But each is necessary in its differing powers.'

'Will he live?'

Hanna got up and stood beside the tall man, not at all dwarfed by him. He could have been one of her sons. 'He is badly hurt. I have set his arm and leg and bound his ribs, but much else is hurt besides, inside and out. Yet he already seems to have survived what would kill most men. He must have a good reason.'

'He does.' Haakon gave a huge yawn, and rose. 'Well, I will sleep for an hour, then resume my watch.'

'Why?'

'Because I need to sleep.'

'No, why so little? They will not return for some days.'

'How can you know this?'

'I see it in the flames' – she gestured to her fireplace – 'just as I saw your coming.' There was confusion in his tired eyes, so she shrugged and continued, 'Friend, you need sleep as much as these two.'

'Nevertheless—'

Hanna raised her hand. 'As you wish. But have a taste of this. It will make your little sleep go further.'

Haakon was too exhausted to argue. He took a long pull at the same elixir Beck had sampled and, finding it good, drained the flask. Then he curled up into a sheepskin on a bench next to Beck.

'Wake me at mid-morning,' he managed before his eyes shut.

'Of course,' said Hanna, then added in a whisper. 'I can always try.'

But she wouldn't. The three would sleep through the day, the sunset and probably another dawn again. *Sleep's Balm*, Hanna thought, *as powerful as anything in my chest of herbs*.

She picked up her tabby cat, Philomen, who had slept through all the excitement with the privilege of his great age, and put him on her lap. Laying another piece of applewood on the fire, she sat back and watched the red slowly creep over it in a series of incendiary flowers. There were answers to seek within the flames. As the heat took the applewood and held it up in crimson and yellow arms, she thought about the savaged man, the strange hand he carried. And what she had said to the tall one had been true: she'd know when the hunt was about to return. She'd see it in smoke and fire.

'Scots pine,' sniffed the tracker, a stocky Bavarian from Heinrich's own manor, handing him the flask. 'We use a lot on bitches in heat to keep away the boar hounds, until we're ready. Then we wash away all but a trace. They love that.'

As a result of their need to rest and Fenrir's steady pace, it had taken the pursuers the rest of the night and until sunset of the next day to catch up with the wolf-dog. Two of their hounds had snuck up on him as he slept in a thicket and had lost their lives as a result. But they had dislodged the flask, before Fenrir finally fled the increasing odds.

Heinrich cursed. 'So we have been chasing a decoy?'

'Someone has helped them trick us, yes,' his fellow German grunted at him, moving just out of range of his leader's reach. His right hand might have been bandaged but he was just as vicious with the left.

Heinrich had taken a step towards the latest man to fail him, but stopped at these words.

'Helped them? Of course. They could not have taken him much further. The prisoner was barely alive.' He paced for a moment. 'They've gone to ground. Back there. You' – he pointed at one of his men – 'ride back to Wittenberg directly. You should meet the Archbishop on the road. We will rendezvous at the crossroads just before we entered the forest. The rest of you scum, mount! We ride.'

The men, with a few scant hours of sleep behind them, had been hoping for a few hours more. But they knew better than to demur or grumble. His tracker, with a little more guile, knew how to ask the obvious question.

'Master, there's much forest back there, off the trail we have come down. How will we know where to begin?'

Heinrich sneered. 'Call yourself a hunter? We watch for a sign. A very obvious one.' He looked at the bottle then hurled it against the trunk of a tree, shattering it. The dogs whimpered, snapped and snarled in their efforts to get away from the overpowering, cloying scent of pine. 'When your hounds start behaving like that again, we'll know we have arrived.'

Heinrich jumped up into the saddle and dug in his heels. The horse galloped off and his men, grumbling louder now at the disappearing back, followed close behind.

Surprisingly, perhaps, Jean was the first of the three to wake. It was not a true struggle to do so, no clambering from great depths, no lung-bursting trawl from the bottom of a sluggish sea. His sleep, as far as he could recall, had been dreamless, certainly untroubled by foes real or imaginary, and no sound drew him forth from the calm of it. It was not as if he could not have slept longer; a part of him, reluctant to stir, tried to draw closed the lashed curtains on the world. But need drove him awake.

He looked for her as soon as his eyes ungummed and he saw her straight away, as someone had had the foresight to put her exactly where he would first glance. Sitting on a pillow beside his bed of boughs, fingers splayed out in that anticipatory way. It was the way she sat that convinced him on waking it was not all part of some relieving dream such as God sometimes sent the tormented. If it were, all of Anne would be there, talking to him as she had in the cell, comforting him. As it was, just the hand lay there.

There was another woman there, a whole woman, sat at a table and humming while she crushed some dried herbs in a mortar, adding them to a pot that bubbled gently on the fireplace. A handsome woman, even at her great age, tall and graceful. She reached a hand behind her, brushing aside the long tress of iron hair that hung there, placing the fingers in the small of her back to rub while she stretched.

He watched her until she became aware of it, at which instant she put down her stirring spoon and came across to him, laying one hand on his head and one on his heart.

'How are you, son?' Hanna said after a while.

'Well,' he replied. 'But I smell a little strange.'

She smiled. 'You smell a lot better than you did when you came to me. I think the poisons are in my bandages now, not in your body. Here.' She went and fetched a beaker of the broth she'd been stirring at the fire and watched as he sipped at it, holding it awkwardly between the few fingers still unbroken and unsplinted.

'Will this make me sleep again?' he asked, sniffing the aromatic steam.

'Do you want it to?' she replied.

'Alas . . .' He did not need to say more.

'It will not. But it will give you the strength to be awake.'

'In that case' – he drained the beaker – 'more, please.'

She brought a beaker of her own and they sat for a few minutes in companionable silence, sipping. Finally, she said, 'I do not want to know much, son. But this hand . . . are you about God's work with it?'

He took a moment to reply. 'There are those who claim only they know the word of God. They would tell you we are not. But the holiest person ever I met gave me this hand from her own body, freely, asking for a promise as she gave it.'

Hanna did not even glance at the hand, just said, 'This person. I think she and I would have understood each other.'

'I am certain of it.'

The silence returned, as comfortable as before. Jean's eyes grew clearer as the herbs within the draught began to take effect, so that when a tousled, boyish head thrust itself up from beneath a pile of sheepskins and blankets, he was fully able to take in the wonder of Beck's yawning face.

She smiled at him. 'I have had the most wonderful dreams, Jean Rombaud.'

'Then I am sorry to awaken you to this nightmare,' he said, bowing a little.

She was beside him in an instant. 'This?' She took his head in her hands. 'This is the best dream of all.'

And she kissed him tenderly.

A huge thump announced that Haakon too had woken up and fallen from his perch.

'Thor's Hammer!' he grunted, from the floor. 'But I am hungry! How long have I slept? One, two hours?'

'More like days, Norseman,' laughed Jean, 'but the rest of us got little. Your snores would make the angels flee paradise.'

Hanna, on the others' awakening, had disappeared, to return with loaves of solid, moist black bread, wheels of cheese, smoked sausages and dozens of eggs she'd simmered in another of her flavoursome broths. Haakon was distracted from his mock anger at Jean's remark and his joy at the sight of the Frenchman's return to consciousness by the plenteous food. He sat down and began to chew his way through platters of it, while the others ate as heartily if less conspicuously. Jean was immeasurably content to let Beck feed him.

'How is it you live so well out here?' Eating and talking caused a soft egg to shed its yolk down the front of Haakon's golden beard. 'I have never seen food like this in a forest before.'

Hannah pushed some more eggs towards him. 'I . . . help the local people and they reward me, that is all.'

'But all this food?' Jean turned his face away from Beck's moving spoon. 'This is a large reward. They will know you have visitors and, perhaps, others will ask them.'

'They will not be able to tell much. No one ever comes up here, I always go to them. They have ways of finding me when I am needed, such as certain calls made by woodland birds that have never flown in the valley below. I hear, I go. Besides' – she fetched some more broth – 'they do not betray me to strangers. They talk to me of any danger.'

Jean saw the concern that contorted the calm brow.

'And what have these birds told you lately?'

Hanna got up and moved to the entrance of the hut, stared out.

'They sing of the hunter's return.' She turned back. 'I do

not want to send you away. I never saw a man more in need of rest and such skills as I have. But I do not want to see you caught by my over-kindness. And I do not think my distractions will hold them again for long.'

'How much time do we have?'

'They will be here by the middle of the afternoon. Perhaps a little sooner.'

'Then this is a farewell feast?' said Beck sadly.

'It is.'

There was a silence as Beck and Jean contemplated again the hard road recently travelled, the hardship of the road ahead.

All except Haakon. For now, he desired to contemplate nothing more than the sausage before him. A sausage he was more than delighted to share when a thin but joyous Fenrir bounded into the clearing.

There were four of them, all dressed in the hip-length coat and leggings of those who work the land. They stood silently at each end of the litter's poles. Four more waited beside it.

'They will take you till the forest ends. It is about a day's march. There, some of their family will carry you for another day on to the border.'

While she was talking, Hanna was pouring a liquid distilled from nettles onto Jean's fresh bandages. He felt the cool slickness of it reach his skin and dissolve beyond that into his body. Again, the pain, which had grown greatly even in the little journey in Haakon's arms down the forested hill to this rendezvous, began to dissipate.

'Do you know where in France that border is, Hanna?'

'Just above Lorraine. You will cross from the Duchy of Luxembourg. Do you know it?'

'I know it. If we are lucky with roads and horses, we can be in the Loire five days later.'

Hanna looked up, concern clear on her face. 'You might not make it so far, Jean. You know this. I have done what I can, but your wounds . . .' She sighed. 'You need to rest for at least a month.'

'And you know I cannot. For all our sakes, I cannot rest until this is done.'

At a nod, Haakon laid him gently in the sling between the litter poles. Hanna turned to Beck standing anxiously nearby.

'This bottle for the bandages.' She handed it over. 'And this one to drink before sleep and whenever the pain is great.' She smiled. 'Do not confuse the two.'

Beck took a deep sniff of the contents of each. 'I will not. Thank you.'

'I have done little enough.'

Beck put her arms around the older woman.

'You have saved his life. It is a debt I cannot hope to repay.'

A wrinkled hand reached up and tousled Beck's curly raven hair.

'Help him do what must be done and you will have repaid me tenfold.'

When Jean was settled, Haakon took his place at the head of the little column. The three horses had been as well cared for as their masters and seemed set fair for the journey, nostrils flaring into the afternoon air. It was a brisk autumn day, but the cruel cold rain had stopped and the sun's rays created avenues of light through the treed lanes ahead.

Hanna came one more time to Jean's side, made some final fussing adjustments to bandage and splint. A broken hand lifted for a moment to rest clumsily on the moving one.

'Enough. You have done all you can, and I thank you.'

She got stiffly to her feet. 'It may not be enough.'

'It will have to be.'

'Go with God, Jean Rombaud.'

Haakon, on a look from Jean, ordered Fenrir forward. The litter men followed, Jean swinging between them, their reliefs trailing behind. Beck brought up the rear.

Hanna watched until long after the party had disappeared into the fading sun. Then, with a sigh, she began to retrace the trail to her hill. Alongside the Scots pine she scattered various substances gleaned from plant and beast. It would not confuse the hunting dogs for ever, but for a time. She knew that every second's delay to the pursuit was vital. That knowledge she did not need to look for in the flames.

# TEN

# LAST STAND

'Are you certain it is them?'

'Certain, my Lord. Their dog has a distinctive howl and it went off to hunt a short time ago.'

'So they have lost their ears and nose? Good.'

It was one of the longer conversations Giancarlo Cibo had had for a week. He saved his strength for the trail and there was little to be said upon it. The fools had tried to make him remain behind, while they went after the hand; they would fetch it to him where he rested. Yet only he knew it wasn't the hardships of the chase that brought the blood cascading to his lips, it was the absence of what he now knew he needed. He had to have her hand in his, resting on his chest, to halt the crimson flow. They might capture it and bring it in triumph back to Wittenberg, but he knew they would be bringing it back to a corpse.

Even this much closer he felt better. Less than half a league ahead, they said, and he could confirm that, he felt the pull of it. So near now; and when it was his again he would never let it go and he would make no more mistakes. Instant death for those who had robbed him of it, as swift and unmistakable as a knife thrust in the heart. His taste for exotic pleasure had led him to delay. No more.

He looked around at his men, slumped against trees, on the ground, snatching meagre mouthfuls of hard bread and dried meat from their satchels. Two thirds of them had fallen away during this chase deep into France, they or their mounts, leaving just these strongest fifteen. So he, the oldest and the sickest, had done well to keep up. To lead. But of course, if they did not have his weakness, they also did not have his motivation.

Franchetto had again seemed as if dead, his huge body curled around in the position he had slept in since Marsheim. Now, without opening his eyes, he said to the tall German before them, 'Then let us attack now. Let us end this and get back to the civilisation of Siena.'

There was still a pretence that the men were under Franchetto's command. Heinrich could never keep the contempt out of his voice when he paid lip service to this pretence.

'They are awaiting your orders, my Lord.'

Franchetto heard the tone, rose to glare into the destroyed face. Yet before he could speak, the soft voice, the silkiness frayed now, spoke first. 'No orders. Creep down there, cudgel them in their blankets, take the hand. When you are sure you have it, slit their throats.'

'My Lord.'

Heinrich kicked and cursed his men to standing. It was early evening and they'd been hoping for a few hours' sleep, but hearing that their quarry had been sighted and was within reach, even the most tired of them roused themselves and checked their weapons. The chase had gone on long enough. It was time for the kill.

It was Fenrir's quick success in hunting that saved them, his sudden return, rabbit in mouth, disturbing the soldier who had taken up a position astride the dog's path. The wind came from behind the approaching hound so before he could smell the man he was upon him, seeing his sword glimmering in the light of the rising full moon.

Rabbit dropped, dog leaping, a man's cry of pain. They were all instantly awake under the willow by the little pool where exhaustion from the last three days' riding without sleep had dropped them. Jean it was who'd suggested they spend the few hours till moonrise there, knowing there was only this little shelter between them and the crossroads, if they were to avoid the village, craving this little rest to give him strength for the final stage of the journey.

Dulled senses had not warned him that their pursuers were so close.

Haakon rolled from a sleeping position to his feet in an instant, his axe clutched in his hands. Beck was on her knees, a stone already fitted to sling, leather and rope whirling as Cibo's guard burst screaming from his shelter in the tree line, Fenrir's jaws clamped onto his arm.

'Take them now!' came Heinrich's cry as another man emerged and fell, a stone lodged in his forehead, and the rest of his men burst from cover. He himself ran for the one position he knew had not been filled yet – the road out of the valley.

It was eighty paces from the tree line to their clearing and Haakon, under cover of the stones, used the scant time to pick up Jean and hurl him over a horse. Jean's scream of agony was drowned in the war yells of the approaching guards. Haakon was astride his own horse in a moment.

'Beck, to me!' he cried, thrusting his axe into the sling of his cloak, spurring his animal without waiting to see the result of his cry. He had seen something else. A large man running to block the exit from the little valley.

With one hand on his own horse and one on the rein of the horse that bore Jean, Haakon had no weapon other than speed. Heinrich was swept aside by the rush of horses and man. Hurling himself at the horse that followed, the German grasped at the reins for an instant, but Beck hit him hard on his broken wrist and the sudden sharp pain caused him to let go.

'After them!' he raged, spitting mud at their receding backs. The horses galloped towards a bridge that lay downhill, spanning a stretch of river ribboned in silver moonlight, swollen now by the autumn's near incessant dowsings. Glancing back the three hundred paces to the little outcrop, Haakon could see the first of the guards emerge from the defile. They did not ride down yet, gathered their strength. He reined up on the bridge.

'How far to this village, Jean?'

'It is over the next hill, the crossroads a league beyond. We are so close.'

'They will catch us in minutes,' the Norseman said.

Beck, looking back, nodded. 'We will have to make our stand here then.' She made to get down from her horse.

Haakon spoke as he dismounted. '*We* will not. *I* will.' Their eyes met, halting her protest. 'There is no time to argue about this. The river is wide but this bridge is narrow. I can hold them here for a while. Long enough, perhaps.'

Jean, who had somehow managed to wriggle around so that he was astride the pack horse, looked down and said, 'No, Haakon. Your loyalty does not extend to dying here alone.'

'Who said anything about dying? And if I do, what better way than against impossible odds with my axe in my hand and my war hound at my side? What a story it will make, like one of the old tales. The Valkyrie will have to bear me to Valhalla at the end of it, that's for certain.'

Jean could not help but smile, though something seemed to catch in his throat.

'You truly are a pagan, Norseman.'

Haakon returned the smile. 'This from a man who seeks to bury a hand at a crossroads.'

Fenrir snarled. They could hear the shouts from the hill, the first men riding down, hunters' delighted cries for a quarry still in sight. The gleam of the impending fight shone in the dog's strange square eyes as well as in his master's.

'Ride, now, or you make what I do here in vain.'

Haakon swiftly slipped on the metal undershirt and

breastplate he had bought at Munster. The helmet rose to cover his flowing gold locks, a strip of metal over the nose.

'We will try to honour your gift.' Beck turned to grab the reins of Jean's horse. 'As Januc would say, Allah protect you.'

'Januc.' Haakon's eyes darkened for a moment, then cleared with a smile. 'You know, you can't blame him. I'm glad at least one of us remained true to the mercenary code. All this self-sacrifice is hard on the purse.'

'Hoch, hoch!' Jean called out as Beck, angrily brushing a tear off her cheek, led him away.

Haakon stood at the bridge's centre, his axe inverted before him, its head resting on the ground, his huge hands lightly on the butt. As the hoof beats disappeared behind him, the ones before him slowed down.

'Surrender, dog!' yelled Heinrich. 'Surrender and we'll make your death a swift one.'

Haakon tipped his head to one side. 'Hmm. Lots of words there I don't understand. Perhaps you'd like to come over here and explain them to me.'

A horrendous spluttering of blood accompanied the next words.

'Take him!' screamed Giancarlo Cibo. 'Rip him apart!'

They could only come two at a time along the narrow bridge – one for Haakon and one for Fenrir. As they grappled with the first of them, others waited their turn behind.

Haakon's giant axe flashed, a scything crescent in the waxing moonlight, impossible to stop. They were strong warriors, the elite of the Archbishop's guards, but they died as they came and each body underfoot made it harder for the next pair to advance. Four lay there before someone thought to bring boar spears from the horses, and their thrusts began to force Haakon back across the bridge. The points could not pierce his armour but one finally caught Fenrir in the chest and Haakon could do nothing as his friend was lifted from beside him, snapping and snarling still, to fall under a thunderstorm of blows. Then the thrusting forward began again, and though Haakon cut and sliced the heads off many of the spears, there were always others to replace them. He was pushed back the length of the bridge and knew that once he reached the end it would all be over.

One spear thrust, slipping beneath his breastplate, snagged in his chain armour; it pulled him forward, off balance, and a sword cut down and bit into his left arm just above the wrist. Another snickered in and cut him in the exposed leg. Roaring, Haakon dropped to one knee. Hurling his axe forward, he saw it lodge in the forehead of a man too keen to take advantage of his fall, but the sword he drew barely parried the three that came at him. Someone had managed to slip round him at the bridge's end and he only half-parried the blade dancing in at his side, turning the force from a death to a wounding blow, taking it in the other arm.

Forcing strength into his cut leg, Haakon stood and with a cry of 'A Haakonsson!' he hurled himself into the heart of his tormentors. There he was immediately pinned by two spears, then two more, his mighty body lifted on them and swept up and over the parapets of the bridge.

Haakon spiralled down and hit the water flat. Instantly caught in its maelstrom he was tumbled downstream to clatter into the rocks. Out of sight of the bridge, an eddy caught and held him in its whirling embrace. Round and round he spun, as the water around him turned red.

*Strange*, he thought, *but where are the Valkyrie? In the tales, this is when they come.*

Then he felt their hands upon him, dragging him awkwardly from the water, and he knew he was bound for Valhalla, the only heaven he could desire. The hands felt a touch rougher than he'd expected – they belonged to blonde maidens after all – but, he thought, you probably had to be that tough to be a Valkyrie. As this world faded away, he looked forward to the other side, to an eternity of feasting and fighting until the last battle. But most of all he looked forward to seeing his father there. For at last he had a tale worthy of his hearing!

'Shh! Is that them?'

The whisper was so close to Jean's ear that her lips actually touched it. He shifted just slightly, raising his head to the gap in the barn wall. Even such a tiny movement gave him pain.

'I don't think so,' he gasped. 'Haakon has held them well.'

He sank back down, glancing around the unfamiliar barn in the familiar village. Pont St Just! Was it mere months since he'd first grappled with Death at the inn here? It seemed an age, a lifetime before, too many other reminders of his mortality since.

'Then I should go. Pick my position.'

Beck made to rise but the slight pressure of a broken hand held her down.

'Beck . . .' He did not know what to say. 'Rebecca.'

'You agreed. It is our only chance.'

'You decided. What chance will you have? You against however many Haakon has left.'

'I have a stone for each of them.' She rattled her pouch. 'Besides, they are warriors for the open field. The streets are mine.'

'This is not Venice, my love. No alleys and canals where the Sicarii can lurk and strike. One street, twenty houses.'

'Are you trying to weaken me?'

'I am trying to make you see sense. You have succeeded in your cause, your father is safe and waits for you. This way we will all die.'

'Only they will die.' She raised the slingshot into the moonlight slanting through the barn's uneven planks. "When despair comes, I concentrate first on my cause – you – then on my good right arm." Remember that time, under that awning in Toulon, when I said that?'

'I remember the peach juice on your lips. I remember it confused me greatly.'

Smiling, she bent those lips to kiss him now. As she pulled back, he reached up and held her neck.

'Will you not obey me in this, woman?'

'When we are married I will, of course, obey your every command.'

'Somehow,' said Jean, 'I doubt that.'

She stood above him, moonbeams striping her. 'Can you get yourself onto the horse?'

'I will have to.'

'Wait till you hear me crow like a cockerel. I will either be victorious or taken then. Either way, ride to the crossroads. Fulfil your vow.'

Then she was gone.

Jean sank back into the hay to wait. Behind him the horses chewed slowly, the barn door unlatched and began to bang in the light wind. He lay there, waiting for the cockerel's cry and the false dawn it would announce. Waiting for a beginning and an end.

At the eastern edge of Pont St Just, the roadway narrowed between a house and its barn, the longer stalks of their thatching meeting to entwine over the gap. It was barely wide enough for a farm cart or two men riding abreast. Twenty paces beyond Beck waited, beneath the eaves of the next house, the rope taut in her hands, her thumb pressing the stone firmly into the leather pouch.

There were hoof beats and then the moonlight revealed the shape of two faces so she aimed for the nearest. The whirring was like the wings of an owl beating in the still night air, the whistle of stone its last cry as if giant talons had reached down and wrenched Bruno-Luciano from his saddle, so suddenly did Franchetto's bodyguard leave it.

'Jesu save me!' the younger Cibo cried, spurring his horse through the gap, crouched low with his head behind his horse's neck. Four of his men did the same and rode to a house in the middle of the village. The fifth was too slow to push through and, when he attempted it, joined his comrade, face down and dying in the dust.

Heinrich took shelter in the lee of the first house. He saw the shadow flit between the buildings but he made no move to stir. Twice already he had taken a stone from that slingshot and the pain in his head, and especially in his wrist, was still with him. He was not going to risk any more.

'He's behind the house to the left!' he shouted. 'Flush him out!'

'I do not take orders from you!' screamed Franchetto. 'And I want the Frenchman!' He turned to his remaining men. 'Search the houses! Drive the people out into the street!'

The first dazed villagers had already struggled forth, and they were joined by the tardy, driven from their beds by the flats of Italian swords. They gathered in shivering groups before their doorways, terror plain on their faces, increasing when one soldier suddenly cried out in shock and agony to plummet down at their feet.

The barn was the last structure on the western edge of the village, and Jean could see that, despite Beck's successes, it was only a short time before he was discovered. *Cockerel or no cockerel it is time to move*, he thought, and he began the agonising process of shuffling towards his horse. This was the most docile of the three, the packhorse, but the night's shrieks had made it nervous and, try as he might, Jean was unable to mount. He had no strength to hold it steady. It whinnied and moved round and round the barn, evading him.

He had just succeeded in pinning the beast in a corner when the doors of the barn were flung open and there, framed in the moonlight of the doorway, stood Franchetto Cibo.

'At last!' he yelled in triumph. 'Your head is mine, Frenchman.'

His long legs carried him across the barn floor in two strides, his sword rising as he came, up and over in a giant killing circle. Jean had no weapon with which to defend himself and no strength to lift one if he'd had one. He could only watch his death descend, flashing through the silver moonbeams.

Then a strange thing happened. Something else flashed, and the unstoppable blade stopped just above the unmoving head. Stopped in a scream of metal on metal, in a flurry of sparks shooting into the darkness. It was like a short, sharp cry in the night, followed by a drawn-out wail as the arrested sword began a swift descent down a curving blade, all its frustrated power causing it to bury itself deep in the wooden rail of a cow stall.

'Not yet, I think,' said Januc.

Twisting the scimitar from under the heavier blade, the janissary plunged it into the younger Cibo's chest. Januc couldn't decide which face before him bore the more astounded expression, but Franchetto's changed the swifter as he died.

'Januc!' Jean had stumbled forward in shock, and the two men were close. 'How? Why?'

'I don't know.' The Croatian lowered Franchetto's body to the barn floor, then pulled out the scimitar. 'Once I had my money safe with some bankers in Augsburg, I . . . I became curious. I needed to know what became of you.'

'Loyalty *after* payment? You have changed, mercenary!'

'Shh!' Januc ran his finger nervously along his moustache. 'Do you want everyone to know?'

Just then, a cockerel crowed, loud, near, suddenly cut off.

'He's up early.'

'It's Beck. Can you help her?'

'Of course I c— Her?'

'Too long to explain now. Can you?'

'I can try. And you?'

'If you will help me onto this cursed horse, I must ride for the crossroads.'

Shouts grew nearer, Franchetto's men seeking their master out. Januc lifted Jean easily into the saddle.

'Oh, I have something for you.' Reaching up, the janissary

436

pulled something long from behind his back. 'Your sword, Master Executioner,' he said, and Jean saw the grip, the green leather strapping he'd so carefully retied the last time he had used the weapon for its true purpose. In London, a lifetime before.

'Where . . . ?' was all Jean could say before the first of the Italian guards ran around the corner, his cry of 'My Lord!' cut off by the sight of the body on the ground. The man, seeing the janissary drop into fighting stance, turned and ran, crying for reinforcements.

'An Englishman I met.' Januc handed the sword to Jean. 'But that story will also have to wait. As will the one about Haakon.'

'You saw him die?'

'I saw him.' Returning voices rising in alarm, 'Later for that too. Ride, Frenchman, ride to your destiny. And I will try to find Beck.'

With that, he slapped the horse's haunch and the animal bolted, scattering the four men approaching the doorway. They quickly regrouped and advanced into the barn.

*Four!* thought Januc calmly, left hand forward, sword arm back, making a large circle of sinew and scimitar. *I can take four.*

The pouring of distressed villagers out onto the streets had made Beck's task easier, and harder. Her darting form was less easily spotted among the throng, but it also made her targets harder to select. Nevertheless, she had managed to kill another of the soldiers that followed her. She didn't think there were many left.

It was while trying to work her way back down towards the barn where Jean lay that she was caught between houses and hit by a metal bar flung hard across her chest. The man who did it thought it enough, and he bent over his victim close enough to take the full thrust of Beck's long knife, his dying weight forcing his body down upon the blade and upon her. She was struggling to shift his weight when she heard the voice above her, the voice she most dreaded to hear, accompanied as always by the now ragged cough, and this time by a little pricking of steel under her ear.

'Well, well, my Salome. Together again at last.'

The body was pulled off her, the blade she tried to extract and stab with again was turned aside by a gauntleted fist, and her face was turned and pressed into the mud.

'I'll kill her now, my Lord.' Heinrich's knee pressed into Beck's bruised chest, causing agony to pass through her limbs. He reached for the knife at his belt.

'Kill? My Salome? When she still owes me the finale of her performance?'

'My Lord—'

'When we have the hand, Heinrich, I told you. Not before.' A handkerchief, once milk white, now nothing but vivid red, was raised again to his lips. 'Bind her. Bring her. We must look for my brother.'

It was then that Beck threw back her head and let forth the cockerel's cry. Heinrich swiftly cut it short with a backhand to the face.

'You will not be crowing soon,' he said, and swiftly bound and gagged her.

Mounting, with her before him, he followed the Archbishop to the barn, the last building in the village. He found him gazing down at the six bodies there.

'Who is that?' Cibo was pointing at the stranger who lay in the centre of a circle made by four of his brother's men.

Heinrich swiftly checked the fallen. 'It is strange,' he said, 'but this man fought beside me at Munster. He helped us take the gate.'

'He has also helped my brother to hell.'

Cibo leant forward, blood now running unchecked down his chin. There was no time for sentiment, even if he was capable of feeling any. If he did not get that hand back he would be joining his brother soon enough, and then they would have an eternity of flames together to lament their swift exit from this world.

'Jean Rombaud is not here. He must have gone to the crossroads. Let us ride!'

As the horses departed, Januc opened his eyes. There was nothing more he could do here but die, he supposed. Which was a pity, but at least he was dying a rich man, so one of his ambitions had been achieved. He'd meant to die in a bed though, at a venerable age and surrounded by at least five young wives. Still, maybe he'd be carried away to that place the pagan Haakon was always talking about. It wasn't the feasting – from what he'd seen Norse table manners were appalling – and, of course, he never drank liquor. But all those beautiful maidens would be fine. With so many drunk Vikings about, he'd be able to take his pick.

*Haakon*, he thought as his eyelids slowly shut. *Wish I'd had time to tell Jean about Haakon.*

# ELEVEN
# THE RECKONING

Ragged clouds scudded across the face of the moon, striping the gibbet in silver. Gusts of wind, in sudden sharp surges, stirred the metal cage and, having no occupant to steady it, the frame swung back and forth on its hook. Metal grating on metal produced a steady scraping, like the faintest cries of the damned.

It was as cold as he remembered it, this desolate place, but at least this time he was on the outside of the cage, though his limbs, broken as they were, felt as imprisoned. He remembered how he had done a survey when he'd first woken up here, a closed-eyes battlefield study of his wounds. He would not do that now. He would not know where to begin the tally. All he did know was that he was so tired the urge to slip from his horse onto the cold earth to sleep was almost irresistible – and the task of digging almost impossible.

Glancing up, he tried to draw strength from the moon-beams. He saw, as he had done ever since he was a child, a face in the moon. He had heard others describe the man up there, but for him it had always been a woman gazing down, one neither young nor old and who seemed, in the fragments of moving cloud, to be speaking to him, telling him secrets. Tonight, with the wind and shreds of grey cloud, the move-ment was more than that, not merely a mouth transformed but every feature: eyes, nose, brow, ears, all shifting, realign-ing into faces, imaginary to start with then increasingly familiar. It was as if the moon were a chronicle of his progress from this spot and his return to it. Showing him the people he had encountered.

The dashing, heretical Count de Chinon developed Da Costa's toothless grin. Maltese Gregor smiled insincerely, while Big Nose raised a cloud pomander, lowering it to reveal Ake's pleading eyes. Lucrezia of the Scorpions gave way to Mathias van Frew, beckoning him back to Montepulciano, and mercenary became mercenary with Makepeace's bald head gleaming. A mad prophet led out his enemies, the twisted distortion of von Solingen, the brutal features of Franchetto Cibo, the refined ones of his brother, a tear-drop cloud streaming like blood from his mouth. At the last, his friends came, led by the Fugger's mad smile: Januc with a gleam of gold in his eyes, Haakon with his equivalent lust for battle. And at the very last, the moon returned to womanhood, to the beauty of his Beck and finally, and for longer, the offset eyes of his Queen, Anne Boleyn.

He half fell from the horse, reaching up to pull at the turf-lifter Haakon had carried ever since Munster. It slipped past too-weak fingers and in its fall dislodged the sword that Januc had thrust up into the saddle bags. He managed to catch that, even draw it slightly from its scabbard. Leaning it against the upright of the gibbet, he bent down for the turf-lifter, dragging it the few paces to the exact centre point where the four roads met.

He had barely begun to dig when a horse's neigh alerted him. He only just made it back to his sword by the time they rounded the bend from the village.

'Well, Executioner.' Cibo's words rode out on a smoky plume in the frigid air. 'Here we are again.'

'Indeed.'

Jean tried to stand upright, resting his hands on the pommel of his sword. He saw Beck was alive, twisting against her bonds, against the gag that held her mouth.

'The hand. Give it to me.' The words were wheezed out.

'You are too late. It is buried. See?' Jean held up his shovel.

'Then you will dig it up again. Or you will watch your friend here die.' At Cibo's gesture Heinrich dismounted and pulled Beck after him, throwing her to the ground. 'But wait! I don't believe you have had time to bury it yet. Nor the strength.' That cough again, the blood unchecked at the lips. 'You, of course, will die very soon. But I can yet live. All I need is the witch's hand. Search him, Heinrich. Find it. Then kill him.'

'At last.' As he crossed over to Jean, Heinrich von Solingen was almost smiling.

Jean raised his sword, letting the scabbard slide off. Von Solingen simply took the weapon from Jean's strengthless hand and thrust it into the midden heap where, swaying slightly, it cast the moonshadow of a moving crucifix onto the ground. He reached behind the Frenchman's back and pulled the hand from its hiding place.

'Now, may I kill him, my Lord?'

'Yes, Heinrich. And I will kill Salome.' Cibo had pulled his hunter's crossbow from his saddle bags, was fitting a bolt into the notch. 'Alas, I am disappointed not to be able to experience the end of her performance. But let her see her reward before she dies, at least. Cut his head off and bring it over here.'

Heinrich von Solingen placed Anne's hand on top of Jean's sword, then awkwardly drew his own with his unbroken left hand. 'I have been waiting for this moment.' The two shattered faces were a hand's breadth apart. 'The last of your cat lives.'

'Oh,' said Jean wearily. 'I'll see you in hell,'

A shadow passed between the moon and the rising sword, and a black shape settled on the gibbet's crossbeam. They had all seen the bird, or one much like it, somewhere before, and when it opened its beak and squawked the word 'Hand!' two of them realised where.

The word made the German pause, sword on high, and in

that moment something erupted from the gibbet midden, bursting from the very depths of the muck, soiled scraps and bones picked clean. Only the gleam of two eyes split the blackness; that and the moonlight flashing on the stiletto blade that flew straight up, like an arrow shot from hell. Its flash was the last thing Heinrich von Solingen saw before the dagger entered his left eye and his head exploded in white light. The midden creature rose as the German fell, accompanying him all the way to the ground.

'Fugger!' yelled Jean, and the mud animal leapt backwards from the body, knife still clutched in hand.

'Ogres pursue me! Devils bite my legs!'

The cry of shock from the Archbishop drew the Fugger's gaze to the horses. All he saw was a mounted demon, blood streaming from his ghastly maw. *The blood of his last victims*, the Fugger thought, *with me destined to be the next meal*.

'You shall not have me!' he cried, raising the dagger.

A bolt flew, passing through the Fugger's palm and on into the wood of the gibbet beam, pinning his one hand there.

'Oh, Daemon, oh my dear!' the Fugger cried as he sank down to his knees, his hand stretched out above him, a crucifixion half complete.

On his horse, Cibo tried once more to slot the string into the trigger notch of his crossbow. But as soon as he took his hands from the reins, his high-spirited horse began to circle around and his weakened fingers kept slipping on a string made slick by his own blood.

'Come on,' he muttered. 'One last bolt for the executioner.'

Jean saw his death in the string creeping slowly to its notch. Then, looking down, he saw something else. For the moon had finally cleared the last great bank of cloud and its beams shone on the sword thrust into the earth, and on the hand that lay atop it. These, he realised, were the three central elements of the journey to this crossroads: the hand of the Queen, the sword that had taken that hand, and a full moon's light. The alignment came together in his mind, then in his vision again, for he saw the hand shift on the pommel, grip it. Beyond the hand, an arm led up to bare shoulders, and above them, fixed upon him now, were the question and the answer in the eyes of Anne Boleyn.

She was dressed in a simple shift of silk, and her brow was encircled with a wreath of meadow flowers.

'You see?' Her voice was soft. 'I promised we would meet again.'

Jean reached out and took her hand, felt that strange and wondrous pressure, and it filled his limbs with a surge of power.

'Listen to me, Jean. Use all your strength now and you will not need to use it ever again in my cause. I will help you. Lift your sword.'

It would not shift at first, despite the eleven fingers pulling on it, then it came from the earth in a rush. Ten more fingers interlaced over its leather grip, just as he heard the click of a string snagging a notch, the sound of a bolt dropping into a groove. Just as he realised what they must do.

'Now, my Queen?'

'Now, Jean Rombaud.'

'Give me the hand!' Cibo cried, levelling the crossbow at the man now standing there with his square-tipped sword raised before him and the object of all Cibo's hopes clutched against the grip.

'Gladly,' said Jean and Anne together, as he bunched his once powerful muscles in that familiar curl and then released them. The sword flew along a moonbeam towards the man on the horse; a crossbow bolt met but didn't deflect it on its flight. The heavy blade took Cibo in the neck, just where the weapon was most keen, in that little space on the front edge no more than the breadth of two hands. The sword made no pause there but passed on through to land, tip first, in the soft earth beyond, just before the Archbishop's head reached the ground. The head rolled over twice before ending face up towards the sky, the eyes wide as if looking for shooting stars.

A moment later, a hand fell upon it, a small sixth finger settling near the parted lips. Blood no longer flowed through them. But for Giancarlo Cibo, Archbishop of Siena, the healing touch was, of course, too late.

# TUSCANY, AUTUMN 1546

It was late when he set out on his quest, driven by the promise he had made her. As he walked down the avenues of vines still bulging with fruit, the setting sun fired the forest ahead of him, the ochres, umbers and brilliant siennas of the trees burnished to a flaming gold. Above, all alone in the impossibly azure sky, one small fist of a cloud was beginning to bruise from purple to grey.

He limped into the forest under the canopy of a copper beech, metallic leaves like spear points thrusting down on him. Here he paused, swishing his stick through the heads of the tall grass, considering the nature of what she had asked him to do, his twin tasks. He knew that he had been observed in his walk through the vineyards, that they would not have retreated far into the trees before setting up their ambush. Probably just ahead, where the little trail widened out through a grove of chestnut. There would be plenty of ammunition and steep slopes to give the advantage of height. It was where he would have chosen, were he the ambusher.

There was nothing for it but to move steadily forward. The light filtered sideways through the trees, dappling the undergrowth, but there were still many leaves on them. The summer had been endless, no great wind sweeping in from the Maremma to shake the foliage down. This was the first day he had felt even a hint of something cooler in the light breeze, though his old wounds had sensed the season's change first, as they always did.

There was the snap of a stick, the slightest of rustles to either side and even . . . was that the hint of a whisper swiftly cut off? He advanced boldly for he had his mission, and the only way to accomplish it was to draw them out.

The first projectile that struck him was from above and he thought *Gianni*, because the boy loved to climb, was never out of a tree. The second was harder and more accurate, the chestnut catching him just below the ear, and with some sting to it. That would be Anne, because she had her mother's arm, her unerring thirst for the target. After that it was impossible to guess at the thrower, so heavily did the missiles come, in single bullets, in concentrations like cannon shot. He staggered under the storm, as was required of him, and finally fell forward onto the forest's mossy floor.

When they rolled him over, he saw they were all there, four faces staring solemnly down at their victim as if wondering what to do with him next. He knew Erik would favour more bloodletting, while Maria-Carmine would be keen to practise some sort of forest medicine. You could never tell which way Gianni would lean, his mind would already be on to something else. How to climb even higher, probably.

But it was Anne who decided, of course. Though a girl, she was still the eldest and the strongest, and she had a ruthless quality to her. *Another trait from her mother*, he thought, rubbing under his ear.

'You are our prisoner. We will take you back to our castle, and there the Queen will decide your fate,' she declared.

'As long as the castle lies homeward, I will surrender my sword to your power, my Lady.'

Jean smiled at his daughter, and reached up with his stick. She grabbed the end of it and tugged, helping him to his feet, where he spent a moment rubbing his knee.

'And the Queen has a request of us. Gather your weapons, for she is going to make us a chestnut pie this night.'

This produced a cheer, for Beck's pies were famous. When they had a sufficient quantity of the tufted brown nuts, they headed back through the wood and along the vine-lined avenues. The heads, fair and dark, kept popping up amid the thick clusters of fruit. Only Maria-Carmine walked with him, her little hand thrust in his. She was a quiet child, very like her ever-thoughtful father.

'Well,' said Beck, studying the bounty of the forest spread out on her table. 'A good crop indeed.'

The moon was full that night, the sky clear and their way well lit across the valley to the Comet. They had a delay at the next house, for Maria-Theresa did not know where her husband was.

'Always fiddling with something. He may be in the barn, Jean, you could look for him there,' she said.

While the women compared their offerings for the feast and the children resumed the game of the day, Jean went around to the barn. The door was open and a swath of moonlight spread across the floor to the olive press.

'Albrecht? Are you there?' Jean called.

There was a shifting from under the huge metal and wooden frame, and a creature's head wormed its way out. Even in the moonlight, Jean could see the creature was covered in oil.

'Oh Fugger!' He leant on his stick and laughed. 'Haven't you had enough of lying in the dirt?'

The Fugger pulled himself out from under the press and began a futile effort at wiping himself down.

'It's blocked. Again,' he explained, rubbing his sticky hand on his smock.

'My friend, Maria-Theresa is going to kill you.'

They left husband and wife there, little Maria-Carmine trying to scrape the oil from her father's clothes and skin, the hapless German standing unprotesting between his scolding wife and child. As they walked down through the Fugger's

448

olive groves, their footfalls were accompanied by the rhythmic fall of an axe. It came from within the walls of the inn ahead, and when they got closer they could see, through the gate, the gleam of a curved blade as it rose and fell.

It was the little Norseman who wielded the weapon. The larger one sat to the side shouting encouragement while he played with the ears of a big hunting dog that looked as if it might have some wolf in it.

'Is it that time already?' Haakon stretched and rubbed the hound's belly as it rolled in the earth before him. 'Have you seen this lazy whelp? All it likes to do is loll about. His father will be snarling in Valhalla while his fool of a son is having his stomach rubbed.'

'And you the fool doing the rubbing,' observed Beck.

'Aye.' Haakon rose, stretched, then went over to take the axe away from his boy. 'Good work, Erik. Anne, Gianni, why don't you take as much of the wood as you can to Mathias in the courtyard?'

It became a game, of course, and much wood was raised and dropped before the children staggered out under their burdens.

'You can never have too much wood.' Haakon was staring after the children, his mind elsewhere. 'I have something to show you,' he said suddenly and moved towards the house, calling out, 'Michaela, we have visitors.'

Haakon's wife stood in the doorway, rubbing floured hands on a cloth. She was a woman whose eyes always danced with a smile in them, and Haakon always smiled when he saw her.

'Is it ready?' he asked.

She leant into him, her head resting on his shoulder, and looked mock seriously at Jean and Beck. 'He thinks I have nothing better to do than oil his carvings.' She laughed at the slight hurt in his eyes. 'Yes, man. It is ready.'

Haakon entered the kitchen and re-emerged a moment later holding a long, curved object wrapped in a cloth. He shook the material off it, and a wooden scimitar, perfect in every detail, lay in his hands.

Jean ran his fingers lightly over it. 'It is beautiful, my friend. Erik will love it. And Januc would have loved it as well.'

'Aye. Tonight, of all nights, I wanted to remember him with something.'

They gathered in the courtyard and, with Mathias's table groaning under the weight of gifts from all their friends, the memorial feast was greater than any of them could remember.

Lying back later, the fire consuming Erik's carefully chopped wood, the umber stones reflecting back its glow, the young wine from Jean's vineyards as refreshing and uplifting as the best of any year past, it was time again for the tales. Some of the details were left out, because of the young age of the audience and the tendency of children to take their fears to bed with them. But most of the story was there, and its accounts of beautiful queens, devilish enemies, impossible odds, improbable rescues and battles by sea and land beguiled the evening away.

Each child had his or her favourite section of the story, and each knew that part of it by heart and was annoyed when there was any deviation from their version. Erik sat with the wooden scimitar on his knees, straining forward whenever his hero Januc was mentioned. He especially loved the tale of the fight at the bridge, how the janissary had pulled Haakon from the flood and left him with a farmer's family before riding to his glorious end in the village. Maria-Carmine sat on her father's lap, clutching at his one hand as her mother had once clutched at it, tears flowing as she heard of his sorrows, replaced by tears of joy at his redemption. Gianni simply wanted more blood in all the stories.

And Anne? She was fascinated most by the beauty of her namesake, the tragedy and triumph of her life. Jean had discovered a way with words to describe Anne Boleyn that seemed to please the child. For he remembered how once he had lulled his other child to sleep, in the only other time in his life when he had been happy, and how she had always liked it when he was simple and true in the telling.